BROTHERS' WAR

DAVID PAUL EMMA

BROTHERS' WAR

To the late George C. Brauer, whose book *Judaea Weeping*
inspired me to write this story when I was sixteen

To my parents, whose own story made my imagination soar

And to my hometown, where I was touched by the
different cultures that fill these pages

A Letter to the Reader

Little has been written in narrative form about the Jewish Revolt against Rome in 70 AD. For readers familiar with the Bible, the Revolt falls just after the end of the Biblical account in Acts. It is alluded to by Jesus prophetically but is never described. Its impact on Jews and Christians, however, proved profound and irreversible. It signaled the final split between Christians and Jews who, up to that point, were still tied by a common, though increasingly strained, spiritual heritage. It also altered the character of Judaism forever. Judaism morphed from a faith of priests and animal sacrifices centered on a Temple in Jerusalem to a scattered community held loosely together by rabbis, traditions, and local synagogues.

Brothers' War attempts to tell the story of how that happened. Its central hero, young Nathan from Jerusalem, becomes trapped in the maelstrom of the Jewish Revolt and must flee to Sicily, then Rome, to put the pieces of his shattered life back together. Along the way he encounters people, cultures, and adventures that aid, and sometimes inhibit, his quest. But between the politics, spirituality, romance, warfare, sibling rivalry, and natural disasters of Nathan's tale, the reader is brought to an understanding of this turbulent period and how two of the world's great faiths split apart, picking up where the book of Acts leaves off.

Various subplots in this novel shed light on other topics of possible interest to the reader. Nathan's stay on the island of Sicily, for example, describes the continued existence of Greeks in the Roman world, the origin of several famous myths, the untold story of the Sicel tribe after which Sicily is named, and the horrors of slavery forced upon the hapless island during the Classical Age. Other subplots deal with the building of the Colosseum, the eruption of Mt. Vesuvius, Rome's Jewish quarter, the development of the modern book, the controversial character of the historian Flavius Josephus, and the sad promulgation of various anti-Semitic laws, all of which play pivotal roles in Nathan's story.

This novel is the summation of forty-six years of research, writing, and love. Begun when I was Nathan's age at the outset, this story has grown, morphed, and matured alongside me, as though experiencing the protagonist's life changes in real time.

I pray this story leaves a positive mark.

—David Paul Emma
  Author

A Word About Dialogue in This Novel

The dialogues in *Brothers' War* reflect the fact that ancient people spoke with colloquialisms and humor just like people do today. A cursory reading of *Plato's Symposium* or the New Testament reveals a world of nicknames, vernaculars, and quips that are strikingly modern. Some ancient phrases have fossilized due to repeated or ritualistic use, like those from the King James Bible, but in their original settings, lines like Jesus' "take the plank out of your own eye," would have been received as humorous and part of the work-a-day life of a carpenter, just as a modern tradesman's joke might be received today.

Modern readers are rarely exposed to informality in ancient dialogues. Few ancient dialogues have survived, and those that have survived are often translated with a reverence that conceals their original jovial spirit. As you read *Brothers' War*, keep these facts in mind so that you can absorb yourself in the multifarious world as the ancients experienced it, and as we do today, full of sorrow, joy, horror, desperation, contemplation, and everything in between.

"A friend loves at all times,
and a brother is born for adversity."

King Solomon, c.940 BC

ROMAN WO
Nathan's travels throu
ROME
Naples Herculaneum
Enna
SICILY
Syracuse
MEDITERRANEAN S

RLD AD 66
hout Brothers' War
PONTUS
E A
Jotapata
Pella
JERUSALEM

BOOK I
JERUSALEM

I

The city smoldered. Everyone Nathan knew was either dead, captured, or missing. The Temple lay in ruins. The cause was lost. He felt lost himself. Where would he go now? He had to search for his mother and sister. They might still be alive. He and the only other survivor with him had to find out.

"Come on, Ducetius," he said, head lowered, not wanting to move.

"Yes, my lord."

Taking a step into the unknown, Nathan halted. It was hard to leave the home he had loved his whole life and had fought for for so many years. How had it all come to this, when his brother and Joseph had seemed so sure of victory?

He took another step. He thought of that day, that fateful day, when for him the war began.

///////

"Samson, Samson, the Philistines are upon you," Ducetius whispered into Nathan's ear.

"Go away," Nathan grunted, angry to wake so early.

"You're late for your meeting."

"What meeting?"

"The one with your father."

"Oh no. And don't say another word."

Nathan shot across the room to his water basin and mirror. The wall frescoes and floor mosaics around him still hid in the predawn gray.

Washing, he could hear Ducetius mutter as he set out his clothes: "Sandals, belt, loin cloth, skirt, phylactery—is he going to wear that thing again?" In the midst of the critique, the father appeared in the doorway.

"Are you ready Nathan? We have to leave."

"Almost," he responded.

"It was a long night," the father said to Ducetius. "Your young charge should have been with us. Where was he?"

"I am not sure, my lord."

Nathan knew he was being reprimanded second-hand through poor Ducetius.

"With the city so dangerous, you can't let him out of your sight."

"Yes, my lord," Ducetius answered again, thinking how impossible his young charge was becoming.

"Are you ready now?" he called again to Nathan.

"Yes."

"Let me look at you." The father eyed him over, completely disapproving. "You didn't shave? And you're wearing a phylactery? Is that your brother Amram's influence?"

"*Abba*, don't start with my dress. Please." He hated when his father harped on his style. "Only the Romans shave. And the phylactery looks distinctive."

"It doesn't look distinctive," retorted the father. "It looks confrontational. I won't be the only conservative at the meeting with a radical secretary."

"I'll take it off when we get there. Why am I even going?"

"I'll remind you on the way. We have to leave."

Walking down the colonnade along the atrium, Nathan's mother and little sister emerged from one of the bedrooms to bid farewell. "Be careful, Opal. Good-bye Nathan."

"Good-bye, dear," and "Good-bye, *ima*," came the replies. The slave then bolted the door behind them.

II

According to their reckoning, it was the 819th year after the founding of Rome, and the twelfth year of Nero's reign. From a modern perspective, it was AD 66. As Nathan and his father traveled to their meeting by litter across the slowly waking city, there was much to discuss.

"Why am I going with you?" Nathan asked again.

"I need a secretary, for one thing. And two, I can't leave you home with the chance that your brother might snatch you away today."

"He won't snatch me away. I can take care of myself. And ima is home."

"You're only sixteen, and your mother can't stop Amram."

"But why don't you want me to go with him?"

"Because he's a troublemaker. The procurator is coming in from Caesarea today, and Amram, I'm sure, is plotting a riot. I don't want you arrested. The whole purpose of this meeting is to discuss mollifying the procurator when he arrives."

"Will I meet him?"

"Probably not. He comes in this afternoon. However, the men at the meeting this morning are important too. They're conservative, powerful, and will decide whether we have war or peace. If anyone can reason with Florus, it's them; and I want you to know who they are. An interesting young fellow named Joseph ben Mattathias, who is not always a conservative, will be there too. He's a cousin of the royal family. You'll like him."

"I hope so; because really, abba, starting a riot with Amram sounds much more exciting."

"Nathan," replied the father, "don't speak like a fool. Riots and wars sound glamorous when you're sixteen. But they're not. Wars mean people die; even people like ima and your little sister. If real conflict comes here because of men like Amram, you'll wish our side had won out instead. I want you to fight for peace. That's the other reason I want you with me today."

The father could almost hear Nathan's eyes roll.

"Just so you know," the father continued, "war has already begun in Caesarea. We were hoping Florus would quell the situation, but he seems to like the prospect of war. And the Zealots are goading him on. That is why we must try to reason with him today: to let him know that not everyone in Judaea is a Zealot. If we can't persuade him…" He shook his head in despair. "I wish you had been with us last night. You'd already know what I'm talking about. Why weren't you home?"

"I was with Elisheva," responded Nathan.

"At your age," Opal reprimanded, "it's improper for you to see her. It's not like when you were small. You should have been home with us. And how late did you get back? Does Rab Simeon know his daughter keeps such late hours with you?"

"We were only talking," argued Nathan. "With all the unrest, we had a lot to talk about. And Rab Simeon was at our house with you."

"I want you to be more circumspect with Elisheva. I need you to let me know where you are. And I must tell you," Opal continued, looking right into Nathan's eyes, "that plans with Rab Simeon's family have altered."

"What do you mean?" asked Nathan.

"Did you know he is a member of the Way?" the father asked.

"No."

"Not even from Elisheva?"

"No. But how does that change anything? How do you even know it's true?"

"He and I discussed it last night," the father responded, "though I have suspected it for months. And it changes his plans because the entire sect is striking out on its own, en masse. If we have war, they will not be going in with us."

"But that means Elisheva and I will be separated. And we've always planned on …"

"I know," replied Opal. "But there's a possibility we'll be going with them."

"What? And leave the city? We can't do that!" interjected Nathan. "I thought you had made a decision about that a long time ago. When were you going to tell me?"

"When was I going to tell you? You are never around to tell," snapped the father. "You are incommunicado at all hours, for days on end. Your brother Amram has ears all over this city and cannot be trusted. So I have to make plans in secret when I can, with or without you."

"But abba, don't you think there's wisdom in fighting Rome?" asked Nathan. "I always thought there was. And I don't want to leave the city."

"No. There is no wisdom in fighting Rome. They will crush us. Men all over this city, and Caesarea too, are leaving, and we have to make our move as well. I've already made financial arrangements in Joppa, as well as Pella, where Rab Simeon's family is going. That way, whether we move east or west, with Rab Simeon or on our own, we will have means to live."

"I can't believe this!" attacked Nathan.

"Believe it," responded Opal. "And if war comes and you survive it, you may even thank me one day."

"I doubt it," he muttered under his breath.

"I'll pretend I didn't hear that," conceded Opal. "And for the moment, keep an open mind. If the Zealots really make sense in the final analysis, I will not stop you from joining your brother. But I am hoping you will see that that is not the case and that you will see the wisdom, even during today's meeting, of working for peace."

For the next ten minutes, Nathan recapped two thousand years of Jewish troubles in his mind. It struck him that in every era the Jews were in trouble from a neighboring country, a conquering oppressor, an internal dissenter. There was always something. Why was that? Was it because Israel lay in the most crisscrossed, overtrodden plot of real estate on earth, or because Jewish customs stood at such odds with the rest of the world, or because no matter who conquered them the Jews simply refused to go extinct?

"Abba," asked Nathan, "do you ever think we might actually survive Rome?"

"No."

"But we survived the Egyptians, Babylonians, Persians, and the Seleucids. Why wouldn't we survive Rome?"

"Because those survival stories are just stories."

"They are?"

"There's some truth to them. But basically yes. Rome is real and Rome is now. And we will not survive."

But Rome, thought Nathan, is really nothing. It's just the current obstacle to Jewish prosperity. It has no pedigree like Egypt. It has no culture that it didn't steal from the Greeks. It doesn't stand at the vortex of the world like Israel. And it won't last forever. It will fall too, one day, like Goliath to the Jewish David. It will be crushed like the feet of iron and clay in Daniel's prophecy. And then we Jews will emerge victorious.

"And don't think Rome is unimportant," said Opal, knowing exactly what his son was thinking. "Rome has been growing in power since the time of Hezekiah. It has the greatest army in the world. And it has a great deal to offer the Jews. It has brought commerce, a common language, and protection to our nation and dozens of others besides. The Zealots would undo all that for the sake of an isolated independence. And for what? And for how long? Their position makes no sense."

"Where did the Zealots even come from?" Nathan now asked.

"Why?"

"I'm just asking."

"They started under Herod," the father explained, "but took off under the procurators during a tax census. After that, their motto became, 'Death to the Romans and freedom for Israel.' They started calling themselves the followers of the fourth philosophy."

"What do you mean, 'the fourth philosophy'?" asked Nathan.

"The Pharisees, Sadducees, Essenes, and Zealots," answered the father. "Those are the four philosophies."

"I like that term. And I like them. To me, they're the only group trying to accomplish something practical for our country."

"I know you feel that way, Nathan, but destroying Israel for a radical political agenda has nothing practical about it. And don't think the Zealots are the only ones fighting for freedom against Rome. They are not. Faith and patriotism do not always require a sword. There are other options. When I was young, my father took me, like I am taking you, to see the procurator. And I learned a lot about faith and patriotism from that experience."

"What happened?" asked Nathan, feigning excitement.

"Pilate was the procurator; and he was even worse than Florus. He was probably the worst procurator we've ever had. And that year he sent his army from Caesarea to winter in Jerusalem. It was a bad situation, and tempers rose."

"Why?"

"He allowed his soldiers to erect imperial standards around their camp site right in the middle of the city—the poles with idolatrous pictures of the emperor on them. Even though the emperors forbade idols inside our gates, Pilate did not care. I think he tried to provoke us to anger. And as a result, people from the city traveled all the way to Caesarea to have an audience with him; and my father took me with him."

"Was it dangerous?" Nathan was almost genuinely interested now.

"Yes. I sometimes wonder how my mother let me go. But I went. And every day a throng of us would see the procurator while he sat in judgment. But he refused to listen. We were there a week, trying to gain an ear. Finally, he granted a hearing, but while we were petitioning, he suddenly gave a signal with his hand and soldiers appeared all around us—from behind walls and trees, from inside buildings—everywhere. I was terrified.

"Pilate then said, 'You will all die now, or you will all leave me alone!' And one of the men in the crowd laid down on the ground, bared his neck and yelled out, 'I would rather die than have our law transgressed!' Then everyone followed suit. Everyone, the men and the women. My father said to me, 'Opal, do what I do, and do not be afraid. To die for God is sometimes why we live.' I was lying right next to him, with one hand holding my chest and my other hand holding my father's. And I closed my eyes."

Nathan imagined the image. "What happened?" he asked, not feigning at all.

"What happened is that Pilate backed down when he saw how willing we were to die. He yelled out, 'All right! Get up! All of you! I do not need your melodrama. Your request is granted. Men escort these…Jews…out of my sight.' So we left.

"And that, my son, is the kind of zeal our people need now. That's another reason I want you with me today. When I ponder that memory as an adult, I believe more and more that Pilate did not spare us out of mercy or compassion or any sense of justice. I think our willingness to die simply disappointed him. He wanted a fight, but we wouldn't oblige. The Roman is an animal of war. It's all he knows. Often it's the same with the Jew. But now the Romans and the Jews are at an impasse again. And I know these Romans, Nathan. And I know Florus. They want a fight again as much as we want our freedom again. But if we use Zealot tactics, we will have an empire to battle against, and Florus will prolong our pain as long and excruciatingly as he can. If we fight with peace, though—if we show that our ways are not like his, and if we surrender our lives without violence—I think Florus will be so disgusted with us he will leave us alone.

"Florus is a crazed man. He wants bloodshed. Everyone knows it. So we cannot allow the Zealots to provoke him into having it.

"I myself am no longer willing to fight for our law. I may have to die for it, but I will not fight for it. When you get older, you think differently. There is not much I would fight for at all. But I will live for the law, and live for peace, and live to see you prosper, Nathan. So we will see how our proceedings fare today; and if war is inevitable, then at least we have a way out, to live."

Nathan showed his discontent. "We'll see, abba," he said. He knew his father couldn't possibly be right. But he wasn't too sure Amram was right either anymore.

They reached their destination minutes later.

III

The delegation for peace convened in a small, windowless storage vault in a forsaken lower level of the Antonia. It was in this fortress, constructed by Herod the Great and named for Marc Antony a century before, that the high Sanhedrin council met and the procurators resided on visits to Jerusalem. It stood adjacent to the Temple and the entrance to the Second Quarter at the jugular of the city.

Subterranean tunnels connected the Antonia, the Temple, and Herod's palace. It was through one of these tunnels that Nathan and his father wound their way to that morning's meeting.

The storage vault was tomblike and gloomy. Its ceiling was arched, stone benches lined its sides, and torchlight cut deep shadows into its rough-hewn walls. It already smelled of humanity when Nathan and Opal entered from the dark corridor, and Nathan was greeted by a torch and a friendly face a little older than his own.

"Good morning," said the face.

"Good morning," Nathan responded.

Opal directed Nathan to a spot on an outside bench while he took a seat next to Rab Simeon at the table. The young man from the doorway walked over to Opal and struck up a conversation. Nathan suspected, and rightly so, that the young man was the not-always-conservative Joseph ben Mattathias his father had described to him. As Opal, Joseph, Simeon, and all the others around the table talked, some of them rather heatedly, Nathan sat quietly to listen, take notes, and contemplate.

They were people. They were all just people, Nathan thought. During moments of mounting tension in the city over the previous few weeks, Nathan had felt himself part of a drama bigger than life. He was still too young not to be captivated by the romance of war; and now, in this basement vault, in the midst of an eloquent assemblage of nobility and pharisaic propriety about to lay the course of action for thousands it did not even know, he felt awestruck by his inclusion in it. It amazed him that all he had to do was sit and listen, and the future would be decided for him in that room by those who possessed the power not only to speak but to act.

Compared to the gray beards and worldly-minded eyes surrounding him, his father seemed a child by comparison; Joseph ben Mattathias a toddler. If it were not for his bearing, Joseph would have appeared out of place. But instead, his presence added to the elegance of the affair: the wisdom of the aged meeting that of the young. Then when the high priest himself entered the door, the respect and bowed heads with which he was met nearly made Nathan forget the sight before him was no dream.

But, on the other hand, they were people. They were all just people. As the meeting officially commenced and each man spoke his piece, Nathan began to sense in every nervous voice and shaky hand how powerless the giants of his world really were. Great Nero himself, he thought, if seen face to face, might prove no different.

He looked at his hands as they wrote and contemplated the notion that thousands of little such hands could build or destroy a city, lose or create an empire. Was it really true that humans and their little hands were the force behind the events of history? Did how Alexander or Caesar feel on a particular day determine the trajectory of the world? Could the war between Rome and the Jews be avoided if Florus felt differently today, or had been born a Jew, or had never come to power? Or was there an inevitability to history so that eventually one like him would have to be born? If only people realized what prey they all were to feelings, Nathan thought, they could sit back and be at peace with one another. Florus could change the way he 'felt' toward the Jews, and the Zealots could change how they 'felt' toward Rome. There was nothing more to it than that. Why was it so hard to do then, Nathan asked himself, when the fate of millions depended on the outcome?

Because they were people. They were all just people. As Nathan entered back into the discussion, he gained a new understanding of why it was happening and recalled a passage from *Qohelet*—Ecclesiastes—that summed up his thoughts:

> ...the race is not to the swift, nor the battle to the strong;
> food does not come to the wise, wealth to the brilliant,
> nor favor to the learned; but time and chance happen to
> them all.

This filled his mind as the meeting proceeded.

Joseph ben Mattathias arose from his seat. "What I want to know, gentlemen," he began, "is this: if our attempts to placate Florus fail, if war cannot be averted, does Jerusalem have the support of its elders to carry on the fight, or am I standing in the midst of those who would abandon Zion to save their own skins? I am a man of peace; but let me tell you that if I thought for an instant that war could win us the freedom we sought, I would be the first to raise my sword. Are you with me, men of Zion, or do we live for our comfort and riches as our people die without leadership? I am not saying we will have war, or that I desire it. But if we are forced into it, where do you gentlemen stand on the issue?"

"It would not be our war, Joseph," one of the men spoke out. "It would be the Zealots' war. Why should we get involved? We are already doing our part to avert it. Jewish communities all over the world could use our influence and monetary support without us wasting it here on a lost cause."

"That is a good point," added Simeon.

"A good point, Rab Simeon? A good point?" whipped back Joseph. "Jerusalem is never a lost cause, or the Jews as a people are a lost cause. So long as it survives, we survive. When it dies, we die. Who would we be, scattered across the world in foreign communities without even a hope of Zion? When our fathers were captive in Babylon for seventy years, what was their cry? Jerusalem. Why did the psalmist weep at the riverside? He wept when he remembered Zion in ruins. You cannot hope for anything but the extinction of our people and our faith if you take away the only thing that ties us together."

"Joseph," continued Simeon, "is a city what ties us together? Is the kingdom of God so connected with a place that it cannot survive without it? The kingdom of God is one of spirit. It is within, not without. You and I are the Temples of the living God, not the building of stone. I say we do what we can now to save our city. But if war comes to us, we have no obligation to cast our lot with the radicals. Leave the kingdom of God to his care, and let fall to Jerusalem what destruction the Zealots may bring. We survived Babylon while Jerusalem lay in ruins. Faith can survive without the city."

"Rab Simeon," quickly intervened Opal, trying to cover up his friend's alien theology, "is talking about things impertinent to our discussion. But Joseph, we have to make our case clear to Florus and to the whole world, if possible, that all Jews are not Zealots. We cannot join a war in the name of our people simply because a half-crazed sect is out for blood. Florus and Nero must know that their quarrel is with the Zealots alone. If we support the radicals, Jews throughout the empire will lose their credibility among the Gentiles. We have struggled hard enough for our privileges in foreign cities. We must make a distinction between us and them in front of Florus today, before any war commences, and tomorrow as well, even *if* a war commences."

"It is true," said Ananus the high priest, his voice quiet but firm, his old frame shaking a little. "We have nothing to gain from a united front with the radicals. If it were possible to round them all up now and present them to Florus today, it would save us a lifetime of trouble. But who knows a Zealot from another in the streets? For that matter, many of them are in our own households." At that, Nathan thought of Amram and looked over at his father. The high priest looked down at the table as he thought of his own son with Zealot leanings.

"Because of this fact, gentlemen," the high priest continued, "I think it is best that we persuade Florus that the people are peaceably disposed. After all, is it not true on the whole? Perhaps he will listen to us. And if he demands the heads of the seditious, we must at least promise an attempt to bring them to justice. Meanwhile, we must beg him to forgive the few guilty for the sake of the many innocent.

"Rab Joseph, I appreciate your zeal—excuse the term—in wishing to present the world a united people with a righteous cause. But the fact is, our survival is at stake. Our nation has been threatened and conquered many times before, but it has never actually declared war upon any of the great empires around it. We are not Maccabees, and Rome is no mere Seleucid kingdom. Rome is the world. We are only a crumb. We must learn to survive as unostentatiously as possible until a day of greater strength."

Nathan thought for a moment: but Joseph is a Hasmonaean. He *is* a Maccabee.

Another man, a member of the Sanhedrin, began to speak. "I am frankly surprised, Rab Joseph, that this line of discussion has arisen. I assumed we all agreed on the absurdity of the Zealots' position. Our responsibility as leaders of this nation is one of averting national catastrophe, which can only be carried out as far as the people are willing to obey. I have no doubt that if war ensues, the Zealots will attempt to override our government completely; and if that happens, none of us in this room will be in a position to join hands with their cause. We will be the first to die.

"Don't underestimate the Zealots. They will show no mercy to Jew or Gentile who does not conform to their ideals. If war breaks out, our only choice will be to escape."

Throughout this dialogue Nathan could see in the glance of his father the admiration he held for young Joseph. Joseph stood out as one of the few willing to struggle for peace through reason, while at the same time willing to die for freedom through war. He was noted by everyone, having successfully straddled the fence between the conservative and radical parties for years. He had joined, of his own free will, an ambassadorial mission a few years back to liberate a group of Palestinian rabbis unduly imprisoned in Italy. The success of his journey in the name of Jewish freedom gained him acclaim that would not be forgotten by anyone—not even a Zealot.

He even left an impression on Emperor Nero's wife, Empress Poppaea, who met him briefly during his visit. It was clear then that Joseph held a different position than the other men in the room. If war were to ensue, he could viably join hands with the radicals, conservatives, or even the Romans, with little risk to his life. This placed him in stark contrast to men like Nathan's father and Simeon, who held definitive positions in the Romaphile and Christian camps. For a moment, Opal envied Joseph his status in all this and explained so to Nathan when the meeting adjourned.

It had lasted four hours. It was now mid-morning. The procurator was due later in the afternoon.

"Since we have a little time," said Opal to his son, "I want to show you around these tunnels. I suppose you never knew they existed, did you?"

"No. I did not."

"My father showed them to me when I was half your age. For a short time, he was an assistant in the Sanhedrin, and he brought me here once."

"He helped on the council? Another thing I didn't know."

"I wish you had known your grandfather. You would have loved him."

The father and son ambled down the deathly corridors with a single torch between them. Nathan mentally mapped their layout in the hope of returning someday. His sense of direction told him they were heading south. Soon they reached a staircase and began to ascend. At the top of the staircase, dots of faint light filtered through a metal grating on the left-hand side. Once on the landing, the two remained utterly mute while looking out the grate. The landing was very narrow. Nathan mouthed the words "Where are we?" His father silently replied, "the west portico."

The elaborate metalwork grating, about four feet high and two feet wide, was one of several that decorated the portico walls. Nathan had seen them many times but never guessed one of them led to a staircase. The metalwork was close knit so that one could barely see through it from the outside. From inside, though, Nathan noticed the grating was on hinges and had a latch so as to open and close like a door. He also noticed there was a pillar standing in front of the grating about five feet away. He tried to memorize the location of the latch and the surroundings of the pillar for future reference, then motioned to his father that he was ready to leave.

Once they were back on the street, moving among the now awakened populace, Opal looked up at the Temple Mount and pointed. "That's where we were. I know you can't see it, but on the other side of that wall, that's where it was. At the twentieth row of columns from the right. What did you think?"

"I think, if it weren't for all the dirt, that it would be a great place to take Elisheva after we're married."

"Oh, you think?" Opal laughed. "It's funny. I took your mother there once. She hated it."

IV

"Tell me something Elisheva," said Nathan almost tenderly, "are you a member of the Way?"

"Yes," answered Elisheva. "But only recently. How did you find out?"

He paused as in disbelief. "So it's true. When were you going to tell me?"

"I've wanted to tell you since the very first day. But it's been difficult. I've wanted to talk about many things, but we have barely spoken in a week. With the city in an uproar and your family having so many troubles and my own family coming to understand something we had rejected for so long, I have not found the words to express it to you."

Nathan remained silent, as if to imply that what she had said up to that point did not answer his question.

"The one thing I can tell you, Nathan," she continued, "is that I believe it, and that the man Yeshua is the dream of the world come true."

"Yeshua? Really? Do you know how strange it is for me to hear you say the name of that man, realizing that you center your thoughts of God around him? It is blasphemy, Elisheva. You have to help me understand how you could even consider it. If I hear someone mention him I either get angry or am at an utter loss. And here you are, someone I thought I understood and who understood me, speaking about this thing that seems sheer lunacy. Do you really follow that man? Does your brother Joram follow him? Did your father force or delude you into believing it?"

"No, Nathan. Not in the least. I am not deluded. The teachings of the Way are the only philosophy I've heard in years that makes sense. They are hopeful and serious, and for the whole world. They go so far beyond the squabble our nation has with Rome that they make Amram's ideas seem childish. The Zealots' hopes are for the here and now. Yeshua's are forever. I haven't spoken to you about it because the tension in your family is so bad already: your brother on one side, your father on the other, and you in the middle."

"But what I know of Yeshua seems the exact opposite of what you have just described. I think of the scriptures and the Law as eternal and as big as the world. I see Yeshua as just one man who lived in a particular time and is now dead. How can you believe he is other than that?"

"Nathan, what do the Jews really fight for when they fight for the Law? Why do they keep the laws and scriptures alive, and what is their hope for the future? You know it is the mashiach—someone real and forever and not just for the now. I'm telling you, Yeshua is that mashiach. You know he was destined to come. And he has."

"But from what I see of the world today, he could not have come. The world is not what it should be if that were the case."

"And how was it supposed to be, Nathan?"

"I don't know. An olive tree in every yard, the lion laying down with the lamb, good sacrifices offered in the Temple, a world begun again without evil."

"But how would that world come about, Nathan? By leading a Jewish army to defeat the Romans? That is what I cannot follow. Mashiach is to create a new world order: a world of peace, prosperity, and righteousness. But that kind of world cannot be gained by the sword; and the Zealots, the Pharisees, almost everyone in this province, expects God's anointed to lead an army."

"The Lord has always been a God of battle. That has been his way: to fight against the Gentiles with his people and lead the Davids and Gideons to victory."

"But what happens after all the Canaans in the world have been conquered and the Promised Land of the whole earth has been won? The same thing that happened after the first one was conquered. The people will forget about heaven, and the problems of an evil world will continue."

"How do you know so much?"

"Why do you say that? Because I'm a girl?"

"No. I know you're not just a girl."

"It doesn't take a scholar to figure these things out. But because I'm a girl, I know how people work. And I hear my father and brother talk, and I think about the things they say. The type of savior everyone is looking for can establish an empire, but he can't change a single human soul. And if he can't do that, what is the good of gaining the world? There will never be peace on earth until hearts are changed."

"And how are hearts changed, Elisheva?"

"God works on a man from the inside out. But you and the Zealots want to change our world from the outside in."

"But Elisheva, do you think it's foolish to try to better our external life? Is your Yeshua the reason why your father is thinking"—he lowered his voice even further than it was—"is that why your father is thinking of escaping?"

"What do you mean?" Elisheva whispered. "I haven't heard anything about that."

"Well, it's true. Your father discussed it with my father, and my father told me."

"But how can we leave?" asked Elisheva. "We have family and friends and an entire life here. We can't just say good-bye to everything and everyone we know and love. My father has never mentioned any of this to me. Are you sure? I don't know if you heard right."

"Why? Because I'm a boy?"

"Maybe. Boys don't listen very well."

"Well I heard this loud and clear. And directly from abba. Our fathers are schemers, and well-connected too. They have been planning this for a long time. They just haven't told us about it because it's a dangerous world out there."

"They?" asked Elisheva. "Now you're talking about both of them? Are both of our families planning to escape?"

"Yes."

"Really?"

"Really."

"Together?"

Nathan smiled. "Yes. Possibly together. We might be going with you."

"Well if that were the case, I could at least tolerate the idea. I can even understand the need to go. I've been terrified living here this last month. But if we weren't going together, I don't know what I would do. Are you sure it's happening?"

"Not completely. But my father told me a week ago that we might be going with you."

"But what about your cause? The war? Don't you believe in that?

"Yes I do. Though sometimes I don't know what to think. If we can find a peaceful solution, why not go with it? But I can see the point of people like my brother who are sick of straddling the wall between autonomy and servitude."

"You're a pretty fine straddler yourself."

"I know. I see good coming out of either path. If we go to war, we might win. If we escape, I'll be with you. In either case, I hope we'll be together after all of this is over."

"Oh, Nathan, I couldn't think of living without you. We've been friends my whole life."

"I don't like to think of living without you either. But we can't think about that now. And besides, I need to leave. With reprimands from abba telling me we shouldn't see each other like this at our age—and I suppose he's right—we'll have to finish our conversation another time. I need some sleep. And I'm sure," he said, as he climbed up the wall to get out of Rab Simeon's courtyard, "that I'm in trouble already."

"I love you, Nathan."

"I love you, Elisheva."

Nathan jumped off the wall onto the outside and walked silently in the darkness the thousand feet toward his house. In the passage, he felt the city lying as in nervous apprehension for morning. The walls and walks seemed moist with sweat rather than dew, and the quiet was tense instead of peaceful. As the servant opened the gate to his courtyard, he noticed a flame still lit in a window. He halted for a moment and out of curiosity snuck around by the window to listen to what was going on inside. He could hear his father's voice. He was talking to someone.

"What do you want?" asked his father to the voice within.

"Just to talk," came the reply. It was the voice of Amram.

His father responded with belligerence. "You never just want to talk. You haven't 'just talked' to me in five years."

"Where is Nathan?" Amram asked.

His father replied with silence.

"Where is Nathan?" Amram repeated. "I want him. The city needs every good man it can get."

"Don't tell me what the city needs," his father retorted. "Don't talk to me about 'good.' Nathan is my son; his life is his own. But after that, he's mine to protect."

"Don't give me your speech about 'protecting' again," Amram replied sternly. "You're only a father when it comes to *him*. When it comes to me, you don't want to know anything."

"It wasn't like that before you decided to go off on your own."

"Don't thwart me again! Where is Nathan? He's not your baby anymore. He's mine. And you know he believes in our cause."

"I have no idea where he is. I knew you'd be after him sooner or later. I'm surprised you waited this long."

"I heard your meeting with the procurator did not go as you had hoped today. He refused to see you, didn't he?"

"If you know it," snapped Opal, "what is the point of asking?"

"Only to figure out why you even try to placate that fool, why you try to reason with him. Is it simply to save your own skin or to maintain your beloved precarious balance? What has Florus, or any of the Romans, ever done for us?"

"They have given us peace and freedom and prosperity for years."

"Not anymore. That stopped a long time ago, and you know it. The gray beards don't know what they are doing. Once and for all, the Zealots want to have it out with our beloved procurator. If future generations are to live in freedom, some generation has to forfeit its life. And I'm willing to make it mine. Otherwise, this lifestyle of beckoning to Rome will drone on for centuries. Nathan wants to dedicate his life to our freedom too. It's time you realize that. You can't protect him forever. All over the city, men younger than him are ready to fight. Israel has never been so ready, and my brother's honor calls him to it. You and your strategy of changing the procurator's feelings toward us lost credibility months ago, and even more so today. Nathan and I want to do something about that."

"I've had enough of this. If you are bent on war, I'm sure you'll have it. But I've talked enough for one day. You need to leave."

"That's right! That's right! Shut yourself off to everything that's going on around you because you can't be inconvenienced by conflict. Well, it's going to inconvenience you till you can't ignore it anymore."

"No. I think it's *you* who is going to inconvenience me till I won't ignore *you* anymore. What do you think I have been doing these past few months? Sitting in a cave waiting for this little skiff to blow over? I have been working as hard as you have for what I believe and have faced several conflicts to do so. And as for Nathan, he can decide for himself. He has two legs of his own. If he wishes to fight with you, he knows where to find you. But I will not allow the servants to let you through that gate again to harass me or your brother." He waited. "Ducetius, Criton! See Amram out of the house."

"I'll be waiting for Nathan to come to me. He knows I'm right, and he knows you're wrong."

Ducetius and Criton walked Amram out to the main hall, out the door, and through the gate. Opal did not move until he heard the gate shut.

Outside, Nathan waited until he thought Amram was gone. Then he went into the house and walked directly toward his room.

"Is that you, Nathan?" asked Opal from the main hall.

"Yes, abba. It is I. I am safe."

As he slid onto his bed to try to sleep, Nathan wondered just how safe he was. He wasn't sure what exactly he needed to be safe from: his father's out-of-date views, his brother's aggression, Elisheva's heresy, or his own lack of decision. Was there a fifth philosophy?

V

If Nathan thought he could remain neutral, he was wrong. Over the next few months, events spiraled out of control so that even a sixteen-year-old like Nathan could not escape.

"Have you seen all the crucifixions happening, abba?" Nathan said to his father. "Who are those people?"

"Demonstrators who denounced Florus," answered Opal.

"You mean because he stole money from the Temple?"

"Yes. And a mob has overrun the Temple and the Antonia."

"What's going to happen?"

"I don't know. Agrippa and Governor Gallus of Syria are intervening. Agrippa has brought soldiers into the city, but the Zealots are fighting them. Please don't leave the house. Your brother is probably involved, and I don't want you hurt. Even the high priest was murdered by that madman Menahem who captured the Masada fortress out in the desert."

"How did he get from Masada to here?"

"I don't know. But he returned and hunted down Ananus till he killed him."

"So the high priest is dead? The one who was at the meeting with us?"

"Yes."

"How can anyone kill a high priest? Even his son with the Zealot leanings wouldn't do that."

"No. You're right. The son actually slew Menaham. But then he turned around and massacred a contingent of Roman soldiers right afterward. The world has gone crazy. I ask you again to stay home till things calm down."

"I will."

But Nathan didn't stay home. When street fighting broke out at the end of their neighborhood, he fled to Amram to find out what to do.

"Well, little brother," said Amram smugly on Nathan's arrival. "I knew you would see things my way eventually. Have you come to join me?"

Nathan shook his head. He was not ready to commit to anything.

"You say no, but you know who's right, and I know you've been watching what's going on. It's all happening now. The war to end all wars has begun."

Nathan was unsure how to respond. Amram continued. "I know you might be scared. We all might die. But think of it this way: we're all going to die anyway. At least we can let it happen our way, and I can try to keep you safe until then, since I am your older brother. I'm glad you came to see me. It's hard to know whose side to fight on these days. One day a man is your associate, the next day he's your enemy, as our friend Menahem found out. I assume you know what I mean."

"Yes. I heard about the high priest," retorted Nathan, angry that the old man was dead.

"It's a mad world out there," Amram resumed. "I hope abba is coming to his senses about it. He likes to listen to men like Agrippa, all "peace" and "it's God's will." But Agrippa is just a Romanizer trying to save his own skin, and his sister is an incestuous whore who actually sleeps with him. It's disgusting. Besides the Hasmonaean palace, what jurisdiction does Agrippa actually have around here, except a dying legacy from his father and grandfather? And even the palace is practically gone since our men torched it last week. No one listens to Agrippa anymore. One by one, all the little props undergirding dear abba's platform are crumbling around him: Agrippa, the high priest, the palace. I'm sure he sees that. And if he doesn't, you can tell him this: I have the linchpin himself on my side. Joseph ben Mattathias is here with me. Tell him that. If nothing else convinces him that his cause is lost, that fact will."

No. It couldn't be. The young man at the meeting who seemed so promising and wise? Here with the renegade Amram? It was a lie. Why would Joseph scope out a crackpot like his brother? Joseph was of royal descent and had the respect of the entire country. Amram was just a self-deluded king among thieves. But then if Amram was lying, it was an audacious lie that could easily be exposed. Maybe it was true. Maybe Amram wasn't such a mediocrity after all, and Nathan had misjudged him. "You actually know Joseph ben Mattathias?" Nathan asked. "I find that hard to believe."

"No, little brother, I *do* know him. I know a prophet has no honor in his family, and neither do I. But Joseph ben Mattathias…"

"…is right here."

Nathan swung around and saw the young man enter the room. "Rab?" Nathan didn't know what else to say.

VI

Opal was incredulous at the news. Nathan was incredulous that Amram had allowed him to return home. Opal explained, "Your brother is so keen on destroying my spirit that he let his prized possession go just so you could tell me about Joseph."

That was probably true, but Nathan didn't like the feel of it. "I don't want to be anyone's prized possession," he said. "I just want to live. I want to be far away from here and Amram and the Zealots and the soldiers. I want you and *ima* to grow old happily and to see us united as a family again. I want to make a life with Elisheva and bring grandchildren into your world. I want this whole fight with Florus and the Romans to be over. I want to go to sleep tonight and wake up to the world that used to be."

"I don't know if that world really ever existed," responded Opal. "It's just a dream in our minds that we try to get back. I do it by working with Rome for a new procurator. Simeon thinks it can be gained by pursuing a cult. Amram thinks a war will bring it back, and you think it will be sleep. Maybe one of us will be right. But at the moment, we have to speed up our escape plans.

"I told you, Simeon is going north into the Decapolis as soon as he finishes his arrangements. There's a growing Christian population there in Pella, and many of the peace-lovers have already left Judaea to join them. But I'm now staking all our futures on going west, into one of the backwater provinces like Spain or Sicily, where Jews are less noticed. I had originally thought of joining Simeon and his family, but it's too risky now. The latest report from the Decapolis says that Gallus has declared open season on the Jews. Our people are being slaughtered in the streets there. It's safe for Christians. They've distanced themselves enough from us so that no one confuses us anymore—though Nero doesn't like the Christians either—but it's not safe for us to go there. Once we're in Joppa we can decide where to head exactly. But the window of opportunity is closing there too. When the Romans finally attack here, they will certainly go to Joppa. So we need to move fast."

As if the day couldn't get any worse, Nathan was now faced with the choice of following his father west, going north with Elisheva, or staying with his brother in Jerusalem. Whatever choice he made would split his world asunder.

For the moment, circumstances forestalled a decision. Gallus sent the Twelfth Legion, known as the Thunderbolt, toward Jerusalem. Within a few days, he fought his way into Jerusalem and occupied the Upper City. Had he attacked nearer the weakened Hasmonaean palace, the heart of the city would have fallen to him. Rumor had it that he refrained from doing so only because Florus's men wished to prolong the debacle. Others said that the Thunderbolt was so debilitated by the rebel attacks that Gallus had no choice but to hold back for the time being. In either case, it seemed like the beginning of the end. It was escape now or be caught in the maelstrom.

VII

"I came to tell you we're leaving before sunrise," said Simeon. He looked nervous and sullen as he bade Opal his last good-bye. "You can still come with us," he continued. "You *must*. The Romans will overrun this sector in a few days. How much longer can you wait?"

"We can't go with you, Simeon. You know we would be a liability if we did. With Jews slaughtered all over the Decapolis, why would we be spared? I know you would try to protect us, but it wouldn't be fair to you and your family. They are your priority. You're a good man, Simeon. We don't agree on many things these days, but we've been through a lot together. And I always assumed your daughter and my son..."

"I know. I had hoped so too."

"But the world is not ending. As the writings say, there is a future for a man of peace. Maybe when all this is over, it can still happen."

"Perhaps."

"For now, you have to do what you have to do, and I must head in the opposite direction. It is a pity, though. I will always be saddened that it has come to this, that you and I are falling out on different sides of the world. You people of the Way have been one with us for decades. We've never appreciated you and have fought against all your beliefs and rationales since the beginning. But how could we not? You have caused the most serious rift in Israel since Jeroboam. It cannot persist if we hope to survive, because without a common viewpoint, how can our faith stand? And without our faith, how can our nation stand? But now, when it's too late, and we need all the solidarity we can muster, I realize how many ties there are between us and how much we need you all. There are thousands of you. And just now you decide to set out on your own and leave us to fend for ourselves."

"Please," pleaded Simeon, "don't think of it that way. My faith is not a treachery. It's an invitation for you to come along too."

"I know. You explained it all to me months ago," continued Opal, "that your faith is a sword severing truth and non-truth, and that nationality doesn't matter anymore, but only faith. I actually remember the things you said. But I'm getting older now, and there are only so many new ideas I can take in."

"Opal, I'm the same age as you. One of these days I hope you'll understand. There is no greater hope I can have for you, my friend. I do not want to say good-bye to you on any level. Not in any way."

"I feel the same. But I'm planning on leaving here tomorrow myself. And then our new lives will begin, assuming we can escape the city alive. If I could ever keep track of Nathan, maybe we can be on our way sooner."

"If I know him, he's probably at our house saying good-bye to my daughter."

The two men embraced. "The Lord be with you," they said to each other.

Simeon then loosened his grip on Opal. Holding in his emotions, he turned around and walked away without looking back. Opal stared at his figure till it began to merge into the early dusk, then he disappeared into his house.

Opal remained in the street alone, not willing to surrender the moment to history just yet. The division between the Way and the

Jews affected him, though he could have no concept of the ramifications it would have for the future. But his ponderings were cut short. Turning to go back inside, he heard footsteps approach to his left. He didn't want to look, but he had a sinking feeling.

"Are you going somewhere, abba dearest?" a voice asked.

It was Amram.

"Yes," Opal answered. "I was just going back into my house."

"And what are you doing here out in the street? It's dangerous. The Romans lurk around every corner."

"If it's not the Romans, it's you. I don't know which is more dangerous. If you want something, tell me what it is, then go."

"Do you see how my father speaks to me?" Amram had about ten companions with him. Looking at Opal again, he said, "You know why we're here. You didn't think I was returning Nathan indefinitely, did you? Where is he? Inside? Is he at Rab Simeon's house? I know Simeon is ready to leave the city. That's good. We don't need his kind here anyway—maybe he'll have an accident on his way out—but you and Nathan are a different story."

Opal turned to the ten young men and said to them, "Please step aside. I'd like to speak to my son alone."

Amram gave assent, and they reassembled out of earshot.

"Amram, what could you possibly want with me?" said Opal. "And why is a sixteen-year-old so important to you? In a few days most of us are going to die if we stay here. Are you really going to deny your mother and little sister a chance to live? You and I understand each other. We don't agree, but you know where I stand, and I know where you stand. I can even see why you feel the way you do. But at this stage, you need to let them go, or you will be responsible for your family's blood before God himself. You know I don't care whether I live or die. I've lived long enough. But your mother, sister, and brother should be allowed to have a future. You are a man. Let's be reasonable as men."

Amram looked straight into his father's eyes. Opal thought that his words had perhaps reached his son's heart. Amram's next declaration, however, showed how great the chasm between them had grown and how little Opal understood the stranger before him.

"You," Amram yelled out pointing to his companions, "take him inside and make sure he doesn't go anywhere. And the rest of you, go to Simeon's house and get Nathan for me. I don't care if you have to drag him. I want him here. Do you hear me? Right here." He paused. "Now go!"

The young men ran up the street toward Simeon's house. Ducetius, who had overheard the entire conversation from behind the courtyard wall, was already ahead of them, having run behind the row of houses. He caught up to Nathan just in time to warn him, and the boy took off. Elisheva hurried back into the house, pleading with her father to do something. But what could he do? This was the moment Nathan had known would happen for a long time.

Nathan thought of a destination to evade the pursuers and the windiest path to get there he could think of. The Upper City grew more densely populated, however, as he ran north toward the wall that divided it and the Lower City. He had to reach the gate before Amram's men caught up to him. When he looked back, he could see that they were in hot pursuit. He turned a corner and down an alley, but the dusk proved even darker between the buildings, and he wasn't sure which direction he was going till his eyes adjusted. He passed a small tree and broke off a hard, dead twig.

Nearby, and closer than Nathan knew, the young men stopped. "Where is he?" they huffed. "He must have gone down the alley." It was too dark for them to see as well, and it allowed Nathan to gain some headway.

When he emerged from the other end, he was in a market near the wall. Running past the stands and shopkeepers as they closed up for the evening, several of them told him to slow down. He nearly knocked over a little girl and a table of fruit. "I'm sorry! Excuse me!" he said, trying to re-balance the ensemble while still in flight. His phylactery blew off his forehead. He tried to catch it with a flurry of his hands, but it was no use. The little girl ran to pick it up. She called out to Nathan and tried to follow him but couldn't. When Amram's men passed the spot a moment later, the angry banter of the sellers clued them in that Nathan had just been there. "Where is that boy?" they yelled out, panting. An old woman pointed, "That way." The men smiled and dashed off, hitting the little girl as they fled by. She was squatting and holding the phylactery. The pursuers didn't notice.

Just out of their line of vision, Nathan continued to run but stubbed his toe, gasping as the pain commenced. He tried to run faster to suppress the ache but made the mistake of looking down at his foot. It was bleeding, with drops of blood left behind after every few steps. He reached down between strides to wipe off the mess but lost his balance for a moment. From around a corner, he could hear voices. "Look, there's blood on the ground." Nathan regained his footing but needed to move faster. He had a larger-than-average physique but lacked speed, and he was beginning to pant. At least Amram's friends were older and slower than he was, and self-preservation was on his side. Just then a man sprang out in front of him and held him by the shoulders. "Watch it!" he reprimanded. Nathan nearly jumped, thinking he was caught. But the man simply grunted and walked on. Nathan breathed in relief, then continued. The dirtier his foot became, the more the dirt soaked up the blood. He had fallen behind a few paces, but at least a trail of blood no longer gave him away.

Nathan was now out the gate and into the middle-class section at Jerusalem's core. There were more residences and shops to get lost in. He stopped to catch his breath in another alley, holding close to a wall to keep out of view. Within a minute he heard someone yell, "There he is!" He hadn't gained the ground he had thought. He fled right then turned left. He stopped inside a tavern and could see his pursuers regroup and devise a new plan. When they had fanned out in every direction, he waited another few minutes and walked out cautiously. If it wasn't too late, he could still make it to the Temple entrance and into the holy precinct. He tried to keep his calm. The area was especially crowded at that time, since the Temple was about to close, and he worked to lose himself amid the throng. He climbed the steps and entered the Court of the Gentiles. He sensed a million eyes upon him. He walked along the colonnade, trying to move at a normal but steady clip. His mind was racing: *one, two, three.* He kept walking. He was almost sure he recognized one of Amram's men in the crowd now. *Seven, eight, nine.* Hopefully the young man hadn't seen him and he was safe for the moment. *Twelve, thirteen, fourteen.* He was almost there. Out of the corner of his eye, he thought he saw another young man point in his direction. *Eighteen, nineteen.*

Suddenly a crowd of people blocked the pursuers' view of him. There was the twentieth pillar. It was dark enough. He stood behind the pillar out of sight till he felt the moment was right. The filigree metal grate he remembered was right in front of him. He took out the stick he had grabbed, and in one movement defter than he could have hoped, he inserted the stick into the design and loosened the latch. It actually opened. With a creek muffled by the noisy passersby, he stepped inside and closed the grate after him.

He waited behind the metalwork, breathless and afraid to move. Outside, two of Amram's men stopped within feet of him.

"Where is he? I just saw him. It's like he disappeared. I'm going to look around a little longer. You go to the eastern portico."

Nathan waited several minutes before stirring to make sure the men were gone. He turned around on what he remembered was a landing by a stairway, but it was pitch black. He had no torchlight this time to guide him. He lifted his foot and gingerly felt for the edge of the riser, then descended five steps and sat down to recoup.

There's no way they can find me in here, he thought. No one knows this place exists. I'm safe for now, and the Temple will be closing soon.

Of course, once he was sitting for five minutes, he wasn't sure what to do next. He was bored and anxious all at once. Had he really gotten away from his pursuers that easily? He always believed that if his life was truly in danger, he would have to work harder to extricate himself. But then again, the chase through the city wasn't nothing. He was sweating and his body was heaving and shaking from all the activity.

After ten more minutes, he thought, what am I going to do now? I can't just go home and relax now that the game is over. I actually have to stay here. And I don't like it. I'm all alone, people are out to get me, it's dark, I have no food, my toe is throbbing, it's going to get cold soon, and I don't have a plan.

His mind then turned to how he had gotten into this predicament. It was his brother, of course: always the guide and bane of his existence. Amram knows just when to ruin my life, he thought. Why couldn't he have waited just one more day? Rab Simeon is leaving, and we were supposed to leave with him. But no. It couldn't be. I'm only sixteen. I should have a whole life ahead of me. But you had to be my brother, out of all the brothers in the world.

Nathan tried to clear his thoughts but grew more agitated between the blackness, entrapment, and solitude. A tear of frustration formed in his eye. I'm all alone here, he thought. It's not just me against my brother. It's me against the world.

He then turned to the fear that he might lose his father in the midst of all the turmoil between Amram and the upcoming war. Despite Nathan's adolescent feelings about his own greatness, wit, immortality, and good looks, he was more dependent on his father than he wanted to admit. Most of the time, he took his father for granted. Abba was simply a prop that Nathan could always rely on—though in his kinder moments he realized that good fathers probably always seemed like that to their ungrateful sons—and sometimes his opinions seemed myopic. But all in all, Nathan loved his father and wanted to agree with him more than he did. The thought that something could happen to him in the midst of this rebellion, and that they could potentially be separated forever, and that his flight from Amram might have signaled the beginning of that separation, all came flooding into his head.

After several more hours passed and the darkness outside the grate was as dense as the darkness within, he felt like an entire night had transpired. It hadn't.

The Temple was closed now, and nothing stirred but a breeze. Nathan got up and peered through the latticework. He opened the latch and stepped outside. After standing there a few minutes, he slowly walked across the courtyard. He could hear every sound he made as his arms rubbed against his tunic and his sandals crunched on the ground. The moon cast deep shadows all around. He walked into a shadow and knelt in its confines in case someone else could secretly see him. He then began to pray—something he often did, but not with the flow of thoughts that came to him now.

I need to ask you, he thought, who am I, and why am I here? David speaks of being a bird in your house, and here I am, feeling neither nestled nor free to fly. I think sometimes I might be safe in the shadow of your wings, but the circumstances into which I was born make me think there is no safe place to go. Your people are not born for safety, are we? We are caught in the middle of the world, with Babylon on one side and Rome on the other, and we cannot move without being noticed. Is that why you placed us here? So that with every move we make, the rest of the world is reminded we are here, and that means you must exist too?

But this place doesn't feel blessed by you. It feels abandoned. Please protect this Temple where you have placed your name for a thousand years. Are you leaving it? When is mashiach coming? Help me know whether I should follow Amram, my father, Elisheva, or someone else. Do you even hear my prayers? David asked you once how you could even notice man. I ask that too. But somehow I do not feel unnoticed. I think you are there. Please protect my father, mother, sister, and Elisheva. Fight for our cause. Bring us peace. Show us a way out if there is one. Please.

Nathan then returned to the grate and stepped inside. He didn't want to cage himself in again, but he couldn't risk the open air and cold. He climbed down five stairs again, since that was familiar, and he curled up to sleep. He stayed awake for a long time. He slept, but passed the night fitfully.

VIII

"Ngngngngngngngngngngngngngngn!" groaned Opal.

"Cut off another finger if he won't tell us where he is," Amram's henchmen said mercilessly.

Opal shook his head and squeezed his eyes shut to lessen the agony. He couldn't believe what was happening to him. He didn't know what to do but knew he couldn't show weakness.

"What's going on in there!?" Nathan's mother called out from behind a locked door, clutching her young daughter as she pleaded.

Amram's companions had taken over the house for the entire night and were ordered to do whatever it took to gain their prize. Amram had not been around for hours, though, so the men made sport of his father. Ducetius also lay in a corner, bruised and unconscious after a heavy beating. No one knew where Criton, the other slave, was.

After a night of brutality, Amram walked in a little after dawn. He could see what was going on and said to his father, "Well. I think you realize by now that we mean business and that family connections mean nothing. Don't worry. One pinky and some bruising are no great loss. Tell us what we need, and all this can stop." He pointed to one of his men. "You. Wrap up the finger. But keep him tied."

"What makes you think," said Opal, breathing through gritted teeth to absorb his pain, "that I know where Nathan is? Every time you've come to look for him for the last three months, he's been gone. There's no special hiding place that I know of that you wouldn't know of as well." As Opal said those very words, however, he suddenly realized there might be.

"That may be true, but I won't know for certain till a little more prodding has occurred," said Amram. "Don't worry, though. I won't stand around and watch my father harmed. I'll be out of the house."

"You're a monster. How could you be doing this? Your cause has made you the very detestable thing you're fighting against."

"Do you think the Romans are treating us Jews any better up in the north city? They're crucifying people out there, but you still think their cause is more just than mine?"

"No, Amram, I don't. I told you before, I understand why you feel the way you do. But I also don't know where Nathan is. So if you're going to kill me, just do it. I can't and won't help you."

Opal's mind was racing back and forth between wanting to divulge Nathan's possible hiding spot and wanting to protect Nathan. If he remained silent, he might be tortured to death, in which case his wife and daughter would be left defenseless. But if he revealed Nathan's possible whereabouts, he might be killed anyway, and Nathan would be trapped. Neither choice sounded good.

Before Opal had a chance to decide how to respond, Amram asked one of his cronies, "When you tried to catch Nathan, which direction did he run?"

"He ran south, through the gate to the Upper City. Johanan thinks he saw him in the Temple."

"I *did* see him in the Temple," responded the young man. "Mattatiah saw him too. But then he just vanished. We looked for him in every direction. He must have gotten out. And if he did, he could be anywhere."

Redirecting his gaze to his father, Amram said, "All right. I'm giving you one more chance to prove you know nothing. I'm leaving, and the boys will help you come clean while I'm gone. After they're done with you, there's the rest of the family in the other room waiting their turn."

"Amram, kill me, and let them go. There must be some shred of honor left in you. We're your family who raised you. How could you do this?"

"I'm leaving, boys. Do what you need to. In fact, start with the others first. That will make him talk."

Amram left the room and approached the front door, where someone was entering just as he was exiting.

"Joseph. What are you doing here?"

"I came to speak to your father."

"My father? What do you want with him?"

"I need to tell him about something. It concerns you too. If you're not in too much of a rush, please come back in and talk to us."

Joseph and Amram walked back into the atrium where Opal sat tied to a chair next to a small puddle of blood. Joseph was taken aback and said to Amram, "You're interrogating your own father? You'd better not hurt him too much. We need him."

Opal raised his eyes as if deliverance had come.

"Opal," said Joseph in a business-like tone, as if nothing unusual were transpiring, "you have a son who shows more loyalty to his beliefs than any man I've ever met. You have to forgive him that fault, though, since I see he inherited it from you."

"Joseph," Opal asked bewildered, "what is going on? Why am I being held here? And is it true that you have decided to cast your lot with the Zealots?"

"I'm the same as I've always been," Joseph responded. "I'm simply doing what needs to be done. And right now, I need to talk to you. I have a proposition. But first, we have to get that finger cauterized so you don't bleed out."

One of the men took care of the procedure. It was as painful as the removal.

Joseph resumed talking to take Opal's mind off the pain.

"Opal," he said, directing his attention to his words and his words alone, "two days ago, as you might know, the civil authorities fled the city. A provisional government is being set up with some moderates who are sympathetic to our cause," he said, pointing to himself and Amram. "They're asking me to take a military position and to lead an army up into Galilee, where the Romans will probably attack first. I personally think I should stay in Jerusalem, but I see the wisdom in their decision. But while I'm gone, I need someone back here who can straddle the fence between the moderates and the Zealots. And I've requested that *you* be given that seat on the council."

"Him?" whipped Amram, pointing to his father. "Joseph, are you mad?"

"No, I'm not mad. Your father is perfect for the job, despite all your capabilities. I've given this some long, hard thought. Now listen to me, Amram."

"I'm listening."

"First of all, you are in no position to act as a liaison between the Zealots and anybody else. Everyone knows that your reputation is stellar, except for diplomacy. Your father, on the other hand, is a known quantity among the civic leaders, and everyone knows you are his son. What better combination could there be? He can keep the government reputable, and you can keep your eye on him. If I have to leave Jerusalem, I need to know that it's being left in the most capable hands around. If I leave it with the two of you, I know that will happen. Think it through, Amram. It's our best option. You can affect the government more thoroughly by working through your father than you possibly could by causing friction with the leaders directly. Your father is a good man, and so are you. Neither of you should be lost to our cause. And everyone knows that even though the two of you can't agree on anything, you at least understand each other."

Both men thought separately of their conversation on that point the previous day.

"So what do you say, Opal? Oh, and one more thing—and this will certainly make Amram happy—I'm requesting that you let me bring your son Nathan on the expedition into Galilee with me."

"Nathan?" asked Opal, almost faint.

"He'll be perfect. He's young, he's smart, and it will keep you and Amram in communication over your one mutual interest. You're in no position to argue. Nathan is either Amram's to take, or he's mine."

Opal's head fell in exhaustion. How could all this be happening to him at once? "Give me a minute to think it over, please."

Joseph and Amram walked a few feet away and quibbled over some details of the arrangement, but it was obvious from the look of things that Joseph's point of view was winning out. Opal was pleased to see his oldest son put in his place by someone in authority, just to assure him that men like Amram did not always have the upper hand in the world.

As for Joseph's proposition, how could Opal not accept it? Although it was absolutely preposterous, it might actually work on that very score. And everyone came out a winner of sorts. He remained alive for his family, his wife and daughter would have protection, Amram had an important role to keep him content, and Nathan would be out of Amram's control. But what was Joseph really up to with all of this? He was not such a die-hard Zealot that he would fall in with the likes of Amram without some other motive. Was it to influence the workings of the radical party from within? Was it to save his own life? He couldn't be sure.

And why arrange a détente between himself and Amram? Was

it really because he and Amram could provide the best home-team while he was away in Galilee? Was it because it was his nature to develop diplomatic solutions to difficult situations? Was it simply because he was flexing his authority and testing the waters? Or did he actually care about a triad of a father and two sons whose lives were swirling in opposing directions, out of control and to the death, unless they worked together? Opal didn't know.

But Joseph's proposal provided a solution to every one of those scenarios. How could he not respect that? The man was a political genius, and his idea gave Opal's family a second chance to survive.

"Joseph," Opal answered weakly, "I accept your proposal."

"Good, my friend. I'm glad to hear it. It is really the only way our venture will succeed." Turning to Amram, he said, "Amram, please untie your father. He needs some rest. And—" he whispered into Amram's private ear—"I want no more of these coercive techniques. We're civilized men."

One of Amram's cronies freed Opal, who excused himself to his bedchamber. As he slumped away, Joseph asked him, "And where *is* your son Nathan?"

Opal turned around. "I don't know," he said. "But based on what that young man Johanan said earlier, I might have an idea."

IX

Nathan was breaking into a sweat as he heard footsteps. How did they find him? Cramped and stiff from the long night, he climbed down the remaining stairs and walked straight into the blackness. It was the exact opposite of what anyone would rationally do, but he was doing it. He had to grope quietly to find a hiding place as quickly as he could.

He felt along the cold stone wall till it gave way to the nothingness of an opened door. He stepped into it and tried to flatten himself against the wall. Standing still, and conscious of every breath, he heard people calling his name. "Nathan, Nathan. We're here in Joseph ben Mattathias's name. We're not going to harm you. Where are you?"

Nathan tried to figure out if it was a trick or not. Amram would stop at nothing to catch him. The torchlight and footsteps drew nearer and nearer. He could see insects crawling around in the dim light now, and it made him itchy. He had been sleeping among them all night. He wanted to get out of that place. It had been the longest, most uncomfortable night in his life.

Suddenly the light vanished, and the footsteps grew fainter. Apparently the men took a turn down another tunnel passage. They were still calling his name. Were they really there for Joseph, he wondered. If they were, he'd run to them in an instant. But he couldn't be sure. If he was going to get out of there, he had to do it now.

He crept out to the corridor and made his way back to the stairwell. He climbed: one step, two steps. The sun was filtering down the shaft through the grate by now. No doubt the first round of visitors was out in the Temple. Nathan had to risk it, though. Better free in the city than trapped like an animal where he was. Simeon's home might be vacated, and Amram's men might have already searched the place, so he could potentially hide there for a while. And if Elisheva hadn't left yet, they could see each other one last time.

He reached the landing and looked through the metalwork. He had no choice. He loosened the latch and stepped outside. He walked only a few paces. Within seconds, he was surrounded by Amram's men. There was no way out. He had to surrender. Either the group in the tunnel or the men outside were going to get him. At least they reiterated the fact that they were there in Joseph's name and that they meant him no harm. Nathan remained suspicious, however, as they walked him back through the Upper City to the house.

X

Within a week, Nathan's entire life had altered. He was on the road to Sepphoris in Galilee with neither his father nor Elisheva nor his brother, but with Joseph ben Mattathias, a man he barely knew. As the caravan stealthed north along the Judaean highway by night, one foot after another, he wondered how it had all happened. Elisheva and Simeon were gone, Opal and Amram were working on the same side, and he, from a relatively peaceful upbringing, was moving headlong toward the rebel front of an upcoming war against Rome with a military commander.

Sepphoris, an opulent city second only to Jerusalem, was traditionally Romaphile and in full Hellenistic bloom. Joseph's job was to transform it into a Zealot headquarters. A myriad of adventures and scrapes with death awaited he and Nathan there—difficulties caused not so much by the Romans, as one might expect, but by the local populace hostile to Joseph's plans. Since the people of Sepphoris vacillated in their loyalties for and against Rome, and the rebel leaders often vied with each other as well as with Joseph, Joseph and Nathan's stay in Sepphoris would prove complicated and arduous. One of Joseph's most vehement opponents there was a man named John of Gischala. "He's a veritable thief," Joseph explained to Nathan. "He means nothing but trouble. But at least he's not in town at the moment."

From Joseph's first day in Sepphoris, he set to work. He trained rebel soldiers, recruited additional bodyguards, and met with local leaders to establish political councils loyal to the provisional government in Jerusalem. The job went well or badly depending on the mood of the moment. One week a city like Tiberias might clamor for war with Rome. The next, when the city was handed over by Nero to King Agrippa as a political gift, it felt uneasy rebelling against a Jewish leader. The same held true for Sepphoris, which shilly-shallied weekly between fear of reprisal from Rome versus fear of reprisal from the provisional government. As a result, one could never trust the outward mask people wore in either city. Certainly Joseph never did.

As time went by, however, Nathan began to suspect that Joseph might be playing his own two-sided game. He never spoke of it to anyone and continued to put his life in Joseph's hands every day. But he remembered his father intimating that he wasn't sure where Joseph's loyalties lay: with Rome, with the Jews, or with himself. Joseph's talent for counterbalancing opposing views, like those of Nathan's father and brother, demonstrated that he was no ordinary thinker; but it also showed that he was capable of duplicity. Nathan was too fascinated by Joseph, however, to judge him too harshly.

Others felt no compunction. One event after another cast doubts in people's minds regarding Joseph's motives. In one notorious instance, he asked the Tiberian leaders to torch Agrippa's palace in their city. The provisional government had issued the order, and it would show the Tiberians' loyalty if they fulfilled it. After an independent ringleader named Jesus Ben Sapphias burned it down himself without Joseph's authority, however, Joseph swindled the rebel for possession of the looted goods, turning many against him. A faction under a rabble rouser named Justus opposed Joseph's every move and spread rumors that Joseph was not merely buying supplies with the goods, but was stashing them away for himself and writing to Agrippa that he was salvaging the gold for the royal family.

In private talks with Nathan, however, Joseph reinstilled his young adjutant's trust by admitting that all three rumors were true. "How else can I run this campaign?" he explained to Nathan. "If I don't have the money to survive, purchase war supplies, and maintain goodwill toward Agrippa, how can I succeed? The provisional government endangered its ties to the king with their order, so I had to let Agrippa know he still has an ally among us. If Agrippa were to turn against me, our cause would suffer irreparably."

"But I thought Agrippa was a friend of Rome," said Nathan.

"But he is also a Jewish king and my relative," responded Joseph.

Such situations enlightened Nathan on the complexities of war and leadership. Nothing was straightforward. Enemies needed befriending and friends needed probing. Nathan could only sit back and learn from such a master. He became Joseph's biggest fan, and as a result, Joseph grew to rely on Nathan's discretion and loyalty more and more.

So much tension mounted within the rebel party, however, that Joseph relocated his headquarters outside Tiberias, in nearby

Cana, a few miles north. Cana was a smaller, more docile town than Tiberias, and unbeknownst to Nathan, it was the site of a popular event told among the people of the Way.

Although Joseph had fewer distractions working in Cana, Tiberias continued to fester in his absence. The 'thief,' John of Gischala, returned to Tiberias, informing Joseph of his visit, then proceeded to incite the entire town against Joseph in his absence.

Within an hour of hearing the news, Joseph and Nathan were en route back to Tiberias and met with a mixed reception. One supporter said to him, "We've heard you are really a Roman spy working for Agrippa." Another said, "John of Gischala is a lunatic and is spreading crazy rumors about you." Still others asked, "What's going on? Are you still in charge of this city? Is it back in Agrippa's hands? Has John of Gischala stolen power from you?"

To calm things down, Joseph sent word for the town's civic leaders to meet him in the city stadium. When he and Nathan arrived at the stadium, the furor already presiding over the crowd proved difficult to diffuse. But Nathan was about to see Joseph at his best.

Jumping onto a platform, Joseph waved to the crowd to quiet down. He then began to speak. A few words came out, but the noise level swelled again. Joseph shut his mouth and looked down. He motioned with his hands a second time for silence. The mob then cooperated.

"Good people of Tiberias," he began. "I understand that some among you are asking what is going on in this city. Some of you have stirred up trouble by questioning the leadership, and others have cast doubt on its policies. Although your doubts may be understandable, let me set the record straight for you. I am Joseph ben Mattathias. I have been sent here by the government in Jerusalem, and I will answer all your questions. I am a descendant of Jonathan, brother of the Maccabee. And it is I, and I alone, who have been ordered to oversee your fight for freedom and justice in this city; and not just this city, but in the whole of Galilee. My goal is to aid in the orderly liberation of our entire nation; a liberation gained not by random acts of violence for personal gain, as some of you have perpetrated recently, but a freedom won by organized resolve against tyranny that will win the admiration of our adversaries.

"Let no man in this city work toward his own end. Let no one dare think he can take charge, especially at the risk of the thousands of innocent elderly, women, and children among you. Unlike some whom you know, I am working under lawful authority. I ask you to work under that same authority. If you trust the Jerusalem government, trust me. And if you don't trust a government so far away, then still trust that I, who stands right in front of you, am out for your good.

"Whatever you may have heard, I have led and served you loyally and will continue to do so. My actions speak louder than any words you have heard muttered against me …" some noise began to erupt from the crowd, "and I came here as fast as I could from my headquarters in Cana …" the grumbling became louder, "when I heard you were beset with doubts …" he paused—he could now barely hear himself— "I can assure you that …"

His words were drowned out by an uproar as a band of men brandishing their swords moved front and center in the crowd. "In the name of John of Gischala," one of the band yelled out, "you are going to die, you thieving liar!"

With that, screams arose across the entire stadium. What was happening? Nathan wasn't sure. The men lunged forward toward the platform where Joseph stood. As the swordsmen leapt toward Joseph, Nathan was helplessly trapped in the crowd to come to his aid. But he watched Joseph leap from the stage into the air and land some six feet onto the crowd. Some of Joseph's bodyguard reached out to break his fall. Then a dozen men surrounded him, pulled out their daggers, and fought to protect him. Nathan uncloaked his dagger as well.

Pressing through the mob to catch up to Joseph, Nathan barely escaped a blow to his head. Seconds later, one of Joseph's guard blocked another blow to his neck. Nathan felt a rush of adrenaline as he pressed forward, shaken a little by his brush with death. He had to get out of that arena. Unfortunately, everyone else had the same idea.

As he neared the stadium exit, surrounded by screaming and killing, he asked himself, 'Does anyone realize there are no Romans here? Why are we murdering each other?' He momentarily lost track of Joseph but spotted him again as he saw him run out the exit. Nathan wondered where Joseph was going. To the waterfront? But we don't have a boat. He watched as Joseph ran to the end of a dock and jumped into a small, oared craft. Can you wait for me? thought Nathan. I'm almost there.

"Nathan! Jump in!" Joseph yelled over to him a few moments later. Nathan obliged as Joseph slashed the rope and freed the boat from the dock. The boat drifted for two seconds, then the body-guard thrust the oars into the water and rowed feverishly. Before they had gotten far, they could hear a throng at the water's edge. Some were cheering; others shouting threats. It was clear that a few people would die that day in the stadium. He felt guilty that he had made it to safety. Within a few hours, he was across the Sea of Galilee.

XI

Six months had passed since Nathan last saw his parents, brother, sister, or Elisheva. His seventeenth birthday came and went, and he contemplated the changes he had undergone. Half of him missed his former life, and half of him reveled in the excitement of his current situation. Although Joseph kept him on the move, he took time out for himself, reading whatever holy parchments or scrolls Joseph kept at the headquarters. He also sometimes tried his hand at poetry, writing about his trials, successes, and doubts. If David could be a man of action and letters, so can I, he thought.

In the outer world, difficulties mounted. Tiberias and Sepphoris continued to steer on and off the rebel course regularly. Internal struggles within the leadership continued to arise. Perhaps worst of all, news reached Galilee that Nero had chosen a commander to squash the nascent Jewish revolt. The commander, named Vespasian, was already preparing his legions to arrive in a few months. His plan was for he and his son Titus to conquer Galilee first. Then he would wait to attack Jerusalem till the city's own infighting squeezed every ounce of hope from its citizenry. In that way, he would make the final onslaught of the Jews the most enjoyable of his career. Each day, thought Nathan, brought the commander closer and closer to his dream.

Meanwhile, Joseph and Nathan stationed themselves in the area of Tarichaea by the sea. Tarichaea had recently joined the rebel side by revolting against Agrippa's authority, just as Tiberias had. Joseph was there to convince the town it had done the right thing. Nathan continued as his messenger and adjutant there.

One day, a group of rebels from another town overtook a caravan on the Galilean plain and robbed the wife of Agrippa's financial overseer. The woman escaped, but her treasury did not. The rebels were honest enough to bring the goods to Joseph for safekeeping, but Joseph responded in a way that led to new problems for him. He told the rebels that the money would be sent to Jerusalem to repair its broken walls, but he entrusted the plunder to two known friends of Agrippa.

Within a day, suspicions of Joseph double dealing began to arise again.

Nathan tried to justify his mentor's actions, despite his own occasional doubts, but it did little to change people's minds. "What do you know, anyway? You're just a kid," people said. So the rebels' slander spread across town, and tensions rose. By the next morning, an angry crowd filled the streets. Tens of thousands headed for the local hippodrome. People were yelling, "The Romans are coming, and our leader is funding Agrippa!" Others demanded that Joseph be replaced. One group even chanted, "Death to ben Mattathias!" As people flooded the arena, the noise level grew deafening.

Jesus ben Sapphias, who just happened to be in the crowd, rejoiced in this serendipitous besmirchment of Joseph's character. Holding up a Torah scroll, he yelled at the top of his lungs, "This is what our leader is really trying to betray! This is what our leader has forgotten! Death to ben Mattathias! Death to ben Mattathias! Follow me to his house, everyone! Follow me! We will burn it to the ground. Death to ben Mattathias!"

Like misguided sheep, the mob followed ben Sapphias out of the hippodrome toward Joseph's new headquarters. Marching and chanting, they could be heard blocks away. Joseph, still asleep, was wakened by one of his guard.

"Commander, you must get up. There's a mob coming this way, headed by ben Sapphias. They're chanting 'Death to Mattathias.' You can hear them."

Joseph bolted out of bed. "Get Nathan out of here." He threw black clothes on and went from room to room. "Where is everyone? Where's the guard?"

"They've left. All but four of us are gone."

"And Nathan?"

"Benjamin is getting him out the door right now."

One minute later, Joseph fled the house alone without his men. Running down an alleyway to escape the approaching lynch party, he put dirt on his head and tore his black robes. He barely saw a soul along the way since the mob was marching up another street in the opposite direction. He reached the arena while the mob was at his house, but the stragglers who stayed in the arena were as furious with him as the mob with ben Sapphias.

"There he is!" someone yelled as he entered.

"It's the traitor!" A thousand voices echoed the insult. A group of men, some of whom Joseph recognized from Tiberias, ran toward him and stopped just short of attacking him. Joseph's pathetic appearance, between his torn black robes and the dirt on his head proved enough to halt the aggressors in their tracks. The rest of the crowd became curious too, as before them all Joseph suddenly prostrated himself on the ground and rubbed his face in the dirt. He then cried out in a loud voice, "Have mercy! Please listen to what I have to say! Let me speak!"

"I'll let you speak, you filthy scum!" yelled back an onlooker. "Where's our treasure? Where's the money you owe us? I'll let you speak about *that*!"

Another added, "You tried this same thing in Tiberias. We should have killed you then!" Dozens of others chimed in.

"Please," pleaded Joseph, now on his feet with his hands behind his back in humility. "I will tell you all, but please let me speak."

The yelling continued.

"All right," yelled a woman. "Let the man speak! Let the man speak!" As others repeated her words, the noise gradually died down to a murmur.

Just then the rabble outside the hippodrome led by ben Sapphias came back into the arena, having received news that Joseph was there and not in his headquarters. Seeing Joseph, ben Sapphias said, "You escaped, you dog! We should burn you right here, like we hoped to do in your house!"

"Let him speak! Let him speak!" someone yelled. "Shut your mouth ben Sapphias. We want to hear what the man has to say!"

Ben Sapphias, shocked at the indignity, saw he was inexplicably outnumbered in sentiment and that Joseph had somehow won over the crowd in his absence. He stood mute and simply waited.

Joseph looked at his audience. His expression both direct and plaintive, he waited for silence then opened his mouth. Every eye was upon him. At that moment, Nathan and several of the bodyguard entered to see what was happening. Nathan was astonished—though not really—that Joseph was still alive, in one piece, and holding at bay 100,000 violent people who had been ready to rip him apart mere minutes ago.

"My fellow countrymen," Joseph began, making sure not to sound too similar to his last, and all too recent, public plea for his life in a similar venue, "perhaps I deserve to die at your hands. I have lied to you all. I admit it. It is my fault that this entire city has been aroused by my words, and you have acted rightly to want me dead for that." He paused for effect. "But I tell you the truth that I never kept an ounce of the money entrusted to me for myself. Nor did I send a mite of it to Agrippa. That I can promise you! The reason I was hiding money was to repair our city walls—our walls, right here—which are in such disrepair." He pointed outside to the walls beyond. "And the reason I entrusted the money to Agrippa's friends instead of one of you was to keep you all from thinking I was playing favorites among you. And the reason I said the money was going to rebuild the walls of Jerusalem was to keep the Tiberians here from getting jealous of you Tarichaeans and stealing the money, since their own walls need repairs too. You can see how many Tiberians are here in this audience even right now who might be jealous." He waited a moment for people to look around and confirm his statement. "So that is why I had to deceive you all for a little while. Not because I am deceitful or have a plan for myself, but because a leader cannot always divulge his true intentions, in order to maintain the public peace. So please forgive me. I ask your forgiveness. Please."

Joseph's last word met with spellbound silence as the audience soaked in his speech. Then someone suddenly began to clap. Another laughed. Someone else yelled out, "We forgive you!" Still another, "We love you, commander!" The applause grew and people continued to speak. "I knew it all along!" "You did all that for us?" "The Tiberians always think they're better than we are!" "And we were going to kill you." "You're a great leader!" The accolades lasted a full minute or more.

The Tiberians nearest Joseph responded quite differently, however. They were still angry for the stunt Joseph had gotten away with back in Tiberias. "You still haven't returned the money you owe us. You speak of *us* as criminals. You are the one on trial here, not us." "You know our city needs a wall too, so why did you never mention giving money for *our* defense?"

Joseph spoke directly to them to assure them he would rebuild their walls as well. He hadn't offered help before because he felt the Tiberians wanted him out of their city as soon as possible. But if they wanted monies for defense, he would certainly provide some.

Then one of the Tarichaean leaders walked over to defend Joseph. "Oh, leave the man alone," he said to the Tiberians. "We've caused him enough trouble already. Now you know the truth. Be on your way."

"Who do you think you're talking to," responded one of the Tiberians to the leader. "Where would your city even be without us? You only rebelled against Agrippa because we rebelled first."

The interchange blew up into a debate now between the Tiberians and Tarichaeans. Nathan, who had just moved nearer to his mentor, heard references in their discussion to money, loyalty to the rebel cause, who needed a wall more, and which city was better. After five minutes of escalating argument, it seemed the combatants had forgotten about Joseph altogether. One of them said to him, "We'll take it from here," and Joseph shyly bid them good-bye and left.

Once outside the hippodrome, Joseph and Nathan walked for blocks without a word.

"I don't know how you do it, Joseph," said Nathan, finally breaking the silence. "I've never seen someone win a crowd like you can."

"I don't know how I do it either. It never worked with my mother. But I sure can make a crowd angry too. It's been a tough morning. I could use a good bath."

XII

That evening Nathan went for a stroll after supper. Joseph stayed in the house to recoup. Nathan felt relieved to be by himself and think about the long day. The faces he saw in the streets were friendly now, unlike that morning. He was beginning to think the whole episode had been a bad dream, not something that had actually happened.

He ambled down the street thinking about how his father and brother were faring back in Jerusalem and if General Vespasian's plans with his son were materializing against Galilee. Caught between the day and the dusk, the empire and the province, his family and the commander, there was much to contemplate, and Nathan stood poised in the middle, as he always did. Elisheva was right about him. Girls were perceptive. But how would the war end, he wondered. Would Joseph manage to wield Galilee into a bulwark against Rome? Would Israel ever be free? Would he survive the events of his generation? His peaceful walk was rapidly descending into a wallow of trouble. He said to himself, I have to stop thinking about all this for a little while. I need some rest. Let me just put one foot in front of the other and continue my walk without a care. There is a world here and now to enjoy, without any planning for the future or regret for the past or guilt for the present. And I will think more clearly if I can have a moment of peace now.

Then out of the gray came a voice.

"Hello, little brother."

What? What was that? No. It couldn't be. That voice could not be real. Not now. Not in this city. Not in the safety of the now. Nothing else can break through it. I am safe here.

He took a few more steps.

"Little brother," came the voice again.

Nathan turned around, expecting the voice to go silent with his movement or be heard emanating from someone else, anyone else, other than who he thought it was, when his eyes landed on the hopefully empty space it seemed to come from. But it did not go silent, and the space was not empty. Amram stood there in the flesh in the shadows as real as the buildings behind him.

"Amram?" Nathan said half startled, half angry.

"Hello, little brother."

Nathan moved to greet him with a hug, feeling powerless to do anything else. "What are you doing here? Is everything all right?"

"I am here to see how you are doing. And as for everything being all right, that is what I came to talk to *you* about." As always, there was a biting sarcasm in his voice.

"Forgive my surprise at your being here. How did you get here?" inquired Nathan.

"The usual way," he said mockingly. "It's not really that far. In fact, I've been watching your house for three or four hours. I was going to have to knock in a few minutes if you hadn't come out."

"Why didn't you just come in then?"

"I have my reasons."

Nathan was exasperated at the discussion already, and it had only just begun. Was Amram spying on him now? Didn't he know that this city was his and Joseph's world? What was *he* doing in it? "What were you watching for? What do you want?" He could hear the same impatience rising in his voice as he heard in his father's whenever Amram was around.

"Let's go over to the square where we can talk." They walked some paces and sat by a fountain in the shadows.

"So what is the nature of your visit?" asked Nathan, only thinly concealing his perturbance.

"I want to know what's going on here," Amram responded. "I want to know what kind of man Joseph is up here in Galilee. Is he doing what he's supposed to? I hear he's been moving around a lot but not accomplishing anything. Are his tactics working? He seems to cause trouble everywhere he goes. Is he being honest with the rebels' money? There are rumors that he's not."

"You're asking *me* those questions?" Nathan asked. "What do I know? Who do you think I am? I'm a kid hanging on the cloak-ends of greatness and just along for the ride. I live with Joseph, eat with him, talk to him, hope he doesn't get into trouble. What do I know of what you're talking about? I don't analyze his every move."

"Then why do you think I allowed you to come here with him?"

"Why? Because—or so I was told—you struck a deal with Joseph and abba, and the result was that I ended up here."

"No, little brother. It's because you're working for me. And because Joseph trusts you. And because our father trusts you. And that's just what I need. You'll always be true to me because you're afraid of what I'll do if you're not. I know that you're honest with abba because you love him—something I've envied for a long time, though it just can't be between us. And you're honest with Joseph because you admire him. I'm envious of that too. Joseph is an amazing man. But you're exactly where I want you to be, whether you think it was Joseph and abba's choice or not." He paused. "And that is power," he added, as if to remind Nathan of where he actually stood in the overall scheme of life.

"What are you talking about, Amram? You sound mad. And you know a coerced tie never truly has power. As soon as a slave can run, he will."

"But where would you run? You know I'd find you anywhere you went."

"You would never have to look for me if you actually let me live freely. I'm loyal to you because you are my brother, but nothing more. So you will always have to search for me to reestablish our connection. I'm loyal to Joseph whether I'm with him or not because I've never met anybody else like him."

"Well, 'never' in seventeen years isn't a very long time. But I agree with you. I agree." He paused. "But it's not just me that needs to know about Joseph. It's our father and the council. It's the whole movement that needs to know. It's that very amazing quality about Joseph you speak of that makes some think he could be up to no good."

"What do you mean, 'no good'?" Nathan asked mockingly.

"Some of the council wants to make sure Joseph isn't putting on another show behind our backs. He may be writing to Agrippa on the sly, and they need to know if he is. I've got spies all over this city, and I hear reports about strange behavior from your 'mentor,' as you think of him. But no one's been able to say for sure."

"So you want *me* to find out?"

"Who else is as close to him as you are these days? I'm sure he confides in you. You're a kid, and you have no political agenda."

"If I'm just a kid, do you really think Joseph would be telling me things that could place me in a vulnerable position? Why don't you just speak to him yourself? You two know each other. You've never minced words with anyone. Why not confront him yourself?"

"I have my reasons. For one thing, it's more fun finding a rat where he's hiding. And if I spoke to him directly, there'd be no way to know if I was getting at the truth. No. I need to catch him in the act. And it can't be me that finds him. It has to be you. If you were to discover something about Joseph, the council would believe you."

"But Amram, I'm not a spy. I don't know how to lie and hide things from people. You're asking the wrong person."

"On the contrary. You're just what I want you to be. And you don't have to lie and hide things to do what I'm asking. You just have to be yourself. In fact, you could tell me right now just by being honest: has Joseph ever spoken about Agrippa? Does he ever write to him? Has he ever told you that he has?"

Nathan waited, unsure whether to divulge or not. "Yes. He has. He told me he wrote to him a few months ago."

"You see? Your knowledge is already of value to us. It's not so hard being a 'spy.' And you probably haven't told another soul about your conversation, have you? Because you're discreet. You're a natural. You probably know other secrets as well."

"But Amram, that wasn't a secret. He told me that writing the king is necessary in order to dupe him into thinking he has an ally among the rebels. They're relatives, remember? It's all part of his plan. He said he has to keep up the pretense because if Agrippa lost his trust in him, it would have dire consequences for our cause."

"He said that, eh?" Amram pondered. "He may be right. I can see his point. But only if he's telling the truth. Do you think he's telling the truth?"

Nathan waited again.

"You're hesitating, little brother. You have your doubts, don't you. Don't you want to know for sure? Don't you want abba and the council to know for sure?"

Amram was starting to sound like the serpent in the garden. And it was having its desired effect.

"Yes, I do. But I will not be your spy. Joseph trusts me. I don't want to do anything to jeopardize that."

"You won't have to. Just write me now and then about what you know. I'll tell you, the council is set on bringing Joseph in for questioning. You can play a role in deciding whether the council has grounds to do so or not, or if Joseph will be acquitted if they do."

"But if I write you letters—and I'm not saying I will, I'm only saying if—how would I even get them to you?"

"Don't worry about that. I've already spoken to the guard Benjamin about it. He'll take care of it."

"You know Benjamin? How? I was there when Joseph picked him out of a crowd."

"I know everyone I need to know. It's my business to know. And I know that Benjamin is loyal. At least for the moment."

"But you also know Joseph is loyal. After all the time you've spent with him, why do you doubt that?"

"Nathan, people aren't so simple—everyone has his price: Benjamin, Joseph, maybe even you. Joseph is a good man, as men go. But every once in a while, a man's mettle has to be tested to make sure. Don't think my desire to get information about Joseph means he has become an enemy. He hasn't. It's just that I have a war to win, and I think you want that too. And because of that, I need to know who is with me and who is not, who is ambivalent and who is playing both sides. I'm offering you an important role in our cause. Don't think of it shamefully and don't take it lightly. If you don't want the job, I'll give it to someone else. There are plenty of other people I could consider, and plenty of other ways I could play this out. But because you're my brother, and because I have respect for Joseph, and because he has respect for you, I thought I would come to you and try out this plan first. Ultimately, you and I are nothing. We might be dead next week, or tomorrow morning. But I thought I should try you first, so that if we live, at least you'll know we dove deep into what we believed and did all that we needed to do to succeed, whoever or whatever the fallout might be."

For the first time, Amram sounded like he was speaking to a colleague and not a subordinate. The new tone almost had Nathan convinced. He could feel the serpent coiling closer now, and his arguments against taking the fruit were weakening by the moment.

"All right, I'll do it," said Nathan, resentful but resolved. "I'll write to you once in a while. But don't expect great revelations. My goal is to justify Joseph's activities, not to place him on trial."

Nathan's response caused Amram to stare at him with a look of chagrin he had never seen on his brother's face before. "No, Nathan. Your goal is nothing of the kind. Your goal is to find out the truth. That's always been your goal. Don't change that now." Looking down, Amram advised. "And just in case you forget your goal, I'll be asking someone to keep his eye on you."

"That won't be necessary, Amram," snapped Nathan. "I'm your little brother."

Amram was silent for a moment. "That, apparently, isn't true anymore."

He stood up, patted Nathan on the shoulder, and left.

Nathan sat watching Amram depart in the dimming light. He wondered how it was that the more involved he became in the world of men, the more lonely he felt.

XIII

"Those miserable Tiberians. They're nothing but trouble!" fumed Joseph to Nathan one morning. "Did you hear what that messenger just said?"

"Yes, I did. The Tiberians have invited Agrippa back into their city. But how could they? After all their blustering about taking the lead in the revolt and them needing a wall more than the Tarichaeans…Why did they do it?"

"Apparently because I've been too slow in getting their wall repaired. This is payback. And now that half my men have gone home for the harvest, I don't have the manpower to threaten them. I've got to think of something." He went into his room and closed the door behind him.

Nathan yelled through the door, "Joseph, I'm going down to the wharf for some fish. I'll be back in a little while. I'll be thinking of a plan while I'm out."

"Be careful," came the muffled reply.

The fall weather was perfect for an errand, though under the circumstances, and after Nathan's encounter with Amram, he felt less inclined to go out into the city alone.

As he headed toward the waterfront, he devised the first dispatch to his brother in his mind. The day's news about Tiberias and Joseph's reaction to it would certainly indicate to Amram that Joseph was honorable in his affairs. If he were really allied with Agrippa, Nathan would have detected some element of relief in Joseph's attitude about the news. But he seemed genuinely distressed over Tiberias's defection. Unless it was all just pretense. Could it be, though, that Joseph was play-acting for Nathan's benefit? If everyone was spying on everyone else, couldn't Joseph have found out that Amram and he had spoken to each other recently? Wouldn't a man of Joseph's stature and experience keep his true feelings to himself rather than talk to a teenage sidekick? Yes. That could very well be true. It was logical.

But on the other hand, are people always logical? Of course not. Is it even possible to be as superhumanly secretive as Nathan was attributing Joseph of being? No. He had witnessed Joseph use discretion and restraint in all of his relationships except his relationship with him. After all, thought Nathan, was there anything Joseph had done or not done in the year they had been together to which he was not privy? Nathan was familiar with every aspect of the rebel operations. He trained with Joseph's men, knew his bodyguard intimately, acted as a courier, attended meetings with civic leaders, covered for Joseph during absences, ate with him, laughed with him, stood on hand in two stadium riots in which it seemed they would both likely be killed. How could Nathan not know the truth about the man?

He made it to the fish market and browsed through the merchandise a long time. He tried to concentrate on what to buy but suddenly felt like everyone in the city might be the man his brother had hired to watch him. He had to guard every step. He had to be aware of his facial expressions giving away his thoughts. He had to limit his conversation. On top of all that, he had to look like nothing was bothering him. Caught again between the truth and the mundane, it was another hard place to straddle.

He paid for the fish and began heading back to the house. At least he knew what he would write to Amram. He turned around a kiosk, and suddenly there was Joseph right in front of him. Several of the bodyguard were with him.

"Nathan!"

"Commander!"

Nathan tried to act nonchalant but wasn't very convincing. He felt more nervous around Joseph than he ever had before. What was Joseph suddenly doing down at the wharf? Had he found him out? Had he read his thoughts about sending a dispatch to Amram? Did he know he was being spied on so he had to spy on him? Was he there to capture and interrogate him?

"You gave me an idea," Joseph said to Nathan unexpectedly.

"I did?" replied Nathan with surprise.

"Yes. I'll tell you about it back at the house." Still smiling, he took a few steps past him. Nathan sighed with relief. Everything must have been all right, and he was only imagining a problem. Then suddenly Joseph stopped and added, "Benjamin, walk Nathan back to headquarters if you wouldn't mind."

"Yes, commander." Benjamin dutifully obeyed.

As if Nathan wasn't already nervous with the thought of having been discovered by Joseph, Joseph's choice of Benjamin as an escort doubled his fear. All he could think of was that Joseph was sending two guilty culprits back to the house only to kill them once they arrived. Joseph had probably left some guards there with instructions of what to do.

As they walked, conversation with Benjamin was haltingly awkward, all the more because they usually communicated quite nicely. He wasn't sure whether to say anything about couriering letters to Amram or not. On the off chance that they were both being watched by a third party, it might be best not to say anything incriminating. But it would also be best not to be seen walking in awkward silence. If Benjamin brought up the subject of dispatches, that would be all right; but Nathan would not. And Benjamin never did.

That evening after dinner, Joseph revealed his 'idea' to the entire group.

"With the Tiberians defecting to Agrippa's side again," he began, "I have developed a plan to retake them. The eyes of the Jerusalem council are upon us," he said, suddenly looking directly at Nathan, "and we must succeed."

Nathan was now sure he had been found out.

But Joseph continued. "Here's the plan. And believe it or not, it was our young Nathan who put the idea into my head…"

Now Nathan didn't know what to think. Maybe his status with Joseph was still good. Or perhaps Joseph was simply toying with him.

Joseph went on. "There are over 200 ships down by the waterfront. I spent most of this afternoon arranging with the city authorities to borrow them for a couple of days to scare the Tiberians back into submission. I know it seems like a crazy plan. But I think it will work. We have about eight hundred soldiers left in the city, us included. If we were to man each of the ships with just enough to steer us into view of Tiberias, I think we could persuade that wretched city to surrender to us—as long as we don't come so close they see how few we really are. What do you think?"

The men nodded in assent.

And for the moment, Nathan breathed easier.

XIV

The mob on the shore stood paralyzed in panic. Others ran toward the water with weapons yelling out, "The Romans are coming!" "We're under attack!" "To the ships!" "All to arms!"

"What are the Romans doing here?" others said. "Don't they know we're on their side?"

"But those aren't Roman ships. What's happening here?"

Whosoever ships they were, it was the largest flotilla any living citizen in Tiberias had ever seen. Though it was an ad hoc group of vessels, it still wreaked havoc among the people, and they didn't know what to do.

One man yelled out from the crowd, "Who are you, and what do you want?"

From the largest ship a solitary figure emerged on the prow as the hulk approached land. Soldiers appeared behind the figure with bows and arrows aimed at the helpless populace. The mob began to drop its weapons one by one. Some knelt on the ground. Others bowed prostrate. The ensuing silence was unnatural.

The lone figure spoke. "People of Tiberias!" he began, "You have broken faith with your countrymen! You deserve to die! I am Joseph ben Mattathias. I have come to annihilate this city and its populace unless you swear allegiance to us again. How dare you invite the Idumaean king and the gentile empire to rule over you! Not just succumb to their forces but invite them to stay with you! You deluded people! You'd best fear reprisal from your own race rather than from the Romans! Your leaders have led you astray, and you should be ashamed, knowing the justice of our cause. Bring your leaders here to me or we will begin an attack in exactly one-half hour!"

A man on shore yelled back, "Give us the names of the men you want, and we will oblige you. Only promise no harm will come to them, or you will have to fight us!"

"If you fight us, you will lose. Already reinforcements are on their way, waiting for my command. Your walls are breached, and my forces are heading right toward the breach. I will promise you, however, that no harm will come to your leaders if you bring them. These are the ten I demand…" He read off their names slowly and loudly. "Bring them within the half hour, and you will be spared."

A flurry of activity commenced on shore as the leaders were brought forward one by one. Some appeared immediately, others took longer. Joseph gave instructions to his men to treat each of them respectfully as they rowed out to his ship and climbed aboard. One of them yelled back to the crowd, "We're all right! They have assured us we will not be harmed!"

With the last of the leaders on deck, Joseph addressed the crowd again. He waited, as always, for silence. "Tiberians! We thank you for your sign of good faith! As you can see, we only want to be one with you, and for you to be one with us! But because we need greater assurance that you will not defect again, we must make another demand with the same guarantee of safety."

At that, moans and grumbling arose from the shore. But Joseph continued. "We ask for the members of your senate to be brought to us as well. We want to meet with them back at Tarichaea and remind them of their duty to their country. They will not be harmed. They will all be returned to you. But if they are not brought out to meet with us, we restate our intent to attack your city. If we attack, however, we will not renege on our promise to keep your leaders aboard unharmed. They will remain safe. We, unlike you, will keep our word as an example of how you should behave toward us."

A man from the crowd yelled, "But there are more than fifty senators! It will take at least an hour to find them all."

Joseph replied, "Then we will wait an hour. I know you have more than fifty senators, but we will only ask for fifty, since some may be away or indisposed. But we will accept no less than that. You have one hour to find them."

Standing on deck, holding a sword, Nathan thought Joseph may have overplayed his hand. The Tiberians would never submit to such an audacious request, he said to himself. But as the minutes passed, one by one of the senators were rowed out to him, each to a different ship by Joseph's order. The task was complete in just over an hour.

Nathan then readied himself to set sail. But Joseph was not done wringing concessions out of the Tiberians. After some time elapsed, he called for yet another list of names, and another, as the morning now rolled into the afternoon. Nathan looked on incredulously. Joseph was magic. How did he dare to accomplish the things he did? Why did people listen to him? Had he been fashioned by heaven specifically for this purpose? If so, maybe it was a sign that the Jews would succeed. But as Nathan knew from the ancient stories, divine intervention did not always mean an easy task. His ancestors had to labor every step of the way to leave Egypt, conquer the Promised Land, construct the Temple, and survive the Captivity. But they accomplished it. Was Joseph a new Moses? Nathan felt like he was. The fact that some loved and some hated him seemed to confirm his feeling.

By the end of the day, hundreds of Tiberians stood hostage aboard the Tarichaeans' ships, to be kept in Tarichaea till after he had met with all of them. Joseph then gave orders to sail. The day had been like a miracle.

All the way home, Nathan mentally devised his second dispatch to Amram. He had a lot to tell.

XV

"You're always composing, Nathan. What are you working on?" asked Joseph.

"A little poetry," Nathan responded. "I enjoy writing."

"Remember what King Solomon said in Qohelet…"

"Yes, I know: 'the making of many books is endless, and much study wearies the body.'"

"You should heed that warning sometimes. Don't you want to follow the scriptures?" Joseph chided.

"Yes," responded Nathan. "But I need to study them to know what they say."

"Yes; another great irony of life."

Still paranoid a month later that Joseph might be on to him, Nathan wondered why he was noticing his literary activities just now. He had been writing at that same table in Joseph's presence for over a year.

"I've always wanted to write," Joseph said, "but I never have the time. Maybe when I'm old I can set down on a scroll what we have accomplished here. I know it hasn't been much yet. It may take years to achieve. But we have started something significant, maybe as significant as what my ancestors started against the Seleucids. I don't know. Posterity will judge. But I have faith in what we are doing. I know we're battling the greatest empire in history; one that makes even Egypt look unimportant. But circumstances can change in our favor any moment and bring us victory. Nero might be deposed, Agrippa might fight *with* us instead of for himself, a plague could decimate the empire—any number of things could happen. So I hope at some point I can record it all, how it started and how it finished. I would consider writing our tale almost as great an achievement as the war itself."

"So you really think we can win this?"

"Of course I do. Why else would we be here? There may be a point at which we will have to admit it is a losing proposition; but until then, I am all in. History is on our side. I trust you are too."

"I am. I wasn't sure at first. But you make me believe. And it has been my hope for years."

"Keep believing, Nathan. I gain strength from you somehow, though I know you're just a 'kid,' as everyone says. But you have become much more than that to me this past year. If anything were to happen to you, or if I were to find out you were not the young man I thought you were, I think I might give up this entire enterprise."

"Commander, you cannot speak like that," said Nathan. "It isn't fair and it isn't right. I admire you more than anyone I've ever met, except for perhaps my father. And if I were to find out you were not the man I thought you were, I would despair. But you can't think of me the way I am allowed to think of you. My brother always told me he and I were nothing. We are expendable, specks in the greater picture of history. But you are a leader. Thousands depend on you. Your vision can't depend on a teenager or anyone else. How could it? I know you are a human being who needs understanding like anybody else. But you have been placed in a high position, and you have to lead Israel even if everyone else turns traitor. You have accomplished amazing things. No one could do what you do if heaven were not with him. That's what has to keep you going. Not me or anything else."

"Then pray for me, Nathan," said Joseph, uncharacteristically.

"I will," Nathan replied.

So much had happened to Joseph in the time Nathan had

known him that it didn't surprise him he should feel fragile and speak personally to him from time to time. But Nathan was noticing a pattern beginning to emerge in all of his close relationships. Whether his father, brother, Elisheva, or Joseph—they all expressed a dependence on Nathan's goodness and honesty, for which he felt completely unsuited. The way people spoke to him about himself was enough to make him think he possessed moral qualities beyond that of an average human, and certainly the average teenager. The thought stroked his ego—what seventeen-year-old boy doesn't think he is the center of the universe?—but it wasn't true. He knew his own foibles and indecision. It seemed to him everyone merely hoped he was as good as they needed him to be, but he knew he would only disappoint them if they knew the truth. Was there anyone in the world as good as people hoped someone else could be? And if not, what put that hope into people's hearts? He put his faith in Joseph, and Joseph put his faith in him. But both sentiments were, in the long run, unrealistic.

"Speaking of your brother," Joseph added, "have you been in contact with him lately?"

What? Nathan said to himself. Don't ask that question, Joseph. Please. Nathan wondered if he'd been found out. I hope not! So what do I answer? If I say no, I would be lying. If I admit that I'm spying, it would destroy everything. So what should I do? Maybe I'll just keep my answer brief, as the proverb says.

"Yes, I have," Nathan finally answered. "And have *you* been in touch with my brother?"

"No. I haven't," answered Joseph.

There, Nathan thought. I said it. And he seems content with my answer. That wasn't so bad. And here I was worried.

A minute later it was on to another topic.

"Tell me about Elisheva," Joseph asked. "What was she like?"

That was an easy question, even though Nathan hadn't seen her for a year and often tried, uselessly, to put her out of his mind.

"Why do you ask, Joseph?" Nathan responded.

"Because when we speak, you don't often talk about yourself. And because your entire life has changed since you have been in Galilee with me. I'm curious if you ever look back."

"Yes, I often look back, and that is what I write about. But as for talking about the past, you keep me too busy to talk about myself."

"I agree. So tell me about Elisheva."

"Elisheva, for me," he began to explain, "changed over the

years, so it is hard to describe her. I grew up with her always in my company since our families were close. She would play with me and my little sister Adah, and Amram often played with Elisheva's brother Joram. But Elisheva became special to me. She could tell when I was happy or sad, and she could read my mind like no one else in the world."

"Women have that ability, don't they? I have noticed that from my own experience. There are some feelings in a man's life that women never understand—and we them, I suppose, to be fair—but when it comes to the emotions we share in common, they recognize them in us before we see them in ourselves."

"That is true. They are rather different from us, but also amazing. But as I grew older," Nathan continued, "my feelings for Elisheva changed and deepened—though sometimes I feel they became shallower, if you know what I mean. Is being attracted to a woman a deep feeling or superficial one? I can't decide."

"It's both. Continue."

"Over the years," Nathan resumed, "I noticed that Elisheva changed too. Recently her father became a member of the Way and convinced Elisheva to follow it as well."

"Yes. I detected Rab Simeon's unusual beliefs during that meeting where I met you. So that effected Elisheva as well?"

"Yes, it did. And I do not know how to think about it."

"No?"

"It makes me angry, to be honest."

"I can understand that," responded Joseph. "With all of the complications in life, I'm sure it added more."

"What makes me angry is that I do not understand how at the most critical juncture in our nation's history, when it is so important to choose sides and fight for our faith, that she should defect to something so new and meaningless. Rab Simeon and Elisheva are intelligent people. How could they have succumbed to such a thing? How could they not support our cause, and how could Elisheva not want to follow *me*? I thought we would end up together. But now I don't know if I will ever even see her again. I am here and she is who-knows-where—and I mean that geographically as well as philosophically."

"I see your predicament," responded Joseph sympathetically. "The people of the Way are strange. They are one of us, and yet they are not. They follow a different line of reasoning and are so sure of themselves. But how could God in heaven ever become a man like they claim? Have the scriptures ever spoken of such a thing? It is an absurdity with no precedent, as laughable as Zeus taking the form of a bird or whatever suits him for the occasion. If their beliefs could be found in the scriptures, I would give it consideration. But if God did become a man, wouldn't he have led us to victory against the Romans by now? Isn't that what the messiah was supposed to do? The Christian sect makes no sense."

"Elisheva mentioned something to me about that very issue—the messiah and the war—that I often think about."

"What did she say?"

"That our approach to Rome was superficial and doomed to failure because it was trying to change the world by physical means from the outside in. She said that her God and messiah were the only way to bring real change in the world because it was working from the inside out for the whole human race, not just the Jewish nation."

"She said that? Very interesting. Sometimes I think it is doomed to failure myself, despite it all. But how very like a woman Elisheva is. Of course she would think that way. For women the world is unlocked through emotion. For men, the emotion is unlocked through the physical. Maybe Elisheva is right. Sometimes women are in these matters, but they are also often bound by immediate concerns, not the big picture, and they are often uneducated besides. But I do not agree that we can explain the movements of heaven's will in history by analogy with how the human body works. Instead, what I see is that the war we are engaged in has great meaning, and the absurd proposition that a particular man who lived several decades ago might have been God does not.

"And if this war is the event of our generation, then remember that you stand right at the heart of it, and the heroics of it will be told through the ages. This war will either make or break us as a nation. And if we survive like the phoenix through the flames, you will have played an important role. And if it breaks us, we will know that we did our best. So one day when all of this is over and we have either won our victory or at least done our best, you will find Elisheva and bring her back to her senses, and all will be well. What do you think?"

"I am not sure what the future holds," responded Nathan. "I have asked myself many times if this war is signaling the end of an age for us or the beginning of a new one for someone else. Will we survive as the rulers of the future or as a mere remnant like has happened so many times in the past? And if we are rulers, what will we be rulers of? Just Israel? And if it is just Israel, is that enough? If that is all we end up with, won't that mean we have only fulfilled the local and superficial victory Elisheva accuses us of aiming for?"

"Maybe," said Joseph. "Control over Israel might just be the beginning, though. But I can see that Elisheva's words have had an effect on you. If I had known you were thinking this way all along, I would have considered twice the idea of you accompanying me to Galilee. Why were you willing to follow me here if that was the case?"

"I haven't thought this way all along. Elisheva's words didn't make sense to me until now that we have begun to talk about it. All along I have had my hope in this war. But I am thinking now that the hope of a war is much better than its day-to-day reality. It's strange how when I think of the grand sweep of history, it seems so big to me. But when I am actually a part of the sweep, I can only see the part of it that I am involved in, and it seems small. And now I'm not even sure what the big picture is."

"Nathan, the big picture only comes together after living it out day by day. That is how life works. That's why I am always planning and arranging for what must be done in the moment. The moment is of vital importance. Tomorrow we have to do what needs to be done tomorrow, and the day after that whatever task we have to accomplish for that day. I just keep living day by day. Then when we are old and writing about us, we will figure out what the big picture had been. Do you agree?"

"Yes. I agree."

"I need to stop talking now—something I always have trouble doing with you—and we'd better get moving."

Joseph stood up.

"I'm going to finish writing for a few minutes, and I will be right with you," said Nathan.

Joseph left the room, and Nathan finished his dispatch to Amram. When he was done, he got up to look for Benjamin. To his surprise, Benjamin was standing directly behind the door in the next room. Nathan felt a bit uneasy about that. How much had Benjamin heard? Did I say anything I shouldn't have? Had Joseph?

Benjamin took the dispatch, looked directly into Nathan's eyes without saying a word, and went out the door.

XVI

As Nathan's dispatch wound its way to Amram, it paralleled a correspondence from John of Gischala to the Jerusalem council. Rumors persisted of Joseph's mismanagement of Galilean affairs, and John was demanding that the council replace the young commander with himself.

"This is preposterous," declared Opal upon reading the letter. "Gischala is a known criminal. To replace a well-respected and organized leader like Joseph with a rabble rouser would bring chaos in the north in a week."

Another council member, a close associate of Amram, countered Opal.

"You mean," the young man retorted, "that Gischala might actually bring on a *war* within a week, whereas ben Mattathias is stalling for time. Isn't a war what you really mean, Rab Opal?"

"Perhaps. War and chaos often go hand in hand. But looking at it from a logical point of view, we cannot change commanders at this stage, after Joseph has spent so much time training the soldiers and gaining the Galileans' trust."

The young man responded: "I hear from a reliable source that just the opposite is happening. Rab Joseph's handling of the money situation has engendered animosity among the Galileans. And as for the soldiers, he let most of them return home for the harvest."

"What are you talking about?" said Opal. "What 'reliable source' are you referring to that I'm not familiar with?"

"I would like to have a private word with you."

Opal obliged.

"I'm talking about your son."

"My son? Of course. Amram would say anything to discredit Joseph or anyone on the side of decency."

"But I'm not referring to Amram."

"Then who are you talking about?"

"I mean your other son."

"Nathan? What does he have to do with this?"

XVII

"It's true, father dearest," Amram answered snidely.

"You actually set your brother up as a spy? How could you?" asked Opal.

"He knew exactly what he was doing. And he provided just what we needed."

"Not what *we* needed. What *you* needed. Though I'm not sure anymore what that is. I thought you and Joseph had an understanding."

"Yes. We had an understanding that he would fight a war. But that's not happening. At least not from what I can see. It's all in these letters from your dear little Nathan. Read them. You'll see Joseph isn't all he appears to be."

"I have a hard time believing that, or that Nathan would write about Joseph in a negative light."

"That's what I find so astounding about the two of you," replied Amram. "Nathan is so innocent he can wrap a shroud around Joseph without knowing it, and you are so blind you can't see it either. But look closely, if you dare, abba, and you will see what Nathan says about Joseph: withholding money from the Tarichae-ans, writing to Agrippa, sending funds to Agrippa's friends, sending troops home for months at a time, enraging the local leadership, risking Tiberias' entire fleet, causing lethal outbursts in two differ-ent cities—it's all right here. I underlined the pertinent sections to save you time."

"I'm sure there are perfectly good explanations for all those things. Galilee is not an easy region to prepare for war. The people there have been divided in their loyalties for a long time. I'm sure Joseph knows what he's doing. Why are you talking such craziness? What is it that you want? To see Joseph discredited, to have your brother exposed, to put John of Gischala in charge?"

"Maybe," Amram shrugged nonchalantly. "But that would be too simple."

"True. It's preferable for you to keep everyone on edge: to keep Joseph unsure of support, your brother under threat of danger, and

Gischala at your beck and call. That way you still think you're in charge of it all. Isn't that it?"

"You figured me out, abba," Amram answered flatly, so that it could have meant either an affirmation or an insult. Amram continued, "So is the council going to bring Joseph in for questioning?"

"The council is discussing sending a deputation to Tiberias to check on the situation."

"That might be wise," said Amram, uncharacteristically agreeable.

"I don't think it is necessary. But, as usual, I find myself in a minority on the subject."

"Well, what would be the harm in sending a deputation?" Amram asked. "It would alleviate the doubters once and for all. Either Joseph would be exonerated and Nathan's dispatches deemed inaccurate, or just the opposite."

Opal now lost his patience, as was usual when he spoke to Amram. "That's exactly what the harm in a deputation would be! Either Nathan would be right and Joseph found guilty, or Joseph would be exonerated and Nathan in trouble."

"Oh, so that's your problem with it. There's only one winner in the deal. And it's not you. But as I see it, it's a perfect plan," Amram said, visibly gloating.

"We'll see about that," Opal replied, trying to resume his calm. "One would almost think you'd devised the idea yourself."

"But I did," Amram paused for effect. "I did."

Opal stared at his estranged son, trying to hold in the revulsion.

"Once again, abba dearest," Amram said, "you figured me out."

XVIII

The pounding on the door came later than Joseph expected.

"Benjamin, see who it is," he ordered down to the guard.

"We're here to speak to Rab Joseph," the leader of the four visitors announced.

"I am right here, gentlemen," called out Joseph, coming down the steps. "How can I be of assistance?"

Nathan, who was feeling ill and had gone to bed early, woke up half delirious to the sound of angry voices beyond the door of his small quarters off the main room.

"Rab Joseph. We are here from the council of Jerusalem to conduct an inquest into your mismanagement of the Galilean campaign."

Joseph, ignoring the rude introduction, said to the men, "So have you just arrived from the capital? Please let me give you some food and wine. You must be tired after your long journey. You must need a place to sleep for the night."

"Rab Joseph," snapped the leader, "we are quite well provisioned. In fact, we have been here for several days and do not need any assistance from you at all."

"Yes, gentlemen," Joseph spoke, changing his tone. "I have been aware of your presence since you arrived, and have been informed that you expended no small effort in questioning my constituents here. Some of my men tell me that you have deliberately tried to malign my character. So let's not kid ourselves. Your visit here has hardly been a secret. I wonder, though, if this is the type of behavior the council has desired of you or if it has been done of your own contrivance. For instance, were you asked officially to barge into my house at so late an hour when you could have done so at any time over the last few days, or was that some clever intimidation scheme you came up with on your own?"

"We have been ordered to take you, willingly, back to Jerusalem with us for questioning. The hour is of no account. We have armed men with us to see to it."

"And if I do not come willingly?" asked Joseph.

"Then you will not live to see the morning."

Joseph paused. "Oh, I see." He stood motionless for a moment. Then, suddenly letting out the command, "Now!" he grabbed one of the four deputies around the throat with his dagger while several of the guard grabbed the other three. "Who do you think you are?" Joseph demanded of the four men. "Do you have more authority here than I do? I have been sent by the Jerusalem Council, just like you have, to accomplish something here, and I *will* accomplish it! Just try to call your men. Just try! My guard has had them under surveillance for hours. Your measly troop is no match for my men here. So on the contrary, my good fellows, if you do not answer *me* some questions, *you* will not live to see the morning."

"If any harm comes to us," the leader spoke up, "it will only prove to the council that you are guilty as charged. They will send reinforcements within days and have you hunted down until you are dead."

"I doubt that very much, though I admire your faith in our government. I wish I had as much backing from them as you believe you have. But don't think for a moment that I plan to show disrespect for the council or what it is trying to endeavor by sending you. I will speak to you; to one of you. And one of you will speak to me. The other three of you will be my guests for the night—elsewhere."

From inside his room, still feeling groggy but awake, Nathan silently marveled as Joseph yet again managed to turn a death sentence into an offensive maneuver. Had Joseph's men really had the deputation's troop under surveillance? Was the troop no match for Joseph's guard? In the final analysis, it didn't matter. Joseph clearly had the psychological advantage now, and events would go his way, as they always did, whether the council sent reinforcements or not.

Joseph gave out orders. "Benjamin, see to our three guests. Make sure they are kept comfortable, fed, and watched. As for you, young sir," he said to the man still in his grasp, "you will stay here with me to conduct your inquest. I am a man of honor, after all."

Benjamin left with the three deputies, including the leader. The fourth deputy was invited to the table where some of Nathan's scrolls lay strewn. A guard was ordered to bring the man some food and a jug of wine.

"Have something to drink," Joseph ordered. The man happily obliged, then began ripping at the food like a low-class savage. He then downed a second cup of wine. Joseph was surprised at the young man's lack of etiquette and surmised that political and urban life were something new to him.

"So what is your name?" Joseph asked as the man threw back yet a third cup.

"Yehudah."

"Well Yehudah," Joseph continued, "tell me a little about yourself before you begin your questioning."

As Joseph poured him still a fourth cup, he began to talk about himself. "I am new to the council, so I know very little about the case against you other than what I've learned these last few days. I come from a small town in the Judaean hill country." He spoke coarsely and with an accent, just as Joseph had suspected he might. He ate a few bites, then Joseph poured him a fifth cup.

"These days, big men come from small towns," Joseph expounded. "They all think they're Micah of Moresheth or giants of Tekoa. If you came from a small town, how did you become involved with the council?"

"I thought I was supposed to be asking you the questions. But you have been asking me instead."

"Don't worry," Joseph said. "We have all night. There's plenty of time for you to barrage me. But it wouldn't be right for me to remain ignorant of my honored guest from the Jerusalem council. So how did you become involved in politics?"

"Before I answer your question, I'm a little befuddled. From what I can tell, most of your men seem to respect you. So why do we keep hearing about so much trouble in Galilee?"

"Because, my young man, there can only be one leader in charge, and everyone wants to be that leader. It is as simple as that. The men who question my authority and my methods are men who wish to be in charge themselves. You know how it is. You are young. I am sure you sense a great deal of competition in the capital for what few positions are available. So getting back to my original question, how did you manage to align yourself with the council at such a young age, and being from the hill country besides?"

Yehudah poured himself a sixth glass of wine and downed it. He could feel himself growing freer in his speech already, the wine having its effect. He was drawn to Joseph, as many people were, by his seeming honesty and intelligence. "I went to the capital three years ago, maybe four," he explained, "to try my fortunes there. I'm 23 right now, and I think I've done pretty well for myself."

"I'm sure you have. How have you succeeded?" Joseph inquired.

"You know how it is. A man's assets are sometimes in his head and sometimes elsewhere."

"Oh, really. Please go on."

"Well, I've always tried to combine my strengths, playing one off the other, if you know what I mean." The wine was clearly clouding the young man's judgment already, and he was poised to speak as honestly as if he were at a pub with his friends. "To tell you the truth," he continued, "there was this girl I met ..."

He was beginning to ramble a little. "She was beautiful. I've seen some fine girls at home, but these city girls were a whole new thing."

"Have some more wine," said Joseph. The young man was an easier target than Joseph had expected. He had hoped for a little more sport.

"Anyway, this girl ended up being the niece of a council member, and I could tell she wanted me. She was always walking close and looking at me. You know. As time went by, I could tell she was interested." He grinned a devilish grin, which should have been embarrassing to him but was not.

"Really," said Joseph. "The niece of a councilman. That was rather fortuitous."

"When I found out about her connection to the council, I told her I'd do what she wanted if she introduced me to her uncle first."

"She had to talk to her uncle first? You had the willpower to stay away from her until she spoke to her uncle?"

"Well, not completely. But we didn't do anything too serious, if you know what I mean, till she did what I asked."

"Nothing too serious? Good show. This is quite a story. Some people are born into connections, like I was. But you made your own. That sort of resourcefulness is admirable."

"I'd say so." He was losing all sense of proportion now and had to concentrate to counter the alcohol. But as his concentration waned, he drank another cup.

From behind his door, Nathan was listening with rapt attention. He too had to concentrate to counter the effects of what was a low-grade fever. Where was this discussion headed, he wondered. Why did Joseph care about this bottom feeder's background?

Yehudah suddenly lunged his elbows forward onto the table to come closer to Joseph. He was apparently one of those happy drunks. "I like you," he said smilingly to Joseph. "You seem like a nice guy. I can tell why people like you."

"Well thank you. Please continue your story."

Yehudah resumed. "So from there, it all spiraled upward. The uncle used me as an errand boy for a while, then as a personal secretary. And the whole time," he took a moment to pour and imbibe his seventh cup, "I was involved with his niece. It was quite a gig."

From behind his door, Nathan's skin was crawling with discomfort for the young man. How could someone let down his guard as quickly and easily as this fellow was and be such a depraved egotist? May that never happen to me, he mentally petitioned heaven.

Joseph's sense of conscience kicked in too, as he found himself saying to the young man, "But be careful. You could be playing with fire. I assume you intend to do well by the girl in the end."

Nathan thought it sounded like something Joseph would have said to *him*. Joseph, he thought, really was a good man, even when he was playing someone for all he was worth.

"Oh, don't worry about me. I've got it under control. The leader of our group, the mean-looking one, he's the councilor's son, and he knows nothing about what's going on between his cousin and me. I know how to keep things under wraps until I can use them."

"Yes. I'm sure you do," Joseph quipped sarcastically.

"I'll do well by the girl. I even think I love her. You seem like a nice guy," he repeated. "You know what it's like to be in my position."

"Of course, of course."

The two men remained silent for a moment. Then Joseph changed the subject.

"Getting back to your original statement," he began, "you said earlier that you knew very little about the case against me till you joined this deputation. What exactly did you learn about the situation here in Galilee when you were chosen for this auspicious office?"

"Ah," exclaimed Yehudah. "Now we're getting to the real subject. But you're still asking the questions!" In his inebriated brain, he suddenly remembered what they were originally supposed to speak about.

"You're free to ask me questions too," Joseph said. "Please, begin your inquest now if you care to."

Yehudah wracked his memory to recollect a question. "Now what did you ask me?" He clearly was not thinking straight.

"I asked you what you learned about my situation while you were still in Jerusalem."

"Oh yes." He thought long and hard for an answer. "There were some letters we were shown about a month ago, maybe more. They were dispatches from Galilee."

"Really? From here?" Joseph became sincerely curious for the first time in the entire conversation.

From behind his door, Nathan's attention suddenly piqued also when he heard the term 'dispatches from Galilee.' Had he heard that correctly? Could this young man possibly be referring to his own letters to Amram? If he were, he would be ruined. If he were, he would have to stop the interrogation from going any further. He did not want to miss a single word of what was said. He was hoping he was wrong.

"Keep going," Joseph urged on. "What did these dispatches say?

"You'll have to excuse me if I jumble my facts a little bit. But I think I remember pretty well. They discussed how you withheld money from one town and made other towns angry…"

Nathan could remember writing that very thing, only explaining how it was all under Joseph's control.

"That there was a riot in two of the cities because of mismanagement of funds…"

Nathan had written about that too, but with an explanation of how Joseph had saved the day.

Thus far Nathan did not feel too threatened by anything that was divulged. Any number of people could have written to the council about those events. They were witnessed by the entire city.

"There was also something about rebuilding walls…"

Joseph began to probe deeper now. "All of those things were mentioned, eh? Were they written by someone from inside my camp?"

"I believe so. It seemed to be someone who knew a lot about you."

Nathan was beginning to break a sweat now. The conversation was getting too personal for him to stay neutral, and suddenly Yehudah was as clearheaded in his account as he was fog headed before.

"I remember another event was that you got a group of ships together to play a joke on another town. Is that right?"

Nathan was growing faint with nervousness at the mention of this event. It narrowed down the number of insiders who could have written the dispatch considerably, since the ship episode occurred recently and with only a skeleton staff. If that young fool mentioned anything about Agrippa now, or Joseph writing to him, that would give his identity away for sure. As far as Nathan knew, he was the only one privy to that piece of information. He had to do something to save his skin and his relationship with the man he admired second-most in the whole world. Why was this happening? Most likely Amram was behind it all again, and Nathan once again found himself having to undo the knot that his brother had tied him in.

"What else did the letters say?" Joseph continued to ply.

"I don't know. There were lots of things. Oh, they also mentioned that…"

Suddenly, Nathan jumped up and flung himself against the inside of his door. Startled by the noise, Joseph jolted a bit and the young man said, "What the …?"

Nathan then opened the door and stumbled onto the floor in the main room. His hair was matted with sweat, and he was breathing hard.

"Nathan!" Joseph exclaimed. For the previous hour, Joseph had actually forgotten Nathan even existed.

"Joseph," Nathan spoke. "I've been hearing voices, but I couldn't tell whether it was in my sleep or in reality."

Joseph stood up and walked over to Nathan. "How do you feel? It looks like you still have a fever."

"I don't know. I couldn't sleep." Nathan tried to calm down. Although his plan was to fake a nightmare, his actual fear at the moment took over and saved him from having to play act. "I've been tossing and turning with horrible thoughts."

"What about?" Joseph asked almost tenderly.

"That we were all captured and everything was coming to an end," Nathan explained, almost childish in his illness.

"Come over to the table, Nathan, and have some wine. Relax for a moment. It might help you feel better."

Nathan sensed Joseph's hand gently nudge him into a seat at the table. "This is Yehudah," Joseph said to Nathan. "He's 23 and he's from the council in Jerusalem." Then looking at Yehudah, he said, "And this is Nathan bar Opal, my excellent assistant."

"Bar Opal," thought Yehudah aloud. "That's not a very common name these days. But I think I've heard it before."

"Huh," Nathan responded, attempting to sound unperturbed.

Joseph jumped in. "Yehudah and I have been talking about his past, and he has been curious about mine. More trouble is brewing for me in Jerusalem, and I have been summoned to the council for questioning."

"For questioning? That can't be. So my dream was real," said Nathan.

"So it was, my friend."

"But you can't go, Joseph," said Nathan sternly. "This is such a critical time for us, and the Romans are getting closer by the day. If you were to leave now, after having done so much good here, things would fall apart."

"Do you hear that, Yehudah?" asked Joseph. "There's at least one honest voice from Jerusalem who thinks I have done good here."

"You are from Jerusalem?" Yehudah asked. "Then maybe that's how I know your name."

"It could be," said Nathan. "But in any case, Joseph, we cannot let you go to Jerusalem. I will go on your behalf. The council knows me. They know I will tell the truth. I could answer any question they could give me."

Joseph thought about it for a moment. "Nathan, you may be on to something there. And it wouldn't be the first time."

"In fact," Nathan continued, "you could send any number of us, and we would all come to your defense."

Joseph continued to think. Then, turning his attention to Yehudah, he said, "Yehudah, if I were to send a hundred of my men back to Jerusalem to vouch for me and describe the good that I have achieved in Galilee, do you think your fellow deputies would allow me to stay here?"

"That's a tough one. I'd have to ask them."

"Well, ask them."

"But it sounds like you're trying to get away with something. I don't think they would go for it. Especially the mean one."

"But my dear Yehudah," Joseph reminded him, "would the mean one want to hear about what's been going on between you and his cousin? Would that information fare any better with your colleagues?"

As the young man suddenly registered Joseph's words in his head, his mouth dropped open. The conversation of the last hour flooded through his diluted brainwaves, and he realized that in the midst of all the talking, he had been taken advantage of. "What?" he said. "Wait a minute. That was said in confidence. You wouldn't… you wouldn't really…No. That wouldn't be right. Tell him, Nathan. He said he was a man of honor."

"Joseph is a man of honor," Nathan responded. "So I would suggest that whatever bargain he makes with you, you agree with."

"But that's not fair," Yehudah whined. "How could you use that information against me? It's you who is supposed to be brought in for questioning, not me."

"The deal was that I would talk to you, and you would talk to me. It's not because of me that you've been fooling around with the councilor's niece."

"The councilor's niece?" Nathan added wryly, feeling half-relief from the difficult position he was slowly extricating himself from, and still half-ill from the effects of his fever.

"So what do you say, Yehudah?" asked Joseph. "Either you tell your colleagues that we have struck a deal and you will let me send my own deputation back to Jerusalem with you—our fine young Nathan included—or I will feel obliged to convey to your colleagues the information I have obtained about you. Does that sound fair?"

Nathan looked at Yehudah and almost recoiled that the council had entrusted a commission to the likes of him. He could not help but see himself in the pathetic fellow. Did Joseph realize he was sitting between two mirror reflections of young, inept betrayal at the same table? Perhaps he did. It was conceivable that Joseph had even set up the entire conversation with Yehudah just to teach Nathan a lesson. It was unlikely, but possible. In any event, for the moment, the situation between him and Joseph still appeared to be good. If he were able to defend Joseph's policies to the council with success, it might go a long way toward healing any rift between them if Joseph ever were to discover the provenance of the dispatches.

Yehudah sat and thought in silence. "I suppose that sounds fair enough: man to man," he said.

Within a month, the entire affair was settled. Nathan and ninety-nine hand-picked followers of Joseph were sent off to the council. News reached Joseph's waiting ears that Nathan, in particular, had staged an outstanding defense of his commander's policies. And the Hasmonaean was officially re-instated as the general in charge of the Galilean campaign.

Meanwhile, the Romans inched closer every day.

XIX

Fifty-eight thousand troops descended on Galilee in the spring of AD 67 from every quadrant of the empire and beyond: Alexandria, Emesa, Commagene, Syria, Nabataea, and Rome itself. They converged for one purpose: to extinguish Jewish independence. A sea of helmets, javelins, daggers, picks, chains, axes, long swords, shields, trumpets, horses, tents, foodstuffs, mules, siege engines, and slaves covered entire landscapes, causing country-dwellers to flee behind city walls for safety. But there was no safety. The Zealots had wanted war a long time, and now it was upon them.

The city of Jotapata, near Sepphoris and Cana, stood first in line for attack by the Romans. The Jotapatans defeated the Romans, however, making it an imperial moral imperative to return to the town again and destroy it. They succeeded on nearby Gabara, and Joseph mobilized for action. Sending word to the council for reinforcements, neither word nor troops proved forthcoming. Undeterred, Joseph focused on the defense of Jotapata as his singular objective, whether the council paid attention or not. He sped to the city while General Vespasian, described as a bulldog-faced provincial, with the military backing of the largest empire on earth, marched his war machine against him. Nathan, as always, went with Joseph.

The site of Jotapata had great natural fortifications on three sides. It lay on a mound of earth surrounded by deep-cut valleys and peaks to its south, east, and west. Its north face, however, stood vulnerable, sloping downward to be met at its bottom by another hill rising in front of it like the tiers of an amphitheatre. This north side was defended by a turreted wall, powerfully built, and which Joseph ordered renovated and heightened. But of all the four sides, it was the weakest; so logically, it was to that side where Vespasian directed his efforts.

Camping his troops on the northern amphitheatre facing the town, Vespasian's goal was simple: to build up the earth in front of the city high enough to walk his troops right over its wall. It was no easy task, but it was one the Romans had accomplished before, to the terror of its conquered masses.

To Nathan, and to all who lived at the height of Roman greatness, the aspect of the empire that impressed its victims most was not the number of legions it had at its disposal, nor its superior weaponry, training, planning, heartless sense of retribution, or superhuman sense of order—though all those were impressive enough—but its utter genius for altering landscapes as it cut its way through mountains, decimated forests, leveled valleys, and stopped-up rivers. It was an unbeatable juggernaut replete with tools for digging, chopping, filling, and mounting, which matched any mere fighting ability it possessed. Engineering was the true secret to Roman power.

As Nathan watched the Romans at work, it reminded him of a scripture that suddenly took on a terrible twist as he recited it to himself: "Every valley shall be filled in," the line read, "and every mountain made low. The rough ground shall become level, and the rugged places a plain, before the glory of the Lord is revealed." Nathan had always interpreted that line as the removal of all earthly obstacles before a celestial visit, or the softening of the human heart to allow one to see God. But now, he wondered if it spoke of a terrible retribution against the Jews being meted out by the Romans, just as the captivity had been meted out by the Babylonians.

"Do you think," Nathan asked Joseph, "that the Romans ever read the great leveling prophecy in Isaiah?"

"I doubt it," responded Joseph. "But if they did, it would be no surprise they would find a fiendish military application for it. The Roman is nothing but an animal of war."

"Funny," responded Nathan. "My father said that same thing a long time ago. Do we even stand a chance against them?"

"With some providence, yes. And I have a few ideas of my own."

As Vespasian's forces surrounded the city with a ring of soldiers two men deep, allowing no escape in any direction, Joseph had to develop a plan to counter them and keep them from the wall. He regularly sent soldiers outside the gates to disrupt their building activity. It cost the lives of many Jotapotans, but it bought the city several extra days to strategize. "In the matter of a siege," Joseph explained to the stalwart men and women circled about him to hear his plans, "time is generally on the defenders' side. The longer we hold out, the more tired and hungry the enemy will grow. But of course, it all depends on the circumstances."

"The major disadvantage we have to holding out," one of the local leaders explained, "is that there is no water source within the walls other than our cisterns. The cisterns are currently full, but the rainy season has stopped."

"Then we'll need to ration the water," stated Joseph, to the consternation of the crowd.

As the days passed, the practice of sending men outside the walls lost its effectiveness. The Romans already outnumbered the Jotapatans by several thousand, and too many Jotapatans were now dead. Joseph thus ordered the people to mount the walls and pelt the soldiers with stones, a commodity with which the region was amply supplied. This worked for several days, until phase two of the Roman strategy went into effect.

For some time since the Romans had arrived, they had been lumbering trees, which were not plentiful in those parts, and constructing wooden frames. The purpose of this was unclear to Joseph at first. But when the frames were lashed together and covered with brush and twigs to form protective mobile shelters for the Romans to construct their earthworks against the walls, it became obvious.

To counter the shelters, Joseph ordered large stones collected and hurled onto the twig and brush coverings, smashing the frames and maiming the Romans beneath. Shelter after shelter was destroyed by this method, and time after time the soldiers had to repair or rebuild them till the supply of wood dwindled.

The Romans were not to be outdone, however. As though waiting to reveal the next tool in their arsenal, Vespasian ordered the use of siege engines against the men atop the walls. As one after another of the catapult-like engines was brought into play, the Jotapatans were horrified to count a full 160 of them. "How did the Romans drag so many siege engines across Galilee?" Nathan asked rhetorically.

The populace was assembled to man the wall tops, but the defenders had no protection against the engines' constant barrage of stones and arrows, half of which had been furnished by the Jotapatans themselves. "We can't do this!" Nathan complained to Joseph. "The Romans are picking off the men on the walls like it's their target practice. And pelting the Romans with stones and arrows is like supplying them with ammunition."

"I know. I'm coming up with something," responded Joseph.

"The problem is, those earth ramps are gaining a foot almost every day, and every day we delay we literally lose ground."

"I know. I know. That north wall has to be built higher. That's our only solution."

Nathan responded, "But how can we build on top of the wall? We can't even defend ourselves up there, let alone build—unless we train the cows and sheep to defend us while we work behind them."

Within the hour, based on Nathan's quip about cows, Joseph ordered that all available lumber and cattle hides in the city be brought to the inner north wall.

"What are we going to do with these?" one of the local leaders asked.

"We are going to build the north wall higher."

"With cowhides and wood?" the people grumbled.

"No," answered Joseph. "We are going to erect scaffolds covered with cattle hides so we can work behind them to build our wall higher."

The crowd stood agape. "It's brilliant," one man said.

"And if the hides are moist and new, they'll even withstand fire," Joseph added.

"I think it will work," the crowd responded.

Joseph then did what he did best: issued commands, gave inspiration, set everyone to task, and got a job done that no one else had thought of doing.

While the scaffolds went up over the next couple of days, Joseph returned to his original strategy of sending out bands to attack, only this time to destroy the brush shelters from close range. It was largely a suicide mission, but there were plenty of men willing to risk their lives for their families, and a few who survived. It became a competition to see who could stay alive the longest. "They die so they can live," thought Nathan as he watched with admiration.

Once the scaffolds appeared atop the wall, the Romans watched in befuddlement. What were they looking at? What was occurring? The pelting from the engines persisted daily, but the masons behind the hides carried out their work unmolested. They actually built the wall at a faster rate than the Romans could build the siege ramps. Vespasian was growing impatient and feeling bested with every passing day. "Why can't we build better than them?! Do we need to hire Jews to get the job done?" By the end of two weeks, the earthworks had only gained twelve feet while the wall had gained thirty. It was a marvel.

"Who is their leader?" asked Vespasian with his gruff voice as the soldiers wondered who the mastermind behind Jotapata was as well.

"We believe it is the Pharisee-politician Josephus ben Mattathias," one of the general's underlings reported.

"The Jew that Nero's wife was so impressed with a few years ago?"

"We believe he is one and the same."

"How could that be? You must be wrong. If you're not, then his career is off to a better start than mine is. I want you to find out more about him. I thought ben Mattathias was still in Tarichaea."

"No sir. He seems to be here."

"How did he get here so fast?"

With that, the general's motivation to annihilate the city doubled. Not only was Joseph countering his every move in what had become a battle of wits, but he, Vespasian, was in disfavor with the emperor while this renegade Jew had his esteem. He wanted Jotapata destroyed but he wanted to meet Joseph alive.

With the northern wall so high, Vespasian abandoned his earthworks for the moment and concentrated on starving the city out. Unlike Joseph's explanation to the Jotapatans, Vespasian was convinced that time was on *his* side. When it was confirmed to him that the city had no underground springs but only rain cisterns, his confidence grew almost to smugness. Still, his task would not be easy. The defenders were obstinate, and Joseph's brain was still churning with ideas. It seemed illogical to Vespasian that they should continue to fight. There was no way they could win. "Can't they just admit the hopelessness of their situation," Vespasian said, "and give up? Even if they win, what would they win—a barren mound of dirt on a dismal rim of the empire?" But he did not take into account that freedom and one's faith meant more sometimes than life itself.

XX

The soldiers on the amphitheatre slope observed the Jotapatans every day doling out their water rations. For them it was an uplifting show.

"It won't be long now," they said to each other. "Then we can go home."

Then one day, during a break from the bombardments, they watched as the defenders began hanging, one piece at a time, dripping wet laundry over the city walls.

"It's actually wet!" one soldier cried. "You can feel the drops if you stand under it."

From a distance, Vespasian snapped at his men. "Are the Jotapatans mad? I thought you told me the city had no well in it, and that the end was near!"

"There isn't a well, sir," said his underling. "There never has been. So yes. Logically, the end *is* near."

"Well then, explain *that* to me," he yelled, pointing to the dripping laundry. "Either their commander is a complete idiot, this is the most transparent ruse I've ever seen, or the man has somehow managed to find a water source that no one has ever found before. And given the commander's success rate so far in this campaign, which one of those three choices do you think it is?!" His bull-dog face reddened to the brink of explosion.

"That he somehow found a new water source, general?" said his underling.

"Precisely!" he shouted. "You imbeciles! I want this city destroyed. And you'd better get me better intelligence than you have thus far provided about this area, or I'll have you all flogged! Now get out there and exterminate that place!"

Inside the city walls, however, reality was beginning to sink in. Joseph's ploy to convince the Romans of a permanent water source in Jotapata had actually worked. But the defenders knew they could not hold out forever. Already several of the leading citizens were making plans to leave. Joseph himself tried to explain to the populace that he should create a diversion from another town and split the Roman forces in two. "You cannot leave us, commander," one of the townsfolk pleaded. "We would be lost. We wouldn't know what to do. Do you think we could have thought of the things you did if you weren't here? Please. You are our leader. You cannot leave us." The people pressed him so urgently that he felt forced to relent.

"One thing I believe, however," he said to Nathan in private conversation afterward, "is that *you* must leave this place while there is still a chance. You must make it back to Jerusalem and report the desperation here. They will believe you. The council must either put its whole heart into this war or give its life to negotiate a peace. If single towns like Jotapata fight alone, with no coherent Jewish strategy to bind us all together, then single towns like Jotapata will perish alone, one by one, until we are annihilated. You must let them know, Nathan. Can you do that?"

"Of course, commander," responded Nathan. "Tell me when, and I will do it."

Early the next morning—it was about day 40 of the siege, and it seemed like a miracle that the town could have held out for so long—Joseph began deploying guerrilla bands of suicide attackers into the Roman camp on the hillside. Their task was to slash, burn, destroy, and kill until they were killed themselves. There was no other way the city could survive another week if desperate and even illogical measures were not followed. Once again, Joseph was impressed by the number of men willing to embark on such missions. If he had found that much courage in Tiberias, Sepphoris, and Jerusalem, the war could have taken a different turn long ago, and perhaps it would have been Vespasian and not he who was calling on deaf ears and empty coffers for reinforcements.

As the reality stood, however, Vespasian had auxiliary flanks to virtually throw away on the guerrillas rather than use his good Roman soldiers against them. That's what the foreigners were for, after all. For as little as the Jewish guerrillas achieved, however, they wore away at the morale of the Romans to the point that they could not view their campsite as safe anymore. Day or night, at any time, in fog or heat, the guerrillas might attack and welcome death if it meant life for their families. What could the Romans do to stop this crazy little city on the hill?

Vespasian now brought out his next weapon: an enormous battering ram with an iron head shaped like an actual ram. It was time-consuming to set up and difficult to maneuver, but once it found its target, it always finished the job. The soldiers went about erecting the high framework from which it swung, and as the Jotapatans watched in dismay, the soldiers moved it within battering range of the wall, under cover of arrows and stones and slingshots.

BOOM! Silence. BOOM!!! Silence. BOOM!!!! Silence. The ram hit the same spot in the wall again and again and again and again. It did not, and would not, stop until someone did something to stop it.

"No!" the people within the city wailed. "The wall will crumble! What can we do?"

It was Joseph's turn to respond in the war game now. He ordered rope and all the bags of chaff in the city to be brought to him. While the soldiers outside pulled the ram back for the next swing forward, they watched as suddenly the Jotapatans flung bags of chaff over the walls to buffer the blows on the very spot it was aimed for.

"What the …" flustered Vespasian. Was there no end to the evil schemes the Jewish mind could devise to thwart Roman progress?

It seemed the bags of chaff could only do so much cushioning of the blows, but it proved enough so that the soldiers were ordered to move the ram to another location. But once the battering began on the new spot, the chaff bags moved as well.

Vespasian had his men tie scythes to the ends of poles, and running up to the walls, cut the bags down. The bags were replaced by new ones, but eventually replacement became impossible. Joseph then ordered hundreds of men outside the walls with torches to raid the camp, burn the siege engines, destroy the shelters, and find anything else they could set ablaze. They drew enough attention to divert the soldiers momentarily, and it proved enough for a major move to occur. A particular defender named Eleazar ben Samaeas, not even a native of Jotapata, appeared at the top of the wall above the battering ram with a large rock. Lifting the rock above his head, he sent it hurdling down onto the ram, breaking its iron head off.

The defenders raised a sky-lighting cheer as Eleazar then leapt from the wall, picked up the iron head, and ran back, screaming insults at the besiegers. The soldiers shot five arrows through his back in response. Despite the agony of his bleeding body, soon to be a corpse, he made his last living moment a triumph of bravery as he scaled the wall still with the head in his grasp. He looked down, jeering at the enemy, and would have made his victory complete, but as his last ounce of blood spurt from his body, he fell frontward outside the wall rather than in, and the ram's head made its way back to the Romans. At least he did not live long enough to see what happened after that.

XXI

"The time has come, my friend."

Nathan awoke from what little sleep he had gotten the last two days.

"Everything is ready. You have to leave this place now." It was Joseph.

Nathan, still groggy, continued to lie on the ground, bewildered as to his whereabouts and who was speaking to him.

"Nathan, it's me," pleaded Joseph. "It's Joseph. You must get up. You must leave immediately." Placing his hands in Nathan's armpits, Joseph helped Nathan to a seated position as he regained consciousness.

It was dark, but fire light shone through the windows. In the distance, Nathan could hear that the battering had resumed.

"They've fixed it," explained Joseph. "This place is going to fall by morning, and you have to be long gone from here. Get your things and follow me."

Nathan shot up from his mat and followed as best he could till his eyes adjusted. "I'm sure the Romans have let down their guard tonight," Joseph said. "They're rejoicing already, and you shouldn't have a problem. But be careful. One wrong move and all my hopes go with you."

"Joseph. I don't want to leave and know you might not be in this world by morning. I can't do that. You've been the friend of a lifetime."

"And you as well," lamented Joseph. "You were the one, Nathan. You were the one given, and that is what your name means. But don't you worry about me. You know I always find a way."

"Yes, you always do."

"But you are leaving, and that is the task that now has brought upon you. And you must fulfill that task alone."

They came to a covered opening at the base of the southeastern wall, far from the commotion and torches on the other side. "Some of the men just completed the opening a few minutes ago," Joseph explained. "We have to cover it up before anyone sees it."

The two men wrapped each other in an embrace that could not have been long enough to capture the sentiment between them.

"Now go," the commander commanded. "Don't look back. Watch every step. Take the Cana road south till you reach the town. From there you'll be able to find the road back to Jerusalem. It's a four day trek, so heaven watch over you."

Nathan jumped into the hole. "Heaven watch over you too," he said.

Joseph's men filled the hole with rocks and dirt the second he was gone.

XXII

The fall of Jotapata did not go easily. Although the battering ram breached the wall within hours of Nathan's escape, Joseph contrived more obstacles to make the Romans' entrance difficult.

As Vespasian ordered his men through the breach, their trumpets blaring and voices shouting while a shower of arrows pelted hapless defenders on the other side, Joseph ordered the people to boil oil so that the first line of attackers met with a horrible fate. Arranged in testudo, or tortoise, formation, the oil poured through the openings between the soldiers' shields and into the crevices of their armor, and they were fried to death piecemeal, with heinous cries of agony.

Joseph also prepared fenugreek, an herb that grew slimy when boiled, and had it poured over the gangplanks on which the Romans were stepping through the breach. The soldiers slipped and fell onto each other and through the opening in the wall so that the Jotapatans were able to spear them through to the point that

Vespasian had to call off the attack for the moment. Even with a hole in the wall, Vespasian could not get in.

Growling in frustration at yet another setback, the general ordered some of the siege engines disassembled and reconstructed into larger versions sheathed with iron fireproofing. He also ordered the earthworks to be recommenced and built high enough so the new siege engines could catapult directly into the city from next to the wall. All this activity took a day or so and gave the defenders a respite. But the fear of torture that mounted during the lull proved more wearing than the defense.

Once the engines were built and dragged up the ramps to the wall, it was open target on the Jotapatans below. The defenders could no longer approach the wall without being picked off. Some were even sniped near their homes by engines within reach. But still the city held out, and news of its bravery began to reach other towns in Galilee. Jotapata proved a catalyst in raising other cities to the point of revolt. The Jotapatans showed that it could be done, that Rome could be held off. And even if it could not be kept out forever, revolt would send the message that Rome was not the world and that people wanted freedom and the ability to worship as they wanted, even if it meant death.

After such a magnificent defense, it was not Roman brilliance that eventually gained access into the beleaguered city, nor was it Roman siege engines or ramps. It was a traitor from within, the downfall of every good cause.

On a foggy morning, the 47th day of the siege, a defector led Vespasian's own son Titus into the city, where sleeping sentinels could not see five feet in front of them. It was the perfect day for an invasion. Thousands of Romans snuck down quiet streets shrouded by mist into unsuspecting homes. Throughout the city people awoke at swordpoint, and a general massacre of the inhabitants lasted for the remainder of the day. Forty thousand lives ended, some still in bed, others in the streets, some tossed over the walls, others dragged from the cisterns, others by their own hand. Though a number of women and children survived only to face a life of slavery, Jotapata ceased to exist as a living entity. It was left standing a vacant mound of dirt and rubble, a humble memorial to a people who once defied the mightiest empire on earth.

As for Joseph, Vespasian managed to meet him alive. Escaping the city just in time, Joseph hid in a cave with forty others for three days. Somehow all forty of his compatriots died by suicide except for him—or at least that is how the story was told. He emerged from the cave at the general's bidding and prophesied that both Vespasian and his son Titus would one day rule Rome. Had Nathan been there, he would not have been surprised to observe that Joseph had found a way to survive after all.

XXIII

As Nathan reached Jerusalem, he could see that it had changed in his absence. Fallen masonry blocked the streets. Gangs of hoodlums lurked in what used to be good neighborhoods. Sunken faces peered from windows in fear. Dogs and cats wandered homeless. Beggars begged where they hadn't before. The only thing that had not changed was the political discord. Amram still warred with Opal and Zealots still warred with conservatives. And the situation worsened as more factions joined the toxic mix.

Upon arrival within the city walls, Nathan made his way straight to the council and was admitted to the inner chamber despite his unkempt and exhausted appearance. In fact, the guard at the door granted him access *because* of his unkempt and exhausted appearance.

The members of the council sat in heated debate as Nathan stood outside the door waiting for an opportunity to interrupt. He could hear his father and friends arguing on one side and Amram's cronies on the other.

"We've heard rumors for days that Jotapata is about to fall," said one of the Zealots, "so what is keeping us from sending reinforcements to Galilee?"

A conservative responded, "We have no funds left in the treasury for reinforcements, even though I agree that we *should* send them."

The Zealot countered, "If you conservatives hadn't hemmed and hawed for two months, we could have sent thousands of recruits north while we still *had* funds."

"It wasn't we who hesitated," retorted Opal. "It was you Zealots who couldn't decide whether ben Mattathias should stay in charge or if someone else should."

"And now that John of Gischala is in town," another continued, "it will add yet another voice to your infighting."

John of Gischala, wondered Nathan, was in Jerusalem? How did that troublemaker manage to make it back here? I thought his town was under siege.

Nathan could not listen any longer and made his presence known. Peeking his head into the doorway, Opal spotted him and stood up.

"Nathan!" Opal exclaimed. "My son, you are alive!" He walked over to the boy. "My son," he said in a low voice, "it is like a miracle seeing you."

"Father, it is terrible."

"What is terrible, my son?"

"The situation up north."

Opal embraced his son and whispered into his ear, "You will tell me all about it later. I must know. But tell me this right now: has Jotapata fallen? Do you know anything about that city?"

"Thousands have been killed there by the Romans. That is what is so terrible. I just came from there. The wall was on the verge of being breached when Joseph sent me out through an escape hole so I could send for help. I don't know if he is dead or alive, but the city could not have held out much longer after I left."

"You have to tell the council what you know," said Opal. "But," he cautioned, "do not conjecture about anything. Only state the facts that you know for sure. If the city has fallen or if Joseph is dead—or alive for that matter—it could create divisions here that will spin out of control. So remember, only describe the situation as you left it. No conjecture."

Nathan composed himself, and Opal led him to where the others sat. Councilors greeted him from both sides of the ideological divide. "Nathan, it is good to see you," they said.

Apologizing for his unceremonious appearance, he received a dozen questions from them: "What do you know about the situation up north?" "Did ben Mattathias send you?" "Is Galilee about to collapse?" "Do you know what happened to the city of Jotapata?" "Is it still possible to negotiate with the Romans?" "Is Joseph still alive?"

Opal motioned for Nathan to sit down. As he put his hand on his son's shoulder, Nathan could see that his father's missing finger had completely healed over, as if it had never been there. He felt like that was soon to be the fate of Jotapata as he began to speak about what had happened up north.

Nathan answered all the councilors' questions, explaining his participation throughout the Jotapata siege, the building up of the walls, the ruse with the water, the defense with the chaff bags, the breaking of the battering ram, and his own escape by night under Joseph's direction. As for Joseph, he was still in charge when last he saw him. He asked him to deliver a message of desperation about Jotapata's state and for the council to send help.

Nathan's report resulted in hours of further debate. He had expected unity against a common enemy. But no. In the end, nothing was done. The city leadership remained divided, and there was no money left to fund an army. Nathan felt like he had walked all the way to Jerusalem for nothing and that he had somehow betrayed the Jotapatans because he was still alive and most of them were dead—or worse.

When the meeting ended, Opal and Nathan walked home. Nathan stared at the ground in dismay, unaware that his father was leading him home in a completely different direction. "Abba, how could the council accomplish so little?" he complained. "Why did I take all the trouble to come here? Joseph was depending on me to deliver a message and to get reinforcements from you, but you have all abandoned him, and I have let him down."

"You haven't let anyone down, Nathan. You did what you were asked. It is not within your power to get the council to act. Joseph knows better than to depend on Jerusalem for anything but grief. I'm sure he didn't really expect us to come to a decision and respond. That would have been unrealistic."

"Then why did he send me back here? It was terrible there, and Jotapata needs help."

"Yes, it is terrible there. But he sent you back because he wanted you to live. Even if he could not, he meant for you to survive."

"I don't believe that. Yes, I'm sure he wants me to survive. But there was more to it than that. And in any case, I don't want to survive under these circumstances. I need to go back and see things through to the end. I'd rather die in the attempt, as any honorable man would, than live knowing I turned my back on him and our cause."

"Nathan, Joseph *sent* you here. You did not turn your back. And he didn't send you off the battlefield to drone out a coward's existence. He sent you back because the nation needs you. He was not going to waste you in a Roman massacre in Jotapata when you could be alive to help the situation here in Jerusalem. He would have been a poor judge of his assets if he had done that."

"But abba," said Nathan, getting agitated, "I have to go back. I have to. How could I not? There's nothing you could say that will change my mind."

Opal grabbed his son's shoulders. "Listen to me, Nathan. You're exhausted and hungry and frightened and you can barely think straight. Joseph didn't train you this last year and a half to die in Galilee. He trained you to negotiate and fight and survive, and he trained you to use your wits for victory. There is too much work to be done right here in this wretched city, which is crying out for good men like you, for you to go back to that forsaken hillock in the north. The city is probably destroyed by now and Joseph is who-knows-where. But Joseph needs you here. And I need you here."

Nathan remained silent and almost began to see the logic in what his father was saying. They continued to walk, and Nathan, finally noticing the strange route they were taking, asked, "Abba, where are we going? Aren't we going home?"

"Yes, we are. But I've taken up residence in the New City beyond the wall. I was wondering when you would notice. I'll explain when we get there."

Nathan looked around again at the poor state to which the once glorious holy city had been relegated. His father was right. Much work needed to be done there, and if Joseph could have done it himself, he would have. And if he could not have, he would have sent Nathan.

Opal asked, "Nathan, *do* you think Joseph is still alive? Do you know of somewhere in the city he might have hidden? Do you think it is possible, even though the wall might have been breached and the Romans entered, that he survived?"

"It's hard for me to say," Nathan began. "But I think so. I lived with Joseph for over a year, and I watched him turn death sentences into successes several times. But I could not say for sure."

"So he might actually still be alive," he reflected. "I hope so."

"If anyone could find a way to escape or survive, it would be him. He may have dug a tunnel, or he may have been captured by the Romans. But in either case, I would almost wager that he is still somehow with us in this world."

"Nathan," Opal paused, "Do you think it is possible that Joseph could have treated with the Romans?"

"What do you mean, 'treated'?"

"I mean, do you think he might have struck a bargain with them in the end to save his own life?"

Nathan could not answer that question right away. He was not sure if it was because he was appalled that his father would even ask it, or because a year of insinuations about his hero were convincing him that they may be true. Had he been wrong about Joseph all along? Had Joseph not said that if he found the war a losing proposition, he would have to find another way?

Nathan answered, "I don't know. It's possible."

"Yes, it is," responded Opal, dejected at the thought of such a scenario. "I suppose we will find out in the next few weeks. News will eventually trickle up to us whether he is alive or dead, and the news, either way, will have its effect on this city. I fear more for us if he is alive because no one will understand the difficulties involved in the moment he had to face the decision to treat or die—if in fact that was the case."

"Joseph always spoke about having to act within the now," Nathan responded. "So if he had to strike a bargain in order to live another day to think things through for our cause, you're right, no one will understand how that could have been a good thing."

"It all comes down to motives and trust," Opal added. "If Joseph struck a bargain, did he do it for the right motives? And will the people trust him enough that he had the right motives?"

As they approached their new home, Opal pointed it out to Nathan, and he saw that it looked as dilapidated as the rest of the city.

"That's our new home?"

"Yes. It's not as big or nice as where we used to live, but it's enough, and I have my reasons for it. We will talk inside."

"But why is it so unkempt? Don't Ducetius and Criton take care of it?

"They take care of many things. But the atmosphere in the city is not conducive to upkeep these days. I don't want to stick out."

They reached the front wall and Opal opened the gate. "Ducetius!" he called. The slave appeared at the door, and a look of elation swept across his face.

"Young master, you're home! Is it really you?" Ducetius asked. Nathan approached the servant and embraced him like a long-lost relative. "Master Nathan," said the servant, "we have missed you. You are so grown up I almost didn't recognize you."

"It is good to see you too, Ducetius," Nathan said. He had often missed Ducetius's good disposition and helpfulness.

Once they entered the main room, Ducetius said, "Please lie down. You look exhausted. I will get you something to eat."

"Abba," said Nathan, as they began to munch, "where are ima and little sister?"

"I didn't want to speak about it outside," Opal explained, "but I had to get them out of the city and send them to Joppa before the situation grew too dangerous here. They are all right."

"Really? Ima and sister are in Joppa? I can't see them?"

"I wish they were still here. I miss them terribly, and I know they are constantly worried about you, as I am of them."

"Have you at least been able to write?"

"I've kept in touch with our friends now and then, and they have indicated that everything is all right; though that city has had its share of trouble with the Romans too. I have been afraid to contact our relatives or your mother directly in the event that either the Romans or your brother try to threaten them to manipulate me."

"It makes me uneasy with them so far away."

"I had to do what I had to do."

"And has Amram come around recently? Does he know you are here?"

"Does Amram ever stay away? Yes, he knows. I made a point to tell him so he wouldn't think I was evading him. He comes around when he wants to argue. Nothing has changed between us, so we still keep half the city in tension. And now that he is in close contact with John from Gischala, who knows what will happen."

"John of Gischala. That man causes trouble wherever he goes."

"It's the same with your brother. And the Zealots think it's the same with Joseph."

Changing topics, Opal said, "Nathan, there is something you need to see."

Opal led Nathan toward the back of the house to a smallish bedroom. The room looked particularly crowded with furniture and piles of clothes and blankets. It was even dirty.

"What's going on here? Why does it look like this?"

Opal moved the bed and rolled away the carpet beneath it.

"What is it," Nathan asked, "a tunnel?"

"Yes. It's a tunnel. Ducetius and Criton have been digging it for a month."

Nathan looked inside. "It's dark in there. And it looks huge."

"Only the first four or five cubits are big enough to stand up in, in case we need to hide from who knows who. But the rest is just a crawl space wide enough for one person to fit through."

Nathan stood up again and moved everything back into place. "So it has come to this."

"Yes. It has come to this. Just like your experience in Jotapata. I fear for my life, Nathan. Not that I mind dying. I just mind how. I want an escape route in case there's no other way out of the city if we ever fall under siege. It's the main reason I bought this house. It's a hundred cubits from the North Wall and out of the way of most of the looting and infighting in the city. The servants and I sleep in this room every night. You should sleep here too as long as you are home."

"Digging a tunnel is a lot of trouble, especially if you encounter obstructions along the way. Do you think it will really work?"

"I don't know. But I don't know what other option we have."

"Where do you put all the dirt?"

"There's an abandoned well in the garden in the back. It's about two hundred cubits deep. We've been filling it up. That's another asset to this property. And sometimes we just throw the dirt in the garden itself. Since the neighborhood looks unkempt already it doesn't draw attention."

"Abba, why don't you just leave here? If it has gotten to this point, wouldn't it just be better to join ima and little sister? Why do you even stay?"

"You know why I stay. It's for the same reason you wanted to go back to Jotapata. There's a job to be done here, and someone has to do it. What would happen to Jerusalem if we all left?"

Nathan nodded, and the two returned to the main room.

"When do you think Vespasian will attack?" Nathan asked.

"With John of Gischala and Amram both in the city at the same time, I think the two of them will destroy this place before Vespasian even arrives." He paused. "They say that's why the general hasn't attacked already. We're imploding from within. And what more could the Romans want? Once we're completely weakened and demoralized, they will pounce on us like a lion on a fallen deer. They'll make sport of us all they want, and we won't be able to do anything about it."

"Maybe," Nathan agreed. "But I still believe there's hope. Even blind Samson was able to take down the Philistines in the end."

"Yes, he was, wasn't he," responded Opal. "If only we had a Samson. I know you always liked that story, ever since you were little."

"I was raised well," smiled Nathan, half chidingly.

"You know *I* didn't teach you that. I never had the love of the writings you do. But I find that admirable. And in the end, why not know them? But regarding Vespasian, they say he is biding his time because he's waiting for an even greater prize than Jerusalem."

"What do you mean? What greater prize could there be?" asked Nathan.

"A revolt has occurred against the emperor."

"Against Nero?"

"Yes. He may even have been toppled by now. We'll have to wait to hear the news."

"So you think Vespasian may be vying for the throne in a power struggle?"

"I do. That effeminate psychotic Nero left no living heir. And his last wife, if you haven't heard, was a young boy that he castrated and married because he looked like the late Empress Poppaea. So any number of generals, Vespasian included, stand in line for the throne."

Nathan wasn't sure what to think. "Nero gone could change everything for us."

"Yes, but not necessarily for the better. It may delay Vespasian's plans to attack us, especially if he is in the offing for the purple. But it could also make things worse if he gains power and backs up his disdain for us with access to the entire Roman military. We live in a topsy-turvy world. When both the province and the empire are in upheaval at the same time, anything can happen."

"In that case, maybe we will win," said Nathan.

XXIV

Like flies to a carcass in summer, every ideological miscreant in Judaea flocked to Jerusalem in the latter months of AD 68. If Roman generals could contend for the imperial title, Jewish bandit kings could compete for Zion.

At the heart of the city, in the center of a series of concentric circles spiraling out from the holy epicenter of Judaism, the Zealots held control of the Temple, and no one entered or exited the precinct without their knowledge. They especially kept a watch out for Ananus, the high priest, whom they—Amram in the lead—had declared deposed. They felt justified in denouncing the nation's prize officer as well as their takeover of the nation's prize monument. Since the Jewish leadership up till that point had only brought defeat in Galilee, and division in the capital, Amram's followers believed Ananus had forfeited his right to rule—or at least that was their excuse for ousting him. They then appointed a new high priest of their choosing to replace him.

In the next concentric circle, just outside the sanctuary, the deposed high priest camped on the Temple Mount with an army of 6,000 loyal followers. He also kept a lookout for all who entered and exited the holy precinct, ready to pounce on any Zealot who tried to escape. He too felt justified in his position, even if it meant endangering the Temple itself, because his title had been stolen from him, and tradition required it back.

Next in the widening circles, and playing both sides in the Temple drama, John of Gischala maneuvered himself between Amram and Ananus and was not to be outdone by either. Swearing an oath of fealty to Ananus, he secretly provided information and supplies to Amram, who lay virtually imprisoned in the Temple. This placed John in a powerful position, which he, of course, felt justified in filling. He saw himself as the rightful heir of the presumably deceased Joseph ben Mattathias and the de facto leader of the entire independence movement against Rome.

Separated from the Temple conflict but forming an almost equal rivalry in the next widening circle inhabiting the streets and neighborhoods of Jerusalem were the Pharisees, who sided with the poor, and the Sadducees, who sided with the rich. Alongside and practically indistinguishable from them were the pro-aristocratic Peace party, who were deserting to Rome on a daily basis, and the pro-Zealot War party, who were robbing, imprisoning, and killing would-be deserters regularly.

Outside the city itself lay yet more concentric circles and factions. Through the conniving of either Gischala or of some other secret contact, about 20,000 Idumaean freedom fighters one day showed up beyond the city walls ready to fight. They had received word that the Zealots were imprisoned in the Temple awaiting liberation, and came streaming in from their desert haunts toward the beset holy city in numbers that not only rivaled the Romans but struck fear throughout the entire Jerusalemite population. Since the Idumaeans, who hailed from ancient Edom southeast of Judaea, were recent converts to Judaism—Herod the Great's father Antipater being among the first—they wished to prove their fervor for their newfound creed by coming to the city's rescue, or at least to the rescue of the Zealots. They formed the largest single rebel contingent under the Jewish freedom banner, and it was only Ananus's blocking of all the city gates that kept them from attacking Jerusalem in a wave that no one would have the power to restrain.

In the widest circle, beyond the Idumaean camps, roamed the followers of yet another seeming madman with pretentions to greatness—a nomadic ruffian named Simon bar Giora. Living like a desert pirate, bar Giora held such a wild reputation for violence that even the dagger-wielding Sicarii—a band of cut-throats who had recently taken over the impenetrable fortress of the Masada in the Negev desert—found him distasteful. Now he was heading toward Jerusalem along with the rest, as if drawn by an invisible force into the hapless Jewish spiritual capital. The Romans, as if in an amphitheatre surrounding their victims in the arena, sat back to watch and laugh, awaiting the final thumbs down.

The trigger that set the battle in motion between all these factions was a rainstorm. It was the first night after the Idumaeans had arrived, and the downpour was so severe that Ananus's men failed to see when a number of Zealots snuck past them and managed to leave the Temple grounds. The escapees headed straight to the city gate and let the Idumaean army in.

The rains stopped and the takeover began. Under cover of night, the 20,000 newcomers to Judaism ransacked the capital for hours, indiscriminately killing anyone in their path between the city walls and the Temple. They did not stop to inquire of bystander, soldier, rich man or poor which side they were fighting for. Their swords sliced through friend and foe, eventually overwhelming Ananus's troops, who numbered only a third of their force. Thousands were slaughtered that night, including the high priest himself.

Unfortunately, the daylight did nothing to end the carnage. Once the Idumaeans had set the Zealots free, the two groups together rampaged through the city, robbing, burning, torturing, and slaying anyone they thought belonged to the aristocracy.

When the renegades arrived in Opal's neighborhood, Nathan could hear the screams of women and men outside. Fearful that they would be caught and their house ransacked, they put their tunnel to its first use.

"Nathan, Ducetius, Criton, hurry up!" Opal whispered. "Get in!" He pushed the carpet away, and one by one the men crawled under the bed and down through the hole. Ducetius, who entered last and had practiced pushing the rug back into place from underneath, covered the hole. They then sat in the dirt and darkness.

Nathan had a sudden recollection of his night in the Temple catacombs and shuddered at the thought of the insectoid creatures around him. At least he was not alone this time and felt safe with his father and the two servants there.

Only minutes passed before the four of them could hear yelling and vandalism going on in the house. They could only make out what they thought they heard through the wall and the closed bedroom door.

"No one seems to be here," one intruder said.

"All the better for us. But keep an eye out," said another.

Suddenly the sounds of voices, a crashing vase and furniture being overturned throughout the house grew louder as the bedroom door opened.

"What have we got here?" said one voice.

"It's just a bedroom. Nothing's in it."

A third voice joined the other two. "We should get out of here. This is where bar Opal's father lives."

"Then his father must be around here somewhere. He would make a fine prize."

"Shut-up, you moron."

Then the door began to close again, and the muffled words,

"Let's just get out of here," could be heard before total silence resumed.

The tunnel had actually worked, and Nathan and the others went undetected.

Remaining absolutely silent for another ten minutes, Ducetius spoke first. "Do you think they're gone?" he muttered under his breath.

Opal whispered, "I don't know. I think we should wait longer."

Fifteen more minutes seemed an hour. At the end of it, Opal gave the ok for Ducetius to remove the rug.

"I will go first, master," said Criton, the braver of the two slaves.

He crawled out of the hiding place and silently snaked across the room on his belly, peeking underneath the door for any signs of movement.

Nathan poked his head slightly out of the opening and watched as Criton soundlessly opened the bedroom door and went into the hallway. He walked around for several minutes just to be sure, checking various windows and rooms. Then he reappeared.

"The house is clear. I think we're safe."

The father, son and servant came out one by one, a bit soiled, but not too badly. Opal said, "Later today we must resume work on the tunnel. We may need it sooner than we think." As he pondered the whole experience, he wondered why the mention of bar Opal by the intruders had turned them away. He found that curious. Had Amram given orders to spare his home and father before the ransacking had begun?

As the day progressed, the two servants took up digging the tunnel again, using the broken furniture in the house to prop up the dirt walls for reinforcement. The work was slow but steady, and the hope of literally seeing light at the end of it kept them motivated.

Meanwhile, beyond the city walls, tumult broke loose again as the outermost faction, belonging to Simon bar Giora, now clashed with Gischala's men, the Zealots, and the Idumaeans. If Jerusalem found the Idumaean army menacing, bar Giora's numbered twice as many. How a desert outlaw amassed 40,000 followers was a mystery, but his promise of leadership, loot, emancipation for slaves, and freedom for all from the Romans proved a powerful attraction.

For months, and well into the next year, power changed hands throughout the city as one or another faction gained temporary hegemony. For a brief time they all found common ground when news of Joseph's capture by the Romans reached them. Since Joseph was alive and had not died for the cause in battle, he was considered a traitor. And since he had been seen accompanying young general Titus, it was assumed that he had turned informant as well. No one considered that he could be, and in fact was, a mere prisoner.

Through all the turmoil, the infighting, and the news of Joseph's survival, average citizens in Jerusalem, like Opal and Nathan, managed to live, work, shop, and sleep between bouts of violence. The faithful were even able to enter the Temple unmolested, whether Gischala's troops, the Zealot ranks, Simon's thieves, or the Idumaean half-Jews happened to be in charge of the precinct that week.

In their push to rule over the city permanently, Gischala's men took to terrorism by dressing like prostitutes, luring the Idumaean soldiers and Gioran thieves into quiet alleyways and slitting their throats once they had them alone. The strategy succeeded for quite some time. Not until the spring of 69 did a new intra-city war break out, with the Idumaeans and Giora's men wreaking vengeance on Gischala's men. But by then the violence was old hat and not worse than before: ransacking homes, catapulting projectiles at the enemy from the Temple ramparts, burning public buildings, and citizenry going into hiding.

Opal and Nathan often discussed the advantages and disadvantages of trying to escape the city before the tunnel was completed. "But son," Opal would always conclude, "here in the city we have a home that has remained fairly unscathed, and a relative who, for whatever irrational reason, has apparently given orders for our protection. Out there, beyond the city walls, we're on our own against Romans, Idumaeans, Sicarii, highwaymen, starvation, and who knows what else."

Nathan always begrudgingly agreed.

/////

One day Nathan went back to the Upper City to see his old neighborhood and Elisheva's house. He half hoped that Elisheva's family had returned. But squatters had taken up residence in both his old home and hers, and he became uncomfortable lingering there. With an increasing population of displaced persons, squatting had become as commonplace in the city as death and disappearance, and Nathan wondered how the four of them—himself, his father and the servants—had survived so long under such dangerous conditions. But really, Nathan thought, was it any more dangerous than Sepphoris, Tarichaea, or Jotapata?

He tried not to look directly at the houses, fearing it might arouse the ire of one of the new residents. Instead, he filled his mind with thoughts of Elisheva and the years of memories he shared with her and her family. Then, all of a sudden, he heard someone call his name.

The call came from Rab Simeon's house, and he did not know whether to respond or to scurry out of the neighborhood to avoid trouble. Did he know one of the squatters, he wondered. Then out of the corner of his eye, he could see a young man running out of the house directly toward him, yelling, "Nathan! Nathan! Is that you? Look! It's me, Joram!"

Nathan turned to see if it could be true, and it was. There in the flesh stood Joram, Elisheva's older brother.

"Joram? Is that really you?"

"Nathan? Is that really *you*?"

Joram hugged him, exclaiming, "I was hoping to see a familiar face. I can't believe you're still alive and that you're here! Even on the same street! How have you been living here all this time?"

Nathan responded, "With difficulty. But we don't live on this street anymore. We're in the New City now. But Joram, what are *you* doing here? Is your family with you? Is Elisheva here? Are you actually moving back to Jerusalem at the worst moment in history?"

"I know it seems lunacy," Joram answered, "but yes. I have moved back here. But no, my family is not with me. I am alone. Though if my sister had known for sure that you would still be here, she would have risked everything to make the journey."

"Is she all right? I think of her every day. Not a day passes when I don't."

"She is well," Joram answered. "And your thoughts of each other must cris-cross the cosmos every day."

"But I still don't understand," Nathan resumed. "What brought you back here?"

"Our fathers. Your father and mine."

"What do you mean?" They began to meander down the road, sitting every once in a while on a wall or rock.

"A few years ago, when our fathers said good-bye to each other, right on this street, in front of your house," he explained, "your father said to my father that we people of the Way were abandoning Zion just when she needed our help the most."

"He said that?"

"Yes. My father told me about the conversation. So I decided to come back here to make amends for that and to show you all in Jerusalem that you are not abandoned and that you are still loved by heaven and by us."

"You came back here for that?" Nathan asked, half incredulous, half touched.

"Yes."

"I've never heard of such a motivation. It sounds noble, but it also sounds crazy. Your father allowed you to come back here on that pretext?"

"No, actually," Joram responded. "He was angry with me and thought I was being foolish."

"I can understand that," Nathan said. "People are leaving Jerusalem by the droves, either by choice or by death. We discuss leaving here all the time. It is unusual to see someone willingly move into the city instead these days."

"Oh I don't know about that. I was told that thousands of Idumaeans and people from the hill country moved in recently. But I know that's different."

"You have to come back to our new house and see my father. He will be so happy to see you."

They walked back to the New City, and Opal was indeed very happy to see Joram again. They spoke about the family and life in Pella, and Opal invited Joram to live with them. Nathan privately reminded his father about the tunnel and the need for secrecy. But Opal countered that if he could trust its secrecy to anyone, it would be a member of Rab Simeon's family. And, he added, Joram could provide another set of hands to dig.

That settled the matter.

XXV

"What are you all laughing at?" Opal yelled into the hole. Nathan, Joram, Ducetius, and Criton often had too good a time shoveling out the tunnel together, and Opal had to remind them of the urgency of their task. Opal enjoyed having a full house, but enjoyed even more all that a full house could accomplish. In the midst of the war and the trouble, having four young men around provided not only an element of cheer, but efficiency and safety.

Almost every day the four of them would wander the city, picking up stray pieces of wood, often charred from the most recent debacle or conflagration, and bring them home to shore up the tunnel walls. They then took turns digging, strengthening, filling buckets, and dumping dirt. Nathan was sometimes all too aware that a sociological change was occurring among them as a result of the conflict in which they were mutually engaged. The slaves were working with the masters and the masters the slaves, with little distinction between them. But so be it, he thought. He had always been fond of Ducetius. And the tunnel sometimes grew by six or seven cubits a day as a result of their camaraderie.

The tunnel was dark, dank, and depressing. Even when the sun was shining, it was nighttime in the tunnel. After working on it for hours at a time, the boys needed a diversion to stay on task. When they broke for a midday meal, sometimes Joram and Nathan competed by reciting scriptures to each other from memory. It was an impressive pastime to the two servants, since they knew only a bit about the beliefs of their native cultures, and it kept them all awake, thinking, and interactive.

One day they came across a human skeleton in the dirt. After the initial scare, they began to reconstruct the man's life during lunch—assuming it was a man. They surmised that he had fallen in battle on that spot hundreds of years prior since he was not accompanied by any trinkets and his bones were not placed in an ossuary. It sparked an entire discussion about history, warfare, life, and death as they continued to work by candlelight. It was then that Joram began a scripture competition with a quote from Isaiah's writings.

"Nathan, do you know the prophecy about Galilee in Isaiah?" he asked.

"Galilee? Probably," Nathan answered. "But I haven't read it in a long time. I spent a year and a half living in there, so I'd be curious if it sheds any light on my experience."

"I'd be curious too," replied Joram. He then recited. "There will be no more gloom for those who were in distress. In the past, God humbled the land of Zebulun and the land of Naphtali, but in the future he will honor Galilee of the Gentiles, by the way of the sea, along the Jordan—'The people walking in darkness have seen a great light. On those living in the land of the shadow of death a light has dawned …'"

Nathan listened attentively, remembering Galilee in his mind, and thinking about all the hope the war had stirred up north under Joseph. He wondered if the light in the prophecy had any connection to that.

Joram continued. "'You have enlarged the nation and increased their joy. They rejoice before you as people rejoice at the harvest, as men rejoice when dividing the plunder …'"

Nathan continued to think: that doesn't sound like what happened to us at Jotapata. There wasn't much rejoicing. Were we supposed to end up rejoicing? It sounds more like a prophecy about the Romans dividing the plunder. But maybe one day that will be fulfilled.

Joram's voice remained steady. "'For as in the day of Midian's defeat, you have shattered the yoke that burdens them, the bar across their shoulders, the rod of their oppressor …'"

It does seem, Nathan thought, that we have had a respite from Rome these past months, so maybe this prophecy does pertain to the present. People from Idumaea and the countryside are pouring into Jerusalem, the nation seems to have been enlarged by all the foreigners, and the Roman burden has been lifted for a while. But I don't know. Even though the Romans aren't killing us at the moment, we're all killing each other.

Ducetius, who was listening to all that was being said, interrupted. "Excuse me master Joram, but this sounds a lot like what master Nathan went through up north under Joseph ben Mattathias."

Nathan exclaimed, "There is some truth to that, Ducetius." He was impressed by the slave's perception. "But I think only portions of the prophecy are fulfilled. Other parts are not."

"I'll continue, then," Joram said. "'Every warrior's boot used in battle and every garment rolled in blood will be destined for the burning, will be fuel for the fire.'" Then he paused slightly to emphasize the next line. "'For to us a child is born, to us a son is given, and the government will be on his shoulders…'"

"Joram," Nathan interrupted again, "I really think this might be connected to Joseph. I always had the impression that there was something special about him and that he had been born among us to be like another Moses."

Ducetius wondered at everything that was being said.

Joram recited on, "And he will be called Wonderful Counselor, Mighty God, Everlasting Father, Prince of Peace. Of the increase of his government and peace there will be no end…'"

"Huh," grunted Nathan, realizing that he had probably pegged the prophecy wrong. It would be blasphemy to claim the attributes of God to a mere man like Joseph.

Then Joram finished. "'And he will reign on David's throne and over his kingdom, establishing and upholding it with justice and righteousness from that time on and forever. The zeal of the Lord Almighty will accomplish this.'"

After Joram finished, there was silence in the tunnel. The candlelight flickered on the faces of the four, and they were all trapped in thought.

Nathan broke the silence. "Joram," he said, "I find that prophecy compelling. How often is Galilee ever mentioned in prophecy? And it seems to me like it is speaking about the messiah. I thought perhaps we had lived to see it fulfilled in Joseph, but that cannot be correct. Sometimes I think Joseph was a type of messiah. But the messiah is much more than just a war leader in that passage."

"Master Nathan," interjected Ducetius, "that prophecy speaks about your God being born as a child."

"It does, Ducetius," answered Joram.

"How can that be?" Ducetius asked. "I know among the Sicels and Greeks, people tell stories about the gods becoming human, but not among your people."

"It is curious," said Nathan. "It does speak about that." Then he remembered a conversation with Joseph a year ago about the absurdity of God being born a man and how there was no precedent for such a thing in the scriptures.

"It sounds like the beliefs of Rab Simeon," Ducetius recalled.

"I remember him describing it to master Opal late one night a long time ago."

Nathan was impressed yet again by Ducetius's perspicacity. Then suddenly putting two and two together himself, Nathan asked, "So is that where you people of the Way get your idea that the messiah was God born as a man?"

"It is," answered Joram.

"Hmmph," muttered Nathan. The candles continued to cast dark shadows on everything around, lending a contemplative mood. "But," said Nathan, thinking about the topic, "this prophecy couldn't possibly be about the messiah. It is talking about a child coming from Galilee, and the scriptures have always indicated that the messiah would come from King David's family in Bethlehem, right here in Judaea."

"You are right," responded Joram. "But if you know the story of Yeshua, he was born in Bethlehem near here in Judaea, but he lived…"

"In Nazareth," finished Nathan, "which is in Galilee."

"I must say," said Ducetius, who had heard of the town of Bethlehem, if not Nazareth, "I find this most fascinating. Where is it written, if I may ask, that the messiah would come from Bethlehem, so close by?

"In the writings of Micah of Moresheth," Nathan answered. "He was also a prophet. His prophecy says, 'But you, Bethlehem Ephratah, though you are small among the clans of Judah, out of you will come for me one who will be ruler over Israel, whose goings out are of old, from eternity.'"

"There you have it," said Joram. "The messiah would be born in Judaea and live in Galilee. And he would be God, from eternity. That is what I believe."

The four of them just sat there in the flickering light again, thinking about all this. Was it possible for prophecies to come true? And if they could, would they come true in such a bland, matter-of-fact way as someone being born in one town and growing up in another?

XXVI

At the pinnacle of the Judeo-Roman world in late AD 68, General Vespasian sent his son Titus to Rome with King Agrippa. Both men were to meet with the new emperor Galba over the situation in Palestine. The two had much in common, not least of which was involvement with Agrippa's sister: the one man committing incest with her, the other interracial scandal. But the meeting never occurred. By the time they were halfway to Rome, Galba had been assassinated, and a general named Otho had taken his place. No one knew it at the time, but AD 69 would later be dubbed the Year of the Four Emperors, and Otho was only the second in the lineup.

Otho's tangential claim to the throne lay in the fact that he had once been married to the Empress Poppaea, who had divorced him to marry Nero. And now, to strengthen his shaky claim, Otho took up a relationship with Sporus, the poor teenager whom Nero had castrated, and who had, since Nero's death, been acting as 'wife' to the Praetorian prefect who had helped oust the maniacal final descendant of the Julii. Rather than being disgusted by this, the Romans loved Otho for it, since Sporus reminded them all of Poppaea and days of greater peace.

But Otho's days were numbered. A new contender arose among the Roman legions in Germania in the form of Vitellius—a fat, jolly, ambitious general whose men now acclaimed emperor, not even realizing that Galba was dead. Vitellius marched his way south toward Italy while Otho, having heard the news of this northern treachery, marched his way north. Otho proved too late, however. Vitellius had already crossed the border onto the Italian peninsula, heading toward his opponent.

Then Otho did the unexpected. Rather than plunge the empire into another civil war like the ones that had plagued so much of its pre-imperial history, Otho awoke one morning after a good night's rest in his tent, and with his entire army camped around him, plunged a dagger, hidden under his pillow, into his heart. His attendants found him already dispatched to the Elysian Fields when they entered for his wake-up call.

Vitellius then marched to Rome in victory and took up the imperial mantle. Like his predecessors, he too sought out the young Sporus, but not to woo him. It was to exterminate him and wipe the slate clean of the entire Caesar family. He thus scheduled the unfortunate castrato to appear in the gladiatorial arena in a reenactment of the Rape of Persephone, for which the boy was to play the victim. But before the event occurred, Sporus killed himself to escape the public humiliation. He was about nineteen years old. By the end of the year, Vitellius would also be dead.

When news trickled east of the fate of Otho and Sporus, Nathan could not help but draw parallels between their lives and those of himself and Joseph. Though he found the relationship of the emperor and castrato sordid and uncomfortable, there was a heroism to them both that he and Joseph utterly lacked at the moment. For whereas Otho took his life to save the empire, Joseph clung to his by bargaining with the enemy. And whereas Sporus, who was about Nathan's age, had lost his life to save his honor, Nathan had abandoned the cause in Jotapata and continued to exist in a state of gnawing guilt as a result. To Nathan's mind, the fallen emperor and castrato would fare better in the final reckoning of things than Joseph and himself.

As he and his three co-workers continued to dig out their tunnel to freedom, Nathan disported himself with further recitations during lunch from the ancient writings. Contemplating the dirt and darkness around him, he said, "Joram, do you know the psalm of David where he talks about the depths of the earth?"

"Probably, my friend. But please let me hear it."

"O Lord," Nathan began, "you have searched me and you know me. You know when I sit and when I rise. You perceive my thoughts from afar. You know my going out and my lying down. You are familiar with all my ways. Before a word is on my tongue you know it completely, O Lord. You hem me in behind and before; you have laid your hand upon me.

"Such knowledge is too wonderful for me; too lofty for me to attain.

"Where can I go from your Spirit? Where can I flee from your presence? If I go up to the heavens, you are there. If I make my bed in the depths, you are there. If I rise on the wings of the dawn, if I settle on the far side of the sea, even there your hand will guide me, your right hand will hold me fast..."

As Nathan recited, all four young men thought about the places they had gone to, or been taken from, in their short lives. Joram thought of Pella and his return to Jerusalem. Nathan thought of Galilee. Ducetius thought of his abduction from Sicily. Criton thought of his sale in Greece.

Nathan resumed. "If I say, 'surely the darkness will hide me or the light become night around me,' even the darkness will not be dark to you. The night will shine like the day, for darkness is as light to you."

Ducetius, always moved by these recitals, asked, "Is this one of your prophets talking to God?"

"Yes," Joram answered. "Actually, it was King David, from a thousand years ago; the one we discussed the other day. He isn't generally considered a prophet. But he seemed to have many prophetic moments when he wrote."

"So your God can see in the dark, and he goes wherever you go?"

"Yes."

"Even in this cave?"

"Yes."

"My gods have a home in one city or another," explained Ducetius, "like yours does here in Jerusalem. Demeter and Persephone live where I grew up, and the Gate to the Underworld is there too, where Hades abducted Persephone. But the gods do not have a spirit that follows us wherever we go like this poem describes."

"For you created my inmost being," Nathan continued, affirming Ducetius's words with a head gesture. "You knit me together in my mother's womb. I praise you because I am fearfully and wonderfully made. Your works are wonderful. I know that full well. My frame was not hidden from you when I was made in the secret place. When I was woven together in the depths of the earth, your eyes saw my unformed body…"

The four looked at the close mud walls surrounding them and thought about what they were hearing.

"All the days ordained for me were written in your book before one of them came to be."

Their lives then flashed before them. Had it been fate under the auspices of this God that had brought them all together to where they were: all four in a tunnel in a house in a neighborhood in a city in an empire in turmoil in the middle of the world?

"If only you would slay the wicked, O God." It seemed fitting, somehow, that that was the next line, as though the writer could have anticipated their thoughts in this tunnel a thousand years later. "Away from me, you bloodthirsty men! They speak of you with evil intent. Your adversaries misuse your name. Do I not hate those who hate you, and abhor those who rise up against you? I have nothing but hatred for them. I count them my enemies."

All of them could relate to those words in their current circumstances, surrounded by enemies on every side—though Joram thought of his own creed as well, that he was called to pray for his enemies.

Nathan then ended: "But search me, O God, and know my heart. Test me, and know my anxious thoughts. See if there is any offensive way in me, and lead me in the way everlasting."

As always, the ending was accompanied by silent thought, the sound of shovels and shifting dirt.

"That was beautifully done, Nathan," said Joram.

"I will think about what you recited for many years," said Ducetius.

Criton, a young man of few words, simply smiled in affirmation.

A few days later during lunch, Joram said, "I know another psalm. This one is spoken as though David were his own descendant—the one I believe is the messiah."

"You seem to think all of the ancient writings are about your messiah," said Nathan.

"They are," he responded.

"We'll see. How does this one go?" There was something about the work and the fellowship and the dark and the candles and the importance of what they were doing that made Nathan more tolerant of Joram's views than he would ever have been otherwise. If my father knew we were having these discussions, he thought, he would probably be angry. But why am I not angry? I do not believe a word Joram is saying, but I do not mind.

Joram began.

"My God, my God, why have you forsaken me? Why are you so far from saving me, so far from the words of my groaning? O my God, I cry out by day, but you do not answer; by night, and am not silent…"

Nathan had to interrupt already. "You say these words are about the messiah? But how could they be? They sound like the writer is in distress. When would the messiah have been in distress, or far from God, or God from him? What trouble could he possibly have been in?"

"Yeshua was crucified by the Romans, Nathan. He was a light hated by the darkness. And he spoke these words while he was dying. He used the words of his ancestor David because they were a prophecy of what he was going through a thousand years later."

"That is most interesting," said Ducetius. "So it is as though they were the same person, only a thousand years apart."

"Yes, of a sort," Joram replied. "Yet you are enthroned as the holy One," he resumed, "you are the praise of Israel. In you our fathers put their trust. They trusted in you and you delivered them. They cried to you and were saved. In you they trusted and were not disappointed.

"But I am a worm and not a man, scorned by men and despised by the people. All who see me mock me. They hurl insults, shaking their heads, 'He trusts in the Lord! Let the Lord deliver him, since he delights in him!'"

Ducetius spoke up. "So people hated your messiah?"

"Yes. Many people hated him."

"And when he was dying, did people really wait to see if God would deliver him?"

"Yes, according to the eyewitnesses, they did."

"And how long ago did all of that happen?"

"About 35 years ago."

"Hmmph. Please continue, if you would."

"Yet you brought me out of the womb. You made me trust in you even at my mother's breast. From birth I was cast upon you. From my mother's womb you have been my God."

Ducetius interrupted again. "And his birth was in Bethlehem, the town nearby," he said. "I remember that from the recitation you did the other day. But then he moved to Galilee."

"Yes."

Criton leaned over to Ducetius and asked him quietly, "Do you actually believe what master Joram is saying?"

Ducetius gesticulated with a maybe and asked Joram another question.

"But if David is supposed to be like his descendant," Ducetius further questioned, "was David born in Bethlehem also?"

"He was."

"Uncanny," he reacted.

Nathan was rather amused by all this. Joram, too, smiled, and recited on: "Do not be far from me, for trouble is near and there is no one to help. Many bulls surround me. Strong bulls of Bashan encircle me. Roaring lions tearing their prey open their mouths wide against me. I am poured out like water, and all my bones are out of joint. My heart has turned to wax. It has melted within me. My strength is dried up like a potsherd, and my tongue sticks to the roof of my mouth. You lay me in the dust of death …"

"It sounds terrible, Joram," said Nathan. "I have read this psalm before, but I never thought of it as a description of someone being crucified. It could be any type of death—especially since David would not even have known what crucifixion was."

"True," replied Joram. "But the next part is the one that sounds the most like it." He went on: "Dogs have surrounded me. A band of evil men has encircled me. They have pierced my hands and feet. I can count all my bones. People stare and gloat over me. They divide my garments among them, and cast lots for my clothing …"

"Oh my," exclaimed Nathan. "That is exactly what the Romans do at an execution—especially if the victim is nailed instead of tied."

"Was your messiah nailed instead of tied?" Ducetius asked.

"Yes," replied Joram. Ducetius nodded in ascent.

"But you, O Lord, be not far off," Joram added. "O my strength, come quickly to help me. Deliver my life from the sword, my precious life from the power of the dogs. Rescue me from the mouth of the lions. Save me from the horns of the wild oxen. I will declare your name to my brothers. In the congregation I will praise you. You who fear the Lord, praise him! All you descendants of Jacob, honor him! Revere him, all you descendants of Israel! For he has not despised or disdained the suffering of the afflicted one. He has not hidden his face from him, but has listened to his cry for help."

Ducetius had to speak again. "Pardon yet another interruption, master Joram."

"It is perfectly fine," Joram answered.

"But this poem speaks only about the descendants of Jacob and Israel. Is someone from another country allowed to worship your messiah as well?"

"It is ironic that you should ask that. The very next part of the poem, which is the last part, speaks about people from all the ends of the earth turning to the Lord. So yes, people from every race can worship him."

The three continued to listen uninterruptedly as Joram finished the psalm with all its concurrent prophecies about the future of the world and God's people in it.

"From you," he said, "comes the theme of my praise in the great assembly; before those who fear you I will fulfill my vows. The poor will eat and be satisfied; they who seek the Lord will praise him—'may your heart live forever!' All the ends of the earth will remember and turn to the Lord, and all the families of the nations will bow down before him, for dominion belongs to the Lord, and he rules over the nations.

"All the rich of the earth will feast and worship; all who go down to the dust will kneel before him—those who cannot keep themselves alive. Posterity will serve him; future generations will be told about the Lord. They will proclaim his righteousness to a people yet unborn—for he has done it."

As always, the four remained silent afterward till the shoveling resumed in a thoughtful air.

"So in that last section of your recital," Ducetius commented as he continued to work, "the dying messiah is alive again and seems unharmed."

"Yes. That is what I believe. Even though he dies, he is alive again, and his message of hope is spread over the entire world."

"But Joram," Nathan interjected, "how can that be? It is hard to believe that your messiah could rise from the dead—though I suppose if he is God himself, anything could happen. But do you really believe your message is going to spread all over the world?"

"Why not?" Joram replied. "God has scattered us Jews all over the world, and we weren't even trying to spread his word. But the people of the Way travel abroad deliberately, and we are commanded to do so. So it can happen. There are Christians in Rome, in Pella, in Spain, in Galatia, even in Nubia. We're everywhere. I know you and your brother and the Zealots wish to fight for Israel's independence. But what, really, is this little nation compared to the countless believers scattered around the empire and even beyond? Shouldn't that be the hope of Israel? That is my hope for our faith; not a solitary plot of land."

"You sound like your sister," said Nathan.

"She is my sister," replied Joram, "and we share the same faith."

Ducetius was beginning to think he might as well.

XXVII

While the boys dug their tunnel to freedom, Emperor Vitellius dug himself a grave, and General Vespasian discretely clawed his way to the Imperial throne. The chaotic political climate of the day was such that any commander who won enough Roman legions to his side could gain Rome itself. The Jewish revolt furnished a base for Vespasian's political aspirations by providing three legions at his disposal for just such a purpose.

Not that Vespasian sought acclaim from his own men. He was too shrewd to be so blatant. Instead, he wrote to Tiberius Alexander, Prefect of Egypt—who, though a Jew, had risen in the Roman ranks to a position of great respect, even ruling Judaea as procurator shortly before Nathan's birth—and asked if his two Alexandrian legions would support his bid for the throne. This they promptly did, proclaiming Vespasian emperor in July of AD 69. A few days later, Vespasian's troops, seeming to merely echo the spontaneous outcry of the Alexandrians for a new emperor, followed suit.

As news of the defections from Vitellius to Vespasian spread, one legion after another swore allegiance to the latter, falling like dominoes to his sway, from Britain, Gaul, and Spain in the far west all the way to the Danube in the north and Syria in the east. The five Danubian legions crossed the border into Italy and began to march on Rome to defeat Vitellius. Vespasian then sat back and let others perform his dirty work. He wished his regime to gain popular support on its own—or at least seem to—and not be forced by his own hand.

Vitellius, caught in Rome, was terrified. Surrounded by enemies, he sought to abdicate, flee the capital, and live the rest of his life in comfortable obscurity. He wrote a letter of abdication to that effect and walked it over to the Temple of Concord as a gesture of good will. However, when his supporters in the city caught wind of what he was up to, they assembled en masse at the temple and chased him back to the imperial palace. If Vitellius fell, they fell too, they reasoned, and they would not let him surrender without a fight. In the end, however, his supporters were all killed, and his large, blubbery and flailing carcass was dragged through the city streets to the Gemonian Stairs—a place of execution dreaded for its dishonor—where he was struck down while uttering his last words: "Yet I was once your emperor." His brother and son were dispatched as well.

Vespasian thus ascended to the empire, and at his side stood the figure of Flavius Josephus, the emperor's newest creation: the man once known to Nathan and to the Jewish world as Joseph ben Mattathias, the commander of the freedom forces of Galilee and the survivor of Jotapata, who had prophesied that General Vespasian would one day be emperor outside the cave of suicide two and one-half years before.

Although Vespasian's plans to quash Jewish nationhood had not changed, his view of his prisoner Joseph had, especially in the light of his victory over Vitellius. If Nathan could have seen just how much Joseph's situation had advanced since last they had embraced on the hilltop of Jotapata, when Vespasian threatened both their lives, even he would have been surprised. Joseph lived as a Roman prisoner for two years, only to have his chains hacked off by order of Titus—hacked, as opposed to removed, to demonstrate their injustice. He then followed Vespasian and his son as a freedman. He Latinized his name to Josephus, and took the general's family name, Flavius, since it was Vespasian who had freed him. He was given a wife, who soon left him; but that setback meant relatively nothing to him. He was now a Roman and the friend of an emperor. His status within the empire had risen dramatically, even if some thought it had lowered in respectability. He was no longer recognizable as the leader of Jewish independence in the Orient. He was everything he once was not. But he was still alive, despite all odds, and there were some past episodes and relationships he would never forget.

As for Vespasian's ambitions concerning the Jews, he bequeathed them to his son Titus. Within no time after his father's ascension, Titus sailed to Alexandria, bringing Flavius Josephus along with him. He picked up two legions there, as well as Tiberius Alexander, the Prefect. Between his two ex-Jewish commanders and every other Roman legion in the area, Titus assembled an unbeatable team. With their fighting capabilities, political acumen, knowledge of the Palestinian terrain and experience with Jewish culture, their enemies did not stand a chance. Adding Agrippa's men to their ranks, they marched to the holy city 65,000 strong.

The beginning of the siege of Jerusalem coincided with the beginning of Passover. Thousands of pilgrims flocked to the holy city just as the Romans were arriving. Few of the devotees realized anything out of the ordinary was afoot.

Titus's men set up camp around the faithful and unwitting pilgrims. Since the entire northern wall surrounding the New City was of recent and substandard construction, one Roman camp was erected there on the vulnerable northwestern side. Another camp went up on the Mount of Olives, providing an excellent view of the Temple precinct. From there the Romans of the Jericho Tenth could watch the endless infighting between Simon bar Giora's men and those of John of Gischala, cheering the internal breakdown of the Jewish cause as it occurred.

"Why not just wait till they've completely annihilated each other?" quipped Tiberius Alexander.

"It would certainly make our job easier," ruminated Joseph.

"But it would be a whole lot less fun," rasped Titus.

The first skirmish of the siege was opened not by the Romans, however, but by a joint group of Gischala and Giora men in a rare act of accord. Running out of the city walls into the Kidron Valley, they attacked the Mount of Olives so swiftly that the men of the Tenth legion were caught unprepared. Scrambling to get their weapons, the Romans fell one after another to the Jewish defenders. Titus had to gallop over with some troops, fighting personally in hand-to-hand combat in order to save them.

Once back northwest, Titus sent Joseph to speak with some of the Jewish leaders. Opal was not among them. As soon as the Jewish leaders recognized him, they cast a flurry of insults. "Look! It's the traitor!" "Get away from him, he's worse than a leper!" "It's the sniveling dog obeying his Roman master!" "Get away from us, you piece of filth!" "We want nothing to do with you!"

Joseph tried to reason with them, but to no avail. He even yelled out, "And what if you win? Suppose you even win? What then? What have you gained? Who will lead you? How long do you think your victory will last? You can't even get along with each other *now*!"

One of the leaders yelled out, "The Lord will never let his enemies defile his holy city!"

Joseph yelled back, "He already has! Many times! Shishak of Egypt, Nebuchadnezzar of Babylon, Antiochus of…"

"Be gone with you!" came the reply. "We will have nothing to do with you. You are a traitor!"

Those words hurt. Joseph could tell that some of his listeners were affected by what he said; but one man in the audience began to physically push him away. He backed up and returned to Titus, fearing the crowd might kill him.

"All in all," Titus observed, "we are starting off this campaign rather badly."

Not only had the Romans encountered two setbacks already, but their presence was all but ignored by the populace. Within the city walls, life continued after the Romans' arrival much the same as it had before. People worked, slept, hawked their wares, bought goods, worshipped at the Temple, taught their children, cared for their elderly; Simon bar Giora's men speared John of Gischala's men in the streets, innocent passersby were mugged, ordinary citizens were strangled, holiday pilgrims were raped, and everyone fretted in timid stasis for someone to make a move and alter the situation.

Nathan and Opal heard that Joseph was still alive and had been seen by dozens. They did not know how to take the news. Had they heard that he called himself by a new Roman name, it might have made their decision easier. But Nathan, at least, still held out a flicker of faith that Joseph continued to work for the Jewish cause even within the Roman camp. Opal felt differently, but gave Joseph the benefit of the doubt that he would land on the right side of things. The Roman camp lay just outside the wall about four thousand feet southwest from Opal's house in the New City, but even he and Nathan continued life as 'normal,' digging the tunnel, and waiting for something to happen.

Then one day, over the western wall, on a day just like all the others, there poured a stream of arrows, javelins, and large stones. Occupants of the New City going about their daily business were suddenly pelted, shot through, or impaled in the midst of getting water, walking to and from work, shopping in the market, or visiting friends. "It's not Giora or Gischala," someone said. "It's coming from over the wall." Others said, "Run for your lives! It's the Romans!" Craziness ensued for an hour, only to be halted by the most terrifying sound in the life of the ancient urban dweller: BOOM! Silence. BOOM! Silence. BOOM!

Roman presence suddenly sank in.

"A battering ram!"

"No!!!!!!!!!!!!!!!!!!!!"

The news spread like a wave across the New City, clear from the weakening western wall to the eastern reaches of Opal's neighborhood. Nathan went outside to listen to the dreaded rhythm of approaching death. He could not hear it from so far away. But that did not make it less terrifying. Knowing it was happening and not knowing exactly where, it put a pit in his stomach. Ducetius, Criton, and Joram followed him outside.

"Now is the time to leave here," said Nathan. "This is just like what happened to me in Galilee. While the Romans were busy with their battering ram on one side of the city, I was able to escape through the wall on the other. We should leave through the tunnel today, or it might be too late."

The tunnel had taken almost two years to complete. Between boulders, tree roots, the foundation of another house, and constant interruptions, twice the amount of time and almost twice the circuitous digging than Opal had anticipated were needed in its excavation. It was finally ready, however, whenever they were ready to use it.

"But my lord," said Criton, "your father is with the council in the Upper City. We must wait for him. We cannot leave him behind."

"Of course, of course. But we must go get him. Criton, please, you must go," Nathan requested, almost desperately. "Tell him he must get back here. The Romans are going to breach that wall within hours."

Criton, who was already fit, and even moreso after two intermittent years of digging, crawling, carrying, and dumping dirt bags to complete the tunnel, sprinted out of sight.

But hours passed, and he and Opal did not return. "Where are they?" Nathan cried. He had somehow expected that running to the Upper City, locating Opal, and walking back would take a much shorter time than it did. He was nervous with sweat. In the streets outside, people were scurrying to and fro, hollering at each other and weeping.

"My lord," said Ducetius, "maybe we should make our way to the Upper City and try to meet up with them. If the Romans breach the wall and we become separated from your father and Criton, our situation will be worse than it is."

"But if we get separated while they are coming north and we are going south, it could be equally disastrous," Nathan replied. "We must wait one more hour. I know they will come." He didn't know what to do with himself while they waited.

Then Joram spoke up. "Nathan, I'm going to go look for them. They need to get back here as soon as possible. You stay here in case they show up while I'm gone."

"Really? Do you think that's wise?" Nathan asked.

"Yes. Two of us can carry your father back more swiftly than one." He turned to go, running three or four steps. Nathan watched him, much as he imagined his father might have watched Simeon walk away when last they said good-bye. Then, as though that exact same thought had crossed Joram's mind, Joram suddenly doubled back and turned to look right at Nathan and Ducetius. "If for some reason I do not return with your father and Criton, it means something has happened, and you should not wait for me."

"But of course we will wait for you," complained Nathan.

"No. You must not," Joram replied. "Promise me that. I came here to help, not endanger anyone's life. If I'm not back with your father and Criton within a few hours, you cannot wait. You must get out of here. You must assume I am dead, or that I was forced by circumstances out of the city—in which case I will be off traveling to my next destination, wherever heaven takes me."

He walked up to Nathan and hugged him. "And just in case this is good-bye, I want you to know I have loved you and have cherished these many months together." Then, taking Ducetius's hand, he said to both men, "If I make it out of the city alive, I will attempt to reach the land of the Sicels and Greeks, where the people do not know there is a God who can follow them wherever they go, and where the Gates of Hell are . . ." He then started running backward, still looking at both Nathan and Ducetius, and yelling out, ". . . for the Gates of Hell will not prevail!" Then he turned and dashed out of sight.

Nathan and Ducetius watched him as long as they could, standing in place for some time and thinking about his farewell. Like everything Joram said, it meant something; they just weren't sure what. They then went back into the house and continued fretfully waiting.

With the malevolent beat of the battering ram providing the impetus, the two arch enemies in Jerusalem once again came to a truce. John of Gischala and Simon bar Giora met face to face and sent a joint team of men to guard the vulnerable spot in the western wall. They also sent men outside the city, much as Joseph did at Jotapata, to attack and burn the siege engines which had recommenced their shower of arrows and stones. Their attempts met with similar results, however, as the engines were lined with iron. After several valiant forays, the Jewish defenders had to retreat—though not before Titus had slain about a dozen of them himself.

The Romans called their largest battering ram Victor, since it always accomplished its task. As Nathan continued to wait for his father to arrive with Criton, the western wall gave way. Although Nathan could not hear the fateful implosion of the stones onto the city streets, he could see the open sky where once there had been solid wall, and the sound of shrieks from the terrified onlookers actually wafted four thousand feet to where he stood. The neighbors suddenly stopped dead in their tracks, their mouths agape in a horrible silence.

The silence was broken by the even louder, denser, wilder, mercilessly masculine cheer of the Romans, thickening like an invisible cloud above the city as the armored soldiers swarmed through the wall like locust droves. The populace thought the previous moment had been the end of the world. But unfortunately, all of them continued to live and would have to endure whatever diabolical destiny awaited them. No such comfort as death lay at hand.

The defenders fell back to the second wall, which guarded the Lower City, closing the gate behind them. Titus ordered a full attack on the wall, rather than bother with the pedestrians of the New City. Nathan and Ducetius watched with palpitating hearts to see if Opal and Criton had made it through the gate before it shut. After several hours, it appeared that they had not. They were on one side of the divide trapped with the Romans. Opal and Criton, on the other side, were trapped with the Jews.

For five days, Nathan waited to hear from his father. He could not leave the city without him. He felt like they were the longest five days of his life. But really, he thought, did they feel any longer than the days of quiet suspense before the fall of Jotapata? He had been through this sort of lingering half-death before, attempting to deaden any urge to progress or proceed because the timing would not allow it.

He heard that several people in his neighborhood tried to escape under the wall, through one of the gates, or through the western breach at night. Over the next few days he watched in horror as crucifixes were erected outside the breach, in full view of the New City residents. One of the neighbors said he even recognized his neighbor on one of the crossbeams. Titus had ordered that anyone caught trying to leave the city was to be crucified. Up to five hundred escapees a day met their final hours on a Roman crucifix as a result—so many that the bored soldiers began tying up the victims in imaginative poses just to add a little fun.

On the fifth day, Titus penetrated the second wall, breaking into the market area, the city's most densely populated sector. Instead of slaughtering the population, Titus ordered his troops to harm no one and nothing. He hoped to negotiate a peace. But instead, the people sniped the soldiers, ambushed them, and slit their throats in the narrow streets and alleyways. In the ensuing havoc, while Titus tried to regroup his men and retreat behind the second wall and back into the New City, a number of citizens managed to make their way through the gate ahead of them. Among them were Opal and Criton, exhausted and hungry, but still alive.

"Abba! Abba!" cried Nathan, his eyes welling up with tears as his father came into view.

"Nathan!"

Father and son flung into each other's embrace.

"I thought for sure you were dead, abba."

"I did too," he said, wiping his eyes. "But if you had really thought I was dead, you wouldn't have waited for me."

"You're right. I must have still believed."

The servants also embraced.

The four of them were reunited, but Joram had still not returned.

"Did you see Joram on your way back here?" Nathan asked.

"No. Where is he?"

"Days ago he insisted on making his way back to the Upper City to find you. But now none of us knows where he is."

"I'm sure he'll make it back here soon," Opal said. "He's a clever young man. But right now we have to prepare to leave." He lowered his voice. "Is the tunnel ready?"

"It is." The four of them went back into the house. "Why couldn't all five of us be here?" Nathan complained. "Something always has to go wrong."

"We'll wait a few hours, or even a few days," Opal said, "in the event Joram shows up. It doesn't look like the situation with the Romans is going to change any time before that."

But as the days passed, the situation did change. Titus breached the Second Wall again, fighting recommenced, and food began to run low throughout the city. Pilgrims who had come to celebrate the Passover were not allowed to leave, and between their numbers and those of the Romans, it was only a matter of time till the food supply dwindled to nothing. Those who were rich paid a premium for what few morsels they could negotiate, and both the Romans as well as Giora and Gischala's men were eyeing the populace for anyone who still looked well-fed or well-dressed enough to maintain a hidden store.

"Houses are being ransacked," Opal explained worriedly after a brief jaunt through the neighborhood. "Innocent people are getting killed out there for a loaf of bread."

"Abba, we can't wait any longer," responded Nathan. "We have to leave. Joram made me promise we wouldn't wait for him. I've already broken that promise. Now it's getting too dangerous to wait anymore."

For days they had had satchels filled with essentials to carry with them when they escaped through the tunnel. Ducetius and Criton were looking them over to see that they were all in order when suddenly a commotion began right outside the house. Soldiers were attacking every home on the block for food, and the screams emitting in their wake made it clear there was a slaughter going on.

"It's time," said Opal. "We have to go. Now!"

The four grabbed their satchels and hurried into the little bedroom.

"Criton," ordered Nathan, "you go first to make sure the way is clear. Abba, you go next."

Banging began on the front door. Ducetius rolled the carpet away and Criton entered the dark hole. The banging became more violent, and men were yelling to let them in.

Opal went down into the hole next, just as the men at the front of the house began to pry at the door to break it down.

"Roll the carpet and bed back in place," Nathan whispered to Ducetius, "and let's get out of this room." Good-bye abba, he thought, not daring to say anything aloud.

Nathan and Ducetius made their way back into the main hall just before the intruders entered.

"Give us your food or it will be your life," the head intruder warned.

Nathan pushed Ducetius behind him toward the back door, whispering. "Get out of here." Then redirecting his words to the soldiers and pointing to some storage containers far from the bedroom and tunnel, he said, "We keep our food over there. You are welcome to whatever we have."

"Then we will be taking the entire house as a barracks, unless …" he said, unsheathing his sword, "you have objections."

"None at all," responded Nathan. "I was just leaving."

The men then began to lunge toward the containers and started flinging off their lids.

"Hey, there's hardly anything in here!" one of them yelled. They looked back to where Nathan had been standing, but he was already gone.

"What have I done?" panted Nathan as he ran from the house as fast as he could. Where are you, father? I can't believe I missed going with you by seconds. Hopefully you are safe and those soldiers will not discover the tunnel. But by the time they do, you will probably be long gone and on your way to Joppa. That's what has to happen. I can't go back in the house and I can't get out of the city. So I must trust that you made it through and that we will meet up in Joppa when all this is over. Please may it be."

He then looked around desperately for Ducetius. "Ducetius, where are you? You won't last an afternoon out here on your own."

Then suddenly he saw him.

"Ducetius!"

"Master! You made it out!"

"Yes. I made it out. I'm so glad you're all right."

"Where do we go now?" Ducetius asked.

"I don't know."

"Do you suppose your brother, Master Amram, might take us in?"

He might, thought Nathan, but that could be the biggest mistake of my life. After two years of avoiding him, can I just show up at his door? But there's nowhere else to go. Amram would at least try to keep us safe as long as he could. It's either surrender to Rome or surrender to Amram; and hard as it is to believe, we're probably safer with Amram. So, "Yes," Nathan finally responded to Ducetius.

XXVIII

"Well, well, if it isn't little brother coming to visit for the holidays."

"Do you have to be annoying from the first second I see you?" Already Nathan regretted his decision. "Passover ended weeks ago."

"I'm well aware, little brother."

"And stop calling me little brother. I'm taller than you."

"So if you're not here to lend us some belated holiday cheer, what else could be bringing you to our humble neighborhood?"

It was always best to be blunt with Amram than allow him to extract whatever motives one was hoping to hide. "I need a place to stay, and this was the only place I could think of."

"Well, one would think you'd have considered your own home first. Why can't you stay there? Has abba finally seen you for the less-than-filial son you really are and kicked you out?"

"No. I don't know where abba is, and our neighborhood has been overrun by Romans."

"Now that is a surprise, younger brother. Can I call you younger brother?"

"What are you talking about? What's a surprise? That our neighborhood is overrun by Romans?"

"No. That you don't know where abba is. I would have thought that if there was anyone in this whole wide world who knew where abba was, it would be you."

"Don't be ridiculous," Nathan snapped back. "When it comes to spying on people and knowing their whereabouts, the prize clearly goes to you."

"Perhaps. But not in this case. Abba has become boring, and I've lost interest in him. But pray tell how this unexpected misplacement of abba has transpired. Not that I really care"—he turned to his cronies behind him for a laugh—"but it would be entertaining to hear."

"You sicken me, Amram, you really do," countered Nathan with disgust. "Are you going to let us in, or not?"

"Of course, younger brother. Come in. Come in."

Nathan's decision to join Amram proved fortuitous, though

often uncomfortable. Nathan could not expect comfort, either physical or emotional, from Amram. But he could expect excitement. That was something Amram was always good for. Thus Nathan's visit to his brother set him up to be at the very forefront of the Jews' last stand against the Romans at the most fateful moment in their history. That meant that when the books would be written about the war—if anyone besides Joseph survived the war to write them—his experiences would be immortalized forever, though he himself might be overlooked.

The most uneasy aspect of serving under Amram was brushing shoulders with the hateful John of Gischala. Nathan had never forgotten the trouble that man had caused for both him and Joseph; and now that the two were under the same roof, Nathan did not know how to act around him. Gischala was leaderly and thoroughly devoted to the Zealot cause, but Nathan could not look him in the eye and avoided him as much as possible. Amram sensed the bad blood between them, and in his unremitting, brotherly way managed to keep them apart.

Watching Amram at work day after day, Nathan became impressed with his brother's command of both the situation and the men around him—a sentiment he'd had at least once before. But their situation grew increasingly worse, and Nathan could sense it. Despite the tireless planning and bravery of both Amram and Gischala, day by day the Jewish front lines in the city shriveled to an ever-protracted circle within Titus's grasp.

For the next few weeks, Titus's men built earthworks up against the Antonia fortress and the First Wall, the two main Jerusalemite structures that kept him from the city's lifeblood. The one stood adjacent to the Temple, the other ran east to west from the Temple Mount to Herod's palace. Once those two edifices fell, it would lay open to the Romans the last free sectors of Jerusalem: the Upper City, where Nathan was raised; the Hill of Ophel, which was one of the original parts of the ancient citadel conquered by King David a thousand years before; and the precincts of the Temple.

As tensions mounted within the remaining Jewish-held areas, Gischala became paranoid about defeat and sometimes lashed out against his followers to keep them motivated and in line. Amram watched him passively as he performed what became almost a weekly ritual. "Do you see this piece of scum?" Gischala yelled one day as he thrust a poor middle-aged man to the ground in front of a cowering crowd. "He had a cache of food in his house; food he could have been sharing with all of us." His eyes searched every person in the audience to make sure none of them would miss what happened next.

"Well this is what befalls those who do not love their neighbors as themselves!" He raised his sword into the air and swung it downward through the poor man's neck and into the suddenly bloodstained ground below.

The audience remained mute.

"I'm watching every one of you! Bring that scum's wife here!"

She came before him trembling.

"And did you know about this food?"

"Yes, I did."

"And did you know you needed to share it?"

"We did share. But it was our food, so we thought we had the right to most of it."

"Oh you did. And what about your comrades in arms here? Don't they need more than half of what you have? What are you without the rest of us? You're nobody! You're nothing!"

None of the onlookers thought he would strike a defenseless woman. But he kicked her to the ground and hacked off her head too, uniting her with her husband.

The crowd booed. Gischala, for one split second, feared he might have overplayed his hand. But he recovered. "You think I'm a monster? Look outside! Your neighbors are being crucified, and you will be too if we do not all stick together. Don't think for a moment I wouldn't behead my own wife and son if I knew they had betrayed our cause!" He could see that this line began to win the crowd back again because everyone knew it was true. "So do not be surprised that I made an example of this wretch and his wife. You will either die from the Romans' hands, or I will kill you myself. So keep fighting. Keep fighting! KEEP FIGHTING!"

The crowd roared back with fickle approval.

"Now get to the walls! And to the Antonia!"

Nathan and Ducetius followed Amram's contingent to the Antonia, where their directions were to access the earthwork ramps from under the Temple Mount itself and tunnel beneath them. "How ironic," Ducetius said to Nathan.

"Yes," responded Nathan, thinking of their long experience with that line of work, and the subterranean chambers under the Temple. Both thoughts brought Opal to Nathan's mind.

As they dug, they were ordered to line the walls with wood to be set on fire when the Romans climbed on the ramps above. In that way, the tunnels would collapse under the invaders and the siege engines would be ruined.

When the time came, the tunnels under the Antonia caved in as planned. Those against the First Wall, inexplicably, did not. The Romans were thus able to reach over the walls and pelt the people on the other side. As they did, the desperate defenders scaled the walls with ladders, ropes, furniture, and whatever they could find, and slid down the ramps into the Roman camp, burning and hacking in an adrenaline frenzy. The Romans looked up in paralyzed disbelief as the Jews poured on them from above.

Trapped within the confines of the Roman camp in the Lower City, the Romans and Jews butchered each other by the dozens. Somehow, both Nathan and Ducetius managed to survive. Along with their compatriots, they scrambled back up the ramps and into the Upper City, leaving scores of dead Romans and siege engines in ashes.

But Jewish cheers of victory were soon replaced by pangs of hunger. "I'm famished," Nathan complained.

"Me too," sympathized Ducetius.

For Titus's part, he encouraged his men after such a defeat with the words, "This city will soon starve to death." But with the piles of dead mounting, the food supply actually grew due to cannibalism as well as fewer mouths to feed.

"That stench is unbearable!" said Nathan to Ducetius, passing a mound of corpses.

"Then shouldn't we catapult the dead into the Roman camps?" said Ducetius, to Nathan's surprise. "At least they'll still be serving our cause." Days later, John of Gischala developed the same plan; and shortly after, the Kidron Valley was clogged with decaying and reeking bodies, all within nose shot of the Tenth.

Titus worked feverishly in the hope that *everybody* in Jerusalem would soon be a corpse. His men surrounded the city with earthwork walls to keep the people trapped and all supplies out. Within a short time, a dirt and stone encirclement five miles in circumference, with watchmen stationed at intervals, surrounded the strangled holy metropolis.

Once in a while from outside the wall, Joseph's voice could be heard, begging the city to surrender before it was completely destroyed.

"There's your friend," observed Amram to Nathan as he

watched Joseph on one of these occasions, "serving Rome like he always did."

"I think really," responded Nathan, "that he is serving *us*, the only way he can at this point, by pleading for us to stop before we're all dead."

"*He* should be dead," Amram said ominously. "Maybe he soon will be." He turned to a nearby soldier and said, "Knock him down." The soldier then picked up a rock and hurled it at Joseph, hitting him square in the head. Bleeding and stumbling, Joseph fell down, and Amram and his men laughed out loud at the sight. For Nathan, however, it was horrifying. As he watched some Romans carry him away, he wasn't sure if Joseph would ever recover.

As more days passed, more people died, especially the elderly and very young. The old saw their once beautiful city destroyed. The young never knew their city had ever been beautiful. Those who could not be catapulted over the wall were buried in large pits.

As for those who decided to surrender to Rome, an unexpected fate awaited them. One day a surrenderer was caught picking ingested coins out of his feces. After that, the soldiers took to slitting every surrenderer open, despite Titus's strict orders to the contrary. In one night, two thousand Jews were thus dispatched, left to die with their viscera surrounding them glistening and twitching in the moonlight.

Titus eventually took the Antonia in the heat of midsummer. Despite the valiant efforts of Gischala, Amram, Nathan, Ducetius, and many others, a group of Romans scaled the Temple precinct wall under cover of darkness and took the fortress by morning. The Romans pushed the Jews out of the fortress and into the Temple, then the Jews pushed the Romans out of the Temple and into the fortress.

Once in possession of the Antonia, Titus ordered its complete demolition. The Jews found it ironic, since it had stood a symbol of Roman occupation for eighty years. But Titus needed its bricks to construct a ramp to reach the top of the Mount and thus make the need for the fortress obsolete.

Then on August 5—the seventeenth day of the Hebrew month Tammuz—in AD 70, an event occurred that altered the Judaic world in a way it had not experienced since the Babylonian Captivity. On that day, the daily sacrifices at the Temple, which had been performed for a millennium except for the seventy years of the Captivity, suddenly ceased—and this time, for good. There were not enough priests or animals to sustain them, and Judaism would forever change from that moment. The Temple continued to stand for a few more weeks but remained non-functioning. If Nathan was previously unsure if he was living through the end of an epoch or the beginning of another, he knew now. News of the event was met with wailing from every quadrant of the city where stragglers still survived.

Now that the Jews were completely demoralized, Titus reapplied his new diplomatic tool, Flavius Josephus—recently recovered from his head injury—to another round of negotiations with John of Gischala. It was possible that with both their recent losses, the Jews might surrender the city and their Temple without further bloodshed. But Gischala would hear none of it.

"My lord Titus offers a generous term only once," Joseph began, looking eye to eye with his old nemesis Gischala once again. "Surrender the city now, and both the Temple and your remaining people will be spared."

Gischala eyed Joseph with revulsion. "We should have burned you alive in Tarichaea. I have never stopped regretting that we didn't."

"You lost that day," Joseph replied, trying to maintain his diplomatic composure, "and you have lost this day as well. For the sake of your men, look at your situation and come to terms. Do you really want this city and Temple burned? Zedekiah went to Babylon in captivity blinded trying to save this city, but you will continue to fight out of sheer pride. Up until today you have managed to keep this Temple and the sacrifices safe, but that has changed."

Gischala remained stony-faced.

"I am a fellow Jew, and I beg you to desist," Joseph entreated.

Gischala gave no reply.

Joseph continued, "If it is war that you still want, General Titus is willing to set up a pitched battle outside the walls so that the Temple and the remainder of the city will stay intact."

"The God of heaven will never allow his city or Temple to fall to the Gentiles."

"Yes, he will," replied Joseph. "He already allowed it thrice to our ancestors."

"So you can count."

"And so I ask you to be reasonable," Joseph pleaded, almost choked up. "Look at your situation. The sacrifices have ceased!"

"But not me," Gischala grunted. "Get out of here, before I cut your legs off from under you. Get out!"

Joseph left the Temple and reported back to Titus.

"It's no use. Gischala wants the fight to continue."

"They are a hardy lot, your Jews," observed Titus, thinking back to Jotapata and the many months now at Jerusalem.

"A stiff-necked people," Joseph quoted, thinking their persistence might be one of the Almighty's reasons for choosing them.

Titus ordered more earthworks to go up, this time around the porticoes of the Temple itself. The Romans shot at the defenders from the portico roofs above, while from below, the Jews began secretly packing the rafters under the Romans' feet with wood and pitch. After the Romans were crowded on top of the porticos, the Jews hurled torches at the rafters and sent their enemies crashing and burning through to the pavement below to be butchered or roasted alive.

Following the Romans' prescribed attack sequence, Titus now called for battering rams and siege engines against the Temple Mount. But the massive Herodian stones that constitute its base would not budge. The Romans then scaled the walls with ladders, but were repulsed by the Jews, who pushed the ladders backward and cast their adversaries screaming to their deaths.

Up until now, Titus had tried to save the Temple from major damage, but he was rethinking his strategy. His superstitious Roman side reminded him that the Temple had offered sacrifices on the emperors' behalf for decades. Would its destruction mean his own demise and that of his father, who had become emperor just as the Jewish Josephus had prophesied? It might, and Titus cringed at the thought. But on the other hand, Titus's military side warned him that so long as the Temple stood, the Jews would continue to fight. So in the end, he decided, the Temple must go. It did not matter that his many Jewish associates—Agrippa, Berenice, Tiberias Alexander, and Josephus—might disagree. They would simply have to understand.

Titus thus ordered the burning of the great silver-sheathed gates that admitted worshippers into the outer courts of the Temple precinct. The fire melted the silver and set the gates' wooden cores ablaze. The conflagration spread to the adjacent porticos, and the hearts of the Jews sank in total dejection upon seeing it. Nathan, Ducetius, even Gischala and Amram, stood in mute shock as the flames destroyed what was considered the undestroyable.

The fire continued all night and the next day until Titus himself ordered it put out. He was having second thoughts about burning the jewel of the Orient. Even his officers assumed the Temple would be left standing as a trophy in Rome's showcase. But as the Romans tried to quench the flames, the Jewish defenders attacked, starting yet another battle.

The Romans and Jews hacked away at each other in wild abandon for several hours right on the holiest parcel of real estate in Palestine, and perhaps the world. The stakes were high at this point, and either victory for the Romans or defeat for the Jews was within reach. Nathan, fearing for Ducetius's life, directed him toward the entrance to the Temple's subterranean chambers, which was exposed now that the western portico lay smoldering in ruins. Ducetius managed to find it and hide himself while Nathan pressed on.

Nathan had never fought in a major battle and came to grips with the fact that he could die at any moment. He entered the fray and proved braver than he expected. He slashed and stabbed and saw Romans dying because of his actions. Strains from victorious Davidic psalms made their way into his head, but he tossed them aside, knowing that now was a time to act and not to think.

In the midst of the mayhem, a Roman soldier hurled a piece of flaming debris at the sanctuary. Standing atop another soldier, he aimed high, and the piece penetrated a gold-framed window, entering the inner courts. Within minutes, the periphery of the sanctuary was beginning to glow with flames. Another soldier ran to Titus's tent to inform him of this newest turn of events, and the general, clearly distraught, soon appeared on the scene.

Titus managed to look inside at the sanctuary just before it burned—an inner sanctum no Gentile had purportedly ever seen. Its beauty and magnitude, which surpassed any reports he had ever heard about it, stunned him. He could barely sustain the thought of so much loss and ran out of the chamber in the hopes of still salvaging it. His men, as well as the Jews, could see him motioning to stanch the flames, to stop fighting and do what he said. But no amount of yelling, signaling, or emoting had any effect. Both the fire and the battle had taken on a life of their own. For the moment, Titus was no longer a Roman general and the son of an emperor. Like Nathan, he was simply a young man lost in a turbulent whirlwind of violence and heat over which he had absolutely no control. It was the anniversary to the day when, some six and a half centuries before, the Babylonians had burned the first Temple, built by Solomon. Fate seemed involved, and nothing Titus or anyone could do would stop it.

After Titus and the commanders retired for the night, one of Titus's men set the hinges of the inner gate on fire, with no direct orders to do so, and the Holy of Holies itself began to burn. The lone soldier watched in the heated amber light as quantities of gold he could hardly fathom began to turn red hot on the sanctuary walls, while vast untold treasures in the storage rooms around the perimeter melted into shapeless mounds.

In the midst of the fighting just outside, Nathan managed to spot Amram, engaged in his own struggle with the enemy. He was not faring well. He screamed over to Amram that he was on his way, but just as he did so he saw his brother fall below the line of visibility and near the flames of the sanctuary. Was he wounded? Was he alive? Was he still fighting from the ground? Would he jab his sword into the belly of the soldier standing astride him, or would the soldier dispatch him first? He tried to reach the spot where he fell but could not.

Seeing Amram possibly downed made Nathan feel utterly and terrifyingly alone. It was not the loneliness of his teenage years, when his politics had pitted him against his father and brother, or of the desolate night in the Temple sleeping with the vermin, or of his lone escape from Jotapata. It was the very real presentiment that everyone he knew and loved had left him. Elisheva lived in another country. Joseph had defected to the Romans. His mother and sister were hopefully in Joppa. His father had disappeared into the tunnel with Criton and may have perished on a crucifix. Joram had vanished. Ducetius was separated from him. Amram was probably dead. Even Gischala was nowhere to be seen. Who was left for him to turn to at that moment? Who would see him fall if he fell? Who in this crowd even knew who he was? All the giants of his world were gone.

As soon as he found a moment to extricate himself from the fighting, he ran toward the tunnel opening where the twentieth pillar of the western portico had once stood. A carcass lay underfoot every step of his way—squishing if it was dead, moaning if still alive, spurting up blood if dismembered, or giving him a bounce if whole. Every carcass was someone's father or brother or son. But he couldn't think about that now. He had to find Ducetius without someone killing him first.

Once he made it to the opening, he descended into its Dark-alfheim depths, with flames and heat all around him. He was not alone. He could not see Ducetius, but the fact that others were fleeing in his same direction gave him hope that he would find him soon.

Half in a stupor, he emerged from what felt like Sheol onto the Hill of Ophel and stumbled about till he found a dark, lonely corner where he collapsed into sleep.

XXIX

The next morning Nathan awoke to a sight he had never imagined: the Temple Mount without a Temple. The Temple was gone. It reminded him of his father's hand with no finger or the hill of Jotapata with no town. The sight looked unnatural and rather eerily *too* natural. No one in living memory had ever seen the patch of sky—gray and smoke-filled as it was—that now replaced the once and glorious spot the Temple had occupied for a century. The open vacuousness gave him an uneasy feeling like being perched over an abyss. Not only were the heroes of his life gone, but a fixture he had thought was the center of the universe had crumbled.

Although at this stage Nathan was wearied to the point that he was ready to surrender Jerusalem to the Romans so he could get some rest, more battles for the city still lay ahead, and many more people would die before the end could come.

Over the next few days, every quadrant of the Jewish-held Upper City and Hill of Ophel was rife with looting and death. A false prophet arose who lured some six thousand innocent Jews back onto the Temple Mount to await God's deliverance. Once they were there, the Romans lit the remaining porticos on fire, and every one of those poor souls perished. Some were consumed by the flames, others were crushed by falling masonry, while still others plunged to their deaths after jumping from the burning platform.

Simon bar Giora and John of Gischala were still at large in the streets, fomenting chaos and rallying support for their losing cause. At one point, Titus came out to speak to them from the roof of a building adjacent to the Mount. The Romans were clustered together in one grouping, Gischala and bar Giora and their men in another, and between them lay a bridge that connected the Mount to the Upper City. Titus delivered a speech to the rebels in which he once again vouchsafed the lives of most of the populace of Jerusalem if John and Simon would surrender what remained of the city to him.

John and Simon had sworn that they would do no such thing. However, if Titus would allow the lot of them safe conduct out of the city with their wives and children, they would stave off fighting and not return. Then the city would be his.

Although the two rebels thought their request reasonable enough, given the parameters of the oath they had taken not to surrender, Titus became infuriated by their audacity.

"You are out of your minds to dare make such a request," Titus yelled down to them from the roof. "You have been responsible for the misery and destruction of your own people, your holy city, and your great Temple. And for what? You follow a cause of your own making, which is of no account to the rest of the world, and which no one else watching could possibly support. You have neither understood the times in which you live, nor the power of Rome, nor the nature of your own pathetic weakness. You are already my prisoners. You are surrounded on every side, and you do not have a hope of victory. And yet you have the temerity to negotiate with me for your lives, as if you had an ounce of leverage.

"I draw the line here in the sand. There will be no more quarter for you and your men. No one will be spared if they come out to us to surrender. And as for the rest of this city, I am ordering that it be completely plundered and burned. You have dug your own graves. That is all I have to say."

A third of the crowd was stunned into silence, a third into sobs, and another into action. Gischala, who knew that even a moment of contemplation would give an appearance of weakness to the enemy, barked out orders to his followers. "To the Herodian Palace! Now!"

The herd of them under Gischala's direction rushed into the Upper City and headed toward the palace, where thousands had already taken refuge and hoarded whatever goods they had managed to keep or loot.

Nathan followed at a distance. He had not returned to the Upper City since the day he had run into Joram. Could Joram still be there, he wondered. No. He would have returned to them if he were still alive and in the city. But as he neared his old home, the front gate of which was hanging on by one hinge, he heard a familiar voice.

"Master."

It was Ducetius, coming out of the house to greet him, as if no time had elapsed since his childhood. But the wan and dreary look on Ducetius's face brought Nathan back to the sad present.

"Ducetius! You're still alive. What a relief." He hugged his faithful servant. "I haven't seen anyone I know for days."

"I haven't either. I've been worried."

"When did you get here?"

"After I left you on the Temple Mount, I didn't know where else to go, so I came here. Some of the refugees inside have been kind and helped me. I wanted to look for you, but I became ill."

"Yes," responded Nathan, "I can see that."

"The only food we have are mice and insects, but I think some of the people are feeding off the dead bodies."

"Yes. We all are. I have partaken myself. I know it is unclean, but God has never expressly forbidden it. Maybe he knew we would be in this type of situation."

Ducetius smiled. "Please come in, my lord. There's room in the back."

"Yes. I need to sleep. There's a mob heading over to the palace. Who knows what's happening there. But I need to sleep a little before I find out."

The two walked into the house together, through the once-tranquil atrium that was now a congestion of people surrounded by smoke, fire, and trash. It smelled appalling, even though the atrium opened to the sky. They walked past his bedroom, which was now being guarded by a dark, sinister-looking man, and the other rooms of what had once been his home. He knew he could not express the feeling of ownership he still had for the place nor his disdain for its current occupants. If anyone knew he had been heir to such a home, they would try to kill him.

He and Ducetius arrived at the back of the house, just outside, but still under a roof. There Nathan fell asleep with Ducetius keeping watch.

Meanwhile, all chaos broke loose in what remained of free Jerusalem. A battle ensued at the palace, with the newly-arrived mob killing the eight thousand who were already there. Outside the city walls, the Idumaeans were treating with the Romans, and bar Giora had the Idumaean leaders assassinated when he found out. The Romans in the lower city were burning every structure, pillaging anything of worth, and murdering anyone they saw. And the remainder of the Roman soldiers were erecting dirt, wood, and stone ramps to reach the Upper City on the west, while Syrian recruits, working under Rome, were busy doing the same on the east. The work was difficult, especially since there were few trees left that had not already been transformed into siege engines, crucifixes, or other ramps. But Titus knew it was just a matter of time. No matter how high the walls were from the surrounding valley floors, his soldiers would eventually build to the very tops of them, and he would have his way. Jerusalem had no hope. He would then crush the rebel army and the idea of Jewish nationalism completely, once and for all.

As the end drew near and even Gischala and bar Giora did not know what to do anymore, they led a mad scramble for the various sewers and tunnels that networked under the city. Their plan was to survive the onslaught and emerge after the Romans were gone. But there was no escape. The Romans ferreted out thousands, slaying and burning so many that eventually they could not go near the tunnel openings due to the stench emitting from them. So much death pervaded the city that even the soldiers became spooked.

A few days later, it was over.

XXX

"Commander says to take this one."

The soldier looked down and growled. "Get up!"

Nathan's body convulsed as he was kicked in the side. "What is it?" he said, jarred out of sleep.

"Get up!" the soldier demanded.

"Who are you?" he responded groggily.

"Your mother."

Nathan's eyes adjusted to the light. It was morning, but not a good one. He was surrounded by Roman soldiers, who grabbed his arms and twisted them as they raised him to his feet.

"What's happening?" he said in pain.

"What's happening?" the soldier mocked. "Are you kidding?

Get a load of this guy," the soldier said to his companions. They all laughed as they pushed Nathan inside through the rear door of the house and into a lineup of fellow captives. He wondered why they hadn't killed him.

"That bugger's got a dagger," one of the soldiers said, pointing to the prisoner in front of Nathan in the lineup. "Slit his throat."

A soldier took his sword and swiped it across the prisoner's Adam's apple without a thought. The prisoner's body collapsed in front of Nathan, who tripped over it.

"There's another one with a weapon," said a different soldier. Within seconds, that prisoner's body lay in a heap on the ground as well. No armed prisoner was spared.

Nathan dragged himself at sword point to the front door. Once outside, he saw numerous other lineups of forlorn wretches like himself being herded by Roman soldiers in an easterly direction.

As the lines continued to move, the soldiers continued to kill selectively. "There's an old man. Kill him."

"Why?" said another soldier.

"Those are orders. What are we going to do with an old man?"

"Maybe just leave him alone?"

"Kill him."

Within seconds he was dead.

They walked past a little girl. "There's a little girl," the soldier said. "Kill her."

The other soldier protested. "Why? I can think of plenty to do with a little girl."

"Not now, you imbecile. You're on duty. Kill her."

Within seconds she was dead.

But what was happening, he asked himself. Was the war over? Had the Romans simply won? Had his side simply lost? After four years of courage and effort and planning and fear and Sepphoris and Tarichaea and Cana and Jotapata and Joseph and abba and tunnels and Gischala and bar Giora, had it really just come to an end? Couldn't the Romans just shake on it and say it was a good match and let them all go home?

The death, destruction, burning, smoke, stench, insects, rodents, cruelty, loss, hopelessness, defeat, blood, mud, crud, all around made it hard to breathe or feel. Nathan only moved because he happened to still be alive. If the Jews had really lost the war, there was no good reason for him to live. He simply inched forward because the soldiers prodded him forward. But where was he going?

The Temple-less Temple Mount? It loomed in front of him. Was he really going there again? Why? I just left the Temple a few weeks ago, Nathan thought. Now it's gone. Why am I going back to it?

As his particular line of forlorn wretches approached the massive Herodian stones, which alone stood victorious against the onslaught of the Roman battering rams and night of fire, the other lines of captives began to merge with his from the side. He hoped that somehow one of those lines might contain Ducetius, who couldn't have been far from the house when the soldiers arrived. He would have survived as long as he didn't have his sword on him—which he probably didn't, Nathan thought.

Then he heard Ducetius call him quietly. "Master."

"Ducetius," Nathan whispered. "You're still alive."

"Yes, my lord. And you too."

"I guess this is it."

"Yes."

They walked together, breathing sighs of relief, and for two seconds clasped each other's hands.

Once they arrived at the entrance to the Mount, they were corralled and shoved through the gates and up the stairs to the still ash-covered and body-strewn courtyard, barely cloistered but by a few remaining pillars. The smell of smoke and decaying corpses was strong. The sight was overwhelming. A sound of moaning arose from one quadrant of the square where women and children were cordoned off.

As the lines of newcomers came into the courtyard, they were unceremoniously thrust toward one grouping of victims or another by a forbidding-looking soldier named Fronto. "You, over there, to the right" he barked, manhandling the tall, handsome fellow preceding Nathan. When Fronto saw Nathan and Ducetius, he commanded, "Get to the left." They dutifully complied, walking toward a group of young men of mixed sizes and looks.

Nathan stood in his section and scanned the crowd, trying to figure out the logic of everyone's placement. He conjectured that each was destined for a different horrible fate. The women and children were probably marked for death or slavery. The pretty teenage girls were headed for—he didn't wish to think it, though he could see why. His own category remained unclear. He assumed he was in the male counterpart to the pretty teenage girls. But observing more closely the brawny and lean mix he was in, illustrated even by he and Ducetius, he realized they were probably destined for the gladiatorial arena, where some would fight and some would die.

Over the next few hours, as more and more newcomers were crowded into the space, he overheard one of the soldiers speaking about captives for the triumphal procession back in Rome. From that, he concluded that perhaps the tall, handsome fellows were slated for that: fine specimens to be displayed in chains behind the conquering heroes, to evoke tears from the women and inspiration for the men.

Though nervous about the impending doom awaiting him, Nathan was relieved that at least he had been chosen for the arena rather than slavery or exhibition, if one had to choose. The ring was the only one of the three fates where one could prove himself and have a chance of being set free. Slaves, on the other hand, ended up in mines or quarries, where they simply served the Roman machine till they expired. They had no hope at all. But to be chosen for the arena meant he might survive, and—he couldn't help but think it for a moment—that he looked strong.

No sooner had that misplaced thought crossed his mind, when suddenly, out of nowhere, a whip cracked him on the neck and slashed his earlobe.

"Kneel!" soldiers began yelling. "Kneel, you dogs! Every one of you!"

Another whip lashed about him, but this time Nathan covered his head with his hands.

After all the captives were on their knees, Titus came onto the Mount with his bodyguard and his new companion, Flavius Josephus.

"Look up, stay kneeling! Look up, stay kneeling!" the soldiers yelled.

Nathan could see Titus motion to Joseph with his finger to enter the crowd. He had not seen Joseph up close for two years. He was unaware that Joseph had taken on a new name and wondered if Joseph would still recognize him past his unkempt long hair, scraggly beard, and filthy clothes—if he saw him at all. He assumed Joseph was going to speak to the crowd about the fall of their city and their capture as being the will of God. But he did not utter a word to the crowd. Instead, he walked among the captives accompanied by soldiers, and whenever he pointed to someone, that person was helped to their feet by the soldiers and allowed to go free.

Joseph walked around the entire complex looking at everyone.

There were men he chose, women he chose, children he chose. Would he notice him? Of course, he started on the side of the crowd opposite where he and Ducetius were.

When he finally reached Nathan, Nathan dared not look directly at him. He could not appear to be begging. But Ducetius looked up at him, and Nathan heard his name being called.

"Nathan."

Nathan then looked him in the eye.

"Joseph, is it really you?"

"It is, my friend." He then spoke to the soldiers: "He's one." Then he asked Nathan, "Is this Ducetius?"

"It is," Nathan responded.

"He is one too," Joseph said to the soldiers.

Nathan and Ducetius were both helped to their feet. When Nathan saw the face of the soldier lifting him up, he realized it was the very one who had kicked him out of sleep earlier that morning. The soldier, however, showed no sign of recognition.

Nathan and Ducetius were both given small *ostraca* granting them safe passage out of the city. As Nathan stood up, Joseph looked directly at him, or rather into him. Taking Nathan's hand, Joseph said to him, "You need to know that your father did not make it. I asked that he be taken down, but he did not make it. He was brave. He suffered terribly. But he would go through what he did a thousand times to know you are still alive. And so would I. So you have to live, my friend. You have to live. You must leave this place forever. That is what you must do."

"Joseph!" They hugged each other. "Thank you." Those few words had to suffice as the soldiers motioned for Joseph to move on. Nathan trusted Joseph knew the millions of words behind those few.

As the two walked away, Nathan looked back once to see Joseph looking directly back at him. His glance seemed both touching and stern, as if his eyes said he wanted Nathan to stay forever to talk about life and war and love as they once had, but that he needed to go and never look behind him again. Nathan understood, but wondered how it had all come to this.

He and Ducetius exited the Temple Mount and walked north. They went through the Hill of Ophel, the Lower City, the First Wall, and the northern suburb. They picked up whatever they could find from their ransacked home and left Jerusalem forever. Nathan felt like Abraham, who, two thousand years before, had struck out from his father's house and traveled west to whatever fate awaited him.

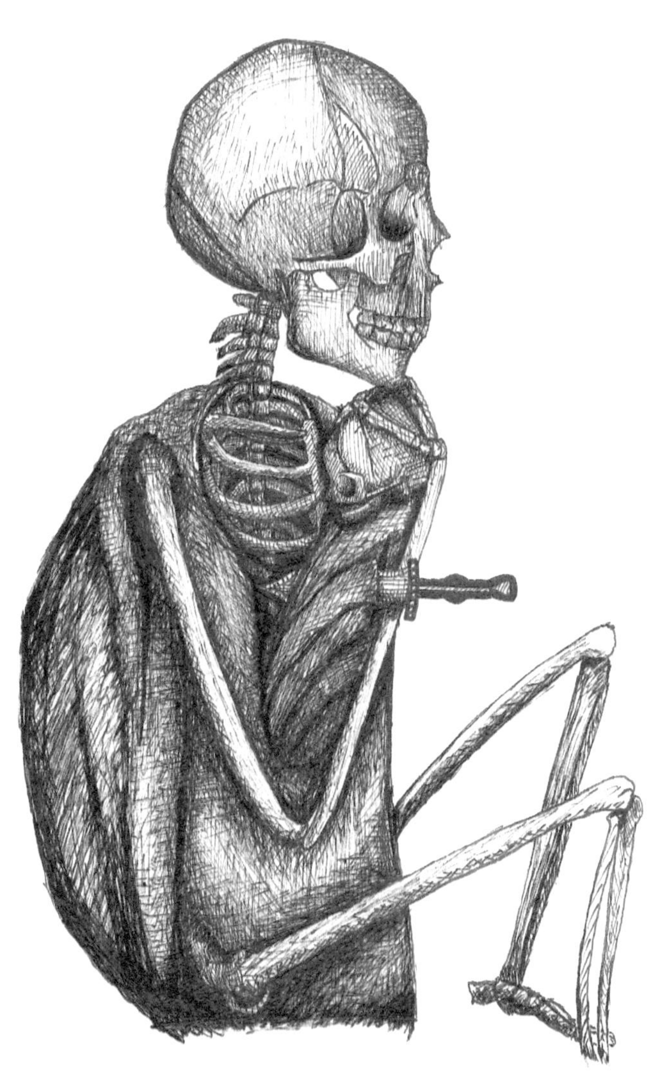

BOOK II
SICILY

I

"To live. That is what you must do."

Nathan often recalled those words. It is easy enough to live, he thought. The heart beats, the lungs intake air, the eyes blink. Anything that has life in it can live, but anything that doesn't cannot. But why can a tiny gnat live while an enormous mountain cannot? And why do living things exist for such a brief time while inanimate mountains last for eons? And why is it that mountains cannot sense the eons passing but only the briefly living can?

Though Nathan wished to probe life's mysteries further, he had immediate concerns to attend to. After leaving Jerusalem, he found his mother and sister in Joppa and booked passage to the island of Sicily, where his father believed it was safe and obscure enough for Jews to live. He hoped that would prove true. Ducetius's Sicilian background would give him a jump start in settling there. But could he build a new life in such a backwater after the excitement of the war, Galilee, and Jerusalem? The stretch of Sicily he and his family had trekked across thus far offered little promise of it.

"I wish my father had not died," Nathan said to Ducetius.

"I also, my lord."

"He should be with us."

"It was his idea to come here, after all."

"What do you think my brother would say if he found out abba was dead? It's been three years."

Ducetius could not answer.

"I think he would he say," responding to his own question, "that abba had it coming. That it was poetic justice that his beloved Rome had killed him. He wouldn't shed one tear for the man who had kept him safe through such a tumultuous turn in history. That is what I think."

Ducetius continued to listen.

"Do you believe there will be a final reckoning, Ducetius, to right all the wrongs of the world?"

"I thought you always believed there would be, my lord."

"But with all the evil we've seen, should I have less faith because things are so bad, or more because the idea of 'wrong' is illogical if there is no final reckoning?"

"Time will tell. Perhaps we will find out here."

"In Sicily?"

"Home has a way of bringing out truth."

"But Elisheva once told me that truth does not reside in any one parcel of land."

With that, they stopped talking to figure out their next steps. Thus far they had traveled three weeks at sea to reach Sicily, then found a caravan into the interior of the island along the Syracusae-Thermae royal road. They had walked fifty-five miles over another two weeks. And now they were approaching Ducetius's birthplace, a city on a majestic butte rising from the island's central hill country. The city was called Enna, a site more ancient than Rome.

"It's beautiful," exclaimed Nathan's mother.

"And not unlike Jerusalem or Jotapata," said Nathan.

Nathan's sister Adah, who was now sixteen, said, "That's our new home? It's about time we got here."

Ducetius, who had not seen his birthplace for twenty years, could not speak. Nathan put his hand on Ducetius's shoulder. "Does it look like you remember?"

Ducetius simply nodded with his mouth open.

As Nathan reckoned, Enna lay at the geographical midpoint of Sicily, and Sicily near the midpoint of the empire. But for all its centrality, it was considered the most invisible Roman province, and hence the perfect place to escape Rome's antagonism.

In its heyday, Sicily had been important: the most coveted land in the Mediterranean. Carthaginians colonized it from the west and produced Palermo. Greeks colonized it from the east and produced Syracuse. The native tribes caught in the middle—Elymians, Sicani, and Sicels—lost their independence to both. Then Rome swooped down from the north and took them all. Sicily became Rome's first overseas province and relegated it to subservience for the next seven hundred years. The island became a mere granary to feed the new empire's ever-expanding population, and it imported slaves from every land to work its endless plantations or *latifundia* of wheat.

"A long time ago Enna was full of heroes, my lord," Ducetius told Nathan as they neared the butte. "It was once a great city."

"Really?"

"We learned about it when I was small."

"Tell me some of it. I would like to know," said Nathan.

"I love stories," added Nathan's sister.

"There was a slave named Eunus who rebelled against Rome," Ducetius began.

"So Jerusalem was not the only place to defy the empire," Nathan commented, intrigued.

"Certainly not. What I remember about him is that he came from another country and was a magician. He prophesied once that he would rise to power, and a few years later he did. He killed his master and all the latifundia owners and became king in our city. It took the Romans years to put him down."

"I wish I could meet him," said Adah.

"And before Eunus," Ducetius continued, "there was a leader of the Sicels, my people, named Douketios. He rose up against the Greeks to keep my people free."

"What happened to him?" asked Nathan.

"He was vanquished too, but not before he ruled Enna and our part of the island for years.

"Your names are similar."

"Yes. I am named after him. Douketios is my actual name."

"So is Enna a Sicel city?"

"Yes, and we are very proud of it. But it is not great like it used to be—or so the old people reminded us when we were growing up."

Enjoying this unexpected facet of his future home as well as of Ducetius, Nathan commented, "So you come from a long line of renegades."

"I suppose so," responded Ducetius.

"But you have always been loyal to me and my family."

"Of course."

Since arriving in Sicily, Nathan, his mother and Adah had discussed Ducetius's loyalty to them and the idea of setting him free. It did not seem right to any of them that he should return to his hometown in servitude. In Nathan's view, Ducetius was one of the finest men he had ever known and deserved to be free again.

"Ducetius," Nathan said, "before we enter Enna, we need to make a change in our relationship. I wish to offer you manumission so you can enter your hometown a free man."

Ducetius looked at Nathan unsure of how to respond. It was completely unexpected. Was his master actually offering him his freedom? He and Nathan were certainly not the typical master and slave, but shared a brotherliness one only heard about in other

Roman emancipation stories. They lived together, worked together, talked together, supported one another; were comrades in arms, fellow fugitives, and fellow captives set to fall victims together in the arena at one point.

"Really, Master?" asked Ducetius.

"Yes," Nathan answered.

"But how? How could I be free?" he asked incredulously. "I have served your family since I was ten. And what does freedom even mean? What would I do if I were free?"

"I suppose you could do the same things that you do now. Or something completely different. Being free means that you can choose."

"But Master, do you really want that?"

"Yes, I really want that. Don't you?"

"I don't know," Ducetius answered. "I suppose all people wish to be free. But I have never felt particularly *un*free; so being something other than I am at this point sounds frightening and burdensome."

"There is some truth to that," Nathan responded. "But being free is like becoming an adult. My brother and I always wanted to grow up and be out from under my father's control. But once faced with that prospect—as I have been since my father's death—it has been intimidating and more of a responsibility than a liberation. So I understand what you are saying. But still, you have shared so many responsibilities and troubles with me that I cannot help but think you are ready to be free, and already are. Besides," Nathan added, "since we are heading for the town you grew up in, you have to return to it a free man."

Nathan's mother interjected. "Yes, Ducetius. Nathan is right. He and I have spoken about this many times over the last few weeks. It is only just, after all you have done for and with our family. You must accept it."

"Thank you, lady."

Nathan continued. "You will not be on your own, unless you want to be. But I will no longer be your master. I will be your Patrón, and you can call me that, and you can work with me or for me for as long as you want, or not at all."

"If that is the case," Ducetius responded, "then perhaps I *do* wish to be free. I had always hoped to return to my home a free man. But what about the tradition you have in your own law? Isn't there a ceremony for becoming a bondslave?

"A bondslave?" Nathan asked.

"Yes. I remember hearing about it when I first came into your family, and I wondered if it would ever happen to me."

"You mean taking a slave to the door of the house and running an awl through his earlobe, and the servant swearing that he will be a servant forever?"

"Yes," answered Ducetius. "That is the tradition I remember. So it *is* true. My memory is not incorrect."

"No, it is not," said Nathan. "Are you mentioning that because you want to become a bondslave instead of a freedman?"

"I don't think so, master. But if there were a status between bondsman and free, that's what I would want to be. Because what servant would not want to remain connected to a family that has been as good to me as yours has been? I think I would wish to be a freedman according to Roman law but a bondslave in my heart according to Jewish law."

Nathan was touched by this. It was a magnificent sentiment. Ducetius's sense of his place in the world—Sicel by heritage, Greek by culture, Roman by law, Jewish by faith—showed the complexity of his mind and his worthiness of the new status Nathan was offering him. His mother and sister were touched by it also. Adah remarked, "That is why we will always love you, Ducetius."

"Then that settles it," said Nathan smiling. "You are now free, and I am your Patrón. My mother and sister are witnesses. And if that does not stand up in a court of Roman law because they are women, your whole town will witness that there is no ownership right between you and me."

Ducetius stopped walking and stood in place dumbfounded. "So that is it?" he said. "I am free now? Just like that?"

"Yes," said Nathan. "You are really free. Just like that."

"But will your God see me differently? Will master Joram's messiah see me differently? Is it all right to change status: to be free, then not free, then free again?"

"Ducetius," said Nathan, remembering all the discussions and recitations in the tunnel, "he has searched you and he knows you, and he has followed you from here to Jerusalem and back again. As for Joram's messiah, I cannot speak to that. But as for the Almighty I know, where can you flee from his presence? He knows exactly what is happening to you, and I am sure he approves."

"Then I must approve also, Patrón," said Ducetius, reaching out his arms to his former master.

Nathan's mother and sister completed his act by joining all four of them in embrace.

They continued walking toward Enna, which grew larger and larger before them with each step. Within an hour they parted ways from most of their caravan and continued on alone. As they walked, Ducetius pointed over to the left. "If I'm not mistaken, that is the road to Lake Pergusa, the field where Persephone was abducted, and where they say the Gate to the Underworld is."

II

Ascending the butte of Enna along a circuitous road, the little troupe passed through the city gate and into the market area with a few merchants and stragglers from their caravan. The market was lively, and the streets were lined with kiosks and counters of vegetables, textiles, storage containers, and animals ready for butchering; but the overall infrastructure of the town was run-down and clearly intended for a population larger than it currently held. This was typical of the island as a whole, but especially the inland cities, which were largely abandoned at the time.

Ducetius entered the town nervously.

"Are you all right?" Nathan's mother asked.

"Yes, my lady, but I'm nervous. I don't know what I will find, or who."

Nathan's sister spoke. "It's funny that I am nervous because I've never been here before, and you're nervous because you *have* been here before. That makes us even."

After walking in one direction through the town, and then another, they rounded a bend in the road, with Ducetius in the lead, and came to an unassuming neighborhood where they followed along a wall to an opened gate. Ducetius then stopped. Inside the gate they saw a short, heavy-set woman washing clothes near a well in a courtyard near a sycamore tree. The woman looked up momentarily and saw the strangers standing there. She stared at them intently as though she recognized them. If Nathan could have seen Ducetius's face, he would have noticed the same expression of intensity and recognition staring back.

"Douketios?" the woman suddenly said, squinting her eyes and questioning whether she could possibly be seeing the person she thought she was seeing.

"Auntie Ayathe?" Ducetius asked back.

"Douketios, is that you?" She was speaking Greek. "Oh gods! Oh heavens! Douketios? Douketios! Is that really you??!!" Ducetius entered the gate, and the woman came waddling over to meet him, thrusting him into her bosom.

Ducetius's eyes filled with tears. "Is it really you, Auntie Ayathe?"

"Is it really you, Douketios?!" She hugged him and hugged him as though she would never let go. Then with her eyes closed into slits, out of which poured tear after tear, she said, "I have waited for years, for twenty long years, every day, every single day, to see your face come through that gate again."

She suddenly released him from her bearlike grip and pushed him back saying, "Now let me take a look at you." She wiped her eyes hurriedly as if trying to hide her emotion. "You have grown so much, Douketios. So much! You're a little thin." She sniffed and then wiped another tear that had gotten away. "But you look good. And we can take care of that thinness," she said patting her belly, smiling. "But the face. I would recognize that face after a hundred years." She held his cheeks with both hands in that timeless way of all Mediterranean mothers, as Ducetius withstood the embarrassment of such handling in that timeless manner of all Mediterranean sons.

Her eyes welled up again. "Where have you been all these years?"

She allowed her gaze to loose itself from her darling nephew for a moment, only a moment, just long enough to see that Ducetius was not alone. "But how rude of me!" she exclaimed. "Who are your companions?" She wiped away another rogue tear. "Who are these wonderful people"—she motioned them to come into the courtyard and hugged each one of them—"who have brought you back to us?"

Ducetius answered stiltedly, not knowing what to say. "This is my lord, master … I mean my Patrón … Nathan. And these are his mother and sister." They each introduced themselves.

"Well, come in. Come in! Lord Nathan, and his beautiful mother and lovely sister, you are welcome. Please excuse our humble home, and let me make you all something to eat. You look hungry."

Before they could enter, the neighbors whose apartment abutted Ayathe's courtyard came through the gate to join in her good news. Little was private in the backstreets of Enna, and it took a full half hour before Ayathe could snatch Ducetius into the house.

Nathan had never seen Ducetius in his own world, among people who knew him before he did and who loved him perhaps even more. He watched him vacillate moment to moment between awkwardness and grace, knowing well from years of training how to blend and bend in a crowd but not knowing how to be at the center of attention. Still, he saw him win over all who spoke to him, this sudden stranger from a foreign land whom he thought he knew so well, and he was touched and intrigued by the difference circumstances could make in one's relationship with other people and the world. Here *he* was the ancillary, and Ducetius the beloved son.

News spread quickly that young Ducetius—now thirty—was back. As Ayathe and her daughters prepared food, and as the newly united family ate and drank well past dark, townsfolk continued to poke their heads into the courtyard at regular intervals just to have a peek. "Ayathe, is it true?" and "Little Ducetius is really back?" and "The gods be praised! It's really him!"

And Ayathe would yell back at them all, "Let the boy rest," or "Let him eat," or "You'll have to see him tomorrow," though she appreciated all their good will.

After nightfall, a relative, George, came by and wanted to hear how his young cousin had returned. He had been affected by the taking of Ducetius and his family for twenty years, and according to the townspeople had never been the same since.

"That was a terrible, terrible day," he said, "when we saw you marched out of our city, knowing you would never come back…But you did come back," he added.

Nathan, in his usual way, listened to all that was going on. He too, like Ducetius, knew when to blend into the background after years of conditioning under Amram and then Joseph. But his curiosity was suddenly piqued in a way it never had been before in thinking about Ducetius's enslavement.

After all the guests were gone, Nathan asked, "Ducetius," he hesitated, "what happened to you that day? How did you end up in our home so far away from here all those years ago?" After having grown up and known his faithful servant-pedagogue-friend for so long, Nathan realized there were things about him he did not know at all.

George broke in and answered for Ducetius, not even waiting for him to respond on his own. "The boy can't describe what actually happened to him," he explained. "He was only ten. I will tell you the big picture, then he can fill in the details."

Ayathe then spoke up, but in a lowered voice. "What happened is that one of the latifundium overseers down in the valley, a horrible man name Demaratos, accused Ducetius's father, my brother-in-law, of theft."

George continued explaining. "My cousin was working at the latifundium in the valley at the base of the hill doing repairs on the villa—he was a carpenter and a mason and could do exceptional mosaic work as well—when some valuables went missing. And my cousin was blamed."

"We all know he was innocent," Ayathe added. "My brother-in-law was a good, honest worker, but there was nothing we could do to save him."

"There is no justice in this place," decried George. "If you are new to Sicily, you will soon learn that anything can happen here. We are the closest province to Rome, but Roman justice, if such exists, does not reach us. We are completely ignored. The latifundia owners and managers lord it over this entire island. The peasants and even small-holders like us who have properties around the city have virtually no rights or privileges. We are subject to every whim the local aristocracy can inflict."

"But what happened to Ducetius himself? Can you tell me?"

"The boy can tell you about his personal experience," said George. "But I thought you should know the general background, since I believe that was your real question, and I am not sure Ducetius ever knew."

"No, I did not know," Ducetius said. "I have wondered for twenty years. All I knew was that one night, armed men burst into our home. One group took my mother, another took my father, and another took me. I have tried to put it out of my mind for years. The only person I have ever spoken to about it was Criton. We sometimes compared stories of our capture.

"In any case, I remember my mother screaming and my father pleading for mercy. I was more scared to hear that they were scared than I was of the men themselves. My parents had always been in control of the world, as far as I knew, and suddenly they were not, and it was terrifying. I could not make sense of what was happening. The first time I ever heard of why we were all taken was just now, when Auntie Ayathe explained that my father had been accused of stealing."

Ayathe, with tears in her eyes yet again, asked, "So you really never knew, for all these years, what happened to you that day?"

"No," Ducetius responded. "I did not know; though I figured out from my father's pleading for mercy that someone thought he had done something wrong."

"So does that mean," Nathan asked, "that you never had a chance to talk to either of your parents after you were taken?"

"No," Ducetius answered. "I did not. The men kept us all separate. I never even saw what happened to my parents. I do not know to this day what happened. The last sound I remember from them was my mother screaming and screaming my name, growing fainter and fainter in the distance until I couldn't hear it anymore." He paused with the memory of that silence.

After recomposing himself, he asked, "Have any of you ever heard from either of my parents?"

"No," they each said in their own way. "There has been no inkling or word about either of them. Nothing."

"I have always hoped that they are still alive."

"They may be," comforted Ayathe, "and someday you may see them again. But just like we waited for you all these years, we may have to wait for them a little longer."

As the night went on, Ducetius continued his tale of how he had been marched in chains or transported by various slave traders for miles and days to one of the cities on the coast. From there, he and all his fellow captives were chained in a ship and sailed overseas to Ephesus on the coast of Asia Minor—though Ducetius had no idea that that was the location—and the lot of them were sold to another trader, who sailed them again in chains to Palestine.

The details of the journey—the lacerations of the whip, the rawness of the flesh as chains rubbed ankles bloodier by the day, the harsh words, the lack of sympathy for the fact that he was a child, the manhandling during inspection on every auction block, the coincidental first meeting with Criton, and the final primping and grooming before his own final sale to his ultimate owner, Lord Opal, whose eyes were the only kind ones he had seen in months— all left their mark on Nathan. Nathan wondered why he had never thought to ask Ducetius about how he had become a slave before. But it was simply not a question people asked.

Nathan, like everyone in the Roman world, had grown up with

slavery all around him. It was a fact of life and such an integral part of the fabric of culture and the economy that it was literally unimaginable that civilization could exist without it. A slave-free society was not a thought in the mind of a normal, rational person—even a kindhearted one. It had nothing to do with harshness or compassion. It was a necessity, and one for which no one had offered an alternative. Even slave rebels like Spartacus and Eunus did not fight to overturn slavery. They simply fought to gain their freedom and let others less fortunate serve *them* instead. But Ducetius's explanation of the pain he had undergone during enslavement cast the practice in a whole new light in Nathan's mind. Nathan had never heard a personal account of the process involved; and in Judaea, he had rarely seen the harsher side of it. The Jews had traditional restrictions on the practice in their law, and it was simply not as common in Palestine as it was in the more cosmopolitan regions of the Roman world. Not that despicable Judaean masters didn't exist. But they were not as commonplace as perhaps elsewhere. Nathan's brief exposure to Sicily, however, was slowly revealing the worst of the practice to him: first in the chain gangs he, his family, and Ducetius had witnessed on the numerous latifundia they had passed on their trek to Enna, and now further by hearing Ducetius's story firsthand.

Nowhere in the Roman empire was slavery worse than it was in Sicily, both in kind and in numbers. Droves of captives were brought there from other provinces on a perpetual basis. The island had two attributes which contributed to that state of affairs. One was its central location in the empire. The other was its fertility. Those two elements worked in tandem to fashion Sicily into what amounted to the great breadbasket and granary of the empire, along with Egypt, and made slavery an inescapable component of its agrarian success. Except for the few free peasants and small property holders like Ayathe, George, and their immediate circle, who were slowly increasing in number and in wealth due to changes in the political and economic climate of the Pax Romana in which they unknowingly lived, most Sicilians lived and died in servitude under Rome.

For Nathan, there was no stereotype of what a slave might look like, what ethnicity he might hale from, or what job he might perform. Slaves were shop workers, doctors, hairdressers, teachers, street cleaners, tavern waiters, sailors, cooks, carpenters, masons, teachers, mosaicists—in short, almost anyone who performed a manual task. Sicilian slaves were generally only of two types, house servants and field hands. But throughout the empire the only real, tangible characteristic that distinguished slaves from Romans was their lack of Roman ancestry. A Roman rarely became a slave, but a person from any other ethnicity could become one. Since Criton was a Greek, Ducetius a Sicel, and Eunus a Syrian, each had become a slave at the whim of some Roman citizen who decided to cast them into bondage.

"But," said Ducetius, in finishing his tale late that night, "despite all that happened to my family twenty years ago, I am beginning to understand that bad experiences can sometimes lead to good. I was given a new family who loved me, I was given my freedom, I was able to return home, and I came under the protection of a new god who has been with me wherever I have gone."

Everyone, especially Nathan, looked at Ducetius in admiration as he concluded the evening on that flourish.

III

"There," pointed George. "That is where Hephaestus lives."

George, Ducetius, and Nathan all stood on a precipice along the eastern cusp of Enna overlooking the vast hill country of interior Sicily. In the distance loomed the silhouette of Mount Etna, emitting a continuous column of smoke from its crater. The mountain was not only the home of Hephaestus but the largest active volcano in the Roman empire.

"And here, where we're standing," explained George, "lived Demeter." Scattered about the precipice, named the Rock of Cerere, the three men could see the remains of a temple to Demeter, the chief deity of the entire island. She was both the goddess of fertility and grain as well as the ancient protectress of Enna. Her power was revered among Greeks and Sicels alike.

"After the Romans conquered Sicily," George recounted, "one of the Roman governors stole a great bronze statue of Kore Demeter that stood right here." The governor's name was Verres, and he confiscated half of Sicily's treasures for his villa back in Rome, causing the dearth of artistic culture Nathan and his mother had noticed on the island since their arrival. The Roman lawyer Cicero, after residing in Enna and acting as *quaestor* in Sicily, exposed Verres's corruption in a landmark trial, but to no avail.

"Today," George continued, "the Romans demand that we pray to Demeter for the wheat harvest, but they won't give our statue back. But such is life in Sicily." It wasn't easy for Sicels *or* Jews to live in the empire, Nathan thought.

"And down there," George continued, "in the valley to the right, is Lake Pergusa, where Hades abducted Demeter's daughter Persephone into the underworld."

Hephaestus in the volcano, Demeter on the cliff, Persephone down by the lake, Hades under the ground: Sicily was the isle of the gods to the Sicels and Greeks, thought Nathan, full of wonder and stories—and George seemed to know them all. It was a surprise for Nathan, who had grown up believing the holy land was Jerusalem. And surprisingly, it was Ducetius who gave voice to that very thought as Nathan was thinking it.

"Among the Jews where I lived for all those years," explained Ducetius to his cousin, "their God is very different from the gods here. There is only one of them, and he is not a part of the world, like the volcano or the cliff or the field. They believe their God made the world but is separate from it."

"Separate from the physical world? From all you can see? That makes no sense! How can one know him then?" protested George. "Is it possible to be close to a god if he is not part of the physical world? I have heard that sort of notion from some easterners here, but I have never understood it."

"It is a different view from how you and I were raised," explained Ducetius. "But somehow, after all the years in Judaea, I became used to it. They learn to know God, as they call him—he doesn't actually have a name—by studying their holy writings, which they believe were written by him through various people in history."

"Like the revelations of the oracles or the Sibylline writings, I assume."

"Yes, similar to that. But they are not secret. All the boys among the Jews, and some of the women also, learn them from childhood. They are very important to the Jews."

"But how can one look at all this grandeur and not see the gods or feel their presence in the physical world? Are we not standing on Gaia herself? Do we need a book to teach us that?"

Ducetius responded. "The Jews sense their God when they look at nature, and they feel his presence too, but they say he is greater than anything the human eye can see. As beautiful as all of this is, he is more so."

Nathan was impressed with Ducetius's explanation of his faith. In fact, it was more interesting hearing Ducetius's take on Judaism as an outsider than it was hearing anyone else's. Nathan was coming to realize that there was no one in his entire world quite like Ducetius. Nathan was also impressed with George and the mystical-intellectual approach he had toward the world. He wondered how George had learned all that he had growing up on this island of slaves, latifundia, and peasants. But between the locals' pride in their distant Sicel heritage, the residual Hellenic culture that survived even the Roman conquest, and the use of the Greek language that had been spoken on the island for centuries, there was bound to exist a small Siculo-Grecian intelligentsia—and George and his circle belonged to it.

"Cousin George," asked Nathan, "tell me the story of Hades and Persephone. Ducetius has alluded to it, but I have never heard it myself."

Ducetius seconded the request. He hadn't heard the story for twenty years. And who better to tell it than cousin George? Obliging, George posed on the cliff like a Greek actor while Nathan and Ducetius sat down on the temple ruins to watch.

"Mother Demeter stood perched on her rocky crag," George began, as if he had rehearsed the line before, "with Hephaestus shrouded in the distance and Demeter's lovely daughter Persephone rambling among the flowers near Pergusa." George gesticulated dramatically as he spoke, sweeping the air with his hands in every direction—the volcano, the precipice, the lake—enveloping the world in his story.

"Suddenly the earth was riven. Billows of smoke arose from the flowering field as Hades burst from the underworld in his chariot. 'Come with me, my beauty,' he said to Persephone. 'You are mine!' The girl attempted to fend him off, but her efforts proved futile. Hades lifted her into his chariot and held her tight to his side. The flowers she had collected into her apron fell to the ground, and tears dropped behind her after them. Hades drew his chariot forward and prodded the ground with his staff. A cavern opened below him, and he and Persephone and the chariot all descended back into the earth. When next Demeter looked, Persephone was gone. Where had she disappeared to? Her beloved daughter was gone!"

"Oh my," Nathan emoted.

"From her lofty mount above the valley, Mother Demeter began searching for her daughter among the fields, then throughout the earth. When she could not find her and learned what Hades had done, she raised her arms and let out a cry of such agony that the ground shook. People thought Hephaestus was stirring in Etna's bowels, but it was the anguish of a mother robbed of her child—the greatest pain the world knows.

"Demeter entreated Hades to return what he had stolen. When he would not respond, she cursed the very world. All vegetation began to die, first in the valley, then everywhere on earth. Leaves fell from trees, flowers withered, harvests failed, and the ground became blanketed with frost.

"In the world of men, worship ceased. The gods did not know what to do, so great was the anger of Demeter. Zeus himself came to intervene from Mt.Olympus, coming to Enna and the lake to speak to both parties."

Ducetius looked over at Nathan to see how he was enjoying the story thus far. Nathan sat in rapt attention, anxious to hear the outcome.

"While judging the situation," George continued, "Zeus discovered that Persephone had eaten six pomegranate seeds while residing in the underworld. That meant a part of her was now attached to that world, and even the mighty Zeus could not break her free. Nor did he want to; for Zeus had conspired with Hades to make Persephone Hades' wife. But a compromise had to be made to set the world aright: a compromise between Hades and Demeter.

"Pointing to Hades, Zeus said, 'You may only have Persephone for half the year: one month for each of the seeds she ingested during her stay with you. But while she is with you, all vegetation on earth will die.' He then pointed to Demeter and said, 'And you may only have your daughter back for the other half of the year. And you must swear that all vegetation will live again on earth during that time.'

"The god and goddess agreed. And to this day in fall and winter, while Persephone resides with Hades, vegetation withers. Then in the spring it comes back to life again when Persephone rejoins her mother. Heaven and earth, frost and thaw, death and life: all are in the hands of the gods. For when the gods touch earth, as they have in Sicily, the world is never the same again."

George then stood in silence as the story sank into the hearts of his listeners.

"Opa, cousin George!" exclaimed Ducetius. "Opa!" His face was beaming. Nathan 'opa-ed' in imitation as well.

"So that is how the Greeks believe the four seasons began?" asked Nathan.

"Yes. That is how it happened," answered George. "And it all started right here in Enna, the center of the world."

Nathan and Ducetius cast a knowing glance at each other and smiled.

Afterward, the three men walked the long road to Lake Pergusa, about an hour away. By then it was afternoon, and the hot Sicilian sun beat mercilessly on the trio. Up on the butte of Enna there was a breeze, but down in the valley, closer to the underworld, there was no respite.

The fields around Pergusa were strewn in every direction with wildflowers. Nathan thought to himself that these flowers must be descendants of the very ones Persephone picked in the story.

"So the Gate to the Underworld is somewhere in this field?" Nathan asked. "Does anyone know where it is?"

George answered, "Some say there is a secret grotto or a cleft in the ground kept hidden till Hades decides to reemerge again. Others say it is through underwater caves around the lake's edge, since the lake is fed by submarine springs. I believe, however, that it is the entire field, which acts like a semi-permeable portal between the mortal world and the world of the dead."

"That is an interesting theory, cousin," commented Ducetius. "Do any of the philosophers corroborate it?"

"No," responded George. "Does it need corroboration? It makes sense, doesn't it?"

As they continued to walk, Nathan became desperately sleepy and begged to find a little shade tree where he could lie down for a few minutes.

"Of course, of course," the two others said, agreeing that a nap would do them good.

They found a cluster of small trees, typical of the savanna-like foliage of the island hinterland, and lay down near each other.

As Nathan closed his eyes, they shut tight as if he had no control over them, and one image after another streaked across his inner eyelids in a barrage that would not let up. Then suddenly he felt his entire body begin to vibrate as the ground shook around the base of the tree where he was leaning. He tried to see what was going on but could not move. His body felt like it was being lashed and weighted to the ground. How could that be, he thought. I'm sleeping in a field. He tried to open his eyes but could not.

As the ground continued to shake, the dirt fell away from the roots of the tree near his head, and Nathan could see vapors seeping upward all around him from the base. Was he next to a mini volcano about to erupt? He yelled out for help, forming the names of Amram and Abba on his lips, but no sound emitted from his throat. He knew his companions were still nearby, and he knew those companions were not Amram and Abba. But whoever they were, they were senseless to his predicament, and no one came to his rescue. He was on his own, unable to lift a finger or make a sound. What was happening?

The vapors around him grew thicker and denser and darker with each second. They enveloped him in every direction. From underneath came a rumbling voice so deep it did not sound like a voice at all. He still could not open his eyes, but he could see out of the corner of one of them an unimaginably bottomless bubbling smoking sulfuric pit and something ghastly and ablaze arising from it, reverberating his name in such slow and profound tones that he felt it more than heard it. "NATHAN! NATHAN! YOU ARE MINE! Y O U   A R E   *M I N E* ! ! !

He yelled back, NOOOOO!!!!!!! as loudly as he could, but he still could not utter a peep. He remained voiceless, immobile, weighted and terrified.

He concentrated all his energy toward his fingertips, which weighed a hundred pounds each, and was able to inch them bit by bit closer to the tree. Come on! Grab the tree! Grab it! And finally his fingers wrapped around the trunk, his nails digging into the bark, just as a powerful and irresistible gravity began to pull him downward. The smoke, the blaze, the rumbling, the voice, the weight, the gravity, the struggle: he could not survive. He was disintegrating and being ripped apart, half clinging to the tree, half falling as if tied by his other hand to a millstone into the pit. Neither side would let go. And all the while the reverberation repeated: YOU ARE *MINE*!!!

He was sweating and shaking, trying to re-fuse his two sides together. Couldn't someone save him? Where was everyone?

Then after what seemed forever, someone nudged him and he could hear a voice call him from a distant world, faintly and sweetly and vastly different from the reverberating voice below. "Master Nathan! Patrón! Wake up!" Then he heard the voice say, "The Philistines are upon you."

He opened his eyes, and there was the face of Ducetius welcoming him back to the land of the living.

"What happened, Patrón? Are you all right? You were having a daymare."

Nathan could barely speak. "Yes. I don't know. Am I awake? Are you real?"

"Patrón, I think you were having a terrible dream. But I am here. You are awake. It's all right now."

"Yes. Yes. You are here. Thank you. I was having a terrible dream. But it was so real, Ducetius. It was so …"

"What happened? Were the Philistines really upon you this time?"

"No. No. It was worse."

"How could it be worse? Did Hades try to take you into the netherworld?"

"Yes, Ducetius! That is exactly what happened! How did you know?"

"This is the semi-permeable portal," Ducetius jested. "Anything can happen here." He smiled down at Nathan. "And hell, I think, tugs at us all."

IV

For many months that dream came to encapsulate Nathan's inner life. The Gate to the Underworld loomed in his mind and affected his outlook. In his outer world, life proved simple and predictable enough, and he tried to concentrate on that. He and Ducetius worked with cousin George doing upkeep on the rental properties that George and Ayathe had taken over after the death of her husband and the enslavement of her brother-in-law, so each day took on a basic rhythm of work and family and rest. But Nathan was often subject to melancholy over the losses of the previous few years, and one he could not dispel. Life was a struggle and earth a war zone. The powers of darkness and light, God and sin, justice and servitude, the town and latifundia, Demeter and Hades, freedom and Rome: all swirled in an endless vat, with each element pitted against the others with Nathan attempting buoyancy, while one or the other elements gained ascendency in his life.

And into that vat one day dove Joram.

It had been years since Nathan had seen Joram, his old neighbor-turned-friend. Weeks went by when the thought of him did not even cross Nathan's mind. But when the thought of Joram did enter his brain, he always remembered him saying that one day he would find the land of the Greeks and Sicels. And after so long, he finally did.

Joram's guide to locating Nathan revolved around one simple question: "Where is the Gate to the Underworld where Hades abducted Persephone?" and that question led him to Lake Pergusa and nearby Enna.

When Joram then came ambling into Enna and back into Nathan's life, he caught Nathan hardly by surprise at all. The meeting simply occurred in the market near the city gate.

"Joram! You're here! You finally made it! I always knew you would come," Nathan exclaimed.

The two friends dropped everything and embraced, with smiles as wide as they could stretch. "How does life change so much yet stay so much the same?"

"How true, my friend," Joram responded.

Then Nathan espied over Joram's shoulder the covered figure of a woman in the distance. Thinking nothing of it for one split second, he did a double take when he recognized her outline. He jerked away from Joram, ready to run to who he thought it was. But was it? Could it be? Was it possible? Yes, it was. It had to be. Who else?

"Is that …? Is that …?" he whispered incredulously into Joram's ear.

"Elisheva?" Joram said.

The young woman uncovered her head and lifted her face so Nathan could see her clearly. It was indeed Elisheva.

"Yes, it is," Joram finished replying. But Nathan was already a yard behind him, galloping toward Elisheva like an unleashed colt.

"Elisheva!"

"Nathan!"

"Is it really you?"

"It is."

But as he reached her, something in her manner stopped Nathan cold. He did not know what it was, but it made him unsure of how to proceed: whether to throw his arms around the childhood friend he had missed for so long, kiss the girl he had fallen in love with since adolescence, or stand and gaze at the lovely stranger she had become. He felt at a loss and merely grabbed her hands and smiled with a questioning glance.

The look in Elisheva's eye did nothing to dispel his unsurety. He actually sensed her inch back from him the tiniest bit at his approach, as if the elation he had expressed at seeing her was already socially inappropriate and he dared not show more.

Then rounding the corner just behind Elisheva, Nathan saw a young man walk toward them who both explained the awkwardness and increased it a thousandfold in a moment—a moment that altered Nathan's life forever.

"Hello," the young man said with a happy glint in his eye. "You must be Nathan. I have heard about you from Elisheva and Joram for years. I'm Efstathios."

"This is my husband," Elisheva said, with a hesitant smile on her face.

Your husband? Nathan screamed in his thoughts. How could this fellow be your husband? Maybe I misunderstood.

"A pleasure to meet you, Efstathios," Nathan verbalized.

"And you likewise," returned Efstathios. "But Elisheva," joked the young man to his wife, "I thought you said that Nathan was hideously ugly. He's not half as bad as you led me to believe." And he gave Nathan a once-over with his eyes.

"Oh quiet," laughed Elisheva. "I said no such thing!"

Nathan also found himself laughing, despite himself. He was set on disliking this new stranger who vied for Elisheva's affections. The young man's perusal of his physique also made him wary. But his quip about Nathan's looks intimated that if he was a rival, Nathan was at least a worthy opponent.

Then Joram chimed in. "Nathan, Nathan. Pay no attention to our young jokester here. We have waited for years to see you, wondering whether you were alive or not. You must tell me what has been happening in your life since the last time we spoke. Because if you remember the last time we spoke, back in Jerusalem, it seemed likely there was no way we would ever live to see this day. And if you weren't alive right now, half the purpose of our journey would have been for naught."

"And half the hope in my life," Nathan responded.

"We heard news as we passed through Joppa that there was one last massacre by the Romans back home after the fall of Jerusalem."

"Another massacre?" said Nathan.

"It wasn't in Jerusalem. It was at the desert fortress Masada, where Herod had a palace. It happened several years before we arrived at the port."

"So there were still Jews holding out against Rome even after Jerusalem? Incredible."

"Yes."

"When we left Joppa about three years ago, there was no news about it," said Nathan. "I suppose it had just happened or was happening as we left."

"Some say," Joram added, "that the Romans did not actually kill the defenders, but the defenders killed themselves."

"You mean suicide?"

"Either that, or they killed each other to spare one another the indignity of capture. In either case, they say that when the Romans breached the wall, they were almost all dead."

"Probably better for them, heaven rest their souls."

"But hearing about that event made us all the more desperate to find out whether you had made it out of Judaea alive. So you must tell us, are your mother and sister doing all right? Did your father and Criton and Ducetius make it out of Jerusalem with you? How did you make it out yourself? And how is life on this island? The slave fields we passed mile after mile on the road here do not match how I pictured this place. There is so much I want to ask you and so much that I want to tell you. I know you have questions too. You said before that life changes and remains the same. We have a lot to tell you in that regard and how young Efstathios came to join us. But first you have to tell me how your family is. I must know."

Nathan motioned for them all to follow him back to Auntie Ayathe's house. "We can talk along the way. My mother and sister and Ducetius will be so happy to see you they won't know what to say." He then began telling them about all that had happened since they had seen each other last.

"We waited for days for you to come back, you know," Nathan explained. "You told us not to wait, but there was no way we were not going to wait."

"Yes. I remember telling you not to wait," responded Joram. "I also told you that if I did not return in a few hours, that I would meet you here one day, in the land of the Greeks and Sicels. Do you remember that?

"Do I remember? That is the primary reason I came to this island. My father had told us about Sicily a long time ago, and Ducetius is from here, so it seemed like a logical place to rebuild our lives again; but your promise confirmed the decision for me. If our families ever had a chance to reunite, it would have to be here. And we are all actually here."

"But maybe not all. What about your father?" Joram asked. "Is he here too? You mentioned your mother and sister and Ducetius, but you did not mention him. Is your father all right? Is Criton?

"No," Nathan answered. "My father did not survive Jerusalem. Neither did Criton."

"Your father is gone?" asked Joram, looking earnestly into Nathan's eyes.

Elisheva's eyes reddened with tears. "No, Nathan. Not your father!"

Nathan shook his head.

"I am sorry," quietly added Efstathios. "I have heard about your father."

"He was a wonderful man," said Joram. "I was sure I would see him again. I have seen him many times in my prayers and dreams. I always thought that when that happened, the person was still alive. But I was wrong."

They all stood in mournful silence for a moment.

"And Criton too," Joram added. "He had become like a brother during those days in the tunnel. He didn't speak much, but I admired his silence and strength and listening ears and hard work."

Nathan shook his head again. "It has been difficult reconciling myself to their being gone. It is hard to think about life the same way. But I must say, seeing the two of you brings my father back for a moment, just knowing you knew him and understand how I feel. Thank you for talking about him. People fear speaking of the dead. They think it will make the bereaved uncomfortable. But talking about my father and Criton brings them back to life, and I don't mind at all. So please mention them any time you want. I will always want to hear about them. And what about your family? Are *your* parents all right? Are Rab Simeon and your mother still alive?"

"Yes. They are both alive and well. They are still in Pella. The community of The Way is strong in that city. They have many friends. But after all these years, I tell you, they have never stopped missing you and your parents and wondering how you are doing. When I made it back home from Jerusalem three or four years ago, my parents were more concerned for you and your family than they were about anything else—the war, the empire, Jerusalem, even me. My father will be heartbroken to know that your father is gone, especially since he so much wanted you all to come to Pella—not to mention the kingdom—with us. You really should have come with us. Everyone in our community would have welcomed you. It was not as dangerous as your father thought."

"That was my dream too, Nathan," Elisheva said, "that we would all be together. If your family had come back with us, you would probably all still be alive."

And, Nathan thought, glancing at Efstathios, you would have married me instead of this stranger.

"But Joram," Nathan said, "I must ask: how did you ever manage to get out of the city alive? There were so many soldiers surrounding it at that point, how were you not killed?"

"It was a strange thing," explained Joram. "You will not believe it. I hardly believe it myself. But I almost *was* killed. As I was trying to make my way back to you in the New City, a Roman soldier drew his sword at me to run me through. I shut my eyes and yelled out "Yeshua! I am coming!" and he put his sword back in its sheath. I opened my eyes, and he did something I would never have expected. He drew an arc in the ground right in front of me. I wasn't sure if he meant what I thought he meant, but I took a risk and completed the arc into a fish. He then told me he would escort me out of the city, and he gave me safe passage."

"What are you talking about, that you completed an arc into a fish, and he escorted you out of the city?" asked Nathan.

"Sometimes the people of The Way," Joram explained, "use a fish symbol as a secret sign between them. If I draw an arc in the dirt, and you draw a mirror image of it that dissects it a few inches from one of the ends so that it looks like a fish"—he demonstrated with his sandal—"it means that you are speaking to a fellow secret believer."

"So you are telling me," Nathan laughed, "that you just happen to have run into the only Roman soldier in the entire eastern sector who believed in your messiah, and that is why he let you go?"

"I told you you would not believe me."

"You're right. The chances are highly unlikely."

"But I do not believe it was chance," said Joram smiling.

"No, of course you don't," said Nathan amusedly. "Of course you don't." Joram's obstinacy in his faith could sometimes be annoying, but it could also be entertaining. "But if you came to some understanding with this soldier because of your faith," furthered Nathan, "why did he not let you come back to us in the New City? Why did he escort you out of the city instead?"

"Just as we were speaking, a fellow soldier reminded him to kill me, since the command was to kill every single Jew. But he told his comrade that I was not a Jew, and that he would escort me out of the city immediately. So I had to oblige, if I ever had a chance of seeing you again in this life. And I was hoping that you would remember not to wait for me at the house, and would leave Jerusalem right away through the tunnel." He paused. "But you did not leave Jerusalem right away."

"No, I did not," retorted Nathan. As he spoke, he began to think of all the bad repercussions that that decision and the earlier one not to go to Pella had wrought in his life: his father's death, Criton's death, the years of separation from his mother and sister, and his loss of Elisheva forever. How could one or two wrong decisions, even though decided for the noblest of reasons, have led to so much tragedy? The longer Nathan lived, the more he realized how consequential every decision in life could be. "There are many things I would have done differently," he said, "if I had the chance to do them over again."

With that, he looked directly at Elisheva and she at him.

Efstathios saw their glance, and Nathan saw him see it.

"And what about this young fellow?" asked Nathan, seeming to change the subject, and pointing to Efstathios. "What is his story?"

"Efstathios?" answered Joram. "It's a little complicated, but we will talk about it later, maybe tonight, if we have a chance."

Nathan half expected Elisheva to speak up at this point. She had hardly said a word since they arrived. But it seemed that she and Efstathios must have arranged with Joram to explain their situation since they were not going to explain it themselves. Given the likelihood that Nathan would be surprised at the unexpected turn of events, he could see the logic behind such an arrangement. But it was so unlike Elisheva to shrink back from speaking, he could only conclude that life and her own circumstances had changed Elisheva like it had everyone else in his world.

"For now," Joram said, "all I'm thinking about is seeing your family, and maybe some food. Are we almost at the house?"

"We are. Just a few more turns."

When the two families finally met, it was one of the happiest and most uncomfortable occasions Nathan could remember. The banter continued well after nightfall. Efstathios and Ducetius instantly made friends, Ayathe and her daughters wanted to know everything about the lovely Elisheva, of whom they had heard for so long, and Adah flirted endlessly with Joram, to whom she suddenly took a great liking. She made every opportunity to interrupt his discussion with George as they tried to converse about the gods, culture, and Joram working for him on his rental properties.

As for Nathan, he grabbed a quiet seat in the corner of the room, watching all that was going on, feeling sorry for himself, and having an inaudible conversation with Elisheva in his head.

Is he really your husband? Nathan asked Elisheva to himself. Do you even know him? He is a complete stranger to me. Did you meet in Pella? He's not even Jewish! He looks Greek. You married a Greek? No wonder he eyed me the way he did—those Greeks with their man love. Weren't you going to marry me? That's what our fathers had always planned on. Didn't you once tell me you couldn't live without me? Apparently you could. I, on the other hand, have continued to wait for you. I've waited all these years. I'm still unmarried in the hope that one day we would reunite. But now here you are, and you're married to *him*? He's a pretty boy, he's not even a man. But I am a man and a scholar and a soldier and a fellow Jew. Don't I have what it takes to make you happy? We share a past and hopes for a future that you and this Greek could never share. You and him are like the mixed fabric forbidden in the Law. How could you, Elisheva? How did Joram allow it? You found me all the way in this far-flung corner of the universe just to taunt me. It isn't right.

///////

Later that evening, after the festivities died down and everyone readied for sleep, Joram and Nathan went for a walk, and Joram told Nathan everything he wanted to know.

"How could Elisheva be married to him?" Nathan asked. "Please tell me how that happened."

"I will tell you, my friend. I know it is hard seeing my sister with someone else. But things just happen in life. Somehow between leaving Pella and finding Enna, I convinced myself that you would understand. But that is because I saw the relationship between them develop step by step, and you did not. So when I saw you standing confused in the marketplace this afternoon not knowing what to say to the man or to the woman who had just trampled your dreams, I realized that there was no way you could understand. I felt devastated myself and could not wait to talk to you tonight."

"Thank you, Joram. I appreciate that. Then tell me what happened. I want to know."

"When my family originally moved to Pella," Joram explained, "we rented rooms in the house of Efstathios's family."

"So that's how it started."

"Yes," responded Joram. "But not so simply as that. There was nothing at first. Efstathios's family were merchants who had arrived from Corinth in Greece only a few years before, and they were believers in The Way, just like us. They were very kind to us, but Efstathios and his father were busy men with their business."

So Efstathios *was* a Greek, thought Nathan. I *knew* it. And he was a crazy Christian too.

"But as the months went by, I spent more time with Efstathios and became increasingly impressed by him," Joram continued. "His knowledge of the scriptures, as well as Homer, Plato, Sophocles, etc., led to many conversations. I became fascinated with his Greek perspective on the world, which is very different from ours. Our conversations were wonderful, and Elisheva started joining us when we talked.

"Anyway, when I left my family to return to Jerusalem two years later, I wondered if some attachment might form between my sister and Efstathios while I was gone. But it did not. And after I started living with you and your family and we began digging that tunnel, I began to understand why my sister loved you more than anyone in the world. You are like no one else, especially for my sister. My conversations with you about the scriptures reminded me of the conversations I had back in Pella with Efstathios. But in addition to you sharing a similar intellect, you share a long history with Elisheva, and that always meant a great deal to her. You two have known each other since you were babies. So I was not surprised when I came home from Jerusalem after spending that year with you that my sister had still not gotten married—not to Efstathios, not to another fellow in our community, not to anyone. If she could ever be permitted to marry for love—and my parents were not averse to that idea—you would be her choice."

"So what changed that?" asked Nathan.

"Efstathios became ill, and it seemed like he was going to die."

"That's what happened?"

"In part."

"What was wrong with him?" Nathan asked, half wishing it had finished the job.

"No one knew. Not even the Greek doctors. He had a fever, he couldn't eat, he couldn't keep food down. It seemed like some type of dysentery or food poisoning. But not quite. Some days he would perk up and speak. Other days it seemed like it would be his last.

"In any case, I made plans to go abroad on another mission. I wanted to try to find you and to reach the so-called Gate of the Underworld, and I wanted to meet people and tell them that the savior had been in the world. Our world is corrupt and dying, and everyone needs to hear that there is more to life than Greece and Rome and Jerusalem and whatever personal troubles they may face. I also wanted to see if I could make copies of some of the letters that earlier leaders of The Way had left behind in places like Ephesus, Crete, Thessalonica, and even Rome—letters that explain our faith and demonstrate how it fulfills the Law, the prophets, and the writings. I had heard one or two of those letters read aloud on occasion, and Efstathios had one from Corinth, and I wanted to read more of them for myself and distribute copies to the places I went, even here in Sicily. I know this is another topic, but those letters are seen by many as scriptures themselves—at least the ones written by the leaders who knew the messiah face to face like Paulos and Petros. But if I was going to travel the empire and find you and make those copies and confront the Gate to the Underworld, I wanted to have a partner with me. I hoped it would be Efstathios or Elisheva, or both, but it seemed like Efstathios was not going to live much longer, and Elisheva was too busy nursing him as his illness continued."

Joram took a break from speaking for a few minutes. Nathan had a great deal to think about, yet he still could not fully follow where the story was leading.

"A few months before I decided to leave," Joram continued, "I asked Elisheva if she would join me on my journey. She said she could not go. Although she was quite concerned over whether you were alive or dead and wanted to see you more than anything in the world, she said she had to make sure Efstathios was all right before she made any move.

"So I asked her, 'Why? Are you falling in love with Efstathios?'

"She hesitated and said, 'I think I might be.'

"'Really?' I asked.

"She answered, 'It is difficult to care for someone like him, who is lovable already, and see him in such a vulnerable state and not have my heart moved by him.'

"'Do you love him more than Nathan?' I asked.

"'I don't think I could love anyone as much as I love Nathan,' she said. 'But I do not know what to do about Nathan. My heart tells me to continue to save myself for him, despite the fact that I am growing older, and abba wants me married. But logic and my prayers tell me otherwise. The fact is, I don't even know if Nathan is still alive. I may be saving myself for a man who no longer is.' She became weepy when she said this. 'What a fool I would be,' she said, 'if I continued to hold out for someone beyond this world.'

"'But he may also be beyond me if he decided to marry someone else; and I do not know that either. I have assumed for years that if Nathan were still alive and unmarried, he would send word to me, but he has not.'"

Nathan cried out, "I tried to! I tried to send word every day, Joram! But it was impossible between the war, getting out of Jerusalem alive, coping with my father's death, finding my way to Joppa for my mother and sister, and sailing us in the very opposite direction from Pella. I found a merchant in Joppa who said he would be going to Pella after a stay in Egypt. He promised to deliver a letter from me to you. But now I see he never did."

"We never heard from him," Joram replied. "Perhaps he arrived after the three of us left. It's possible. But to tell you the truth, Nathan, as difficult as it is to say it, it would not have made any difference."

"What do you mean?" asked Nathan, readying himself for what was most likely the core and worst part of the conversation.

"The greatest obstacle for my sister in marrying you, she said, was the faith that you two still do not share. If my sister became weepy with the thought that you were gone, she became equally weepy with the idea that you were still alive in the world but beyond her reach because of the spiritual chasm between you. She told me that if I had heard the tone in your voice and seen the expression on your face when the two of you first discussed Yeshua years ago, I would understand how great the divide was between you.

"I explained to her that you and I spoke many times about spiritual matters while I was living with you in Jerusalem…"

"But she knows me," interrupted Nathan, "and she knows I do not believe as she does."

"Yes. She knows you," Joram repeated, "and she assumed you still did not believe as she does. Her greatest fear apart from you being dead was marrying you and watching the differences between you rend you apart. She said to me, 'how could we ever build a life together, even if he loved me? I know we would try, but eventually we would become strangers. And how could I let that happen? I would have lost the greatest treasure I have in this world, and that would be too much loss for me to bear. I would see my life as a defeat.'

"I tell you, Nathan," said Joram frankly, "I had never seen my sister in such turmoil. She had always known exactly what she was about, up to that moment."

"No," disagreed Nathan. "She still knew exactly what she was about, even in that moment. She was up against her love for God—as she sees him, crazy as that belief is—and her love for me. Most women—most people, I think—would have crumbled under a decision like that and given in to the weakness of their emotions. But not your sister. I would have chosen the lesser path myself. But not your sister. That's why I need Elisheva so much. How could I not love her? I could never have the clarity of thought she has."

"I disagree," said Joram. "But I think you understand the situation. She could either marry you, in which case she might lose everything that was dearest to her in all the world, or she could marry Efstathios, whom she could love with no conflict to her soul."

"So you think," Nathan summarized, "that if I had believed like you do, and if I had gone to Pella when you did, that Elisheva and I would probably be married by now, instead of her and the pretty boy?"

"Yes. I think that likely," answered Joram, chuckling at Nathan's sarcasm.

"But that is not what happened," he said introspectively, though aloud.

"No, it is not."

"Instead, I did not believe, I did not go to Pella, I stayed in

Jerusalem to fight beside my brother, I stayed longer than I should have so that my father and Criton lost their lives, and I ended up on the opposite end of the world, not really knowing where my life is heading anymore. I have no wife, no prospect of one, and no known future."

"I suppose so." Joram paused. "But as to whether your circumstances are 'unfortunate' as you said, or not, that remains to be seen. Do not throw the idea of marriage in with the idea of not knowing where your life is heading. Apart from God, none of our lives are heading anywhere. Do not think that you are a lost soul merely because you are not married to Elisheva. Marriage is not the goal of life. It is a mere detail that happens to some and not to others. You still have a lot to live for. I am not married, and my life has a great deal of purpose."

"I feel like my life has very little purpose. Right now I feel like I am in a holding period, merely keeping life together for my mother and sister and Ducetius," said Nathan. "But nothing really for me."

"To me," responded Joram, "life this side of eternity is always a holding period."

"The one major hope I always had," continued Nathan, "was marrying your sister. But according to you, that one hope would have ended in disaster. But would it have really, Joram?" He questioned the idea in his mind. Was faith really greater than human love, and did it play a more pivotal role in one's life? Was faith surer than the pulse of the human heart? As he pondered that question, the more he had to begrudgingly accede that it might be. He knew that history did not turn on romantic love, that nations were not built on it, and that the war against Rome was not either.

When confronted in that moment with the complexity of human motivations that caused people to act or not act, he concluded that romantic love was merely one cause among many and not the sublime and primary mover troubadours and poets might make it out to be. He knew it had its moment under the sun. Even Qohelet wrote his song to the Rose of Sharon. But he fooled himself, as did most people, that his feelings of romantic love, as his for Elisheva, moved beyond the terrestrial and into the eternal. It wasn't true.

"Romantic love is not eternal, Nathan," answered Joram, seeming to know, as he so often did, where Nathan's thoughts had taken him. "One time when asked about marriage in the kingdom of God, Yeshua stated that in eternity we will be like the angels, neither marrying nor being given in marriage. So all of this trouble you feel over my sister is temporary in the light of eternity."

"You believe that there is no marriage in eternity? How very sad that is to me."

"Is it? It is not sad for all those people whose marriages ended up as empty as they were hopeful in the beginning. And it is not sad for you. Is it not good to know that Elisheva will not be married to Efstathios forever?"

Nathan did not like that question, but he was right.

"There is something hopeful about marriage not being eternal," Joram continued. "There will be something greater than that in the end."

Nathan doubted the veracity of that. Something greater than the feel of a woman's soft body against his own, lost in his largeness, and throwing her lot in with his because she knows he can envelop and protect her? Greater than the power of the push and pulse and rush of his body coursing into hers? Nathan did not think so—even though he knew that perhaps theoretically there might be something in eternity greater than that.

"I don't know," responded Nathan. "It's hard to imagine, even though that may well be the case. As a single man whose hope has been pinned on the joys of a woman's affection and effect on my life, I am too tied here to the earthly in this conversation to be thinking that ethereally. And besides, even though you say human love is temporary, it is a very long temporary. Forty or fifty years seems like an eternity to hold an unrequited affection."

With that, the enormity and weight of all they were discussing reached a point where Nathan could not say another word.

Joram then reached out to Nathan and wrapped his arm around his shoulder in consolation. "Oh, my friend. Do not take it too hard. You are loved by many. As strange as it seems, you will have Elisheva's love your whole life. And you know you have mine. Life is difficult. We can never control who we love, and we cannot even control what we believe. People think we can control those things, but we cannot. Sometimes the person we love and the truth we believe blend together so we can live life without a thought in that regard. But we live in a fallen world, and love is much more likely not to go so easily. Adam and Eve had nine hundred years to argue and bemoan what they had lost in the garden. We'll only have forty, but the trouble is just as great, and maybe even greater with the compounding of the centuries.

"There are many things I wish were different, and this is one of them."

When Nathan lay on his bed that night, a tear streamed down his temple onto the matting below.

V

"I may have found work for the lot of us."

"The lot of us?"

"Yes."

"What is it?"

"A renovation."

Joram, Nathan, Ducetius, and Efstathios all sat in the *andron*, or men's quarters, at Ayathe's house, where they convened every morning and evening, as Joram told them the news. George walked in as the conversation began.

"Cousin George!" greeted Joram. "I'm just telling everyone that I may have found some lucrative work for all of us, including you."

"Me?" grunted George. "My work is already lucrative, and I have plenty of it. In fact, I came by to ask all of you to help me repair a wall at one of the properties."

"We can do that. But this work I found is with the latifundium. It could be important for all of us."

"The latifundium is no friend of ours," retorted George. "I wish you had consulted me first before you decided to talk to anyone from there."

"Why? What's wrong with the latifundium?" Joram asked.

"The head manager, Demaratos, is the man who sold Ducetius and his parents into slavery twenty years ago. We have no dealings with him. He is a dangerous man. I cannot allow my young cousin to go anywhere near that place, so I would suggest having nothing to do with it."

Ayathe, who was listening from another room, interrupted the discussion, startled by what she thought she had overheard. "You found work with Demaratos?" she asked in a worried tone.

"No, no, please everyone," Joram began to explain. "The man I spoke to was not named Demaratos. His name was Vitus, and he told me that *he* is the head property manager at the latifundium. No one named Demaratos ever came up in our conversation."

"Well, no doubt Vitus and Demaratos are connected in some way. I have not heard of any changeover at the latifundium as of late."

"According to Vitus," explained Joram, "there *has* been a changeover. He told me that months ago the latifundium was bought by a new owner and that he came to Sicily with him."

"A new owner?" George started incredulously. "Who?"

"He is the son of a senator named Funisulanus, who acted as quaestor here in Sicily some years ago."

"Funisulanus?" George asked. "I've never heard of him. And you say his father was stationed on the island?"

"Yes."

"What happened to the old owner who has been in the valley my entire life?"

"I don't know," Joram answered. "Maybe he died or needed money from the sale or wanted a change of scenery. Maybe I can ask sometime. But the old owner, and probably the old manager Demaratos, are apparently gone. Perhaps not, but that was the implication."

Ayathe chimed in again, entering the room this time, despite her gender. It was her house, after all. "Well if that is the case," she said, "it makes me feel a little better about the whole situation. But I am not convinced. We need to make inquiries around town. What kind of work does this Vitus want you to do? I do not want Ducetius to go anywhere near the latifundium."

"The work is not at the latifundium. It is a renovation job at the amphitheatre up here in town. He needs contractors, managers, overseers, negotiators for materials, designers, sculptors, grunt workers. He also may be interested in building a villa nearby. The senator's son wants to enjoy a little culture while he is living here."

"There's an amphitheatre in Enna?" asked Nathan. "I've been here for over three years, and I've never seen one."

"It's been in ruins since I was little," said Ducetius. "You have to look for it to find it. I barely remember it myself."

"And this manager Vitus is willing to hire you to help oversee this project even though you have almost no experience with construction?" asked George.

"Yes, because of our connection with *you*. I mentioned that you manage several properties in town and that we work for you. We walked past two of the properties, and he was impressed by the level of upkeep he saw."

"I wish you hadn't mentioned me. I want nothing to do with those people."

"It was the only way I could sell us as an experienced outfit."

"I understand that you may have had good intentions, and you had no idea about the difficulties we had with Demaratos in the past. But you have to remember that you are a newcomer here," George reproved. "You have been a good helper, and I like your spirit of initiative. But you must watch your step and consult me first before you make any moves that involve us all."

Nathan had rarely seen Joram reprimanded by anyone, not even his own father. He was usually in command of every situation he was in—similar to Joseph, Amram, and even Elisheva.

"Cousin George," apologized Joram, "Forgive me if I have overstepped myself. But we are not committed to the work. I have signed no contract. If it turns out that we cannot accept Vitus's offer, so be it. But if you could at least talk to him yourself, you might find the offer a good one and see that he is a reasonable man."

"What seems reasonable about him?" asked George, curious.

"His wage was fair, he spoke respectfully to me, and not in the lordly way I had anticipated, and he was amenable to hiring us no matter what our background was: Jew, Corinthian, Sicel, or member of the Way."

"He asked about your backgrounds?"

"He could tell from my accent that I am not from around here."

"Did he even know what the Way was?" asked Ducetius.

"Yes, he did," answered Joram. "He actually said that he knew members of the Way, and that they were particularly hard workers."

"What a strange thing to say," commented Ayathe. "What does that even mean? Why would a member of the Way work particularly hard?"

"Because work among Jews and Christians—and Greeks, of course—is seen as a virtue, but for Romans it is a sign of servitude."

"How true!" complained Ayathe. "The Romans think that everyone around them should work but that they are above that sort of thing." Neither Ayathe nor George had ever bought a slave. They did their own work. But it was not because they had a moral compunction against the institution. It was really because of what had happened to Ducetius and his family. Still, however, they viewed work in a positive light. "And as if their attitude doesn't make me angry enough," Ayathe continued about the Romans, "the idea of Ducetius working for someone who might possibly be connected to Demaratos makes me even more uncomfortable."

"Auntie," Joram assured her, "We will not embark on this venture if it brings danger to Ducetius or any of us. We will be working up here in the town, not at the latifundium. And I know of no connection between Vitus and Demaratos, at least not as of yet. I thought taking this job might be important for all of us because it would give us steady employ for a while, we could return a portion of all the hospitality you have shown us since we've been here, and it would increase cousin George's notoriety in town as a builder."

"You boys have been helping me and cousin George with the rental properties since the day you arrived," Ayathe said. "It has been a great relief to me, and especially to George, who did most of the work alone for years. So do not feel like you have to look for employment elsewhere. George can keep you busy several days a week, and I am content financially. But if you promise to watch over Ducetius to make sure no harm comes to him, maybe this job could open up other opportunities and be good for us all."

"Or maybe not," muttered George. "Since when does the latifundium hire workers from the city? I don't trust it. They usually run a self-sufficient shop."

"But you told me that your cousin did mosaic work and carpentry at the latifundium," said Nathan. "Didn't *he* live in town?"

"That was different. Ducetius's father was known for his artistry. He was sent there. He wasn't hired. And in any case, I can't think of another worker before or since who comes from the town and has had any connection with the latifundium below. It just doesn't happen."

"Well," said Joram, "it is happening now. If we decide to work for Vitus, he wants us to start next week. Maybe since he is new to the area, he doesn't know the local protocol."

"He must not," said George, "because if he understood anything about this town, he would know that the locals won't step foot into that amphitheatre."

"What do you mean? Why not?" asked Nathan.

"They believe it's haunted," George said.

"Haunted?" they all asked.

"Yes," replied George, telling them the story. "Back during the war with Carthage over Sicily a few hundred years ago," George said, "the Roman prefect here massacred the people of Enna in that very theatre."

"How horrible!" everyone responded.

"It's true," confirmed Ayathe, though she could not have conjured a single detail about it.

"And people still remember that from hundreds of years ago?" asked Joram.

"We Jews remember events from thousands of years ago," Nathan said.

"That's because they're written in the holy books," said Joram.

"The people of Sicily," explained George, "have long memories; but nobody actually remembers the massacre per se. They only know it's haunted.

"As the story goes, the war in Sicily raged a long time, and no one knew if the Romans or Carthaginians would win. But just to be sure, the Romans, who had already taken our city, butchered the people in that theatre. They lured them there to hear an announcement from the prefect. Then he unleashed his henchmen, and they all perished. If any tried to escape, they were hunted and annihilated."

The group of them sat quietly, as if in mourning for a moment.

"That's why from that time to this," George continued, "that theatre has lain fallow. Most people don't even know why the place is taboo anymore. They simply know that it is. The only person I know who went there sometimes was my cousin, Ducetius's father. We read about the massacre together as kids from a Livius scroll—who knows where we got it or where it is now—and it troubled him ever since. I visited the place with him once, but he went numerous other times, especially toward the end, just before he was taken. I say the place is haunted, but it really seemed like it was my cousin who was haunted by that place."

"I didn't know that about my father," said Ducetius.

"He was a talented and often troubled man," responded George. "He let life affect him too much. I miss him."

"I just happened to see the theatre the other day when I tried to find the *palaestra*," said Efstathios. "The ruins run all along the cliffs on the western side of town facing the mountain range. It looked beautiful, but I wondered when I saw it why it was not used anymore."

"It is sad," concurred George. "I myself have always wished

we had a working theatre in town to see Sophocles or Aeschylus or Euripides or even some of the inane phylax plays that are so popular these days. But it has never happened. So maybe it's fate that you have come here to work on resurrecting it. Why should Syracuse and Taormina and Catania all have beautiful theatres and not Enna? This is the most important city in the entire center of the island."

"So does that mean you might work with us on this job?" asked Joram.

"I will think about it. But I really do not have time to take on more work. And as for you, Ducetius, I simply will not allow you to take the job at all until I am convinced you will be safe. I don't care how old you are. I'll have to ask around town if anyone knows anything about this fellow Vitus. And maybe I'll go speak to him myself." He paused. "I just don't understand, though, why the latifundium owner would want to bother renovating anything in this city. The previous owner never stepped foot in Enna proper."

"Maybe he thought there was nothing worthwhile to come here for," said Nathan.

"But now," said Efstathios, "there'll be a beautiful theatre, maybe a villa, and just for good measure, we can even put up a statue of Nathan in all his glory at the theatre entrance."

"Oh yes," groused George. "That would no doubt draw the senator."

VI

One day Nathan asked Elisheva, "Want to see the theatre we're working on?"

"It depends."

"On what?"

"On whether you'll talk to me along the way."

"I might," said Nathan.

"Then that would be lovely," responded Elisheva.

It was the first time they had been alone together since her arrival.

They walked along the north wall of town toward the west. Looking down and to their right, they could see the latifundium sprawling across the valley floor around a promontory that later became the hilltop hamlet of Calascibetta. Although the promontory was inhabited in ancient times, and people dug out tombs in the nearby cliffs, no one lived there at present, and the tombs served as hideouts for escaped slaves.

Despite Nathan's willingness to talk, he only spoke of mundanities. It took Elisheva to broach the real topic at hand.

"Nathan," she said, almost sternly.

"Yes?" he said, happy to end the small talk.

"I know you and Joram have already discussed this, but do you want to know why I came to this island?"

"Please tell me."

"Because when Joram asked me to join him to try to find you," she explained, "I could not think of a single reason to say no. Don't misunderstand me," she paused. "I had plenty of reasons not to leave Pella. There were my parents, I dislike traveling, I get ill on ships, and I didn't want to live like a stranger in a foreign country. But when I thought that you might still be alive and had survived the destruction of Jerusalem, I had to let you know that that mattered to me, to us. Jerusalem mattered to me, and your fight for it mattered to me.

"And for the sake of that place and the childhood we shared and the hope of a new world that we separated over, and even for the sake of my faith, which I will pray till the day I die becomes your faith too, I was willing to risk self and comfort and the simplicity of the life Efstathios and I were building in order to find you, despite my parents' objections, and my new friends, and the distance, and the unknown ahead, and the so-called Gate to the Underworld. That gate is not anymore here than it is everywhere, just like Jerusalem as a particular location is not our hope in the world. The gate follows us like a shadow and is next to us all the time and can be fallen into, tripped into, and dove into by will at any point. I would travel with my brother and my husband and our faith to keep as many people from it as we can. But how could I not be there, not even try to be there, to keep you safe from it? So yes, I had to come here. I had to see you whatever my singlehood or marital status or age was. I had to know that you were safe. Can you accept that?"

"Yes. I can accept that."

"Really? Because I don't want you to be angry that I'm here anymore."

"My acceptance and my being angry are two different issues. I am not angry that you came here. I've wanted to see you for ten years. It was longer than Jacob waited for Rachel. I am not angry that you're here. What makes me angry and what I cannot accept is that after all these years of waiting, the door is closed on our future. We can never be, because you are married to someone else, and even more than that—since marriage can be undone—because you have *chosen* to close the door that way."

"What else could I have done?" responded Elisheva. "Joram explained to you the circumstances that brought Efstathios and I together. You know that if the world were different and everything went as I had hoped, you and I would be together. But you closed the door on us as much as I did. We are partners in that crime. You chose your lot and so did I. But between the two of us, I would say you are more content in the disbelief in my faith that formed a wedge between us than I am content in the choice I made that added to it. Not that I do not love Efstathios. I do, and I chose him. But you made your choice also. So do not lay all the blame on me for keeping us apart. That would not be proper. I came here. You did not come to Pella. I believed. You did not. I made it possible for us to be impossible. You made it impossible for us to be possible. Again we met half-way. If only our meeting could have been on different ground, we would be together.

"Is the door really closed, though?" she continued. "Am I not here? Do we not speak? Do I love you any less than I always did? Yes, the door is closed on us in one way; but doors close, door after door, with each passing year we live. Jerusalem is gone. That door is closed. Your beloved father is gone. That door is closed. I am separated by a thousand stadia from my parents, whom I miss terribly. That door may close by the time I return to Pella—if I ever return. I have been unable to bear a child. I have lost three pregnancies and became dreadfully ill while expecting. That door may also be closed. I do not know. But we learn to compensate for the closures and rework our lives and relationships and ourselves. I am not the same woman I was when last we spoke. I have had to redefine myself: my mind, my behavior, my goals, my dreams. You are not alone in having to do that. And you and I will learn to relate, and perhaps even do it well, under our new circumstances. What do you think? Can we do that?"

Five minutes slipped by unnoticed while they continued their conversation not taking a single step closer to the amphitheatre.

"I don't know," responded Nathan. "I don't know if *I* can. To me, I am living two lives every day: the life I have with you in my mind and heart, and the life of my daily actions, which must at least appear to have nothing to do with you. I travel, but always in the hopes that our paths will cross. I work, but only in the thought of securing some monetary future for us. I dream, but my dreams are all of you. I speak of God, but always in the expectation that he will grant me you to share my earthly life with till I meet him in eternity."

Elisheva began to weep. She was not usually prone to emotion, and Nathan was taken aback by it. His eyes turned red as well. The two of them stood there in place gazing at the ground, then looking straight ahead to the vast barrenness and beauty of the hinterland that surrounded them now—alternating fittingly between barrenness and beauty all at once, like life. They remained there a long time in silence—long enough for their tears to dry and their hearts to calm, for their spirits to come back to physical earth, and for the reality of their situations and the limitations of their minds and conditions to change what they knew they could not.

Elisheva was first to resume speaking.

"Oh, my dear Nathan. My dear Nathan. What are we to do?"

"I do not know."

"Should we continue on to the theatre?"

"Yes," Nathan answered. "We should continue to the theatre."

They walked on.

"We can speak about this again," Elisheva said. "And I think we will have to. I will need help to keep redefining my life regarding you, and you will need help to do the same. But it will happen. And we will learn to find contentment in what is, instead of regretting the things that are not. Yes? That is the only sensible, workable thing to do. Right?"

"Yes. As always, you are right."

As they approached the amphitheatre, they could see Efstathios and Vitus heatedly discussing blueprints at a table. George was teaching Ducetius something about construction. Joram was arranging landscaping and carving tools with another fellow near the theatre entrance (maybe a statue of me *would* look good there, thought Nathan). Dozens of laborers attended to their tasks—some slaves, some hired hands; it was hard to tell except for their chains. There were also a few latifundium bodyguards standing watch over the slaves in ominous silence.

Nathan and Elisheva decided not to disturb anyone with a visit just then. Efstathios was clearly not free to talk. The others waved hello as they passed. She had seen what he wanted her to see. And they had spoken about what he had hoped they would speak about. So they continued inside the theatre entrance and stood on the top row of weed-and-moss-covered stone seats.

"It is beautiful here," said Elisheva.

"Look at these seats," Nathan pointed. "They're carved right out of the mountainside."

"How impressive. I think this whole town must have been magnificent once."

"George told us it once was, but it has gone through many bad times."

Nathan told her about the massacre.

"So this place," she said, "fought the Romans too, just like home."

"Yes. Ducetius told me he's named after a king who fought for freedom against the Greeks too."

"They had a hero named Ducetius?"

"Yes. But you know that on the job we do not call him Ducetius anymore."

"You call him Baropalus, correct?"

"Yes."

"After your father, because you are his Patrón," said Elisheva.

"Yes. But also because cousin George does not want anyone from the latifundium hearing his real name, in case someone recognizes it."

As they continued looking at the view, Nathan thought about the Sicels and Ennans and Romans and this unknown city that had become his home the previous few years. It was so different from where he grew up. Yet so much was still the same for him. The faith he grew up with was not entirely unknown on the island. Rome was still an ever-present reality. And the woman he had loved since he was two years old was there, despite the unlikelihood of them ever meeting again. God, Rome, and Elisheva: that was the world into which he, Nathan bar Opal, had been born. Would it be the same world from which he would eventually depart?

"Let's go back," said Nathan. "I told the fellows I would start working by late morning, and it's almost that time."

"Yes. Let's go back," said Elisheva. "Though, really, you know we can't."

VII

The problem with renovating the amphitheatre was that there was a problem with every aspect of renovating the amphitheatre.

The clay quarry for making bricks was down at the latifundium, and the theatre was up in the city. That meant every brick formed and kilned in the valley had to be transported up the mountain via the one lone serpentine road, then half-way across town to the building site.

How the bricks would be transported was another issue. They could be saddled onto mules or pushed uphill in slave-drawn carts. But the latifundium lacked mules and carts, so they needed to be purchased at a reasonable price. But none of the band of four—Joram, Nathan, Efstathios, and Ducetius—knew where to buy mules or carts or what a good price for them was. They would have to investigate.

Then one of the two kilns at the latifundium was malfunctioning. The one that actually functioned was too small to efficiently fire the quantity of bricks needed. But whether it was wiser to fix the broken kiln or rebuild a new one was a question no one could answer. The band of four needed to find a kilner.

There was also the question of manpower. Did the latifundium have enough slaves to work the wheat fields as well as the brick transport and the renovation itself? If more slaves were needed, it was unclear where to get them, or if they could be borrowed from another estate—in which case, arrangements would have to be made. The project would also require stonecutters, sawyers, sculptors, and engravers, and they would not be easy to find.

Whichever manpower option was chosen, the question arose as to whether or not sleeping quarters for workers or slaves should be erected on the site. It might be wiser to house slaves up on the hill, but it would be cheaper to keep them in the *ergastula* down in the latifundium.

If workers' quarters were needed, wood would need to be purchased, and wood was scarce in central Sicily. The Romans had been depleting the island's forests for centuries to build ships. Even if quarters were not needed, wood was necessary for scaffolding, carts, and rollers. It was a mystery where to obtain it and how much it would cost.

Then there was the question of food. The entire workforce needed to be fed daily. The latifundium could supply the food, but it would have to be transported up the mountain. And if a vendor in town could supply it, it might be easier but it would be costlier.

And lastly, there was the question regarding what play to perform on the opening day, and who should perform it. No troupe had worked in Enna for centuries, and there were no play manuscripts anywhere in the town or latifundium. If the senator's son wished to celebrate a grand opening with a performance, there had to be a performance to perform. Efstathios inquired about manuscripts in Syracuse, Catania, and Taormina, which all boasted fine, recently renovated Greco-Roman theatres, but they would have to be purchased or copied if available at all. And since there was nowhere to house manuscripts if they *could* be found, Efstathios asked Vitus for a small library in town as part of his pay. But the details of that had to be negotiated, and it would take time, money, and more materials.

In the end, it became obvious why, as George had said, there was rarely interaction between the latifundium and the city. But the band of four had to make it work. It was too important to them and to Enna not to.

With Vitus in charge of the project, strict protocols had to be followed. Slaves were to be chained at all times, and females—even believing ones—had to provide relief for the workers. Joram and Vitus often quibbled over the details, but Vitus would not bend. "Be content that I allow you to share your Christian writings with the slaves." And there the debate ended.

As Joram soon discovered, the man responsible for Vitus's positive outlook on his faith was a slave named Sos, a powerful individual captured during Rome's recent conquest of Pontus and who acted as a leader among the growing number of latifundium believers. Sos had been born in the region near where the apostle Paulos had traveled, and he became a convert of a convert of the apostle. After becoming a slave, Sos brought his faith with him into servitude. He was an impressive spokesman for his worldview, having memorized much scripture before his capture, and many of the overworked, death-bound souls around him on the latifundium found hope in his words and surety. He himself believed his captivity had been orchestrated to send him to the most desperate place on earth, and that was why he ended up in the wheat fields of Sicily.

When Joram met Sos for the first time, he understood how he had left a strong impression upon Vitus. Vitus was wary of Sos but also conscious of the benefits he provided. Sos was a force to be reckoned with, but he used his power to persuade men and make a positive difference in his world. If he had wanted to lead another Servile War, he could have done so. But instead he spoke about the messiah, protected the weak from other slaves, led the workers in spiritual songs, and met latifundium quotas set by Vitus day after day. Neither Vitus, Joram, Nathan, nor Funisulanus had ever met someone like Sos. And for the moment, Vitus needed him.

It was curious that during the first century, several men of faith landed amid the backwardness and suffering of Sicily. The apostle Paulos spent three days there in Syracuse while in transport to trial in Rome. And another Pontian, Pancratius, who met Jesus as a teenager and had once befriended the apostle Petros, preached in Taormina till he was stoned to death for his faith.

And so somehow in this complex mix of Sicels, Greeks, Christians, Jews, Romans, managers, slaves, freedmen, patróns, vendors, aunts, cousins, senatorial sons, gods, volcanoes, wheat fields, and semi-permeable portals, life was lived, careers rose and fell, and an amphitheatre slowly reemerged on the butte of Enna.

VIII

"You sure look strange down there," taunted Efstathios.

"Then stop looking there, you freak," grunted Nathan, as he hurled Efstathios to the ground.

Efstathios lay on his back in the palaestra sand with all the naked weight and endowments of his sparring partner astride him. "It always looks like you're erect with your head sticking out," observed Efstathios, "even when you're not."

"Killing you right now," Nathan responded, "would solve a number of my problems."

Efstathios smiled, only to begin choking a moment later as the larger fellow applied pressure to the smaller one's neck.

Efstathios gasped and flailed until Nathan let up on him just enough for him to eke out, "Stop! I give up!"

Nathan rolled off him and lay a few feet away on his side and elbow under the shade of the colonnade. Efstathios pulled himself into the same position in the shade across from Nathan as he recovered his breath. A few older men sat tunic-clad nearby, intellectualizing and occasionally glancing at the younger. Other than that, the gymnasium was largely empty, as it often was.

"I've never understood," Nathan questioned, "since you bring up anatomy," and pointing derisively at Efstathios's, "how you Gentile Christians claim to know God and the scriptures but are not circumcised."

"Joram never explained that to you?" Efstathios asked.

"The topic never came up."

"No, I suppose it wouldn't," responded Efstathios. "And you really want to know?"

"Yes. It perturbs me on several levels."

"Why?"

"For one thing," Nathan explained, "you look like an animal instead of a man. It also bothers me from a theological point of view. And lastly, I wonder how Elisheva puts up with it, being a Jewish woman." Nathan then continued. "If I were perfectly honest with you, Efstathios, almost everything about you bothers me, even though I like you—despite the fact that you're annoying and have ruined my life."

Efstathios rolled his eyes, smiling.

"But right now," Nathan went on, "you have to explain the circumcision conundrum to me. I cannot imagine how you justify it."

"It's not complicated, especially since you have a Jewish background. And there's an explanation for it in one of the books that Joram and I copied on the way here."

"Oh, I can hardly wait."

"It was written by a Pharisee-turned-Christian who was contacting other Christians in the city of Rome."

"You're telling me," said Nathan, "that a Pharisee became a member of the Way?"

"Yes, against all odds—though odds really had nothing to do with it."

"Was he anyone I would know?"

"His name was Paulos. He died a dozen years ago."

"I've never heard of him. Nor am I sure I want to."

"But," said Efstathios, "you've probably heard of his teacher Gamaliel."

"I have heard of Gamaliel. But you are telling me that the famous teacher Gamaliel was the teacher of this man Paulos?"

"Yes."

"And after studying under a rabbi of that caliber, he somehow became a member of the Way? I find that hard to believe."

"Believe it. In fact, Gamaliel is quoted as having defended the Christians at one point in his career."

"But he didn't become a believer himself."

"No. But his student Paulos did."

"And what does this Paulos have to say?"

"Oh, so you *are* curious to hear about him."

"Only so I can dismantle your argument."

"He says that when God first made his covenant with Abraham, according to the first book of Moses, 'Abram believed God, and it was credited to him as righteousness.'"

"Yes, I know the story," retorted Nathan.

Efstathios continued. "Paulos emphasizes the fact that when that interaction occurred between Abraham and God, Abraham was still a Gentile using his pagan name Abram. He was not circumcised, he did not have the Law, and God had not changed his name to Abraham yet. He had nothing but his faith to commend him. So Paulos explains that it was Abraham's faith alone that saved him: not being a Jew, not being circumcised, not knowing the Law of Moses—nothing but his faith."

"So what does that have to do with you?"

"It connects with me," Efstathios explained, "because Paulos says that Gentile believers are in the same situation Abram was in when God first said he was righteous. It's only our faith in God and his self-sacrifice in human form to take away sin that can make us righteous. We do not need the Law, and we do not need to be circumcised to be saved. We are truly the sons of Abraham if we come to faith under the same conditions Abram did."

"That is ridiculous," Nathan responded. "The Law and circumcision were not established yet, so of course Abram was not circumcised. But if God had commanded him to follow those rules, he would have obeyed. And when God finally did tell Abraham to be circumcised, he did it unflinchingly—unlike some in present company." He pointed insultingly at Efstathios's body again. "You're nothing but a Philistine."

Efstathios laughed at the appellation. "According to that book we copied," Efstathios resumed, "it is significant to Paulos that the scriptures discuss Abram's righteousness at a time *before* the coming of the Law, and not after. Paulos says the case for faith alone, apart from merely obeying the Law, is clearly established from that; and that faith in God, and not faith in our own bodies or legalistic righteousness, was God's intention all along."

"I disagree," Nathan argued. "It could not have been God's intention all along. That is why he eventually revealed the Law. The *Law* was his intention, and that is why he revealed it last."

"Not at all, Nathan," rebutted Efstathios. "Rather, God introduced his original intentions *first*: that we can be righteous without following the Law, by faith alone; and that one of Abram's seed— the same one as the seed of the woman promised at the beginning in the Garden of Eden right after the fall—would make that possible. All of the other laws, prophets, and psalms were written to make it clear how impossible it was to be righteous on our own and also make it clear how we would recognize that seed when it came."

"Oh, not that again. You sound just like Joram. You think all the scriptures point to that one man and event."

"But they do, my large, impressive friend. Why do you not see it? Iesous is the long-awaited seed that was promised in the garden and was promised again to Abram *before* he was circumcised as well as many other times in Jewish history."

"So the Law means nothing according to you?"

"No, it doesn't mean nothing. It means a great deal. It points out our sin, it shows us how impossible it is to be righteous on our own, and it gives pointers and guideposts to its true fulfillment, when God would sacrifice himself once and for all in the form of the man Iesous, instead of by continuous slaughters of millions of bulls and lambs."

They both lay there unclothed and silent for a moment. Then

Efstathios said, "And believe me, Nathan, I know my sin and that no amount of sacrifices can atone for it. Only Iesous can do that."

"Hmmph," grunted Nathan. "Yes. I assume that since you are Hellenikos and frequented gymnasia in Corinth, you have many sins to account for."

"What do you mean by that? Why do you always judge me and my being Hellenikos?"

"Because the 'Greeks' have that … reputation …, and I assume that is why you are so aware of my physiognomy."

Efstathios was on the verge of becoming defensive, but he held back. "Nathan, I was raised in a world very different from yours. In Hellas, it was no shame to love another man. Not that I have such sentiments toward you. You are too annoying as well. But love between men was viewed as natural as life itself and was a societal expectation. It was the deepest kind of relationship a person could have: a spiritual as well as physical bond between two equals."

"And can't you have that kind of relationship with a woman?" Nathan asked.

"I am trying," said Efstathios.

"What do the scriptures say?" Nathan responded: "'So God created man in his own image; in the image of God he created him: male and female he created them.' So the deepest relationship a man can have with someone else is with a woman, re-forging the two halves of God's image into one, and finding the other half of ourselves and Godliness in the other."

"Yes. Theoretically I believe that too. I know the scriptures. But I have found the image of God so marred in the relationship between men and women it is difficult for me to experience the oneness you speak of even in marriage."

"You don't know what you're doing in marriage, then," Nathan gibed.

Efstathios resumed. "In some ways, marriage emphasizes the chasm between men and women as much as it brings their complementariness together."

"Are you telling me that you are married to Elisheva and do not appreciate the woman and womanliness that she is and has?"

"I am not saying that at all. I appreciate her very much. And to add the third component of the ideal Greek relationship, Elisheva brings her intellect to it as well. But even with all that, learning to live with a woman and all her differences is a long and difficult process. With a man, there is no learning at all. I can just be myself.

I can speak, act, desire, and it is all reciprocated with no explanation. Two men understand each other in a way a man and woman this side of heaven rarely seem able."

"I might grant there is perhaps some truth in what you are saying, but the fun I could have with a woman during the learning process would far outweigh the difficulty."

"But women are not about having fun, in my experience. Life is serious, and women are attuned to that. Men are fun. They are always doing and willing. Women are less so since they understand the consequences. When a fellow would approach me in the gymnasium, I knew exactly what he wanted and vice versa, whatever the consequences. But to be physical with a woman takes an act of the Senate, and the ambience needs to be perfect, and I have to have achieved some herculean feat to impress her. Women want a reason to engage with a man. Men don't need a reason. Women romance men mostly to conciliate them, or because of what men can give them, like protection or money or status or children."

"And don't men equally only want to be with women for what they can give *them*?"

"I suppose so. But I was always less bothered by taking from another man than from a woman who seemed more vulnerable and was so different from myself."

"That is another thing I do not understand about you Greeks," Nathan complained. "The beauty of a woman is found in the very ways that she is different from a man: the way we can fit together and be so opposite of each other—soft where I'm hard, in where I'm out, diminutive where I'm tall, receptive where I'm aggressive. It's perfect." He reached for his towel and threw it over his middle to hide his reaction. "How can you think the glory and fun of physicality is in sameness?"

Efstathios covered his middle as well. "It is not the sameness that is the attraction, but the mutuality. Physicality between two men is mutual. But I never feel that a woman enjoys my body as much as I am enjoying hers."

"Well look at you. I can understand that."

"It has nothing to do with being circumcised or uncircumcised. It has to do with mutuality. The mutual enjoyment between two men is powerful. But with a woman she is often passive and the mutuality is not there. It is the aspect of my former life that I miss the most in my marriage."

Nathan glared. "It is difficult to hear you speak about women that way, knowing that I could have done so much better by Elisheva than you."

"Oh you think so," Efstathios retorted, almost angrily, though not quite. "But it would be the same with you. Every man thinks he will be irresistible to his woman. But he's not. There's very little that a woman finds attractive in a man's body. To them we are all function, ungainly biology, and fur. Women are not interested in that. Babies, flowers, clothes, food, hair, jewels—those are the things that captivate a woman's mind and heart. A man's body is not even in the lineup. A man's body is just an unwanted accessory of the man the woman otherwise loves. A woman has a great capacity to love a man. Men are sometimes the very center of a woman's life. But it is not the man's body she loves. It is him."

"I completely disagree. A woman loves both. You can see it in their eyes," responded Nathan.

"Look at you," Efstathios continued. "You really think that a woman, even Elisheva, would love the particular parts you have? She loves your height, mass, personality, persuasiveness, intellect, spirit. But the shoulders, the belly, the legs, the prize under the towel—they will impress her only at the very beginning of your relationship. Within a few days, they will be completely overlooked. They will simply become a tiresome ever-craving accoutrement she will wish she did not have to deal with, but *will* deal with because she loves the overall man you are."

"You think women do not like men's bodies?" Nathan asked again.

"No, I don't. They love men's eyes. But otherwise, they don't care about the physical. Men, on the other hand, love women's bodies. Men even admire other men's bodies. Men are all about looks. Women are about emotion and safety. You are more likely to notice a fellow's arms, calves, or other body parts more than almost any women would. Bodies are meaningless to a woman except at first meeting, when those attributes draw her to you. And that is the great deception that makes men think that women care about the physical. But their attraction to your body is all promise with no follow-through. It is merely an initial reaction."

"You scrawny, ignorant pagan," Nathan retorted. "Who do you think you are telling *me* all these things? How are you, who spent so much time with boys, suddenly an expert on women?"

"I'm not. I only wish I were. But my position in life—a married man who spent too much time with boys, as you say—has forced me to think about these issues every day. I am always trying to figure out 'What's missing in my relationship with her? What makes it so different from what I am used to? How can I make it better?'

"I want to be happy in life, but I also want to follow the scriptures; and marriage has brought out the chasm between those two forces as much as it has brought out the differences between men and women in general. So every day I have to rationalize and analyze and come to terms with what I want and how I feel, what my faith tells me is true and what my body craves, and how those two are often completely incompatible.

"For whatever reason, the Almighty does not favor the physical union of two men. I am not sure why. Maybe it's because it would consume all our time if it were permissible, and civilization and his kingdom would not progress. But I have to wrestle with the fact that I believe what the scriptures say, even though I do not want them to be true on this point. So what can I do? The letter that Paulos wrote to believers in my home city says that the body is not made for immorality but for the Lord, and that I am not my own, I was bought with a price; and so I must honor God with my body. And that is how I am trying to live."

The older men looked over at them.

Nathan motioned to stand up. "Come on, Efstathios, let's find another place to talk." They got up and walked down the colonnade, ignoring the stares of the older men at their backsides and found a large and shaded window ledge with a grand view of the Sicanian Mountains west of the city. They climbed onto the ledge and sat on their towels, enjoying the breeze and looking out on the range, which undulated before them like the waves of an endless stone sea. A precipitous drop to the valley below spanned under their feet.

"This island is spectacular," said Nathan, turning to Efstathios.

"Yes, it is. It always amazes me that our troubles take place in the midst of so much beauty."

"Don't be troubled, my foolish diminutive friend," said Nathan, almost caring.

"How can I not be troubled? I think about these things every day. Even though I am married, I feel lonely, because the person I should be closest to does not see me or the world the way I do. Even though I know I am loved by her, my body is mostly ignored."

"When I look at a woman," Nathan responded, "I do not think about what she will do for my body, but what I want to do to *hers*."

"That is how I often feel too," said Efstathios. "But after months of enjoying a partner's body, I want the attention reciprocated, but it rarely is."

"I guess it could be reciprocated if, instead of marrying, you or I simply hopped from one woman to another to experience that initial attraction they have."

"I suppose so," responded Efstathios. "But where would that get us?"

"Happier than we are now."

"True for the short run. But in the long term it would bring complication and instability for us and a trail of broken hearts for them, which is no way for us to live out the idea of loving our neighbor as ourself.

"But I wish women did not present such a predicament for men. Women can find dignified, respectable men who also know how to please them, but men can rarely find reputable wives who are also great lovers. It's unfair. If a woman could remain entranced by a man's body the way she is upon first meeting a man, marriage would be happier for both parties. But as it is, I think some of our Greek heroes, like Achilles and Patroclus, or Alexander and Hephaestion, were closer to each other than most men ever are to their wives."

"There is some truth to that," conjectured Nathan sadly. "Maybe that is why David spoke of Jonathan's love being sweeter than that of women."

"I have thought that very thing," said Efstathios.

"Not that David was as you are. David loved women, and many of them. But there is a certain loyalty and affection men can share with each other that is easier on a man than his relationship with his wife. There is no pressure for friends to be perfect for each other. So I can see why the love of another fellow could be sweeter than that of a woman—just not from a physical point of view."

"That is what I think too. Among the Greeks, a man has both a wife and a male companion. An older man takes a younger companion, since it is disreputable to submit to other older men. But if you have a younger companion, you are considered a teacher and mentor and are fulfilling your obligations to the next generation. So most men live in two worlds: one at home with a partner to raise a family with, and one at the gymnasium with a partner to play and intellectualize with."

"So that is why the gymnasium is so important to you Greeks."

"Yes," responded Efstathios.

"So if you could have the two partners," Nathan asked out of intellectual curiosity, despite his discomfort with the topic, "would you?"

Efstathios sighed. "If women were educated and loved men, there would be no need. But as things stand, I might want to, but how could I? The scriptures indicate that heaven is not pleased when we mix the spiritual, intellectual, and erotic together. So to answer your question, no. I have made my choice. I can still have friends in addition to my marriage, but they cannot be the way they used to be. Instead, as a believer, I am asked in the writings to control my body and learn to live with my one wife and to live honorably with others instead of in godless desire, not taking advantage of any brother in a physical way."

"The Christian writings say that? So they specifically speak to men from the world you came from?"

"Some of them, yes. And they are all written in Greek. But it is not easy following them. If you were a fellow believer, I would ask you to pray for me."

"I believe in a fashion. And I admire the way you have changed your life and taken refuge under the wings of the Almighty, just like Ruth did when she left her homeland and gods behind."

Efstathios thought about that comment. "I have never likened myself to that story."

"I meant it as a compliment, hard as that is to admit. I do not know if I could do what you are doing, and I am sure many fellow Greeks would not understand if you explained it to them. I have held out all these years for the hope of having a woman. If I had to deny myself that, I do not know what I would do."

"The most difficult part of it for me is that I am asked to honor my wife by having no other partner besides her and to see her as an equal."

"Is that so hard?" asked Nathan.

"Sometimes, yes. The writers Petros and Paulos say that a man is to love his wife like his own body and treat her with respect and as a fellow heir of heaven so that his prayers are not hindered. And Paulos says that a husband's body is not his own; it belongs to his wife, and not to another man. And he says the woman's body is not her own; it belongs to her husband. He also says that a man must love his wife the way Christos loved the church and gave himself up for her. So it asks women to be physical with their husbands and men to give their all for their wives. I don't know if there is another philosophy on earth that makes women so equal to men and men so responsible to their wives. When I think about it, it is both wonderful and scary."

"Then maybe I don't want to get married to Elisheva. I always just thought she loved me and I loved her, and it was as simple as that."

"No. Life and marriage are never that simple."

They sat and thought some more.

"So you have never had feelings for another fellow like I described?" asked Efstathios.

"No," responded Nathan. "I have had love for many men in my life: my father, brother, Joseph, Ducetius, Joram; and somehow I am not without sentiment for you. But no. I have never felt what you described."

"Then you are lucky, Nathan," Efstathios sighed. "By the grace of God, you are lucky."

IX

Work on the amphitheatre progressed slowly but steadily. Each of the band of four had his assigned task. Efstathios ordered materials, negotiated prices, and oversaw expenditures. With his trade background in Corinth and Pella, he knew how to deal with vendors, distributors, clients, and even Vitus, with whom he shared a similar vision for the theatre. Despite his youth, his amiable nature, wit, and flashing eyes, which disguised the uncertainty he often felt, won him favor among even hardened merchants.

As for Nathan, he worked closely with Efstathios estimating quantities of goods needed and delivering them where needed: wood, rope, and nails where the workers' shelters were being erected; marble and tools where the pillars and new seats were being sculpted or repaired; bricks where the stage was going up; saws, rakes, shovels, etc. where the invasive underbrush, weeds, and overgrown trees were being removed; and the ingredients for cement wherever it was required. Nathan's time as attaché to

Joseph in Galilee taught him how to be second-in-command to Efstathios—a position that grew uncomfortable after their conversation in the palaestra.

Joram oversaw the laborers, assigning responsibilities, keeping everyone on task, exhorting or confronting when needed, jumping in as an example, assisting with distribution of materials, troubleshooting, settling quarrels between the men, and acting as a general liaison between Vitus and the workforce of 100 employees and slaves. Assisting Joram closely was Sos, filling in wherever Joram could not, and employing the same temperament, humor, certitude, exactitude, and energy that Joram brought to the table and that made Sos indispensable. More than once, Joram asked Vitus if Sos's ankle chains could be removed. Vitus would not consent. But for Sos, he understood why the chains were necessary and never raised the issue.

As for Ducetius—called Baropalus on the job site—he acted as a gofer between Efstathios and Nathan, Nathan and Joram, and Joram to Efstathios, delivering messages, analyzing situations before they became crises, making sure the food and water was apportioned properly, and helping out in any way the other band members needed him when he walked by. And they always thought of something when he walked by.

If anyone knew how to serve an enterprise faithfully and unheralded, it was Ducetius: the slave turned freedman, and the freedman-turned-beloved-young-nephew again. He was the glue that held the outfit together. Conscious of his former status, he often eyed the chains on the slaves uncomfortably. But from watching Sos, who, like a fettered giant, still commanded respect, he felt inspired to be all he could be whatever his condition: slave, free, or somewhere awkwardly in between.

As for George, he not only made inquiries about Vitus in town and went to speak to him as Joram had asked, he went several steps beyond. From the first meeting, he positioned himself as essential to the renovation project. He explained to Vitus the locals' attitude toward the theatre and the potential backlash and obstacles the vendors might present to its completion. He assured Vitus that as a cultured man, he himself supported the reopening of the theatre, but expected he would need to use his influence to change his neighbors' minds on the subject. He had lived in Enna his entire life and understood how things were done there—unlike Vitus, Joram, Nathan, Efstathios, or even Ducetius.

In addition to making himself indispensable, George also positioned himself as the lead contractor on the job, clarifying to Vitus that 'the band of four,' as Joram and his gang liked to call themselves, worked for *him*, and that he would require a percentage of their salaries to lend them out for the job. He might also schedule them from time to time to work on his own properties rather than the theatre, if need be. If those conditions were not amenable to Vitus, then Vitus could not hope to rely on the locals' good will, or his influence with them, or on his connections with the local vendors, or even on his workers showing up in the morning.

George played hardball with Vitus. From his perspective, there was a great deal riding on this project—an upgrade for the town, an upswing in local employment, and an upheaval, though worthwhile, in everyone's life for the next year or so. For himself, there was also the potential to establish his reputation further in town, make connections with a senator's son, increase his monetary status and that of his widowed cousin-in-law Ayathe, and set up another layer of protection around his young cousin-nephew Ducetius.

In some ways, Ducetius was George's greatest concern in the mix of motives that drew him onto the project. He thought of the despair and vulnerability he had felt for years after the loss of his cousin, and he never wanted to be in that position again. His own childlessness and widowerhood had been loss enough in his life, but the enslavement of Ducetius had brought him to the brink of emotional and fiscal ruin for a few tenuous years. Achieving status in the town and on the latifundium for himself and for what remained of his family could offer him a safeguard against future misfortune.

In the end, Vitus agreed to all of George's terms. George became Vitus's 'in' with the local populace to ensure the theatre's success, and Vitus became George's 'in' for a wealthier, more cultured, and safer future. George's professional standing with Vitus soon grew to the point where he even negotiated with him for the small library Efstathios had first envisioned.

X

If relationships between George and Vitus, Joram and Sos, and the town and latifundium were growing stronger, it was unclear how that of Nathan and Efstathios would play out. The palaestra conversation changed their relationship permanently. As a result, it was clear to Nathan that Elisheva's life was being wasted with a husband who was possibly more in love with him than he was with her. And it was clear to Efstathios why Elisheva had been in love with Nathan her entire life.

The conversation also changed their relationship because further reflection on it caused each to resent the other. For Nathan, it was because the 'little complicated half-man,' as he called Efstathios, presented an obstacle between him and the woman he loved. For Efstathios, it was because Nathan knew too much about him and perhaps had lost respect.

As the months passed, however, each found himself more and more in the other's company. Being friends with Nathan made Efstathios feel more socially acceptable among other fellows. And being friends with Efstathios made Nathan feel bigger, stronger, and nicer in the eyes of women. In addition, both men discovered that their friendship pleased Elisheva and kept them in her good graces better than if they stayed apart. So strangely enough, the two actually began to grow closer, despite their underlying resentment. After all, they both shared a great deal in common: they both loved Elisheva, the scriptures, the palaestra, and Nathan. In addition, they worked closely on the theatre project, were about the same age, struggled with their station in life, came from other countries, liked to intellectualize, and enjoyed taking an occasional jab at each other when they could.

The love-hate relationship between them, beknownst only to Joram at first, eventually became apparent to all. One day, as Nathan and Efstathios entered Ayathe's house after walking back from work together, George announced, "There they are: Damon and Pythias."

Sitting down, Nathan asked, "What do you mean, 'Damon and Pythias'?"

Ducetius smiled, knowing another Georgian tale was afoot.

"Damon and Pythias," George began, right on cue, "were two close friends who came to Sicily hundreds of years ago."

"And that reminds you of us?" said Nathan, already in a sarcastic mood.

"Yes," said George, surprised at Nathan's response. "Shouldn't it?"

The two young men rolled their eyes, ready to be unconvinced by whatever George had to say. Ayathe's daughters came in to listen to his story, even though it was in the andron.

"So while Damon and Pythias were in Sicily," George continued, "they visited Syracuse. But Pythias committed an accidental crime and was arrested, charged with treason, and sentenced to death by the king."

"*Now* I can see the resemblance," Efstathios said. "I could definitely imagine Nathan doing something like that."

"So," George continued, "Pythias asked the king if, before he was executed, he could return to his homeland to say good-bye to his family. The king permitted it. 'But under one condition,' he said. 'You must leave your friend Damon here as a ransom.'"

"Oh my," said one of Ayathe's daughters.

"The king then told Pythias that if he did not return by such-and-such a date, Damon would be executed in his stead."

"Did Pythias agree?" asked Joram. "And, more importantly, did Damon?"

"Yes, they both agreed," said George. "Pythias left to go home, and Damon was thrown into prison."

Now it was Nathan's turn to interject. "I believe I am starting to like this story," he said, "especially if I'm the one who gets off free and Efstathios is the one thrown into the dungeon."

Ayathe's daughters laughed.

George, trying to ignore the interruptions, continued. "So days passed," he said. "Days and days and days. Then the day of execution arrived."

"Oh no!" the daughters said.

"The king summoned Damon out of prison," George continued, "bringing him to a field to put him to death."

"No! No! It's not going to end like that, is it Uncle George?" exclaimed Ayathe's youngest. "It can't end like that!"

"I doesn't sound like such a bad ending to me," commented Nathan.

"Cousin Nathan," asked Ayathe's little daughter, "you wouldn't *really* let cousin Efstathios get executed, would you?"

"I might," he answered with a smile and a wink.

"Anyway," George continued again, overlooking the further disruption, "just as the executioner lifted his hand in the air to slay Damon, Pythias suddenly appeared. He told the king that he had tried desperately to make it back in time but that he had been abducted by pirates on his return voyage, the pirates had tossed him overboard, and he had had to swim all the way back to land and then run all the way back to the city."

"He did all that?" said Nathan. "I wouldn't even have bought the return ticket."

The little girls laughed again. "Cousin Nathan, you're so funny," they said.

"I know," he responded.

"In any case," continued George, trying to complete the tale, "the king of Syracuse was so impressed with the loyalty the two friends had shown for each other that he decided to let them both go."

"Yay!"

"I knew it wouldn't end sadly," said Ayathe's older daughter. "I knew it."

"And that," concluded George, "is the tale of Damon and Pythias."

"Opa, cousin," applauded Ducetius. "I haven't heard that story in decades. You told it beautifully."

"Even amidst the vacuous commentary," muttered Efstathios.

Ayathe's daughters showed their approval as well.

"So what do you think, Nathan?" asked George. "Isn't there a little bit of a resemblance between those two men and the two of you? I thought so."

Nathan shook his head. "It is a very nice story, Cousin. Really. But I'd prefer to see us in the story of Persephone."

"Persephone!? There's absolutely no similarity between you two and her."

"I know. But if there were, we could go back to that field some day, have Efstathios pick some flowers, and have him disappear for a while. And I think that would be a great ending."

George was puzzled by Nathan's words, but the girls laughed again and Efstathios shook his head.

XI

"Cousin, tell me about the Gate to the Underworld," asked Joram, as the group walked to the lake together.

"What do you want to know?"

"Is it real, is it scary, is it a place to avoid?"

"I would say 'yes' to all those. But ask Nathan. What do you think, son?"

Nathan responded. "I was terrified when I was there. I don't really want to go back again. I had the worst dream I ever had in my life there."

"Maybe it wasn't a dream," said George.

"What did you dream?" asked Efstathios.

"That hell itself was pulling me in and that there was no escape."

"Then it wasn't a dream," Joram said.

"I knew you would say that," responded Nathan.

"So you agree with me, Joram?"

"Yes, I do. Hell pulls at us all."

"That is exactly what I told Patrón when he woke up," said Ducetius.

"Every one of us is poised on the verge of hell and eternity," said Joram.

"I have always believed the field around the lake is a 'semi-permeable portal' between the physical and spiritual worlds," explained George.

"But it's not just the field. I'd say the entire world is a portal," said Efstathios.

"To a point, I agree with you," responded George, "since there are many gates to the underworld in Greece, where Orpheus descended into the Netherworld, and Cumae where Aeneas descended. And two days' from here is the underworld lair of the Palikoi. I visited there once on Ducetius's behalf. His namesake founded a sacred city there, and the Palikoi protect slaves. But all those places together do not constitute the entire world."

"But my point," responded Joram, "is that heaven intervenes in human affairs no matter where one is, not only at certain designated locations."

"Perhaps so. They intervened at Troy," answered George, "and Kore Demeter intervenes with her protection over Enna."

"And Zeus," added Efstathios, "likes to 'intervene' whenever he sees a lovely young creature pass by."

"Ha!" chuckled George. "I like the way you phrased that: 'Intervene.'"

"What do you mean?" asked Nathan.

"Zeus makes a hobby of seducing beautiful women and fathering children by them," explained Efstathios. "There are dozens of tales about his escapades with Leda, Europa, Io, Callisto…"

"My favorite is Leda," said George.

"Why?" asked Joram.

"Zeus seduced her in the form of a swan."

"A swan?" laughed Nathan.

"Yes. Could you imagine all the ways a swan could make love to a woman?"

The thought made them smile.

"What other forms did he take?" asked Nathan, curiosity aroused.

"He carried off Europa as a bull."

"I can relate to that one," responded Nathan

"With another he took the shape of the woman's husband."

"Now I'll bet you wish you could do *that*, Nathan!" laughed Joram.

"I do, but I don't think I could morph as small and lovely as our little Corinthian here," said Nathan, nodding toward Efstathios.

"So is that the issue between you two? You're jealous?" asked George, suddenly understanding Nathan's response to the Damon and Pythias story.

"A bit," Joram said.

"Don't worry Nathan," counseled George. "The world is full of beautiful women, and one of them will want you."

"Then again, they might not," said Efstathios, for which Nathan put him in a strangle hold. "I mean, of *course* one will," corrected Efstathios.

"If you're clever like Zeus," continued George, "and he is the inspiration for all of us who love women—you can capture a female's attention by an endless variety of methods."

"Give me another example," asked Nathan. "I need an idea."

"With Callisto, he took the form of the goddess Artemis."

"Another woman? I don't think that would work for me."

"It was the only way he could gain Callisto's affection. She swore never to be with a man."

"But isn't there a method I could actually use?" asked Nathan. "My Artemis imitations aren't very good."

"There really isn't. That's why they're stories about the gods. The methods are so strange I wonder how even the gods thought of them."

"Which is the strangest?"

"I think Danae."

"Why?"

"Her father, the king of Argos, locked her in a chamber with no doors or windows so she couldn't have a baby. It was prophesied her baby would kill him some day."

"So Zeus had to find a way into that chamber?"

"He's always up for a challenge, and when Zeus wants something, he gets it— unless his wife Hera finds out about it first."

"So how did he 'intervene' with Danae?"

"He turned himself into gold dust and rained down through the chamber to enter her body."

"And did it work?"

"Of course! He's Zeus! He can do anything. Danae gave birth to Perseus, one of the greatest Greek heroes.

"So I assume Perseus then killed the king?"

"Yes. But it was an accident."

"But why did he always have to disguise himself?" asked Joram.

"Mostly to hide from Hera," said George. "But also because the women would explode if they ever saw his true lightening glory."

"That's what happens to women when I meet them," said Nathan.

"So did any of his lovers explode?"

"Semele, the mother of Dionysus, did."

"Then how did she become a mother?"

"Zeus found the baby in the cinders before she completely disintegrated."

"Oh, of course," said Nathan. "That makes perfect sense."

"And what about *your* god?" asked George. "Did he ever take on different forms and come to earth?"

"Here we go," whispered Nathan to Efstathios. "Did Joram *pay* George to ask that question? How does he always manage to turn every conversation to this topic?"

"He doesn't," whispered Efstathios back.

Joram answered. "Yes, the Hebrew God *did* visit the earth. And he impregnated one woman, one time. But it wasn't because he was in love with her or wanted a dalliance like Zeus. He is not like that at all, and has no physical attraction to humans and other creatures like the Greek gods do."

"He doesn't? Then he must be a very distant god."

"He is not distant. He is very near and involved."

"But he doesn't love people, or probably even hate people, the way our gods do."

"He loves people very much and occasionally hates, when justice requires it. But he is described in our holy writings as embodying love itself."

"But what kind of love? Zeus loves people as friends or as children or as lovers. But the love of your god sounds passionless and limited."

"It is neither, I assure you," said Nathan.

"But what does he love?" asked George. "And if, as Ducetius once explained, your god made everything in the world, who or what did he love before he made those things? Or did he only embody love after he made the world?"

"That is an insightful question," responded Efstathios.

Joram attempted an answer. "Our holy writings describe him as having a mysterious quality of threeness to him even though he is one. It is tough to understand. It is like if a man, his son, and their actions were so intertwined that when you saw the man, you would be seeing his son; or when you saw his son, you would be seeing his father; or if you saw their effects in the world, you would be seeing all three, though they are really one and the same."

"So what does that have to do with your god being love?"

"The threeness always existed, according to our writings. So even before he created objects to love, the three loved each other. So, in short, he did not embody love only after creating. He is love eternally. He couldn't be eternally love if he wasn't at least two; but our scriptures indicate that he is three. It is funny. His eternal love is our favorite and easiest-to-believe aspect of him, and his threeness is the most mysterious and hard-to-believe aspect; but the first quality could not exist without the second."

"The threeness is not so strange," said George. "I have heard of something like that from the east. They say there are three gods who function as one, or one who functions as three…"

"I have heard that too," added Efstathios, "from traders returning from India and the Red Sea trade and the overland route from Bactria to the Decapolis. The idea is not exactly the same, but it is similar. I do not know enough to say. But I am not surprised that other people in the world have the concept of the threeness. If something is true, there are always people who know it; but sometimes the truth gets passed down through generations in a bastardized form, so people have many different beliefs."

"What do you mean?" asked George. "Give me an example."

"I think Zeus intervening is a good example."

"Explain."

"The hope that the gods would love us so much that they would take on another form to reach into our world, like Zeus did with all those women, is a hope I think humans have had in their hearts for centuries. Not that we wish to be dallied with by the gods, but that they would care enough to be with us. We don't even know we have that hope inside of us until someone articulates it. Then all of a sudden we realize, 'Ah, that is what I was hoping for all along."

"But you said before," observed George, "that your god did not have any attraction to the woman he impregnated or have any dalliance with her. So why did he impregnate her, and what form did he take?"

"It was to save the human race."

"How could impregnating her do that? Was the child going to save the world?"

"Yes. That is exactly it. Our writings contain a prophecy from thousands of years ago that our God himself would enter the world through a woman and grow up a man to die as a sacrifice to save the human race. And that actually happened."

"It did?" responded George. "I don't know that story."

"It's not a story," Joram answered. "It's history. It happened in the country we come from, and recently."

"How recently?"

"About eighty years ago, during my grandfather's lifetime."

"That is absurd," responded George. "You believe an event like that could actually happen recently? You think your god lived in your country 80 years ago? I don't believe that. The gods don't still touch our world. We still sacrifice to them and they occasionally answer our prayers, but all of the stories we tell about them are ancient, before anyone who is alive now can remember. I do not believe stories about the gods still happen. How could they? Why should they?"

"Because we still need them," continued Efstathios. "And because when prophecies are fulfilled, we cannot control at what point in history they occur. What we call the past was 'now' to some earlier generation, and our 'now' will be the past to some future generation. True events have to happen at some point in time, or they are not true events. That is the difference between myth and history. If a prophecy is fulfilled, it is fulfilled in history, or it is not really fulfilled. And what is wrong with now? When you speak about Kore Demeter and her daughter Persephone, you speak about them with such longing, as if you wished they still noticed you and cared, that I think you wish their stories could still be happening right now."

"I do," assented George with hesitation.

"And you mentioned Orpheus before," Efstathios continued. "When you hear the story of Orpheus's descent into Hades to bring back Eurydice, don't you wish in your heart that a god would descend to where you are, trapped in this world, to take you by the hand and lead you to freedom?"

"I have never thought of that story that way," answered George. "But as you said, once someone articulates a hope, perhaps we find that it is what we desired all along."

"But unlike Orpheus, the Israelite God did not look back at the last moment and lose Eurydice forever. He plowed into this world and into death and freed any captives who would follow. And he himself left the netherworld and is alive again."

"You really believe that? And you say this all happened 80 years ago?"

"The time he died and revived took place closer to 50 years ago. But, yes. And whereas Orpheus had to return to Hades to be with his beloved Eurydice since he did not succeed in bringing her back, the God we try to follow made it through Hades and death and came out of it on the other side alive."

"So you consider your god greater than Orpheus?"

"He must be. He did what Orpheus could not. He loved and died in a way that even Zeus did not. Zeus never entered the world to sacrifice himself. Quite the opposite. Our God is not just a story from a long time ago that people repeat. His entrance into the world was recorded by many people and was the fulfillment of prophecies that were written and kept in our scriptures from centuries before."

"That is much too much to believe. And how unimaginative it all sounds!" exclaimed George.

"What do you mean?" asked both Efstathios and Joram.

"The stories of our gods make the mind and emotions soar," explained George. "They are outside of reality and time. They elevate our minds out of the humdrum of the here and now. They give hope. They entertain. They give us something to tell our children and share with our neighbors. But what you are telling me all sounds cold and calculating. It is all written and delineated. You say such-and-such happened because it was prophesied, or that your god's love is a certain type because that is how it was penned. You say he is a particular number because your scriptures say so. There is no freedom for the mind to take over and embellish, like in our stories. Here among us, our minds and experiences teach us about the gods. We merely need to see a flash of lightening to see Zeus, or the silhouette of the volcano to think of Hephaestus, or walk a field of flowers to remember Persephone. And concerning love, we merely have to feel what humans feel to understand the many loves the gods feel. Just living brings us into connection with the gods. It is all intuitive. It does not need to be written."

"Is knowledge really intuitive, though, cousin?" Efstathios asked with earnestness. "You are the great storyteller of Enna, so you know how important the written word is. You didn't learn about Demeter and Zeus or Damon and Pythias, or about the massacre in the theatre through intuition. You learned those things because you read it or heard from someone who read it earlier."

George nodded his head slowly, recollecting all those stories. "Perhaps," he said.

"And it is not so calculating," Efstathios continued, anxious in his youthful way to set the record straight. "When we see our scriptures fulfilled, it is a wonderment in our eyes because of the very fact that it really happened. Who could imagine that the written word could come to life? It is like Pygmalion's statue beginning to breathe. Maybe more than any other people on earth, those who believe like Joram and I marvel that the things written on pages thousands of years ago can suddenly come true in the here and now."

"It is true," Nathan corroborated. "I do not believe the way Efstathios and Joram do, nor will I probably ever, but I can attest to the wonderment they feel, and I think Ducetius too, when they see their scriptures manifested in the physical world."

"You believe the way they do, Ducetius?" asked George, saddened by the news.

"I think I do, cousin," responded Ducetius. "Joram's words tug at me much more than Hades."

"Speaking of Hades, we are almost at that infernal field," said Nathan, "and I am telling you I do not want to go there again."

"I almost want to turn back myself," said Efstathios. "It's so warm near the lake. Look at the mosquito bites I have on my arms already."

"I thought those were your biceps," said Nathan.

"If you didn't want to go to the lake again," Joram asked Nathan, "why did you come along?"

"Because I wanted to go for a walk with everybody—not really Efstathios, but everybody else. There was nothing better to do today. But I'm getting that uneasy feeling like the last time I was here, and I don't like it."

"Really, Nathan?" responded Joram. "I've never heard you speak like that before."

"I've never felt like this before."

"It is a beautiful field, the flowers are budding, and the lake is shimmering in the sun. What could you be afraid of?" asked Efstathios.

"That my biceps are going to start looking like yours."

"I think Nathan senses the dark presence here," interjected George. "He wouldn't be the first."

"You think Nathan is sensitive to the spiritual world?" mocked Efstathios.

But Nathan no longer came back with a clever remark.

"I think he's serious," said Joram.

"I *am* serious," said Nathan. "I'd like to leave, Joram. You've seen the field and the lake, and that's what you came to Sicily to see. If Hades shows up again, please don't let him take anybody—except maybe Efstathios."

They then headed back before a chariot emerged.

XII

The workmen gasped.

It was the end of the day, and they were clearing underbrush from the edge of the amphitheatre. They removed a large pine branch that was growing downward along the southern theatre wall. Then suddenly...

"Sos! Master Joram!" they yelled.

Joram, Nathan, and Efstathios were standing in the middle of the theatre talking. All the family women—Auntie Ayathe, her daughters, Elisheva, and Nathan's mother and sister—were there too, having visited with a special snack for the men.

Joram, Efstathios and Nathan walked down the theatre stairs between the seating sections to the lower level where the workmen were huddled. Sos joined them a moment later.

Efstathios motioned for Elisheva to stay back.

"Look!" the workers said, making way for the foremen to see.

And there, against the wall, covering a section of the outermost stairway, lay a skeleton curled up in a fetal position. It had tatters of clothing still hanging on it here and there—enough to tell that it was a female—and had a dagger going through its rib cage. On closer inspection, it turned out to be two skeletons: one of a woman, and one of a baby held close to the woman's chest. The dagger had pierced both their rib cages.

"It looks like a mother and child," said Joram.

"Could it possibly be from that massacre three hundred years ago?" asked Nathan.

"It seems unlikely that it could have been here so long," commented Efstathios. "But whenever it was, how sad."

Sos motioned to the two workers. "Thank you for informing us. You should get back to work now. Over there."

The workers hesitated for a moment, waiting to see what everyone would say about their find and regretting that they had 'informed' the authorities so quickly. But Sos gave them a stare that set them in motion, and they walked dutifully away.

From the middle of the theatre Elisheva called down, "Is everything all right?"

"Come and see," said Nathan. "But keep the girls up there with mother and Auntie."

"I will."

Nathan's sister complained to Elisheva, "Of course *we're* not allowed to see. We can never have any fun."

Back in the huddle, Nathan looked at Joram and asked, "Do you remember the skull we found digging in the tunnel?"

"I think about that moment all the time. That was the catalyst for weeks of discussion."

"It seems like a long time ago. And only three out of the five of us are still here."

At that moment, Elisheva arrived. She spotted right away that the remains were of a mother and baby, and she sat down near it with a distressed expression. Looking at her, Nathan thought about the fact that Elisheva had lost three pregnancies, and the woman lying in death had actually given birth to her child, only to lose it before dying herself.

Sos, standing near Elisheva, muttered a line from the writings of Loukas so that only Elisheva heard him. "This child," he loosely recited, "will cause the thoughts of many hearts to be revealed; and a sword will pierce your own soul too."

Elisheva turned and looked at Sos. "How do you know those words?"

"I have read them and believed," he responded.

Elisheva was surprised and touched.

Continuing to look at the skeleton, she suddenly espied something underneath it, and said, "Efstathios, do you see those two little pouches next to her? What are those?"

Efstathios and Nathan walked to the other side of the skeleton and saw a pair of matching, fancy, discolored little bags.

"Can I touch them?" asked Nathan.

"They look like silk," said Efstathios. "But there couldn't possibly be silk in Sicily if this is from the massacre."

"What's inside them?" asked Joram. "Let's take a look. I'll be respectful."Elisheva reached down and gently picked one of the pouches up, apologizing to the skeleton, woman to woman, for handling her things.

She opened up the pouch and said, "It's a little statue."

"May I see?" asked Joram. He took it out and showed it to the rest.

"It's a Roman *lar*," said Efstathios, "a little household idol."

"It looks like it's made of gold," observed Nathan.

"I'd say it is," exclaimed Elisheva. "But why would this woman and her baby come to the theatre with a little golden idol?"

"It seems unlikely she would have," observed Efstathios. "People do not usually take lares out of the house to walk around town."

"So why did she have this with her?" asked Elisheva.

"I don't know. It seems odd," said Efstathios.

"What's in the other pouch?" asked Nathan.

Elisheva picked up the second pouch. From the feel of it she could already tell what it contained. She opened it and said, "It's a bag of money."

"How much?" asked Nathan.

She and Joram rifled through the contents and estimated. "I'd say it's about a month's wages. It's full of denarii and sestertii."

"Are they old? Are they Sicel or Roman?" asked Efstathios. "Can you tell? If they are from the war with Carthage, it would confirm that this woman died in the massacre, unlikely as that is. It would also mean they are worth a lot of money to a collector."

"Oh, Efstathios," said Elisheva, "how could you think of that now?"

From the middle of the theatre again, Nathan's mother called down to the huddled circle. "Nathan! We're coming to take a look. The girls are restless up here and want to see."

"All right, mother!" Nathan yelled back.

As the girls approached, Nathan prepared them for the spectacle.

"Wow!" said Nathan's sister. "A skeleton?"

"Yes," said Nathan. "But please, keep your voices down. We don't want the whole world to know. And don't touch anything. Just stand there quietly."

"Yes, sir!" his sister mocked. She complied, however, and contented herself with simply watching Joram and every move Joram made. He noticed her looking at him and did not mind.

Elisheva inspected some of the coins. "The coins do not seem old at all."

"So they're not Sicel or from the Republican era during the war?" asked Efstathios.

"No," responded Elisheva. "They are mostly from the reign of Emperor Claudius."

"One of them, at least, says Tiberius," remarked Joram.

"So when was this poor woman killed?" asked Nathan. "I thought maybe she was murdered during the massacre three hundred years ago."

"Now that I've looked at her a little more thoroughly, I would say that she *was* murdered then," responded Efstathios. "Look at the condition of her clothes. And look at that pugio dagger in her rib cage. No one makes pugiones like that anymore. It looks like the old Iberian type."

"The old Iberian type? How could you possibly even know that?" asked Nathan.

"I think Efstathios has a huge brain," said Ayatha's youngest.

"That's the only huge thing you've got," Nathan whispered to Efstathios,

"I'm grateful," interjected Joram, "that at least someone here knows about Roman pugios, household lares, and silks, or we'd be completely in the dark."

"I was just about to mention all those things," jested Nathan, "but little mister 'I-know-everything' beat me to it."

The girls laughed.

"But seriously," Nathan added, changing tone, "if the dagger and clothes are from the Carthaginian War, then what are coins from Claudius's reign doing next to her? The little statue and the silk pouches look recent too. The statuette almost looks like Emperor Gaius, as if the 'lar' was based on his looks. There is something strange going on here. Those pouches next to this skeleton do not match the time of her death. Not that it really matters. But I find it interesting."

"I agree," said the others.

Although they lived in a milieu in which sleuthing was uncommon, the entire group of them grew curious about the circumstances of the woman's death. None of them was willing to simply discard the bones and continue with the renovation. Additionally, Joram wanted time to figure out how best to dispose of the corpse so as not to arouse suspicion, affront Ennan practice, or create a local stir.

"So what do we do?" asked Elisheva.

"I think," Joram said, "that we should cover up the woman and the pouches again with the branch until we can figure out what to do with her. I would like a few of us to camp here in the theatre tonight to make sure no one disturbs the site. I will volunteer. And Sos and Nathan, could you volunteer as well?

"Certainly," they said.

Nathan's sister wished she could volunteer too, so she could speak more to Joram. But she said nothing.

Joram continued. "We should not mention this incident to anyone. It should be a secret until we know more about it."

"I will tell that to the two workmen," said Sos.

XIII

Of course, it was all they could talk about till they fell asleep that night. In every domicile—Ayathe's house, where she lived with her daughters and Ducetius; Ayathe's small auxiliary apartment next door where Nathan, his mother and sister resided; and George's rental property a block away, shared by Efstathios, Elisheva and Joram—every conversation every minute always reverted back to "Who was she?" "She must have been incredibly rich." "She wasn't rich you idiot; those weren't her pouches, remember?" "How *did* Efstathios know about Iberian pugiones?" "Has anyone told cousin George yet?" "How could someone just stab a mother and baby like that?" "Ducetius, Ducetius, you're not going to believe what we saw today!" "If those pouches weren't that lady's, whose were they then?" "I wish we knew her name." "What's a pugiones?" "If people in the town find out about this, it will put a stop to the whole renovation." "I think she looks like a Silvana." "Do you think she could have been an ancestor of ours?" "Maybe she wasn't married and somebody killed her because of the baby." "Maybe she *was* married, but it was someone *else's* baby." "Are those workmen going to give it all away?" "Are you *girls* going to give it all away?" "Do you think she could have been hiding behind that tree when she was stabbed, and that's why she was never discovered till now?" "Those pouches just don't make any sense." "What did the Romans do with all the other bodies that were massacred?" "If you found a pouch of coins and a gold statue, would you dump them behind a tree next to a skeleton?"

There was no end to the speculations and comments.

The very day after the discovery, Vitus already knew about it. How he found out, no one was sure, and no one was bold enough to ask. Even George hadn't heard yet, but Vitus had. Perhaps it was one of the bodyguards who had informed him.

"I would like to see it," he said matter-of-factly, showing up at the theatre first thing in the morning.

Joram, who had not slept well during the night, roused himself and removed the branch with Sos's help. Nathan woke up as they did so.

Vitus examined the skeleton, pugio, and pouches. His interest surprised everyone. However, there were practical concerns behind it, as well as some intellectual curiosity. "Everything is exactly as you found it?" he asked.

"Yes," answered Joram. "We looked into the pouches but put them back where they were. Nothing has been removed."

"And what are your conclusions about it? What do you think may have happened?

"We think there might have been two separate events that occurred."

"Two?"

"Yes. We think the woman was the victim of a massacre that took place in this theatre during the Punic War hundreds of years ago; but we think the money and lar were placed here much more recently."

"And on what do you base those conclusions?"

"Efstathios is well-acquainted with all the accoutrements we found near her: a lar and pugio and some coins. He believes the pugio is ancient, but the pouches and their contents are recent."

"By pugio, I assume you mean the dagger."

"Yes."

Just then Efstathios showed up on the scene.

"And what makes you think the pugio is older than the coins and lar?" he asked Efstathios directly.

Efstathios, surprised and annoyed to see Vitus there so early and already asking questions, tried to answer nonchalantly. "I have rarely seen that style of pugio on the market. It is an outdated model that no one makes anymore. Based on the condition of the fabric on the skeleton, which appears more worn out than the silk fabric of the pouches, and the ancient style of the pugio in contrast to the recent dates of the coins, mostly from the reign of Claudius, it seems logical that the woman's death and the placement of the pouches are separated by hundreds of years.

"How do you know," retorted Vitus, "that the woman's dress is not simply made of a less durable fabric than the silk? And how can we be sure that someone in town did not simply own an antique pugio and use it in a recent murder?"

"I do not know either of those things for certain," responded Efstathios. "But the style of the pugio is the same that Republican soldiers would have used about the time of the Carthaginian wars, and the corrosion on it leads me to believe that it was left outside for centuries rather than housed in someone's private collection indoors."

Nathan, who stood there silently with sleep still in his eyes, marveled at the astuteness of both questioner and answerer, especially so early in the morning.

"That sounds reasonable," responded Vitus. "You are a good, clear thinker, Eustatius. What we need to do now, however, is to keep this entire matter under wraps and dispose of the skeleton before the whole town hears about it."

"I will bury it in the woods just over the theatre wall," offered Sos.

"No," retorted Vitus. "The remains are to be burned. I want no trace."

"As you wish," responded Sos.

"I will take the pouches," said Vitus. "You take care of the body." He began to walk away, then saw Efstathios looking at him out of the corner of his eye. "And *you* can keep the pugio if you wish," he added.

"Thank you," responded Efstathios. "It is a fine piece."

"If you sell it," added Vitus, "I will take some of the proceeds."

"I may not sell it, since it is of historical value. But if you would like, I will sell the lar. That would fetch a good price."

"No. I'm sure Lord Funisulanus would like it for his lararium. I will offer it to him instead. He would like it more than anyone else."

With that, Vitus turned and left.

After he had gone, Efstathios looked at his three compatriots. "We cannot burn that poor woman's remains," he said, urgently and unexpectedly. He spoke quietly, as if Vitus could still hear him.

"We have to bury her—I mean, *them,* she and her baby—like the old Greeks or Sicels would have done."

"Why?" Joram asked.

"That is how it should be done. She was Sicel. She would want to be buried. It is disrespectful otherwise. What does Vitus care how we dispose of the body? He's a Roman. He thinks burning bodies is normal."

"But why do *you* care how we dispose of the body?" asked Nathan.

"To be honest, this skeleton and the massacre bothered me all night. I could not wait to come here this morning to give that woman a proper burial. It irks me that Vitus beat me to it. But after all she went through, dying at the hands of the Romans along with her child, we should show her this one last kindness. It is no trouble for us, and it is more fitting for her. And I would not just do it for her. I would bury her on behalf of all the people who died in this theatre that day."

"It seems unwise and unnecessary, Efstathios," said Joram.

"It is not unwise or unnecessary. It is honorable. And there is a precedent for my caring about it."

"What precedent?" asked Joram.

"You know the story of *Antigone*?"

"*Antigone*? I can't wait to hear this one," said Nathan, finding it no longer too early for sarcasm.

"It is the story of a Greek woman who flaunts a king's edict to bury her dead brother."

"I always knew you were a Greek woman," chided Nathan. "But are you going to insist on burying this skeleton because of a story? That borders on lunacy."

"It's not just a story. It is a matter of honor and respect. It is one of the most famous tragedies in the entire Greek world, and it was written by Sophocles. I am trying to acquire a copy of it to have it performed for the opening day of the theatre. Please don't tell me you have never heard of it before."

"I have never heard of it before," said Nathan.

"I have heard of it," said Joram, "but I did not know the story behind it."

"How did things end up for the woman in the story?" asked Nathan.

"She was executed."

"Then, by all means, let's bury that skeleton," responded Nathan.

"I rest my case," said Joram. "We should not go against Vitus's directive."

"Let me deal with Vitus," said Efstathios. "If it bothers you to bury this poor woman and her child, I will bury her myself. But I cannot let it go. There are few times when a person can set a wrong right, and for me, burying this woman can bring a decent and humane end to an inhuman event that has cried out for resolution for centuries. It is frustrating to me that Vitus threw an obstacle into my plan. And I am surprised that you two are so ready to acquiesce to him. Where is your sense of adventure, not to mention right and wrong?"

"I guess my sense of adventure doesn't include digging ditches," said Nathan.

"On the contrary," argued Efstathios. "I have heard you and Joram discuss that tunnel you dug many-a-time."

"He's got you there, Nathan," said Joram. "That was an interesting period in our lives. But, Efstathios, I still think this is a bad idea."

Ignoring Joram's words, Efstathios bent over the skeleton and gently removed the pugio from the woman and baby's rib cages. He then said, "Sos, would you mind helping me carry the remains into the woods? I understand if you do not wish to go against your master's bidding. But we have to carry her into the woods whether we burn or bury her. We can't light a fire here. It would discolor the stone."

Sos began to pick up some of the bones, and Joram bent over to help him, to Efstathios's surprise.

"Here," muttered Nathan, also making a contribution. "Take my blanket to wrap them in."

Sos and Efstathios walked the remains out of the theatre to the adjacent woods to the north while Joram and Nathan stayed in the theatre and slouched down on the seats to relax.

〰〰〰

Half an hour later, George arrived in the theatre, and Joram and Nathan told him what was going on.

"It sounds like the story of *Antigone*," George said.

Joram and Nathan chuckled with amazement. "That is exactly what Efstathios said."

"It is strange, though, what you are telling me," George continued. "You say you found a skeleton here in the theatre? Right here, where that large tree branch used to be?"

"Yes. She was behind the branch."

"I told you this place was haunted. But I didn't know there was literally a corpse watching over it. How did it survive all these years, unnoticed? I guess the old timers were right. And you are certain that she was one of the massacre victims?"

"Reasonably sure, based on what Efstathios said." They described Efstathios's theory to him. "And there were two little pouches right next to her," they added. "One had money and the other had a little gold lar."

"What did you say?" George asked, suddenly looking disturbed by that additional information.

Joram repeated, "There was a bag of money next to her, mostly from Claudius's reign, and a little golden lar."

"How much money was it?" George asked.

"About a month's wages or so."

George's face suddenly turned ashen. He stared blankly in front of him with his mouth hanging slightly open, as if a horrible thought had entered his head.

"Are you all right, cousin?" they both asked.

"What?" he responded, trying to recover himself. "Yes, yes. I am fine. Some money and a gold statue you said?"

"Yes. Some money and a little gold statue."

As if he were in another world, George asked, "And where are those items now? I don't see them."

"Vitus took them."

"Oh. Vitus took them?" he repeated absent-mindedly. "Vitus took them," he repeated a second time. He then sat down on a stone seat, looking pensive.

"What is it, cousin?" they asked again. "Does it bother you that there was money and a lar found next to the body? Does that mean something?"

"No, no. Not in the least. It doesn't mean anything. I was… simply remembering something I have to do today. I'll be back in a couple of hours. I am working on one of the apartments." He got up to leave. "I will be back." He walked up the theatre stairs, stopping every now and then as if he were too lost in thought to take the next step. Then he disappeared out the exit.

"I wonder what's wrong with him," said Joram.

"I don't know. You'd think he knew the woman," responded Nathan.

XIV

Ayathe was not herself that evening. As the boys returned from work and the girls finished dinner preparations under the pergola in the courtyard, she barely said a word to anyone.

"Where are Ducetius and cousin George?" Nathan asked her, trying to make conversation. "We haven't seen your nephew in two days, and we only saw cousin George for a few minutes this morning."

Ayathe tried to put a pleasant face over whatever troubled her, but it was not convincing. "I expect they will both be here soon," she said. Then, lowering her voice and drawing the boys inside for a moment away from the girls, she said, "Cousin George asked me to request that you not mention a word about your discussion with him this morning to anyone until he has had a chance to speak to you about it first."

"Of course, Auntie," they all said. "We won't say a thing."

They sat down in the andron, and the girls began to serve them. Shortly after, George and Ducetius entered. Before George took a seat, he cast a glance toward Ayathe, who winked at him to convey she had passed his message.

As they ate, the boys did an admirable job avoiding discussion about the day's events. But it was not easy. Even though the girls, including Ayathe, Elisheva, and Nathan's mother, ate separately from the men by tradition, the only topic the girls wanted to discuss was 'the skeleton lady,' as Ayathe's youngest daughter had nicknamed her. The girls had looked forward all day to hearing an update on the situation from the men, especially since they were strictly forbidden to discuss the matter outside the house; but Ayathe put the kibosh on that entire line of inquiry.

"Let the men eat," she said several times. "Don't bother them. Maybe you can ask them about it a little later."

Of course, Ducetius was curious for an update too, and it was hardest of all to keep him in the dark. He had only learned about the skeleton from his little cousins the night before and had not seen it himself at all. If he were to ask a question, no one would want to withhold an answer.

George described the barest facts he thought were safe: that Vitus had come to the theatre and asked that the body be disposed of. He also shared his surprise that a body had been found at all and that somehow everyone else knew about it—even Vitus—before he did. He retold the story of the massacre and asked Efstathios to show everyone the pugio. In that way he managed to steer the conversation clear of the real issue at hand, which as of yet had not been disclosed to anyone but Ayathe.

"So we can't see the skeleton lady anymore?" asked Ayathe's youngest.

"No, we can't see her anymore," answered George. "You heard what master Vitus said. But we can talk about it amongst ourselves, and maybe someday we'll figure it all out."

As it grew dark, everyone readied for bed, but George quietly asked Nathan, Joram, and Efstathios to take a walk with him outside.

It was a moonlit night, and the streets looked eerie as the four made their way through the northeast sector of town. The light and shadows reminded Nathan of his night in the Temple.

George led the three of them to the Rock of Cerere, where he had first told Nathan the story of Persephone. He now began a very different tale.

"Nathan," he said, "you already know the circumstances under which my cousins were enslaved."

"Yes," he answered. "You told me when I first arrived on this island that Ducetius's father worked at the latifundium when some items went missing. And that is why Ducetius's whole family was arrested and sold."

"You have a good memory." He hesitated to speak further, looking all around him to make sure they were completely alone.

"For all these years," he continued, "I have lived with the belief that my cousin was innocent of the crime of which he was accused.

I was tortured by the thought that he had been enslaved unjustly, and that there was no one to appeal his case to. He and Ducetius, and my cousin's lovely wife, Ayathe's sister, were falsely accused, or so I thought, and sold into servitude." He stopped again.

The three remained silent and stared into George's eyes shining in the moonlight, waiting intently for what he was going to say next.

"But today," he resumed, "I learned that my cousin was probably not innocent after all. The items that were found in the theatre by the skeleton…" he paused… "…they were the very items that went missing from the latifundium…" He began to get choked up. "…They were the very items that my cousin was accused of taking." He paused again, hurriedly wiping each eye as though that might hide his emotion.

"Do you mean," asked Joram, "that your cousin killed that woman, and she was not a victim of the massacre?"

"No," George responded, surprised at the misunderstanding. "That's not what I'm saying at all. My cousin did not kill that woman. He didn't kill anyone. But he stole those items, and their location next to that skeleton incriminates him with more proof than I ever thought existed."

"But I don't understand," commented Nathan. "How does their placement convince you that your cousin was the one guilty of the crime? Why would those items being there, as opposed to somewhere else, make him seem guilty in your mind?"

"I told you," George explained, "that my cousin was haunted by the story of that massacre—even a little crazed by it. I believe he actually stole those items in reaction to it. I think my cousin found that skeleton behind that tree years ago. He never told me about it, and even the one time I visited the theatre with him late at night, he never showed it to me. I think now, in hindsight, that he was going to show it to me, but I grew uncomfortable there and impatient with him and thought we should leave, so I never saw it. And he kept it a secret till the day he was taken. But he became obsessed with that massacre, and he often talked about taking whatever revenge he could on the Romans for what they had done to our people and still continue to do."

"So what are you thinking?" asked Joram. "That your cousin stole the money and the lar out of some act of vengeance against the Romans at the latifundium for a massacre that occurred centuries prior?"

"Yes, that is precisely my thought. My cousin was not a thief.

I never knew him to be greedy for money, and he was not dishonest in the least. Theft for theft's sake was not in his character. He was content with his family, his art, and his ideas—though as I've told you, his ideas often troubled him. So I know he heisted those items for some other reason, with some plan, or at least some idea, warped and illogical as it might have been. His mind was not always quite right."

"If he was normally an honest man, as you say," conjectured Nathan, "then what you say makes sense, looking at the evidence. If his goal was merely to steal in order to get money, he would not have left the loot where he did—by the skeleton, outside, exposed—rather than hidden in his home. And if someone else had stolen the items, it would have been completely illogical for them to have left the items there as well."

"I agree. That makes sense," said Joram, "But if it was your cousin, why *did* he put them there then? If it wasn't safe, and he couldn't even use the money while it was located so far from his home, it would serve no practical purpose being next to the skeleton..."

"Except," interrupted Efstathios, "as a symbol for something."

"A symbol?" asked Joram. "Of what?"

"Maybe of Rome?" surmised Efstathios.

"Seriously? A symbol of Rome?" questioned Nathan. "Does anyone really think that deeply or convolutedly?"

"Yes," exclaimed George. "My cousin did. And that is exactly what I was thinking. He was not an ordinary fellow. I completely believe that his theft was a symbolic gesture. Everything he did had an artistic or dramatic flare to it. I can easily see how the money and the god are symbols of Rome. I can even see how the mother and child he put them next to could be symbols of Sicily—a type of Kore Demeter and Kore Persephone—destroyed by Roman greed. Is that going too far? Perhaps I am reading into it too much in my attempt to make sense of it."

"You might be reading too much into it," said Nathan, "but it sounds interesting. Keep going."

"I don't think it sounds farfetched at all," exclaimed Efstathios. "To me it all makes perfect sense."

"Of course it makes perfect sense to you," responded Nathan. "But so does defying Vitus because of a Sophocles play."

"What can I say?" said Efstathios. "I too believe in symbolic gestures. So I think I can understand how cousin George's theory is entirely plausible."

"What do *you* think, Nathan?" asked Joram.

"I see the theft on a more basic vengeance level. Stealing Roman money and a Roman god would be the perfect way to make a Roman angry."

"It is. But since you mention it, that is also what makes them so believable as Roman symbols," said Joram. "They hit at the very heart of the Roman character. That is why their loss made the latifundium owner and manager angry enough to enslave an entire family over them, including a young child."

"Aach," said Nathan in disgust. "Their pride was just affronted, and they couldn't let the thief go unpunished. I think it's as simple as that."

"But what did Auntie think of your theory?" Joram asked George. "Based on her behavior at dinner tonight, you clearly discussed it with her before we got there."

"Yes, I did. When I first told her about it, she did not connect the contents of the pouches with my cousin's theft. But once I reminded her, she found my theory completely plausible, given my cousin's state of mind at the time. Once we started talking about it, she even remembered him ranting about taking revenge on Rome."

"Then that almost settles it for me," affirmed Joram. "Ayathe is as good a judge of character as anyone I know. If she believes your theory, I probably do too."

"But what preoccupies me most right now," continued George, "even more than having found proof of my cousin's guilt—and that is bad enough—is the thought of what might happen if someone at the latifundium sees those items and remembers what they are, connecting them back to my family and to me all over again. When you told me that Vitus took the pouches, all I could think of was that someone at the villa might recognize them so that the entire issue could reopen. Ducetius could be incriminated a second time, and something worse could befall him, or I could be held responsible. But my greatest worry is Ducetius. If something happened to him, I couldn't bear it. It was difficult enough the first time around. A second time would kill us, especially Ayathe. It's not safe here for Ducetius anymore. I may have to send him away, but I don't know where. It would break Ayathe's heart to part with him, as it would mine. He is like the son neither of us ever had. But there may be no other way, and I am sick with worry about it."

"I noticed you hardly ate tonight," said Efstathios.

"I could not eat. It was all I could do to play the bard until I had a chance to talk to all of you."

"You played it well," complimented Nathan.

"I think for now," said Joram, "it might be best to act as if nothing has happened. There may be no one left at the villa who even knows about the theft, let alone anyone there who ever saw those items. Is there anyone you can think of?"

"No. The former owner and Demaratos are both gone, as far as I know, and the turnover in slaves is fairly regular. It's possible there is still a house slave who might remember the incident, but most likely the new owner brought his own batch with him, and the old ones are gone."

"We can find out tomorrow whether the items meant anything to anyone at the estate house."

"What do you mean?" asked George.

"Efstathios can ask Vitus tomorrow how his master liked the little lar, and he could perhaps offer to sell it again. Then we can gauge from his answer whether anyone at the latifundium attributed any significance to the items. And if Efstathios is able to wrest the lar from Vitus's hands to sell it, then no one else on the latifundium will ever see it, and we may have dodged a major incident."

"That is a brilliant idea," responded Efstathios. "I was planning on asking him that very thing tomorrow anyway."

"But," continued Joram, "I would keep Ducetius away from the theatre job for the next few days. Keep him busy on one of the other properties—anything. If you can spare me at the theatre, I'd like to stay with Ducetius just to make sure he's safe."

"No," said George. "I don't want Ducetius out of my sight."

"I don't think that would be wise, cousin," said Nathan. "You two should stay separate. That way if the issue arises, it will be harder for them to find both of you if you are in different locations. You should stay with Auntie."

"Maybe you're right. That might be better. And Ayathe needs protection as well," George agreed. "And no doubt there are plenty of things to keep me busy at her place. But I must have your word that you will say nothing of this to anyone, particularly Ducetius. I may have to tell him the story at some point, especially if I make plans to send him somewhere. But you must leave it to me. He cannot hear it from anyone else. Do I have your word?"

"You have it," they all responded.

They stood on the rock silently, looking into the night and to the east, where the brooding silhouette of Etna loomed like a patch of starless sky near the horizon.

XV

As the projected time approached for the reopening of the theatre, much needed to be done and much needed to be undone. Among the tasks needing to be done was the acquisition of a theatre troupe and a play manuscript to inaugurate the opening day. Concerning the latter, Efstathios had already set in motion the process of procurement, having spoken with Vitus, who discussed the matter with Funisulanus, who contacted his friends back in Rome, who suggested he communicate with the praetor in Syracuse, who had connections with the two main actors' guilds there, who then spoke to each other: the one guild being the Artists of Dionysius, and the other the Artists of the Jolly Aphrodite.

Of the two guilds in question, that of the Jolly Aphrodite was the more responsive. Though both guilds specialized in mimes, the guild of Dionysius sometimes performed plays in Latin for Roman colonies. The guild of the Jolly Aphrodite, on the other hand, sometimes performed among Greek colonies in Greek. Since Enna was largely Greek, the Jolly Aphrodite made preparations to perform there, though none of its members had ever been.

The process of acquisition took a full half year. In addition to the slowness of the courier system from the interior to the coast, as well as ships back and forth across the Tyrrhenian Sea, the messages themselves had to wade through bureaucratic channels before they could even reach the Praetor, then from him to the guilds, and from the guild masters to the librarians of Syracuse, who housed the best copies of the Greek plays.

Had Funisulanus desired a Roman drama, he would have found a manuscript more easily, since those of Seneca were still in current circulation. But he thought it important, unlike any of his predecessors, to ingratiate himself with the local Sicels by trying to stage a play in a language they could understand. Latin had made some inroads among the coastal Sicilian cities, especially in the Roman colonies in Syracuse, Catania, and Taormina. In Enna, however, there was scarce a Latin speaker apart from the latifundium owner and manager. Even George could only read it, not speak it.

Funisulanus followed in the rare ilk of Cicero and the writer Pliny the Elder, who both took notice of Sicily's plight in a Roman world that generally ignored it. Not that his main concern—or Cicero's or Pliny's for that matter—was completely altruistic or would ever amount to a shred of real change for Roman Sicily, but the idea of improving the town next to his estate even for his own selfish ends gave him something productive to do during the years in which he intermittently resided there, and it had some benefit for the Ennans as well.

Funisulanus's quest to find a good Greek tragedy was complicated by the fact that little survived from the classical tragedians. Of the hundreds of works penned by Aeschylus, Euripides, and Sophocles—all of whom had dominated the various Dionysian festivals with award-winning scripts in past centuries—only tens of them still existed by the first century AD, and that number would continue to dwindle. The sole survivors were mostly those that found their way into Roman curricula during the imperial era as examples for students. Otherwise, everything else except for an occasional title or pithy phrase embedded in another written work perished through disuse and copying inertia.

Efstathios put in a special request for a script of *Antigone*, one of the few surviving classical tragedies. Vitus handed the request to his master, not even knowing what the play was about, and Funisulanus, with the zeal of a convert excited to know the title of any Greek play, included its name in his letters. At every step, it was clear that there was no guarantee *Antigone* would ever be found. In fact, the Aphrodite guild master sent word that a manuscript from the *Oresteia* might be both easier to access and more popular with a Sicilian audience since Aeschylus briefly lived in Syracuse and died in Gela, where he was buried.

In the end, a copy of *Antigone* was, in fact, procured. But by then, circumstances were such that Efstathios regretted his original request. And thus began the long list of items that needed to be *und*one.

The burial of the skeleton lady was chief among them. Word had gotten out about the workers' find, and the entirety of Enna was abuzz with the news. "So the theatre really *was* haunted all these years." "I hear the Romans tried to burn the body to get rid of the evidence." "The theatre can't be reopened now." "It has a curse on it." "Did you hear where that woman is buried?" "I certainly did, and my niece placed a little offering on top of the grave."

When Vitus caught wind of the fact that there was a rumor circulating, he flew into a rage. "How does the whole town know about that blasted skeleton? And why wasn't the body burned like I asked? I knew this was going to happen! You cannot leave a morbid relic like that in a superstitious backwater like this! Whose idea was it to bury that thing? I blame *you!*" he howled at Efstathios. "You will pay for that slip up!"

Back on the latifundium, Vitus began the process of having every one of the slaves whipped to extract a confession from the mole who leaked the information. The slaves were called out en masse to one of the fields to watch the bloody spectacle. When the third victim, a lovely weeping teenager named Lois, was about to be tied to the whipping post, Sos suddenly spoke up and confessed to the crime. He hadn't actually done it, but he could not stand by and watch that poor young girl, who had just arrived in chains at the latifundium the previous week and was terrified as it was, be torn by the lash. Instead, he submitted himself to such a brutal lacerating that skin was hanging off his back, protruding through the blood, and he was thrown unconscious into an iron chamber in the hot Sicilian sun to starve and roast to death. The latifundium managers referred to the chamber as the Brazen Bull, after a horrific legend of a Sicilian tyrant named Phalaris of Agrigento, who cooked criminals in a heated cast-bronze bull, the internal mechanisms of which transformed its victim's screams into the bellowing of the animal. The latifundium chamber was not shaped like a bull, but just as Vitus was contemplating the idea of recasting it as one, a delegation from the town arrived and interrupted his malevolent scheme.

"What do they want?" Vitus asked his assistant angrily.

"They wish to speak to Lord Funisulanus to stop the theatre renovation, sir. They say it is bringing bad luck to the town."

"Bad luck to the town?" He stomped over to speak to the men: a motley and elderly crew, though possessing a certain dignity Vitus did not anticipate.

"We would like to speak to Lord Funisulanus," they said.

"I am Lord Funisulanus," said Vitus. "What do you want?"

"Pardon me, sir, but you are not Lord Funisulanus," said the leader. "We have never seen Lord Funisulanus, but we know you are not he."

"No one speaks directly to Lord Funisulanus. I am the manager here. What is it you want? Be quick about it."

"The town has sent us to ask you kindly to put off your renovations of the old amphitheatre."

"For what reason could you possibly desire that?"

"We believe, good sir, that it is bringing ill fortune upon our city."

"Ill fortune? The only good fortune this town has experienced in two centuries is its Roman lord, who cares enough to overhaul the town's greatest monument. When was the last time you had a functioning amphitheatre?"

They answered, "Not since the unfortunate incident commemorated by the recent finding."

"What are you talking about?"

"We are referring to the massacre that took place in the theatre some centuries before and the last remaining skeletal victim from it, discovered the other day."

"Who told you about the skeletal victim?"

"The entire city knows of it. People are visiting the victim's grave."

"I daresay that is more than the town will do for any of you. And what of the victim and the grave? Can you not see what a boon the renovation will be for this town?"

"Frankly, sir, we cannot. The skeleton is an ill omen."

"It is nothing of the kind," Vitus responded with patrician disdain. "Surely you can raise your thoughts above such common superstition. The skeleton is, in fact, a good omen: it is the last victim of the massacre speaking to us from the past, putting her blessing on our entire current endeavor."

"Perhaps that is a possibility. We will have to discuss that point of view amongst ourselves," said one of the elders. "I am not sure I can readily concur with you, with all due respect; but there may be some merit to what you are saying."

Vitus grew further impatient, wondering why he should continue such an inane conversation. "There is a great deal of merit to what I am saying," he said haughtily. "But of course, you hadn't thought of the incident in that light. You and your townspeople are too preoccupied in your downtrodden misery to think of it that way—the only town in Sicily without a working theatre, while Syracuse, Catania, and Taormina all boast splendid ones. You hadn't thought of the fact that perhaps we, who are trying to elevate your status to that of the other cities on this forsaken island, are the best fortune to befall you in generations. The problem with you provincials is that you don't know a good thing when you see it! My master has poured his own personal fortune into this town, and you respond as if you were being massacred all over again! Now be gone with you. And you can be sure that I will convey your sentiments to my lord."

"We meant no offense, sir," said one of the men. "We rather thought the generous attitude of your master might promote an understanding between us."

"You thought sending a delegation of this nature might promote an understanding? Rather, it demonstrates that you have none." He called for one of his assistants. "Escort these gentlemen off the premises."

And so they left, disgruntled, and Vitus assumed he had gotten rid of them.

The next day, however, Vitus showed up at the theatre, and there was a mob near the entrance blocking his access.

"What in Hades is going on here?" Vitus asked Efstathios. "Why aren't the men working? And what are these townspeople doing here?"

Efstathios answered, "The men are afraid to work. Their neighbors are clamoring for us to desist in the renovation."

"We shall do nothing of the kind!" Vitus retorted, raising his voice above the din. "Did you try to speak to them?"

"Yes," replied Efstathios, also straining his voice. "But I made little headway. We need Sos. He could convince them that we should continue. But I have no idea where Sos is. Where is he? Do you know?"

"Forget Sos. Where are Joram, George, and the others? Not one of them is here!"

"Nathan went to find George, and I don't know where Joram or Ducetius are, but I wish Sos was here."

"Who is Ducetius?"

"What?"

"You mentioned someone named Ducetius," said Vitus. "Never mind. I will speak to this rabble myself." Vitus tried to cut through the crowd to speak from atop the outer theatre wall.

Just then Nathan appeared with George in tow.

"Thank the gods you are here," said Vitus to George, pulling him aside. "You need to speak to your superstitious neighbors. The town sent a delegation to me yesterday to stop the renovation because of the skeleton. You need to explain to them that the skeleton is a good omen for the theatre, not a bad one. I told them yesterday the woman was left as a messenger from the past to the present to bless our endeavor. You must corroborate my story."

"I will do what I can."

George climbed onto a ruined lower portion of the outer theatre wall, right where Efstathios had joked about erecting the statue of Nathan. Vitus called for the silent bodyguards to brandish their swords. Efstathios and Nathan stood by in mute support, waiting for what George would say.

In a moment that reminded Nathan of one of Joseph's stadium speeches, George raised his arms to ask for quiet. The madding crowd quelled.

"My fellow townsmen," George began, "Aristo, Abantes, Thoőn, please allow me to speak." He waited for silence, in good theatrical form. The three neighbors he had just called upon helped calm the others down. "You know our good Lord Funisulanus has graced us with the funds and manpower to resurrect this theatre—a monument of which our ancestors were once proud. We have been left without a theatre for centuries because of the unfortunate event that occurred here so long ago. But now we have received a sign from the gods that this theatre can be reopened to give our people pride again and perhaps even a little entertainment in the midst of our toil."

"You call that skeleton a sign?" someone from the crowd interrupted. "I call it an omen of death!"

The crowd started yelling again.

George waited for the right moment to resume. "Yes, I call it a sign. You should have seen her face. It wore a smile, even after all these centuries, telling us that she approved of what we were doing, and that future generations—like the little child she held at her bosom—were not meant to stop living but to rebuild their lives and the town. And that is what we are doing now."

Nathan was impressed. How did George come up with that tale? "And he never even saw the skeleton," he whispered to Efstathios.

Vitus was impressed too. He suddenly reached into his satchel and pulled out the lar that was still in it and, looking to George for an in, jumped onto the wall beside George and said, "And this

Roman lar was found at the woman's side: a talisman indicating her approval of Roman help in rebuilding your town and this theatre."

The appearance of the lar made George very uneasy, though no one in the crowd could possibly have seen it before or associate it with his cousin's theft. It looked like any one of a thousand other lars, except that it was gold. But George swallowed his fear and put on a good face for the crowd, actor that he was.

Vitus continued. "From now on, let this theatre stand a tribute to the friendship of Rome and Enna. We know it has stood a monument to enmity and cruelty for all these centuries. But now the gods want it to stop. They have given us the sign of their unity—Roman gods and Sicel gods together: Demeter and Persephone right next to the lar of Mars."

Vitus did not mean a word of what he was saying, but his analysis of the find was so frighteningly close to George's own take on the skeleton's symbolism of Demeter and Persephone that he began to sweat. Was it possible that Vitus had overheard their conversation on Cerere the other night? Nathan and Efstathios had the same thought and looked at each other in worry.

Someone yelled out from the crowd again, however. "If you thought it was such a good sign from the gods, then why was it kept a secret until now?"

Vitus thought fast on his feet again. "It was not kept a secret," he responded. "We were simply unsure what it all meant when we first found it. We had to make inquiries and auguries as to the nature of the sign and were prepared to follow whatever conclusions they led us to. But now that we know, we have no issue with letting others know as well. We simply had to be sure ourselves first."

Despite the utter discomfort George felt, he could perceive that his co-speech with Vitus was having a positive effect on the crowd. He, Nathan, Efstathios, and Vitus could all see people beginning to smile as they lowered whatever implements they held up as weapons down to their sides.

George made a few closing remarks, then he climbed off the wall to speak with some of his neighbors. Vitus, despite himself, walked over to one of the faces he recognized from the delegation the day before and said, feigning diplomacy, "I trust, then, that we may have your support for this project. And I, on my part, will convey the town's thanks to my lord, rather than the sentiments I am now grateful I did not have the opportunity to mention yesterday."

The elder was a bit skeptical of the Roman's friendliness, but he responded, "I too trust that this might inaugurate a new era for Enna."

///////

After the crowd dispersed, Vitus directed everyone to get back to work. While the laborers resumed their stations, several of them asked where Sos was.

"He is not here today," snapped Vitus. "You—" he pointed to one of them—"take charge in his place."

Efstathios then walked over to Vitus and complimented him on his laudable performance before the mob. "How did you ever think of that story, and so quickly?"

"To vouchsafe this theatre," Vitus responded, "I could perform a tragedy, a comedy, a satyr play, whatever it takes. Acting has its uses—though Romans do not generally respect it, and I myself have little patience for it."

Efstathios then asked Vitus about the lar. "And did Lord Funisulanus like the lar you so ingeniously employed in your little show? Or hasn't he seen it yet, since it is still in your pouch?"

"He has not seen it yet," replied Vitus.

"Will you be showing it to him tonight?"

"I don't know. Why do you ask?"

"No reason. But I was thinking that if he is not interested in keeping it, I would still like to see what price it might fetch on the market."

"I thought we discussed that already, and I said I did not wish to sell it."

"You did," responded Efstathios. "But after all you went through yesterday and again this morning because of this incident, I thought I would make the offer again, since a little extra income off the whole ordeal might seem attractive to you."

"Well, it doesn't," snapped Vitus.

Efstathios, frustrated by Vitus's sudden intransigence, and unwilling to lose the battle over the lar, foolishly pushed the issue further. "But I think it really would get you a very nice return," he said.

"Not as nice a return," seethed Vitus, "as denying you the satisfaction of a sale. If you had simply done what I had asked in burning those remains, yesterday and this morning would never have happened. So the answer is no. The only reason I'm not contemplating the termination of your employ at this very moment is because that little lar brought me luck this morning, and I'm feeling magnanimous. I might even keep it for myself in my satchel for good fortune, if that is not too sacrilegious. But don't press your luck with me any further."

Foiled in his attempt to wrest the lar from Vitus, Efstathios tried to hide his feelings and changed the subject back to Sos, which he thought was neutral and safe. The topic of Sos, however, riled Vitus even further, since he did not wish to discuss or justify his placing of the renovation team's most valuable worker in a roasting pot.

Thus, when Efstathios innocently asked, "Where did you say Sos is today?" Vitus flew into a rage again.

"Nowhere that concerns you!" Vitus barked. "I told you not to press your luck with me any further! He'll be back in a few days, when *I* choose him to be." And with that, he turned and left.

It was clear from Vitus's reactions to Efstathios that Efstathios had dug himself into a hole. Not only did he now wish he could undo the entire burial episode—except, perhaps, to switch places with the skeleton lady—but he wished he could retract his long-posited request for the *Antigone* play, which would now seem like another slap in the face to Vitus's directive once he saw it performed. He knew it was unlikely that a copy of the play would be found. But in light of the new downturn in his fortunes, it was entirely likely that it *would* be found. But what could he do? Should he talk to Vitus about it? That did not seem like a good idea. Vitus was already annoyed with him. Should he proffer a trip to Syracuse to ensure that another play, perhaps from the recommended *Oresteia*, be found instead? That seemed too complicated, and his life was already chaotic. Besides, he couldn't leave Enna with the date of the reopening so near.

But how had he failed to get the lar out of Vitus's hands? It was such a simple task! He thought of a thousand ways he could have reworded his conversation with Vitus, but now he had to face George, Joram, and Nathan with his bungle. And Nathan would remind him, no doubt, that his devotion to *Antigone* was the source of Vitus's antagonism toward him.

So much needed to be undone, Efstathios felt like he was drowning. He had even let Ducetius's name slip out, which could never be taken back. And on top of all his other problems, Elisheva was pregnant again.

Not that pregnancy in and of itself was a bad thing. But in Elisheva's case it was because she always became dangerously ill. During the current instance she was fine for the first trimester, with no more than the usual morning sickness. But now, at the end of the second trimester, her health was worse, and she began to look emaciated. And everyone looked askance at Efstathios as if he were to blame for Elisheva's condition.

Of course, Efstathios was, in fact, responsible. But was it not normal for a man to sleep with his wife, and wasn't her expectancy something that should have gained him respect among his fellows? But in his case, it did not. Efstathios, it seemed, could not do anything right in people's eyes. Not even romance. If he practiced it as he used to, it was perversion. If he engaged in it with his wife, it was murder. He sometimes felt like the abused land of Sicily: not really good in and of himself, but only there to do others' bidding. And heaven forbid he should step beyond anyone's expectations to make himself happy, whether it be to bury a dead woman or to make love to a living one. He had a function to fulfill for others, and there was nothing in it for him. He was overlooked, especially when compared to brilliant Joram, adorable Ducetius, sagacious George, and Mr. Marvelous Nathan. He received little admiration for any of the fine qualities he himself possessed.

Although he held great promise, and could be brilliant, charming, good-looking, and knowledgeable about trade, theology, history, and culture, Efstathios had never found a home in the world. He had moved from the debauchery of Corinth to the religious community in Pella to the boondocks of Sicily, and he had succeeded materially in all three places. He also had made a friend in Joram, a partner in Elisheva, and what seemed like a healthy competitor in Nathan. But his life seemed worthless after his discussion with Nathan in the palaestra—or rather, that discussion revealed to him just how tenuous his position in life really was. He already knew his wife was close to Nathan, but he did not realize just how far he lagged behind Nathan in the contest for her affections. While he and Elisheva had lived in Pella, and Nathan was a distant memory, Elisheva's love for Efstathios seemed real and focused, and he thought he had found something to replace the former life he had lived. But now in Sicily, with Nathan a very physical presence in all their lives—in Joram's, his own, and Elisheva's—he was reminded all too keenly of the life he had left behind and sometimes missed, and he perceived how much he stood in second place in the hearts of both Elisheva and

Joram, a thought almost too painful to bear. He came to the conclusion that he had been merely a Nathan-substitute for both of them during the Pella years, and now that 'perfection' had come, he, the imperfect, could disappear.

Nathan often spoke to Efstathios, despite the tension in their relationship, to try to comfort him. Efstathios believed he was always in second place with the people who meant the most to him and that there was no one in the world for whom he was the most important. But Nathan, who had lived in the shadow of giants like his father, Amram, and Joseph, also knew what it was like to feel unimportant. Here in Sicily, his status had changed, and he was revered by everyone—Ayathe, George, Joram, Elisheva, and Efstathios himself. But that had not always been the case, Nathan informed Efstathios, and there was no irrevocable destiny to which they were all assigned—some to greatness, some to obscurity, some to mediocrity. Life was not a Greek play, but time and chance happened to them all, Nathan reminded him. And even if that were not entirely true, and the Almighty spun their stories from his lofty position from beginning to end, men were not privy to such designs, and it was none of men's business to think about them. People were given enough latitude in the scriptures to make of themselves what they could in this life. "So don't worry, my dark-cloud complainer," Nathan told Efstathios. "There is always hope. Things can change in a moment in heaven's economy. The mighty city may become a ruin, the slave may become free, and the nobody can become a hero."

XVI

Two marriages took place in the midst of all the turmoil. George wed Ayathe in the spring of AD 79, after years of everyone wondering, 'Why don't the two of them just get married?' and, 'They've been friends and business partners for years, and she's a widow and he's a widower.' And the same day, Joram wed Adah, who had been scheming for that eventuality with Joram's passive consent since the moment he had arrived three years prior.

Adah sometimes wondered why she was so in love with Joram now, when she had never felt that way about him as a child back in Jerusalem. Maybe, she thought, it was because she was only six and he was twelve years her senior, he was Amram's contemporary, and his association with her older brother cast him in a negative light. But it was hard to believe that that could have been the reason, since maturity and forbidden fruit often have a great appeal. She also thought that maybe it was because he was a neighbor and was simply part of the scenery. But he was part of the scenery now, and she very much noticed him. Eventually she concluded that he must have been very different when he was younger than he was now— uglier, stupider, or something. What else could it have been? She couldn't remember. She hadn't seen him since she was six, and now she was eighteen. Not that the first thought anyone had of Joram, even now, including her, was that he was strikingly handsome. He wasn't striking, at least not particularly. But he was manly, interesting, gentle, leaderly, utterly dependable, and always knew exactly what he was talking about. And he certainly wasn't unpleasant looking. In her view, and as is often the case between friends, he was on par with Nathan, who, despite possessing every obnoxious quality a brother could possibly posses, also had an undefinable 'something' that made him attractive. Besides all the attributes commending him, Joram was also the only eligible bachelor she knew in Enna besides Ducetius, and she couldn't possibly marry Ducetius. Although she had always loved Ducetius—everyone loved Ducetius—it seemed socially inappropriate to marry one's freedman, and she didn't think her mother or Nathan would allow it. And so she married Joram. Everyone loved Joram too.

As for Joram, he found Adah possessed of all the wit and fun and prettiness he never thought he would find in a partner. Not that he had been looking for anyone. He had always been content with singlehood, unlike every other person anyone knew. Perhaps that was another quality that made him attractive. But Nathan's sister was the first girl he had ever met in his life who even made the thought cross his mind that 'perhaps, maybe, it would not be the most terrible thing in the world to get married.' She was absolutely adorable in how she followed him around, and he never minded. She was bright, but she was not intellectual the way Nathan, Amram, Efstathios, and Elisheva were. Her education had been interrupted by the war, her sojourn in Joppa with her mother, and her family's migration to Sicily. But she was always eager to learn.

The most endearing quality she had was that she would simply ask Joram questions, and Joram loved that. For instance, one day she asked him, "You knew both my father and my brother for years, and I know they both always fought. Who did you agree with more?" And he explained how his views had changed over time from that of her brother to that of her father; but, in short, that he at one point or another had agreed with both. Another time she asked him, "Solomon had a lot of wives. Which one of them do you think was his favorite?" And she listened as Joram expounded on the possibilities of the Shunamite, or Pharaoh's daughter, or Naamah the mother of his heir, or perhaps even the Queen of Sheba, though the scriptures did not mention a romance between them. In her own opinion, she liked the Queen of Sheba option best because it sounded the most exotic (had she known any Ethiopians, they would have concurred). And another day, while she was preparing food under the makeshift pergola in the courtyard, she asked him, "Why do you think that man you talk about was the messiah?" And the answer to that question, which she did not find nearly so unbelievable as her brother made it seem she would, attached her to him like nothing else and sealed their matrimonial trajectory. But even with that question, as with all their discussions, she was conscious not to overstay her welcome in Joram's presence, so that after they talked for what seemed like the perfect amount of time, she would politely excuse herself to attend another task—until the next time she had a question.

Nathan's mother was thrilled, and a little nervous, to discuss the possibility of her daughter marrying Joram: thrilled to have Joram as a son-in-law, and nervous about Nathan's reaction to the whole idea. "If only my husband had lived to see this day," she told Joram. "He always wanted a union between our two families, and now it is going to happen." But to Nathan, in private, she said, "My beloved son, do not let it bother you that Joram and your sister are getting married. Your father and I always expected that you and Elisheva would be the ones to bind our families together. That, for the moment, however, is not the case. But please do not hold a grudge."

"There is no grudge, ima," he responded, though the irony of it all was not lost on him. And so Adah married Joram, and she loved him, and he loved her, and she never stopped asking him questions.

As for George and Ayathe, the debacle of the skeleton lady solidified for them what everyone around them already knew: that they shared a long past together and had everything in the world in common, including their beloved Ducetius, and there wasn't a reason in the world why they shouldn't get married. Even Ayathe's daughters would sometimes say they wished Uncle George could be their father. Everyone else had a father; why couldn't they? They had lost their father when the younger was three, and they loved Uncle George, who was a daily fixture in their lives, especially at dinnertime. He and Ayathe did not look like the model couple. She had grown prematurely stout and matronly, and he always had that disheveled middle-aged bachelor look that cried, 'I need help getting dressed.' But shortly after George began spending his days working at Ayathe's house, people noticed that Ayathe began to lose a little weight, and George started to look a little neater. Within months, their affection for each other, as well as that of Joram and Adah, became public, and wedding plans were in the making.

Of course, given the uncertainty of the times, the plans were made discreetly and on a small scale. It all had to take place on Ayathe's property for privacy's sake and for that of Elisheva, who wished to attend even if lying ill in bed. Thus Ayathe's courtyard was decorated for the occasion.

Although Ayathe and George could afford a lavish middle-class double wedding, they invited no one from the outside except two of George's oldest and most guarded friends and their sons to fulfill the required ten witnesses at a wedding. One of the friends had officiated at local weddings for years, and would play that role again. Customarily it might have been appropriate to invite Vitus, but everyone was afraid to do so. And though it would not have been appropriate, everyone wished they could have invited Sos.

The food for the wedding banquet was prepared with so much love by all of them that it could not have been anything but sumptuous: goat and lamb seasoned with garlic, onions, and sea salt from the shores around Palermo, where salt was first harvested in ancient times by the Carthaginians; a stew of spelt and pulses (dried peas, lentils, chickpeas, and other seeds), a favorite of the Greeks; cheeses made from goat and sheep milk, including a form of pecorino; a bread dip called moretum, borrowed from the Romans, made with some of the cheeses by mixing them with garden herbs till it had a greenish tint to it; bowls of grapes, apples, figs, pears, pomegranates, peaches recently available from Persia, and olives; garum, a fermented fish paste for seasoning food, popularized by the Greeks throughout the empire and made out of aged anchovies, mackerel, and sprats; a few expensive lemons and citrons just to add a little flavor and class; various wines from local vineyards, as well as a small amphora from the west coast, where the ancient Phoenicians and Elymians before them grew grapes that would develop into Marsala; wheat pancakes with almonds, dates, and honey, usually eaten for breakfast but specifically requested by Ayathe's daughters for the occasion; pork sausage, which Elisheva and Joram tried for the first time in their lives, while Nathan, observing *kashrut*, graciously declined; numerous loaves of fresh-baked bread, including one divisible into eight slices and covered with cheese; a vegetable assortment of lettuce, endive, radishes, celery, leeks, cucumbers and asparagus; and a type of egg custard cooked with honey.

If Plato had once complained that Sicilian Greeks were obsessed with food—apparent in the waistline and eating habits of Ayathe after the birth of her second daughter and her subsequent widowhood—one could have pointed to the wedding banquet in this quiet unassuming neighborhood in Enna as proof. The one culinary category absent from the affair was seafood, despite the fact that the oldest cookbook in the world, written by a Sicilian Greek, called for a special fish recipe with cheese. But seafood rarely survived transport to inland Enna, so George and Ayathe had to forego the idea—though it was perhaps serendipitous, since the *second* oldest cookbook in the world, *also* penned by a Sicilian Greek (Plato must have been right about the islanders' obsession with food), stated that Sicilians typically ruined fish dishes with cheese. In the end, fish or not, there was such an abundance of food at the wedding, featuring flavors from all over the empire and beyond, that the participants ate and ate until well into the night.

The marriage ceremony itself was by necessity anomalous and non-traditional, not only because it was a double wedding, but because of the single venue at which it was held, the single day on which it would occur—as opposed to multiple days for both Jews and Greeks—and the differences in faith between the two couples. There was no set ritual at the time for members of the Way, and Enna had no synagogue or house church other than Joram's to consult. Thus a combination of Greek, Roman, and Jewish customs was followed with modifications. Joram set about figuring out what those modifications might be, and George's discreet old friend discussed Joram's ideas with him. The friend was amenable to an eclectic ceremony; and where he was not, George asked him to be flexible. George trusted that whatever Joram masterminded for the ceremony would be agreeable to all the parties involved; and, in fact, it was. Joram discovered, however, that in some Roman traditions, the groom did not need to attend the wedding so long as the contracts were signed. He jested to his betrothed about taking that option, but she, of course, smiled and forbade him to even think about it.

Greco-Roman weddings commenced with an augury to bestow a blessing on the couple. On the wedding morning, George and Ayathe performed that ritual in Ayathe's house, while fifteen feet away, in the auxiliary apartment, Joram and his bride recited scripture and prayed for the day's success. Elisheva was there next to her brother, lying on a stretcher Nathan and Efstathios had constructed.

After the initial ceremonies, the two couples emerged from their respective houses, and stood under the makeshift pergola, which for Nathan's sister acted as a wedding canopy, and which for Ayathe was simply a novel and quaint idea. The younger bride wore a plain white dress; the elder, her finest outfit. In Greek fashion they both wore a veil. The old friend said a generic prayer to ward off evil and request a smooth transition from singlehood to marriage.

Since neither bride had a living father, they followed the Roman custom of the matron (in this case, Nathan's mother) giving her daughter away. For Ayathe, they used the Jewish custom of the male next of kin, Ducetius, to do the same for his aunt. The husbands then spoke some recited lines from their respective traditions to their wives. For the bridal response, which was usually something like the Roman phrase, 'Ubi tu Gaius, ego Gaia'—loosely meaning that where the husband leads, the wife will follow—the two brides agreed to simultaneously recite the words of Ruth from the Hebrew writings, which rendered the same sentiment in a longer form: "Where you go, I will go, and where you lodge I will lodge. Your people will be my people, and your God my God. Where you die, I will die, and there I will be buried. May heaven deal with me, be it ever so severely, if anything but death separates you and me." For Nathan's sister, they were endearing words she had heard her whole life. For Ayathe, the words were new and lovely, and she was happy to say them.

The climax of the ceremony came with the removal of the veils.

This occurred next. Once they were removed, it signified that the wife was no longer under the protection of her old family but under the protection of her husband's. With that, the husband was then permitted to kiss his new bride, and the ceremony came to an end. Afterward, everyone signed the two marriage contracts. The contracts loosely stated that the undersigned had witnessed the proceedings on such and such a date and that the marriage partners had entered into their relationships of their own accord. Had any of them been Roman citizens, especially a century earlier, the contract might have included mention that each of them possessed *conubia*, the right to marry under Roman law, since they were members of the same class and were neither slaves nor active soldiers at the time—both of which were denied the right to marry, according to Roman law.

Once the proceedings ended and the feasting began, there was no way to keep the occasion a secret in a neighborhood where everyone knew everyone's business. The neighbors heard laughing and singing and musical instruments. Efstathios, of course, knew how to play the lyre, and George and the girls all had flutes. Everyone on the block joined in on the celebration, and Ayathe welcomed them all. Ayathe and George were worried that the news might reach the latifundium, but as the days passed, it apparently never did. Vitus never indicated that he was cognizant of the event, and no one in the neighborhood was quick to tell of it. After all the difficulties the Sicels had been through in their history up to that point—and thousands of years of trouble still lay ahead—they had already begun to develop that mistrust of outsiders that has always been one of their hallmarks.

By the end of the evening, everyone was a little drunk, a little gorged, a little jovial, and a lot tired. Even Elisheva slept with contentment.

XVII

From the look of Sos's back, Vitus was clearly on the war path.

"What happened?" asked Efstathios, upon the slave's return to work two weeks prior to the wedding.

"Don't ask," snapped Vitus.

"I'm asking!" exclaimed Efstathios. "Is it right to whip the workers we need to a pulp and not at least consult with me first about it?"

"It was a latifundium matter," Vitus replied. "The slaves are latifundium property to be dispensed with as I see fit, just as you and your increasingly incompetent 'band of four' are under the direction of George and can be taken on and off the job as he sees fit."

"Yes. I understand all that. Still..." He looked again at Sos's tunic, with blood seeping through and dripping down the back of his legs. "He's going to soil the stonework. Don't you at least care about that?"

"The blood from the massacre disappeared, didn't it?"

It was due to Vitus's increasing belligerence, his treatment of Sos, and other reasons, that it was deemed unsafe to ask Vitus or Sos to the wedding. The main reason, however, was that George did not want Vitus to know how any of the members of the band were connected other than through mere employment. If Vitus discovered that Ducetius was his cousin's son, or that Joram, Nathan, and Efstathios were all brothers-in-law of a sort, it could lead to trouble for the entire group if the truth behind the lar and pouches was ever disclosed.

In the event Ducetius ever needed to escape, George sent a letter to a relative in Herculaneum on the Italian mainland, asking if Ducetius could stay with him if need be. Since he never heard back from the relative, George assumed the answer was yes, or that the relative was dead, or that the letter never reached its destination. Such was 'mail service' in the first century. Whatever the case, George felt he had a plan for Ducetius if things went awry. The hard part was informing Ducetius about his situation.

The news about his father left Ducetius distraught. He did not blame his father for what happened, but tried to understand his motivations instead. Ducetius trusted George that his father had been a good but troubled man, and he was consoled that George said there was a similarity between he and his father. If Ducetius were never to see his father again, at least he knew there was a bit of him in his face. And regarding his mother, George said she was a great deal like Ayathe, and that there was a strain of his mother in him as well.

George's warning about renewed danger from the latifundium came as a surprise to Ducetius. George told him he was arranging for an escape if necessary, and he assured George that he would be ready at a moment's notice with a satchel on hand. "But if I have to make my way to the mainland," he asked, "what would be the best way to get there?"

"It depends," George explained. "If you depart on good terms, then the royal road you used to come to Enna is the best route. You would follow it back east to Syracuse and book passage to Herculaneum. Herculaneum is a major port city, so you won't have any trouble getting there.

"However," he continued, "if you have to escape in secret, you must travel west, past the promontory down in the valley and over to the 'hill of tombs' where you can hide a few days. Then when it's safe, you can pick up the northern leg of the royal road from there, near one of the ancient pyramids, and continue up to the port of Thermae. You can book passage to Herculaneum from there also."

"So I have to hide in some tombs?" asked Ducetius.

"Yes. And that's where it gets tricky," George responded. "The tombs are dangerous because other escaped slaves might be hiding there too, but they're safe from the authorities because they're too risky and expensive to bother with. Rome has lost a lot of men fighting slaves on this island, so for years there has been an unspoken truce between the latifundia and the tomb gangs. The latifundia don't bother them, and the gangs don't bother the latifundia. But if you have to hide there, we need to figure out some way to get Sos to go with you. No one would bother you with Sos."

"But involving Sos would be tricky too," Ducetius said.

"Yes, it would," George concurred. "But if you leave under good circumstances, Vitus might allow me to borrow him for a few weeks to accompany you if I offer him collateral. But even then, I don't know. Vitus watches Sos like a hawk.

"But if we cannot get Sos, your Patrón is the next best choice. He's got a little brawn and he's resourceful, and he kept you alive all those years during your war. But he's complicated too. He might be unwilling to leave here as long as Elisheva's fate is unsure and her baby unborn." He paused and suddenly asked, "It's not his baby, is it?"

"Not that I know of, cousin."

"Just wondering," said George. "I only ask because I heard Elisheva lost several babies before she arrived in Sicily, but since this baby seems to be surviving, I thought maybe it had a different father."

"It's possible, cousin, but I doubt it. Patrón and Elisheva are honorable. As much as they might have wanted to, I've seen no hint of any affair. Patrón is not good at keeping secrets. He is protective of Elisheva because he loves her, not because the baby is his."

"Sorry. I had to ask," apologized George. "In any case, I hope you can leave on good terms. So far, things are quiet regarding the lar and pouches. I do not sense any immediate danger. But if you have to flee quickly before Nathan knows the outcome with Elisheva and her baby, we will have to rely on Sos, and I may have to surrender my life or business as collateral to Vitus to make that happen—especially if I ask for the key to Sos's ankle chain so he can walk. But if that is what it takes to keep you safe, my wonderful boy, that is what it takes. You are my greatest concern."

"But frankly," George continued, "I think if you end up leaving here, your Patrón will eventually follow you to Herculaneum or wherever you end up."

"Why do you say that?" asked Ducetius.

"Because your Patrón loves you. In all the changes that have happened in that young man's life and all the losses he has sustained—and he may have to sustain much more in these upcoming weeks—you are the one constant, with all of your losses too, who has remained at his side. He is the Patrón, but my guess is that if he were to lose you, he would not know what to do with himself. And I feel the same way."

"Thank you, cousin. You have been to me like the father I have not had all these years. I am grateful."

They hugged.

"So we have a plan?" said George.

"We have a plan," responded Ducetius.

XVIII

Meanwhile, Sos was hatching a scheme of his own. He clearly needed to escape Vitus if he was going to live, and he wanted to take young Lois with him.

When Vitus's guards released Sos from the iron chamber, thanks to Efstathios's unwitting intervention, he was in a terrible state. If the weather during his incarceration had not been cloudy, he would have putrefied beyond recovery. But even as it was, 30 hours of exposure and untreated wounds left him in need of serious care. A man of average constitution would have died under similar circumstances. Sos only lived because he was Sos.

The guards, who had respect for the Pontian mammoth—how had he not been sold to a gladiatorial school, they always wondered—made sure he was washed and fed. They put him in a side room under lock and key in the ergastulum that was cleaner than the main cell, and it had a cot. They were given strict orders to nurse him back to good health in a few days. Eyeing Lois in the fields, they grabbed her to do the nursing for them. When they took her, she assumed she would be ravished again, as she had been many times since her arrival. But the guards delivered her to her new charge unscathed.

Entering the room where Sos lay, they said, "This ought to perk you up, Sossy boy. Look who we brought you."

Sos opened his eyes, saw Lois, and smiled.

"Did you see that?" one of the guards said. "I believe he just smiled."

"I think he's on the mend already," said the other guard. They then left the room, returning every few hours to check on him and bring him food, water, clean bandages, or anything else he needed.

"Thank you for your kindness," said Lois.

"Kindness?" said the guard. "We'll be expecting payback later. We'll let you know when."

By the next morning, the guards had not made good on their threat, however, and a fellow slave brought in the morning gruel, water, and fresh bandages instead.

When Sos was strong enough to speak, about midday, he asked Lois to come closer to him so he could talk to her. She moved nearer and he said to her, "Don't worry about those men. You're safe with me. I know you are from the same country I come from. I hear it in your voice. And you share the same faith that I do. I heard you say the Name when they were going to whip you."

Lois, incredulous at what she was hearing, began to weep. "You too?" she asked. "How is that possible?"

"He sees everything. Even you and me."

She kissed him on the cheek, and her tears wet his face. A tear poured out of his eye as well and rolled over the bridge of his nose and down onto the matting under his cheek. He was smiling again, but his eyes were shut. He then fell asleep, as if even their few words had expended all the energy he had. Lois watched over him and prayed that he might recover. There was something magnificent about him, she thought.

Sos had never married back in his homeland. He was taken captive in his early twenties. On the latifundium, he remained chaste among the female slaves for a year because he believed it was the right thing to do. His example inspired some of the other believing male slaves to do the same. But it was difficult to sustain. Slaves were not allowed to marry under Roman law, but Sos learned that there was a type of common-law marriage among slaves sometimes recognized by Roman society. It could be broken up at a master's whim, and a slave family could be sold separately to the four winds. But a common-law marriage was better than nothing, and something had to be done not only to provide a quasi-legitimate outlet for the males but also provide protection for the believing females. So Sos took one of the young believing women who seemed to like him and declared that she was his wife. Before God he promised her protection and faithfulness, and she, before God, promised him affection.

Once Sos set that example for the other slaves, many of them followed his lead, and in no time, it became the hallmark of the believing slaves on the latifundium that they had common-law wives to whom they remained faithful. Of course, the Roman overseers and guards still took advantage of the so-called married women, and no one could stop them. But Sos remembered a line from one of Paulos's writings that he had heard back home, which provided comfort for them all under their difficult conditions. It said, "Each one of you should remain in the situation which he found himself when God called him. Were you a slave when you were called? Don't let it trouble you—although if you can gain your freedom, do so." And from that line, he devised two applications. One was to encourage the slave women not to be overwhelmed with feelings of guilt for unfaithfulness when the Romans attacked, as these attacks were beyond their control and a reality of female slave life, and sometimes male as well. The second was to inspire the believing men, especially, to seek freedom by gaining the respect of the latifundium overseers, by being obedient, and by being kind to each other—which seemed like a taste of freedom—until such time as they could obtain their goal, if ever. And remarkably, over the years, the reputation and clout that Sos and the other believing males gained on the latifundium brought about the result that the overseers and guards began to think twice sometimes before they preyed on the believing women.

There was no one like Sos on the entire island. If Sicily was a land that epitomized the worst in ancient slavery, it was also one that produced heroes like the rebel Eunus, king Ducetius, and Sos, who rose above the rest to improve their lot and that of those around them *because* of the difficulty of their circumstances. Sometimes, like Eunus, they used horrific means like mass murder to achieve their ends; others, like king Ducetius, used military strength; and Sos—the most unusual of all—his faith.

By the third day of his recovery in the ergastulum under Lois's care, Sos was sitting up on the edge of the bed and talking, plying Lois with questions about her past, explaining the marriage situation on the latifundium, comparing notes with her about their common faith, telling her about his slave wife who had died a year prior, and probing to see if she would ever want a husband to watch over her. "Because," he said, "if you would like one, I might actually know a fellow who wouldn't mind too much having a wife like you."

Lois, taken by surprise, smiled for the first time since her arrival. Playing along with Sos, and intrigued by the turn the conversation might be taking, she looked right into Sos's eyes, and asked, "And who is this fellow you're talking about?"

"Well," he replied, "he's not doing very well at the moment, and the boss doesn't like him very much. But if you are fond of heavy chains and interlacing whip designs on backs, he might be just the man for you. He's got a lot of each. One day, he hopes to change the world. And when he does, he would very much like to have someone like you by his side."

Lois couldn't stop smiling at what she now knew Sos was trying to tell her. It took her aback to see that he had a playful side—similar to what the guards had felt. But she responded, "Then you must tell that fellow that I wouldn't mind in the least having a husband like him."

He looked intently at her, trying to ascertain if she was really thinking along the same lines as he. "Really?" he said, with a glint in his eye.

"Really," she replied.

Then he kissed her with such a kiss they forgot for a moment how far they were from Eden.

"Tell me," Lois asked when the kiss subsided, "was it really you who spread that rumor about the skeleton in the theatre? I barely know what the story behind it is, but it doesn't seem like the type of thing someone like you would ever bother to do."

Sos hesitated. "You're right. I was not the one who spread that rumor."

"But you were brutally punished for saying that you did," she said.

"Yes."

"Then why did you say it?"

"Because I saw you crying, and you were next in line."

"What?" she asked, startled and incredulous again. "You took the blame for me?" She began to weep all over again.

"Yes. I thought to myself as I looked at you," in an attempt to make her smile again, "'maybe I'd like to have that woman as my wife some day, if she would ever have a dog like me; and if that is the case, I don't want her to have whip marks all over her back.'"

Lois laughed, as she wiped her eyes.

"I don't generally like interlacing back designs like you do," he continued. "But I will tell you that, if you ever get any, I am sure I will change my mind."

She kissed him again, and this time there was no doubt as to her intentions. A couple of believing slaves walked in with bandages and food just at that moment, interrupting the mood. But Sos, seeing it as a godsend, said to them, "What excellent timing you have, my friends. I would like to marry this woman, and I need a pair or two of eyes to witness it."

The couple smiled with assent, being familiar with the drill. They watched as Sos swore, before God, fidelity and protection to Lois, and as Lois swore, before God, affection to Sos.

After the brief ceremony was over, Sos turned to the couple to say thanks. "And now, if you will excuse us…" he added, smiling. And the couple left the room.

Within a few minutes, despite occasional setbacks from the scourges, Sos and Lois entered nuptial bliss on the ergastulum cot.

Afterward, Sos recited his favorite proverb. "There are three things that amaze me," he declared; "four that I do not understand: the way of an eagle in the sky, the way of a snake on a rock, the way of a ship on the high seas, and the way of a man with a maiden."

Lois laughed again. "I think you found your way, my love."

The next morning, the original guards returned to check on their charge. Upon entering, Sos and Lois looked like patient and nurse again, as if nothing had transpired except that Sos was sitting up, and Lois sitting in the little seat across from him.

"He looks pretty good," said one of the guards to the other.

"It was an ingenious remedy," the second guard said. "You should be a doctor."

The first one said, "And she looks pretty good too."

At that, Sos glared at them as if ready to pounce.

"Oh come on, Sossy boy," said one of them. "Don't take offense. You're not really going to keep her all to yourself, are you?"

Sos lifted himself off the bed.

"After all the help we've given you?" the other said.

Sos stood up, and the two shrank back.

"All right, all right," one of them said. "Calm down, Sossy boy. Calm down. No one is going to do anything. Listen, we have orders to take you—both of you—up to the city. Today. Right now. So we have to go. No harm done. Right?" He waited while Sos calmed himself. "Lord Vitus is waiting," the guard added.

Sos and Lois were then walked out of the ergastulum, put in a donkey-drawn cart, and escorted up to the butte by the guards. Neither Sos nor Lois knew why they were going. They asked the two guards, but they only responded, "We were just told to drop you off at the workers' quarters."

Sos and Lois concluded that that might be a good thing, if Vitus wished to keep Lois nearby to take care of Sos. It could also be a bad thing, if Lois was assigned to the quarters for the relief of the laborers.

Once they reached the work site, Lois was escorted inside the workers' quarters, and Sos was escorted to the theatre, where Efstathios and Vitus proceeded to have the conversation about what had happened to Sos's back.

It was not until the end of the day, when Sos was chained into the slave's quarters without any sign of Lois, that he knew Lois was in trouble. Fortunately, Ducetius was finishing up his rounds for food distribution, and Sos asked if he could tell him anything about the new girl in the workers' quarters.

"What new girl?" Ducetius asked. "And what happened to your back?"

Sos explained the entire situation: who Lois was, how he was whipped and partially roasted, how Lois nursed him back to good health, and how the two of them had made a marriage pact.

"You did all that in four days? I haven't acquired a wife in thirty years. I'd say Patrón and I need to spend more time with you! But how can I help with your new wife?"

"Tell me if she is safe and what is happening to her."

"I will," replied Ducetius, "but I will not be able to give you a full report until tomorrow."

As soon as Ducetius left, he returned to the workers' quarters and spoke to the guard about Lois. The guard replied that she was in a special room that was cleaned per Lord Vitus's request, and that Vitus had visited her several times during the course of the day.

"Thank you," Ducetius replied matter-of-factly. "I will make sure she is given an extra portion of food in the morning."

During the course of the next day, Ducetius gathered info about Lois on his rounds. The most important piece was that, although there were plenty of women in the barracks, Vitus consorted with Lois alone and posted one of the silent, menacing guards in front of her door to keep her for himself. Another fact was that Lois was the brunt of ridicule from the other women in the barracks. This was because of her special status with Vitus and because of her scruples. Lois was sweet and attractive, and Vitus did not care in the least that she might be 'married.'

As promised, Ducetius came to Lois's door with an extra portion of food. "Open the door," he said to the silent guard, who was not the same one as the previous night. As soon as he entered the room, Ducetius, like most men who met her, became instantly smitten. He left the door slightly open to avoid scandal, then introduced himself and told her that Sos was inquiring about her welfare. The mention of Sos elicited a reaction from her he did not expect. Lois suddenly latched onto Ducetius's arm and became weepy.

"Is Sos all right?" she asked.

"Yes. He spent the night in the slave's quarters, and he's back at work today. But he wants to know if your situation is tolerable."

"By comparison to being attacked at the latifundium, yes. But I have been shut up in this room since yesterday, and the only person I have seen besides you is Lord Vitus. And if Sos wants to know, Vitus hurts me just like the guards and other slaves back on the latifundium."

She showed Ducetius her bruised arms and legs. "How long do I have to be here?" she asked. "I'm scared. I have been scared since I came to this horrible island. Is there any way you can help me? Is there any way I can see Sos?"

"I cannot say right now," Ducetius answered, "but I will see what I can do and will let Sos know how you are."

"Don't leave me," she begged. "I am afraid to be in this place alone. The women taunt me through the wall, and the guard says lascivious things or joins the women in hurling insults. If there is anything you can do to help me ..."

Ducetius's heart broke as he listened to her. He wished he could save her, along with every slave in the world, but he knew that was not possible.

"I feel so dirty and guilty," she told Ducetius. "I have been reduced to prostitution, and I knew nothing of that life before coming here."

Lois had not been born a slave. She came from a free family with loving parents and brothers and sisters and had been captured during the same Roman campaign that cast Sos into bondage. But unlike Sos, she did not and could not see the good in her current situation. As a female, she did not have the least chance of gaining respect or a modicum of agency like Sos had. She saw her relegation to Sicily as the life sentence it actually was, with no hope of escape or improvement except by death. Sos had been the only good thing to happen to her since her arrival; and now there was Ducetius.

Ducetius did not know how to respond, except to commiserate and say that he would check in on her every day. That, at least, brought her some comfort.

As he left her room and closed the door, he spoke to the menacing guard. "You may tell your Lord Vitus, as I will tell him myself, that I came here to ensure that his merchandise was safe and well-maintained. If I catch wind of you touching her or abetting the other women in their abuse of her, Lord Vitus will hear about it from me. I will check in on her again tomorrow."

The guard nodded in obedience without a word. Ducetius then left, hoping he had accomplished some good and that Lois might spend a less troublesome day than before.

He found Sos at the amphitheatre and described Lois's situation.

"I must get her out of there," he said. "She is my wife."

"Be careful, Sos," responded Ducetius. "Vitus almost killed you already."

"Are we not supposed to sacrifice our lives for our wives as he did for us?"

And thus Sos began to hatch his scheme.

XIX

After the wedding, Elisheva's health deteriorated. She could not keep food down. "I knew we shouldn't have had that sausage," quipped Joram at her bedside.

Everyone was worried. It was two months before the scheduled opening for the amphitheatre. The troupe had arrived in Enna and was practicing all five plays to be performed. The marble columns, carved for the backstage area by Ennan artisans, were being polished and set in place. Vitus ordered announcements about the event posted throughout the town, and Funisulanus sent messengers to the prefect of Syracuse and other notables. But no one was sure if Elisheva, who was beginning her third trimester, would live to see the day.

Efstathios, Joram, and Nathan were so preoccupied with her condition for all their various personal reasons—husband, brother, soulmate—that they found it difficult to concentrate at work. In addition to the women being in attendance over her, each of the band of four took shifts at the house.

Efstathios was terrified at the prospect of losing Elisheva.

Besides his feelings of guilt for causing her condition, he was plagued by horrible hypothetical scenarios in his head. If the child lived and Elisheva did not, what would happen? Who would raise it? Would he have to marry again? How could he find someone as lovely and intelligent as Elisheva, who cared for him and had known him for so long? Could he even bring himself to find another woman? Would he be alone for the rest of his life? What if Elisheva and the child *both* perished? Who would he have left in the world? Would it be worth staying in Enna if that happened, or would he feel compelled to leave? If he left, would he return to Corinth, where he would probably fall back into his old life patterns? Would he return to his parents in Pella defeated and empty-handed, assuming his parents were even still alive to take him in again? He didn't know. And somehow the scenario of both Elisheva *and* the child surviving did not enter his head as a serious option. Joram reminded him that it was entirely possible that that could be the case.

But Efstathios had other difficulties weighing on his mind as well. They were not personal in nature but had major ramifications for the family, his circle, and the entire city. At the top of the list was the performance of the *Antigone* play. Efstathios did not want Vitus to see it. He was sure its content would cause a permanent rift between he and Vitus, and neither he nor any of the band could afford bad blood with the manager at this point. Issues of great import were afoot. Final payment for the renovation was being negotiated, including manuscripts for a local library. Discussions about hiring Efstathios and George to oversee a villa that Funisulanus wished to construct near the amphitheatre were being finalized. And Vitus announced that Funisulanus was so proud of Enna and his amphitheatre that he asked his father to petition the Senate to raise the status of the city from civitas to municipium. Although the status change was honorary, it was significant, and Senator Funisulanus himself was slated to attend his son's opening day all the way from Rome to judge whether the city warranted such a bestowal. Thus a great deal was riding on good relations with the Romans at this juncture, and Efstathios felt responsible to ensure that nothing threatened that.

In an attempt to occupy Vitus's time during the *Antigone* performance on opening day, Efstathios concocted a scheme by paying a visit to the architect who was Vitus's top consideration for the villa project. He told the architect that the plans for the villa needed to be completed for the day of the play and that if he wanted the job, he should present the plans while Vitus was in good spirits during the performance itself.

"You want me to interrupt the play?" the architect asked, confused.

"No," replied Efstathios. "Come and find me in the theatre after the first performance has ended and before the second one has begun. It should be about mid-morning. I will look for you as well. Then we will both talk to Vitus."

"But he might miss the second play," said the architect, concerned. "I will have a great deal to show him."

"If I know Lord Vitus," Efstathios assured the architect, "he will be looking for an excuse to absent himself for a while at that part of the day."

"If you are sure," replied the architect, "then I will be there."

"Yes. I am sure. Please contact me if you have any other questions. There is no need to bother Lord Vitus until then."

"I will do that. Thank you." The architect was a Sicilian Greek, but he had spent several years in Rome. Vitus liked that.

With that arrangement taken care of, Efstathios prepared for the difficult days ahead but felt uneasy on many fronts. Between the burial fiasco, the lar in Vitus's satchel, the mention of Ducetius's name, Elisheva's illness, the tension with Nathan, plus his dependence on an appointment with the architect to keep Vitus occupied during *Antigone*, Efstathios felt that his life could unhinge at any moment. If Ducetius was the glue of the group, Efstathios felt he was the wrecking bar. How could someone like himself, who always tried to do good, instead always manage to ruin everything? Maybe he tried too hard, he thought. Other people strutted through life with ease, like Joram and Nathan, and accomplished great things. But he could never just be himself and accomplish anything. He knew that his zeal, meticulousness, and hard work had produced an amphitheatre that was the pride of central Sicily, but his overanalysis of life led to difficulties, especially with relationships. None of his relationships were good, and largely because he could not just be himself around other people. No wonder, he thought, he had such a hard time finding a home in the world.

He promised himself that if he were given the grace to live beyond the next three months to see the pregnancy and the opening day through, he would try to change and think less about things.

But for the moment, he had to deal with his current reality, the chief concern of which was his wife. Ayathe kept Elisheva in the far room on her first floor so it would be private but accessible in case there was need, and Efstathios slept in the room with her.

Although Elisheva was only six and a half months pregnant, Ayathe was in touch with the local midwife to see what her prognosis of the situation might be. It was not good, according to her. It was possible both mother and baby would survive, but more likely that one would live to the exclusion of the other. When the midwife asked which choice she preferred, Elisheva insisted on saving the baby. When Joram tried to convince her otherwise, she told him, "What would my life be if I continued? For what? For whom? I cannot be a good wife for Efstathios if pregnancy causes a problem every time. And even if I could end up with Nathan, which can never be, it would be the same situation. At least having a baby will allow me to depart knowing I fulfilled my role as a woman and mother in the world."

Joram dropped his head, not knowing what to say. He did not want to lose his sister.

"Joram," she said, looking at him earnestly as he returned her glance, "would you and Adah take care of the baby if it survives? I would leave content knowing it was in your hands."

"Well, certainly we will, but …"

"I know Efstathios will try, and he will love our child. He is a good man. But he is complicated. You know. And he is young. He will need all the help he can get. And if I know he has the two of you to fall back on … The two of you are a wonderful couple … Please talk to Adah and consider. I have to …" She faded back into sleep again.

For weeks, she barely spoke. Her conversation with Joram was the longest she had had for a month. She had to save her strength for a similar discussion with Efstathios to let him know that Joram and Adah would help him, as would the rest of the family. She then fell silent for another couple of weeks, as if conserving her energy again for perhaps a last conversation with Nathan, which would be the hardest of all.

When Nathan walked into her room one day to check on her, his mother was at Elisheva's bedside, talking to her.

"I was just telling Elisheva," she said, "that I had a few terrible pregnancies myself. They were all in the years between you and your sister. I was healthy when I was expecting you and Amram, but with those pregnancies I did not know whether I was going to make it or not. The babies did not. But I did. And eventually your little sister was born." She smiled down at Elisheva and took her hand, trying to encourage her with this anecdote.

"Is that why there are so many years between Adah and me?" questioned Nathan.

"Yes."

"Why didn't you ever tell me that before?"

"You never asked. But that is why. So our dear Elisheva, there is always hope. One never knows about these things. Do not despair."

Elisheva looked up at the gentle face of Nathan's mother, who had been a politician's wife, raised three children—one of whom was a renegade—had lived through a war, been relocated twice, relegated to a house a tenth the size of what she had been used to, and never complained. Although she was a quiet woman and often in the background, Elisheva admired her and envied her acceptance of whatever life brought her.

Elisheva, on the other hand, had been so sure about so many things for so long that she could not help but feel disappointment that life did not end up the way she had expected. She still had her faith, but life had been unpredictable and a reason to rely on that faith.

Nathan's mother saw Elisheva smile back at her, conveying that her story had had its desired effect. Then the mother said to both of them, "Now I will leave you two for a visit."

When Nathan's mother was gone, Nathan sat in the chair beside Elisheva, and Elisheva motioned that she had something to say. Nathan came closer.

"It's time we talked," she said. "I may recover, but I don't think so. And just in case, you need to hear me."

"Elisheva, don't speak like that," responded Nathan.

"I am going to speak like that. When the last door is about to close, I can say whatever I need to. And you will hear me. Do you hear me?"

"Yes. I hear you."

"First of all, I have loved you more than anyone in my life." She stopped as tears fell down her cheeks. They fell down Nathan's as well.

"But that love," she continued, "did not play out as I had thought it would. Maybe real love never does. It is funny how when someone loves someone else, it is not all sunny days and warm feelings and hopeful prospects and happy endings. Instead, my love for you caused the most thought, planning, pain, and utter redirection

I ever had to face in my entire life." She had to pause to regain her strength. "Living without you was significant for me. You left a mark. And I don't know how it is that all of life's wonders and changes, places, experiences, and mysteries could end up coalescing around just one other person in the world, and that one other person can take up so little space but fill up the universe with so much meaning so that life hardly seems worth living unless that one other person is around. How can that be? How can someone like myself, who had such a good education and learned theology and languages and history and shared so many profound thoughts with so many people in three different lands, still have to realize that, when all else is stripped away, there was only one other person in the world who made the difference for me, and that person was you?" She had to pause again. "Nothing else has been able to erase it: not the war, not travel, not a husband or a brother. And I am ashamed of that. Perhaps a baby would have. They say there is nothing you will love more in all the world than your baby when it comes. Maybe that is why the soul of this island is wrapped around Demeter and Persephone. Maybe that is why the finding of a mother skeleton shielding a helpless infant halted even the Roman progress on the theatre. But I will probably not live to experience that. I will probably not be granted the knowledge of a human love in this world greater than mine has been for you." She paused again. "As I lie here day after day thinking about my life, I feel very much that I have failed: that I neither had you nor didn't have you and was not able to let my love for anyone else eclipse you; that if I didn't have a child, it would be my undoing; and if I had a child, it would still be my undoing. I have met with failure at every turn.

"But I have loved you, and that is how it has been. I have loved others too, and have always been faithful, but it was a struggle to give them the place they should have had in my life. Don't misunderstand. You are not my hope. There is another who holds that rank. But in this sphere, I have tried but failed. Yet if when next you and I meet, if my love for you will have inspired you to follow me into the kingdom of the only one in the cosmos who loves you more than I do, then at least, even with all its concomitant troubles, my love will have had a purpose. There is a feast promised in that kingdom; and when it happens, I hope you can be one of the three sitting next to and across from me. So be sure you make it there, Nathan. You have to make it there."

She stopped and closed her eyes for longer than a minute.

Nathan would have grown alarmed except he could still see her breathing.

She opened her eyes again and said, "Be good to Efstathios, Nathan. He loves you, and he has always been good to me. Help him succeed. He told me that some of the talks you had helped him through some difficulties. You are a prince among men for that, Nathan. But I am not holding you to it. When I am gone, you may not stay here, and he may go in the opposite direction. But if you stay, do not be competitors in your hearts anymore. Remember that if we meet again in the kingdom, I will not be married. I will be free and you will be free and he will be free, and all of us who make it to that day will love the Maker and each other forever. And that will be the glorious end of our story, and it will be a blessed, unencumbered time. If you let it happen."

She paused once more, then said, "I have to sleep again, and I do not know when I will awake. But if I do awake and linger here and have other conversations and faces before me, then this conversation and your face will not be the last I experience in this life. But I tell you that yours will probably be the last face and words on my heart and mind other than his when I depart here."

"Elisheva!" he exclaimed. And he wrapped his arms around her diminishing frame and kissed her face with all the love he had held back for years. If someone else had seen it, they would have thought he was smothering her and that she would not survive. But she did survive. At least for the moment.

XX

Opening day began a comedy and ended a tragedy.

At daybreak, throngs of Ennans appeared before the entrance to the theatre. The placards and announcements in town mentioned that admission was free through the gracious beneficence of Lord Funisulanus. Few in Enna had ever seen a lord, and even fewer a Greek play. Thus every type of person in the vicinity showed up for the spectacle: men, women, old, young, slave, free, vagabond, wealthy, middle-class, cook, vinedresser, farmer, prostitute, inn-keeper, bee-keeper, tailor, cobbler, smith, kilner, ceramicist, carpenter, sculptor. And if anyone could recognize him, there was even an escapee slave-gang leader from decades before.

In the area in front of the theatre, dozens of merchants set up kiosks to sell their wares to the incoming crowd: pancakes, wines, fruits, nuts, and garum to eat; cushions and mats to cover the hard stone seats; hats and little awnings for shade; mini theatre masks and little terracotta characters for souvenirs. The figurines were generic, since none of the artisans who produced them knew the plays. But there were little female versions that could represent either Antigone or Electra, regal looking men who represented Oedipus the King, little satyr statues, and farmers as well.

The day's theatrical fare included the three surviving tragedies of Sophocles: *Oedipus the King, Antigone*, and *Electra*; a bawdy satyr play by Aeschylus named *The Net Fishers*, featuring Danae, of the gold dust fame, and her heroic son Perseus washing up on a beach; and a finale titled *Agrostino*, by Epicharmus, the father of Sicilian Comedy, about country life. Altogether, it promised to be a long and enjoyable affair: eight hours of performance, music, dancing, food, pageantry, nobility, and, no doubt, a few requests like 'mommy, I want to go home.'

It was typical in the days of classical Attic theatre centuries prior that the three main plays during a festival be written in trilogy format by the same author. The primary plays presented in Enna that opening day in 79 AD did not form a trilogy but were all written by Sophocles. The more educated Ennans had at least heard of Sophocles, and the less so were excited that Epicharmus was described in the placards as a comedian born in Sicily, and Aeschylus a tragedian who had died there.

After the hordes of humanity poured into the auditorium and found seats—women and children mostly filling up one side and men the other—Funisulanus and his father made a dramatic entrance. They were carried in litters and surrounded by guards, some of whom blew trumpets and others of whom waved large banners. The master of ceremonies down on the orchestra floor pointed to the procession and led the masses in a loud cheer. It was the most splendid civic moment Enna had witnessed in centuries.

The senator and his son took their seats, specially carved to look like stone thrones for the occasion, near the front. Several of the guards set up an awning over them and sat down in the surrounding rows. Just behind the Funisulani sat Vitus, with a friend from out of town, surrounded by yet more guards. And nearby, two rows behind Vitus and to his right, along the exit stairs, sat Joram. No special seating had been arranged by Vitus for George or any of the band of four; nor, realistically, could any have been expected. This was a Roman affair, with only Greek trappings, and the Romans were much more class conscious than the Greeks. Still, at one point when Vitus turned his head and saw Joram sitting nearby, he motioned to him and smiled. He seemed quite pleased with himself.

Joram smiled back. Within a minute, some acrobats came onto the stage, performing amazing feats that drew everyone's attention. While the audience was spellbound, the master of ceremonies took advantage of the silence and interjected his introduction to the day's program. Every single person in the theatre could hear him due to the genius of Greek engineering. The audience murmured how impressive it was. Between the beauty of the theatre, the splendor of the Sicanian Mountains beyond, and the outstanding acoustics, people were intrigued.

The actors then came out onto the stage as the acrobats exited and took their positions. There were fifteen masked choristers, as is typical in Sophocles plays, arranged in a rectangular formation on the left side of the orchestra. In the center was a large, masked actor with a few others facing him. All the actors and choristers were male, even if they were to play a female role. It was an actor's mask that determined his gender as well as his major character trait: hero, villain, old man, young damsel, etc. Sometimes characters would change masks. But typically there were only two or three actors on stage at a time. Extras were occasionally added in, as was the case in the opening scene that morning.

As if he were welcoming the audience and the characters before him, the main actor, playing King Oedipus, called out, "My children … what purpose brings you here?" And so began the performance.

The audience sat riveted as the plot unfolded: a plague and blight on the land was being caused by a man who had murdered his father and married his mother—an unheard of, monstrous deed. As the tale continued, the chorus sang commentary on it to the music of trumpets, drums, cymbals, and lyres. The choristers danced in military unison as all fifteen turned their heads together or raised an arm at once or swayed to and fro simultaneously. Later in the plot, the patricide was found to be none other than King Oedipus himself. Upon learning this, the viewers' mouths dropped open. It was then later revealed that Oedipus's own beloved children, including Antigone and Polynices, were actually the products of incest. Upon this second disclosure, the audience sat aghast. That meant that the mother of Oedipus' children was one and the same as the mother of Oedipus himself. But how could that be? The audience cringed in repulsion. As the story drove on, the chorus clarified that all these awful events had been preordained by the gods. Upon hearing this, the audience sat despondent. And finally, at the end, King Oedipus blinded himself in response to all the abhorrent things he had done. The audience sat horrified, weeping, and asking itself if such a thing could ever occur.

The play ended and catharsis took place, even without the aid of much scenery or many props. It was the artistry of the dialogue in a Greek play that fed the imagination—and the imaginations of the Ennan onlookers had become completely absorbed. Vitus and the Funisulani looked around as the 'opas' arose like a surging wave across the entire auditorium. So far, the morning had been an unparalleled success. The Senator was convinced already that Enna should be elevated to a municipium, his son was contemplating what special gift he could award to Vitus, and Vitus had decided that George and Efstathios would oversee the new villa project.

/////

Then everything unraveled.

Vitus and his out-of-town guest stood up as the exhilarated crowd rambled about happily during the intermission before the second play commenced, and they began to walk up the stairway near to where Joram sat.

"And I owe all the success of this morning," Vitus said in Joram's hearing, "to *this*." Vitus reached into his satchel and retrieved the little golden lar that was in it, showing it to his out-of-town friend.

The friend looked at the lar, and said, "What do you mean?"

"It is a lar that I found," responded Vitus. "It has brought me a great deal of luck."

"Let me see that lar," said the friend, turning it about in his hand. "I have seen this very one before. You say you found it?"

"Impossible. How could you have seen it before?" asked Vitus.

"It has the same marking on the bottom as…Remember I was telling you…"

"Oh, just a moment," interrupted Vitus in the middle of his friend's sentence, as he realized Joram was sitting right next to where they were standing. "I also owe this morning's success to this fellow. He is a Judaean but a most knowledgeable young man. Joram, I'd like you to meet an old associate of mine, the former manager of the latifundium, Demaratos."

"I'm very pleased to meet you," Joram responded smiling, feeling satisfied with the morning's proceedings as well.

Then, suddenly, a shiver of terror ripped through Joram's entire frame as the name of the out-of-town guest registered in his head. Had he heard the name correctly? And didn't Vitus just say the man was the former manager of the latifundium? And hadn't the man just said that he recognized the lar that Vitus was showing him?

Joram couldn't believe it. This clearly wasn't just any Demaratos he was meeting. It was *the* Demaratos.

"Is everything all right, Joram?" asked Vitus, noticing Joram turn pale.

"Yes. I mean, no. I am not feeling well this morning," responded Joram. "But the show is going marvelously, is it not?" he added, looking directly at Demaratos, trying to hide his anxiety. His heart raced as he realized the seriousness of the situation George and Ducetius were suddenly in should Demaratos recall either of their names from the past. Pressure mounted inside him with every passing second he delayed running across town to warn Ducetius.

"Yes, quite," answered Demaratos, showing disinterest in small talk, especially to an individual of no rank.

Demaratos then turned back to Vitus to resume their conversation about the lar. Joram, excusing himself, left their company and headed out of the theatre as quickly as he could. He was feeling uncharacteristically frantic, trying to tell himself to regain his composure. As he hurried up the stairs toward the theatre exit, Efstathios, at that very moment, was hurrying down the stairs to meet with Vitus at the prearranged time with the architect. Joram's shoulder actually brushed up against Efstathios as they passed each other. But between the crowd and urgency of their separate missions, neither man noticed the other.

Efstathios reached Vitus with the architect just in time—yet again—to interrupt any revelations Demaratos might disclose about the lar. With Efstathios's arrival, Vitus's attention was now completely redirected to the architect and the villa. Vitus could barely wait to speak about it and show off to Demaratos his newest plans for Lord Funisulanus. "We can talk more about the lar later," Vitus said to his colleague. But it would not be long before Demaratos would grow impatient enough to say what he wanted to say about it.

In the meantime, Vitus smiled at Efstathios and introduced him and the architect to his colleague. "Ah, my good men, let me introduce to you my old friend, and fellow latifundium manager, Demaratos." When Efstathios heard the name of the friend, and that the friend was a fellow latifundium manager, his face also turned ashen as Joram's had done earlier. "What is the matter with all of you?" Vitus asked him.

"What do you mean?" answered Efstathios.

"You suddenly do not look well. And neither did Joram when I just spoke to him a moment ago."

"No. I am fine," responded Efstathios, trying to hide his true feelings. As if his ruse of bringing the architect to occupy Vitus's time during the *Antigone* play did not make him uncomfortable enough, now he had to deal with the possibility during the next hour that he might be in the presence of the very man who could undue all their lives in a moment, should Vitus show him the lar in his satchel. He prayed that such a thing would not happen, not realizing, of course, that it already had. "Perhaps I am just a little anxious about your reaction to the villa plans."

They began discussing the plans right then and there on the theatre stairs. But noticing that the second play was about to commence, Efstathios gently nudged the three of them toward the exit and out into the street to the proposed villa site itself. A decrepit building already existed on the site. The plan was to partially renovate it and substantially add to it. The four men entered the building to look around.

Meanwhile, Joram ran back across the north side of town to warn Ducetius, who was spending the day alone in his apartment trying to keep a low profile.

Joram was breathing heavily from exertion when he pounded and called at Ducetius's door.

"What has happened?" asked Ducetius, opening the door.

"Demaratos is here. You have to leave."

"What do you mean? *The* Demaratos?"

"Yes. He is at the theatre talking to Vitus. Go get your satchel."

Ducetius showed Joram his satchel, which was already in his hand. "It's already in my hand," he said. And the two of them bolted.

Joram then ran in the lead in the direction of Ayathe's house. "Where are we going?" Ducetius asked.

"We have to get cousin George," Joram responded breathlessly. "Cousin George has the key to unlock Sos from the slave quarters." George was not permitted to have the key for Sos's ankle chain, but he was given the key to unleash Sos from the slave quarter wall, in case George needed him while Vitus was at the latifundium.

"I know my cousin has the key," responded Ducetius, equally as breathless. "But isn't George at the theatre? I assumed you left him there."

"I did not see him there," said Joram. "I was at the theatre all morning saving him a seat, but he never showed up. I assumed he was still at the house."

When they got to the house, Joram burst into the men's quarters, sweating like no one had ever seen before.

"Where is George?" Joram heatedly asked Ayathe.

"What has happened?" responded Ayathe. "Is everything all right? George is at the amphitheatre."

"At the amphitheatre?!" Joram exclaimed. "Ducetius has to leave Enna immediately, and we need Sos's key from cousin George."

"What is happening?" she asked again.

"I just met Demaratos. He is here …"

"Oh dear gods!" exclaimed Ayathe. "*The* Demaratos?"

"Yes! And he is talking to Vitus right now," Joram continued. "They know each other after all. And when I just left them, Vitus was showing Demaratos the little lar, and Demaratos said he recognized it."

"Oh dear gods," cried Ayathe again. "How could this be happening? I knew it was dangerous. I knew it. Why did we ever get involved?"

Nathan, who was sitting just outside the third room, on shift with Elisheva, heard the conversation, feeling utterly torn between his two favorite people in the world. How could he not jump to leave with Ducetius? But how could he not stay to watch Elisheva, who was helpless and possibly at death's door?

"We have to go, Ducetius," commanded Joram. "Come on!"

That made the decision for Nathan, who stayed by Elisheva's side.

Joram led Ducetius out of the house and back toward the west side of town to the amphitheatre.

"I can't believe George is at the theatre," Joram said angrily to Ducetius as he became more and more tired in the course of what was becoming a marathon. "I did not see him at the theatre at all this morning. If he had simply come to the theatre on time and sat with me, you and Sos would already be out of the city and on your way."

Ducetius didn't know how to respond. He figured cousin George had had a good reason for being late, but his lateness was causing a great deal of confusion.

Upon reaching the theatre entrance, Joram said, "Stay here, and stand behind these bushes. I have to find George. I can't risk Vitus seeing you if he's still in there. Though who knows if he is still in there, or if he is already looking for you in the city. If you see him, hide. Then run."

Ducetius dutifully obeyed as Joram made his way into the theatre for what almost amounted to searching for the proverbial needle in a haystack. "I have no idea if he is wearing a hat or is covering his head with a sheet." He looked to and fro, not only for George, but to see if he could espy Vitus as well. He crossed the back of the theatre to the right side and glanced over every seat. He then crossed to the left side and glanced over every seat there. "Where is he!!" he said to himself. But the more terrifying question that gnawed at him was where in the world was Vitus? Is he gathering up his henchmen to track us all down?

When Joram turned around to look at the right side of the theatre again, he bumped into Ducetius, who had crept up right behind him. "What are you doing here?" Joram reprimanded him. "You should not be in here."

"I just saw Vitus," Ducetius answered, with a worried look in his eye. "He is outside the theatre."

"What is he doing there?" Joram whispered loudly.

"I could only see him in the far distance, but it looked like he was with Efstathios and at least two other men, whom I could barely see."

"What was he doing?"

"I don't know. They were by the villa site. Maybe they are discussing it."

"Did he see you?"

"No."

"I haven't seen George anywhere either. Where could he possibly be? Maybe by some miracle, he's already at the slave quarters unlocking Sos."

They exited the theatre. Joram looked in every direction to find George, and Ducetius looked in every direction to avoid Vitus.

All of a sudden, Joram saw George in the distance. "Cousin, is that you?" he called out. "It is! Thank heaven!"

George just happened to be taking a jaunt after having sat in the theatre all morning, never having found Joram to sit next to. "I'm sorry I was late this morning," he said walking toward Joram, "but at least the play is going well."

"Never mind that," said Joram. "Do…"

Then George interrupted Joram, suddenly seeing Ducetius next to him and realizing that something must have gone terribly wrong. "But what are you two doing here?" he said. "And especially *you*, Ducetius?" George now broke into a panic. "Did something happen with the lar?"

"Yes," said Joram. "That is what I'm trying to tell you. Demaratos is here. *The* Demaratos."

"No!"

"Yes," responded Joram. "Ducetius has to leave Enna right now, and we need to get Sos out of that slave quarters. Do you have the key? Please tell me you have the key."

"Yes. I have the key." He reached into his waist purse. "Thank the gods."

The three men hurried to the slave quarters.

"Vitus is at the villa site right around the corner," Joram warned George as they arrived. "We have to make sure he doesn't see us."

"Wait here," George said as he turned the key.

Once the door to the slave quarters closed behind him, George took a mere minute to speak to the guard and unfetter the Pontic giant. For Ducetius and Joram, however, that minute felt like an hour. When the door finally flung open again, it wasn't George they saw but Sos, who came flying out and jettisoning toward the laborers' quarters, ankle chains and all, before anyone could stop him.

"Where are you going?" called out George, appearing behind Sos in the doorway, seconds later. "What are you doing?"

"What *is* he doing?" Joram mimicked.

"I don't know."

"I think I know," said Ducetius.

Within a minute, Sos appeared at the door of the workers' quarters carrying Lois.

"Sos, what are you doing!? You can't take her!" yelled George.

"Baropalus, meet me outside the city gate," Sos yelled back.

"Go!" said Joram, pushing Ducetius into motion.

"You can't take her!" cried George, dropping his head. "It's my life!"

Joram looked on as Sos, one of the mightiest creatures ever made, ran toward freedom with a 105-pound woman on his whip-scarred back and a 13-inch chain connecting his ankles—the mastery of which had become a sport to him. For as long as Joram and George watched him, Sos never looked back. "Lord, help them," Joram prayed.

Before they were out of view, Vitus, Efstathios, Demaratos, and the architect walked up to Joram and George, who were standing near the slave quarters gazing intently into the distance. The expression on Efstathios's face as he approached them made it clear that the cat was now out of the bag—or rather, the lar was now out of the satchel.

"What are you looking at?" Vitus asked them. Following Joram's eyes, he turned to see Sos's hulking form running in fettered pizzicato with Lois on his back. Ducetius fell long behind him, even though he was running on two free legs.

Vitus could not believe what he was seeing. "What is going on here??!! Is that Sos? And the girl?" he demanded to know. "Is this entire island a den of thieves? First my associate tells me that someone from town stole this golden lar from the latifundium twenty years ago, and now I find *you* trying to steal my property." Turning specifically to George, he said, "Is that why you so earnestly needed the key from me: to steal my property?"

"No Vitus. Certainly not," insisted George. "I am not stealing anything."

Then Demaratos, scrutinizing George's face, suddenly realized he recognized him. He said to Vitus, "Vitus, you know this man?"

"Yes. He is George, the chief contractor on the theatre job that I have been telling you about."

"*He* is the chief contractor?"

"Yes," Vitus responded. "Why? What are you trying to tell me?"

"Isn't it obvious?" said Demaratos. "You are witnessing him steal your property right before your eyes, and you wonder why I question it?"

"I understand he is stealing my property," countered Vitus, "but you speak as if you know him from somewhere else."

"I do."

Demaratos slowly circled around George, glaring at him from every angle. "You were part of that thief's family twenty years ago," he asked, "weren't you?"

Demaratos paused to see George's reaction to the charge. Vitus was a bit confused but could clearly see George cast his glance downward, as if he felt guilty and that Demaratos was onto something. The former manager then continued the interrogation. "You came to beg for that thief's freedom after he stole that lar and all that money, didn't you? And you pleaded for your little nephew too. I know it was you. I remember your face."

"Are you sure about that?" queried Vitus. "I have been working closely with George on the theatre project for two years. Although something is afoot with his usage of my slaves at the moment, which I fully intend to get to the bottom of, you really think he had something to do with that theft from twenty years ago?"

"Yes, I do. I know his face. And his name is not George, as you say with your Latin accent," said Demaratos, remembering everything now. "His name is Georgios." Then turning to George again, he questioned him directly. "It is Georgios, is it not?" he said. "Yes; that is your name," he said, answering his own question. "And your young nephew was Douketios. I remember his name too, after that pathetic old Sicel hero."

Then suddenly Vitus's brain formed a connection between the theft of the lar, the theft of Sos and Lois, and the name Douketios, all in one moment. The enormity of the connection was so monumental that Vitus did not believe it at first. He had thought he was dealing with two separate thefts: one from twenty years ago by someone who was long gone, and one now by George—a man whom he had come to know and trust, as much as he trusted anyone, at least on a professional level. But now it was becoming clear that George was connected to both thefts. It was too incredible to be true. But to be sure, he had to know the answer to one pivotal question. Turning to George, Vitus asked him, "So is Baropalus really your nephew Douketios?"

George shook his head in disbelief at the question, and in utter despair that the present circumstances were framing him as a criminal. "Yes," he stiltedly answered, as he watched with relief as Ducetius disappeared from view.

"By the gods!" exclaimed Vitus. "Then it is true."

"How did you learn his name is Douketios?" George asked Vitus.

"Our friend Eustatius here called him Ducetius one day," Vitus replied. "I thought nothing of it at the time. But now it all comes back to me, and I see the connection, and why you might have been hiding his name all along."

Efstathios now looked so guilty and remorseful for having let Ducetius's name slip out all those months ago, it seemed he would perish right then and there.

"These Sicilians never learn," said Demaratos. Then, nodding at George, he said, "I should have enslaved you along with your nephew twenty years ago along with the others. You're a thief, and you come from a family of thieves."

Joram jumped to George's defense. "Lord Vitus, you know George is not a thief."

"Quiet, Joram," said George, cutting him off.

"But maybe it's not too late for justice to be meted out," said Vitus. "He'll only last a few weeks in the mines or galleys at his age, but it would be a satisfying way to end his miserable life."

"And what about his nephew?" said Demaratos. "He's getting away as we speak. He needs to be recaptured too and sent off with his uncle. He'll last quite a bit longer, and it will give him plenty of time to ruminate on the lowlife father who put him there, especially after he watches his uncle die."

"Leave the boy alone," begged George. "I gave you *my* life as collateral, not his. You lent Sos to me for three weeks. That was the deal. You gave me three weeks. If Sos does not come back in three weeks, I will go wherever you see fit."

"Fair enough," said Vitus.

"Not fair enough," said Demaratos. "What about the girl? Did he ransom his life for the girl as well?"

"No, he did not," replied Vitus.

"Then I will put up half my business properties for her," George begged. "If Sos does not come back in three weeks, my freedom and half my properties are yours. But I tell you the truth: I did not steal Sos. I borrowed him. And I did not steal the lar and the money. That was my cousin. I played no part in it. And I was not hiding my nephew's name. His name really is Baropalus. He is the freedman of Nathan Bar Opalus: the Nathanus who works with us, whom you know. And I did not steal the girl. That was Sos's idea. He surprised us all with that one. I had nothing to do with that either."

"We will see about that," said Vitus. "But far be it from me to be unjust. I have always prided myself on reasonability. If the theft was Sos's idea, the guards will tell me. We will talk to them right now to see if what you say is true."

Asking George to describe what happened in his own words, Vitus led the group into the slave's quarters to see if the guard's story matched George's. Vitus asked the guard exactly what happened and who was there last. The guard's description corroborated George's description as if they had rehearsed it. They then went to the workers' quarters and did the same thing.

In the workers' quarters, they found the guard knocked out with a bloody wound on his head. Asking some of the female slaves about it, they described how a huge fellow in chains burst into the place, bludgeoned the guard, and broke down the door to 'that woman's room.' They could all see how the door was hanging by only one hinge.

When they went back outside again, Vitus said to George, "So it seems you are telling the truth. And if so, then this is how things will play out: if Sos comes back in three weeks, which he will not, I assure you, you will keep your life and your freedom, but I will take half your business assets for the girl. And, needless to say," he laughed, turning to Demaratos for backup, "you and your company of miscreants are off the villa project. But if Sos does not come back, which is almost as sure as death, you will be sold to a mine or a galley. And I will leave you the choice as to which."

"But the old man might try to escape before then," said Demaratos, always ready with a malevolent suggestion.

"True," responded Vitus. "Then, my sorry friend, I am afraid you will have to spend the next three weeks chained in the slaves' quarters. There is no way around it. Guards! Incarcerate this fellow in Sos's place."

They obliged him. Joram and Efstathios stood speechless. Efstathios's eyes began to water, but he stanched them.

"These Greeks are so weak," said Demaratos. "The Romans did the world a favor by conquering them. And you Jews are no better," he added, looking at Joram. Based on his name, everyone thought Demaratos was a Greek himself, but apparently he was not.

Vitus stood there silently, thinking about all that had just transpired. It was really no surprise, he thought. After all the interactions, professionalism, and outstanding results produced by George and the band of four, it was clear that provincials, after all, could not help being provincials in the final analysis. They proved themselves the very street urchins Vitus had assumed they would be upon his arrival on the island—though they briefly bamboozled him into believing otherwise. Provincials could perhaps build a theatre. But that did not alter anything else about them or the world in which Romans and provincials lived, despite a lord's or a manager's best efforts toward their improvement. Rome was Rome, and the provinces were just the provinces, and that's how it should be and always would be, and justifiably so.

Joram and Efstathios stood there silent as well. But for them, everything had changed. The day they had all been working toward for so many years was ending now in catastrophe. George was going to prison, half his properties were going to be confiscated, the contract for the villa was cancelled, and the presence of Demaratos meant the loss of Ducetius, and most likely Nathan as well. With so much loss, they did not know what to think or where to turn.

"You can go home now," Demaratos said to Joram and Efstathios, disrespectfully shooing them off like small children.

"Yes, you can go home," reiterated Vitus, but in a slightly more polite tone. "I, on the other hand," he added, "have a show to attend."

As Joram and Efstathios turned to leave, however, Vitus called out to them again, as if he remembered, for at least a moment, that after all their work and the success of the morning, the band of four and their boss were worthy of some modicum of respect—a sentiment Demaratos would never concede even *for* a moment. "If you wish to visit George," Vitus said to them, "and provide for him these next three weeks, you may do so."

They thanked him and began to walk home.

Vitus and Demaratos then reentered the theatre to finish out the day there, having completely missed the *Antigone* performance.

XXI

Back at Ayathe's house, Nathan was still on shift with Elisheva. While Nathan paced around the bed, Elisheva opened her eyes for the first time all day, and Nathan bent over her. Looking into her eyes, he spoke to her in words that he had practiced beforehand in the event he ever had a chance to speak to her again.

"Can you hear me, my dear Elisheva?" he said. She seemed eager to hear what he had to say. "I want you to know," he continued, "that you should never think for a moment that your life was a failure. It was not. You have been a bright spot in the lives of everyone who has known you. For me, you have been the sun. And you've given me the half of my life that heaven didn't give me at birth." He paused. "And I want you to know, that if I ever make it into your kingdom, it will be you who will have brought me there, and you will have achieved what you had hoped for, after all."

When he was done, she smiled and lifted her arms up, with her elbows still on the bed, as if she were reaching for something. Looking straight at Nathan, she stared at him and never took her gaze off him. But after a minute of staring, he suddenly realized she was gone. There was only eternity behind her eyes. Elisheva, the love of his life and the center of his terrestrial universe, was dead.

With that, Nathan let out a wail that filled the house. Upon hearing it, his sister came running into the room, knowing that cry could mean only one thing. The midwife ran into the room behind her. The midwife had been at the house for hours at Ayathe's request, in the event she was needed. Nathan's mother, Ayathe, and Ayathe's daughters came into the room as well

"You have to find Efstathios," his sister said to Nathan, more clear-headed and unemotional than he could possibly have been at that moment. "We should have found him hours ago," she added, "but it seemed like Elisheva was stable."

Nathan, who would have been utterly lost in anguish if his sister had not given him a concrete task to perform, mindlessly found himself heading across town to the theatre, occasionally having trouble seeing through tears. Every few minutes he stopped in his tracks, his mind unable to convince his lower half to move. His reality had changed as well, and the motivation to take one more step had fled him. Where did he really need to go, anyway? What did anything matter? Elisheva was gone. Had he understood the concept of gravity, it would have made as much sense for it to be gone from the world as Elisheva. But no, he had a job to do. His sister had said so. He had to find Efstathios. Efstathios had to know. He did not know why. Did Efstathios really matter? He, Nathan, was the one who mattered. But propriety dictated that Efstathios should know. And so he found a reason, shallow as it was, to propel himself forward another few steps. Within a block, by coincidence, he happed upon Joram and Efstathios, who were morbidly skulking in his direction after the debacle at the theatre.

"Ef?" cried Nathan. "Ef!"

"Nathan?" answered back Joram. "What is happening?"

"Ef!" That was all Nathan could say. He looked at them as through water.

"Oh no. No!" Efstathios exclaimed, suddenly realizing in the midst of his own mental turbulence why Nathan was trying to find him. "She isn't...she isn't...did she?" he asked.

Nathan put his hands around Efstathios's. "Ef!"

Joram's mouth dropped. "Oh no," he said.

"She seemed fine," cried Nathan. "But..."

The three of them stood transfixed in place. If all the world had suddenly ceased or exploded into a conflagration around them, they might not have noticed.

After several minutes, another thought entered Efstathios's brain, and he asked, "And the baby?" He paused. "Is the baby...?"

"I don't know," Nathan responded. "I ran...the baby..."

"It was still unborn?" Efstathios said. "We have to go." The three of them, energized by the prospect of the birth, though knowing it might be bad news as well, bounded back to the house, as if enough had not befallen them that very worst of days. As soon as they entered the andron, they could hear the plaintiff cry of a baby through the length of the house.

"The baby is born?" Efstathios asked Ayathe, who was guarding the door of the third room.

"Yes, love," she said. But as he reached for the knob to enter the third room to see it, Ayathe barred him. "You cannot go in there, my dear," she said.

"But, isn't Elisheva all right?" Efstathios asked, illogically believing for a moment that the birth of the baby meant that Elisheva had been able to deliver it herself.

"No love," answered Ayathe. "She is gone, my sweetheart."

"But…but," Efstathios stuttered.

Ayathe, trying to understand his confusion, said, "The midwife had to deliver the baby from Elisheva's body after Elisheva was gone. Elisheva could not help." She hugged Efstathios, and Efstathios began to blubber.

"Come here," said Ayathe. "Let's sit down together. All we can do is wait until the midwife is ready to bring the baby out."

"So Elisheva is gone, and I have a baby?" Efstathios asked.

"Yes, love," comforted Ayathe. "You have a baby, and Elisheva is gone."

"I thought I would be there when…"

"I am sure you were. I am sure you were."

A few minutes later, Nathan's sister came out of the room carrying the infant. She walked right over to Efstathios and showed it to him. Tradition dictated laying the newborn at the father's feet, giving him the option to accept it as his own, reject it, or decide to expose it in the case of deformity. Nathan's sister dispensed with that and placed the baby directly in his arms. "You have a son, Efstathios. A little son." The baby was a few weeks premature and small, but it was alive and as healthy as could be expected.

"O, Lord," he said. "I have a son." He lowered his head to the baby's little face and held it close to him. "Hello, little fellow," he said. As Efstathios looked at him, he wasn't sure, but he thought that maybe at that moment there wasn't anything in the whole wide world that he loved as much as that little, tiny boy. Maybe it was its sheer helplessness or the fact that it seemed to love him back without any judgment or question. It just rested in his arms and felt at home there like no one else ever had. He didn't know. But that is how he felt. Elisheva had said that that might happen, and he said to her, as if he could share the moment with her somehow—"You were right, Elisheva. You were right…as always."

XXII

There was so much to tell after the events of that terrible day, Joram and Efstathios—the only two who knew the full scope of what had happened—did not know where to begin. The immediate task of calming and caring for the newborn until a hired wet-nurse arrived, as well as washing Elisheva's lifeless body in the bloodied third room, kept them occupied and silent until there was a lull in the activity.

When that lull finally came, Joram approached Ayathe to break the news, as gently as he could, that George was under guard near the theatre. He added the good news that Ducetius had escaped Enna safely and that he was in the protective company of the powerful Sos. But the news about George, in tandem with the departure of her beloved nephew, hit Ayathe hard.

The life-changing events of that one fateful day were almost too much for any of them to take in. Elisheva was dead, George was in chains pending execution, a motherless baby had been born, and Ducetius had fled with what was construed as two escaped slaves. Who could bear so much loss? But withstand it they did, learning to live under the aegis of a new reality, as some of them had already done many times before.

Nathan, who had no idea what had happened to George until Joram told Ayathe, offered to take Ayathe right then and there to the slave quarters. Joram, who mentioned that they had Vitus's permission to visit George and take care of him, offered to accompany them. Ayathe gathered some food together, stoically setting aside her emotions, especially for the sake of her daughters, and the three of them set out. The others stayed home with the baby.

When they arrived at the slave quarters, the guard, who knew Nathan and Joram, kindly brought them over to where George was. Upon seeing them, George tried to smile. But it became apparent he had suffered some type of mini-stroke during his afternoon of incarceration. He could still speak and was elated to see them all, but his face sagged a little on one side, and he felt terribly weak. Joram spoke to the guard and asked if he could send a message to

Lord Vitus, requesting that George be nursed at home under house arrest so that he wouldn't die. Vitus, who was still at the theatre, answered with refusal—no doubt at Demaratos's insistence—but said that members of the family could stay in the slaves' quarters with George if they so wished. To that end, a guard brought in two cots. They put George in one of them, and Nathan offered Ayathe the other. Nathan stayed with them and slept on the hard floor.

Over the course of the next few months the many difficult circumstances that the family faced would eventually be sorted out and brought to some type of conclusion: good, bad, or horrific.

Elisheva was buried on a forested hillock north of the theatre on the northwest side of town. Her grave lay within view of the spot where Efstathios had buried the Skeleton Lady near the amphitheatre. Everyone thought it was a fitting location, since Elisheva had felt an affinity for that poor ancient mother the moment she laid eyes on her remains. Elisheva's burial on that hillock started a trend among the Ennans—or rather Efstathios's burial of the Skeleton Lady really began the trend—of using the mount at the northwest corner of the town as a necropolis. To this day, the beloved dead are buried there. As for Elisheva, although her marker stone is lost to the ages, her memory lived on for many years within the family. And the three men closest to her throughout her life—Joram, Efstathios, and Nathan—would never fully recover from her loss.

As for Vitus, he led celebrations at the latifundium for days pursuant to the success of the theatre opening up on the butte. The senator and Demaratos stayed in Sicily for two months of festivities and relaxation before returning home. The festivities, however, did not redound to the city itself. After Vitus and Demaratos recounted the sordid tales of theft they had each experienced among the Ennans, Funisulanus rescinded his request for a change in the city's status. Enna would remain a lowly civitas till the Roman Empire collapsed four hundred years later. He even stopped his plans for building the villa up on the butte. "Sicily is a beautiful place," he said, "but its people are dogs." Within a decade, even the theatre, which had been reinaugurated with so much fanfare, trouble, and vicissitudes in fortunes, began to fall into disuse and was all but forgotten by the next generation.

As for George, he waited the full three weeks for Sos to return. The family prayed, hoped, hired a second wet-nurse for the baby, sent Nathan back and forth with supplies for the incarcerated couple, and prepared for the worst.

Then on the morning of the twenty-first day, Sos returned to the latifundium. His chain was gone and Lois was not with him, but he had returned nonetheless. Vitus and the other overseers were shocked to see him. They never expected that he would keep his word, though his fellow fieldhands suspected he would.

Notice was sent to the slave quarters up in the city that George could be released and that half of George's business assets and properties were now under the ownership of Funisulanus. Initial documents had been drawn up to that effect, including a receipt of sale for Lois the slave.

It took many weeks for George to recover from his ailment and much longer to recover from his economic setback. But partially recover, he eventually did. After his release from prison, one of the first signs of his returning health was his suggestion that Elisheva's baby be named after Giorgias, a Sicilian philosopher described by Plato as also having been born posthumously from his dead mother's body. But Ayathe pointed out that having a Georgios and a Gorgias in the same household would be untenable, and so the baby remained unnamed.

Greco-Roman tradition forestalled naming a child till its eighth day, in the event it did not survive its first week. But as whole weeks went by in the case of Elisheva's unnamed baby, something had to be done. Then one day, after a month of private mourning, Nathan announced that he planned on leaving Sicily forever, just like he had left Jerusalem. And Efstathios decided then and there to bestow on his little son the name of his long-time competitor. Even though Nathan had vied with Efstathios for Elisheva's attention all those years, Efstathios was always thankful to Nathan for how he had helped him through difficult times, talked to him about deep, intellectual, and personal topics, sparred with him in the palaestra every week, walked home with him every day from work, lent him a hand in defying Vitus's orders, and in the final analysis, had honored his marriage to Elisheva despite his every natural inclination to the contrary. He also wanted to do it to honor the life-long love his little son's mother had always had for Nathan. And lastly, it was because Efstathios was going to miss his friend. So the baby was named Nathan. And everyone, including Nathan's sister, thought it was a sweet gesture, even if unusual.

As for Sos, a diabolic fate awaited him for his selfless return on George's behalf. Vitus recast the iron chamber into the form of a bull, as he had wanted to do for months. No one knew how to replicate the mechanism that produced the sound of the bellowing, but Vitus was otherwise satisfied with the contraption. He would be able to hear Sos's yelps of agony for what they were.

On the day of the execution, all the slaves on the latifundium were forced to watch as Sos was placed in the bull and a fire lit beneath it. But as they listened for the squeals of anguish to begin, Sos remained silent—a cause of great consternation to both Vitus and Demaratos. The onlooking slaves hailed it as a miracle, and perhaps it was. But Sos had always exhibited almost superhuman self-control. He died in his faith as he had always lived it.

When George learned weeks later how Sos had perished, he marveled while talking to Joram at what a living myth the Pontian had become. "He rescued Eurydice," he said, "he came back to save Damon, and he died in the Brazen Bull." To all who knew him, Sos was a hero of classical and biblical proportions, the likes of whom most people would not encounter in a lifetime. Sos's memory never left George, and he found himself talking to Joram about Sos for years, trying to understand him.

"Sometimes old stories really do come true," Joram always concluded.

Meanwhile, the time had come for Nathan to bid Enna and his family farewell. He joined up with a small caravan trekking its way north on the royal road to Thermae. From there, he booked passage on a ship to mainland Italy. As he traveled, he thought about how much he would miss his family and Sicily itself, along with all the adventures he had experienced there: encounters with Greek gods, the latifundium overlords, the beloved aunt and cousinly bard, the Skeleton Lady, the amphitheatre, and the Gate to the Underworld. But he needed a change, if for no other reason than to help him forget what he had always hoped for and had still not attained. His plan was to strike out for Rome now and try his fortunes in the capital of the world. But before reaching that destination, he had first to pick up someone along the way in Herculaneum.

It was August of AD 79, and Nathan was thirty years old.

BOOK III
ROME

I

The column of smoke had been spewing skyward for an hour.

"It won't stop!" yelled Nathan.

"I'm scared," said Lois, rubbing her belly.

"I think we need to leave the city, Patrón," said Ducetius.

Ducetius's old relative Aristo, who was still alive after all, and as crotchety as they come, called out from his bedroom where he had been napping all morning. "What is going on?" he demanded to know. He looked out the window and shrieked. "Aaahh! What's that smoke coming out of the mountain?"

Nathan, entering old Aristo's room, replied, "We don't know what it is. In Sicily there was a mountain that smoked every day, but it never did anything like that."

"Yes," replied Aristo. "I grew up seeing Etna. Remember? But this looks like the world is about to end."

"I'm going to ask the neighbors if they've ever seen anything like it," said Nathan.

"Well, of course they've never seen anything like it," bellowed the old curmudgeon. "I've been living in this town for forty-two years, longer than most of them have been alive, and I've never seen anything like it."

Nathan could say nothing right in current company.

"We've been getting tremors for years, and now this!" Aristo complained. "I still haven't repaired my shop from a tremor a decade ago. Maybe you and Ducetius could make yourselves useful and fix it one of these days during your 'visit.'" He glanced out the window again. "Look at all that smoke!"

Nathan simply nodded, not knowing how to respond.

Aristo then looked directly at Nathan and demanded. "Well, aren't you going to ask the neighbors about it?"

"About what?" responded Nathan.

"The mountain!" he blustered.

"But you just said…"

"Nevermind what I just said," he responded. "Go talk to Kaliphon. He lives nearby. He'll know what's going on. He's the magistrate's freedman. If he doesn't know, nobody will."

Nathan walked outside to see how the neighbors were responding to the situation. He did not know who Kaliphon was. But one of the neighbors—maybe Kaliphon—was standing in the road gazing up at the smoke.

"What do you think?" Nathan asked.

"I don't know," he responded. "My wife is terrified. From what I can see, it may not affect us at all. But who can say? I know we've had a few tremors this week, but that has almost become the norm."

"But that column of smoke is enormous," observed Nathan. "If the wind changes and starts blowing our way, it could completely envelop the town."

The Bay of Naples, where Nathan was now situated in the city of Herculaneum, was, and is, the most seismically unstable locale on the entire continent of Europe. Caught near the collision point of two tectonic plates, the beauty of the bay's cliffs, promontories, port cities, and islands belie its dangers. Upon sailing the Tyrrhenian Sea to reach Herculaneum a month prior, Nathan saw half a dozen volcanoes and volcanic islands to his right like Stromboli, Vulcano, and Lipari. The captain of the ship made note of them. But lurking beneath the sunlit waves lay a brooding world of submarine volcanoes as well. The mountain currently spewing, which stood on the mainland beyond the beach-front boathouses and terraced villas near where Nathan disembarked upon reaching Herculaneum, was about to become the most lethal and famous volcano in the entire world.

"I am new here," said Nathan to the neighbor.

"Yes. I know. You are staying with the old fuller, Aristo."

"Yes, I am" answered Nathan. "So perhaps I am misspeaking; but my inclination is that we should try to get out of the city. What do you think?"

"I agree," the neighbor replied.

"And we should leave soon."

"That depends on conditions," the neighbor replied. "I believe you have a boat, correct?"

"Yes. Or at least Artisto has one. It's down by the boathouses."

"If you have a boat," continued the neighbor, "then you should attempt to reach Naples or Misenum to the northwest by water." He glanced toward the waves and grimaced. "But it looks like the current is beginning to pull in the opposite direction from there, toward Oplontis and Pompeii. And that is the same direction the wind is taking the cloud of smoke.”

“So you think traveling by water is *not* the best way to go?”

“It may be the only way to go. Walking up the coast would not be advisable. If you need to leave the area quickly, you’ll never accomplish it by walking. But to sail, you have to either wait for the wind to shift in your favor or hug the coast as you sail north to avoid the current. If you go too far out into the bay, the current will pull you in the exact opposite direction you wish to go and drag you toward the dark cloud.” The neighbor paused. “But if you sail too close to the coast, you’ll have to deal with possible shoals and shallows when the wind whips up, and your boat will be dashed to pieces by the incoming waves.”

“So,” said Nathan, with a half-sinking, half-challenged feeling, “there is no easy way out of this.”

“No, there isn’t, my friend. Like life. But you know how to sail.”

“No,” responded Nathan. “I have never sailed, and neither has the friend I came with. Aristo is too old to sail, and my friend’s wife is pregnant and has probably never sailed either.”

The neighbor shook his head.

“Would you mind then,” asked Nathan, “if we worked together to leave? I do not think I can make it without help.”

“No. I would not mind. But if you can reciprocate by taking some of my friends and family on your boat, I will make sure you reach land safely.”

“I would appreciate that,” said Nathan.

“But how is it,” asked the neighbor, “that you have never sailed?”

“My family is Jewish, and I am from Judaea,” Nathan replied. “The only sailor I have ever heard of in our entire history was thrown overboard in a storm and swallowed by a giant fish.”

“That is a sorry national record,” commented the neighbor. “But then you are sure to fare better than he did.”

They smiled then looked back up uneasily at the ceaseless torrent of smoke.

“By the way,” said the neighbor, “my name is Kaliphon.”

“I am Nathan,” he said, extending his hand in greeting. “Aristo has mentioned you. It is a pleasure.”

Nathan liked Kaliphon. Aristo was right that he seemed to know everything.

“We should prepare,” said Kaliphon. “You should tell Aristo

and the others that as soon as the wind shifts, we will try to leave. Until then, they should gather a few essentials to take with them."

"I will," replied Nathan.

As Nathan turned back inside, he thought to himself how unsafe life had become yet again. No matter where he went—Jerusalem, Galilee, Enna, or Herculaneum—life-threatening circumstances arose either from war, riots, employers, or nature. How much tumult could one survive? He was only thirty, and life had sent more than his share of difficulties. He thought he had escaped to a new life only to run into the jaws of more chaos than he had left. He knew he was not alone in his troubles and that others had experienced much worse than he had. The only person he knew who seemed unscathed by life was Joram. No matter what happened, Joram somehow managed to rise above the fracas.

As usual, the line from Qohelet that 'time and chance happen to us all' entered Nathan's brain again. Not, he thought, that life was completely arbitrary and that there was no one at the helm overseeing the affairs of men. But it seemed to him that the helm was unsearchable and gave no guarantees to men other than the fact that he would exist whatever betide them. So, as Joseph would say, Nathan had to do for now what the now required of him. And that meant, for now, that he had to go back inside, fortify old Aristo, expectant Lois, and gentle Ducetius to keep their wits about them, and survive what might promise to be the worst catastrophe of their lives. He only hoped that he himself would survive.

/////

What promised to make the catastrophe even worse for Nathan than he could possibly have imagined was the fact that on the day before the eruption, the old latifundium manager Demaratos arrived at Herculaneum. He was not there to sightsee or rest before finally returning to Rome. Instead, he entertained one diabolical and outrageous purpose in his evil head: to hunt down Ducetius, whom he had watched run to freedom back in Enna, and resell him again into slavery.

For two months prior, the black-hearted former latifundium manager had remained in Sicily with Vitus, bemoaning the fact that young Ducetius had gotten away. "I have hoped my whole life," Demaratos once said, "to recapture a freedman and return him to slavery." That, in his estimation, was an endeavor worth living for.

Upon seeing Ducetius escape Enna, he already felt compelled to give him chase, not even knowing he had once been a slave. But discovering that Ducetius was a freedman, and the very boy he himself had sold into slavery at the age of ten, the prospect of recapturing him became "so delicious" that he took on the challenge as one of the major aims of his deranged life. He wished to bring George to justice as well, and longed to hear of him being skewered through slowly at the end of a pointed rostrum while chained to an oar in the stinking bowels of a Roman galley. Or if not that, to starve alone in the asfixiating darkness of a Numidian mine collapse. But Vitus would not hear of vengeance on George. During the weeks that Demaratos remained in Sicily, he argued with Vitus about having allowed the two to go free to the point that Vitus grew angry with his old comrade. He would not let Demaratos touch George, whom he said had paid his debt in full as per arrangement. However, in Demaratos's mind, Ducetius was a different story. If he could find out where Ducetius had escaped to, he could pursue him on his own without Vitus ever knowing about it. And so he began secret interrogations and torture sessions among the slaves on the latifundium, without Vitus's knowledge, to see if Sos had left behind some clue as to the whereabouts of his beloved Lois and his accomplice Ducetius. As things ended up, the demoralized fieldworkers gave in easily to the sadist's persuasions now that Sos was dead, and Demaratos found his answer within an hour. And so Demaratos, forestalling his return home from Sicily to engage in a little sport, had come to Herculaneum.

Demaratos's first stop in town, the very morning of the eruption, was to speak to the local magistrate, Kaliphon's former master. Demaratos had many connections in Herculaneum since his own Roman lord, the prior owner of the latifundium, had a vacation home there. The lord was not in town, so Demaratos had full run of his house and plenty of henchmen to help him capture Ducetius. But he needed to keep in good standing with the magistrate so he could perform his manhunt surreptitiously.

"So tell me what's new in town," Demaratos said as he entered the magistrate's office. "Any newcomers, important people, lovely ladies?"

"Why do you want to know?" the magistrate answered. "What nefarious plans do you have for this trip?" He knew Demaratos too well to trust him, but he sometimes found him useful.

"Just wondering," responded Demaratos. "I'm in town for only a few days, and I want to know who I should go out of my way to meet or go out of my way to avoid."

"Ha!" laughed the magistrate. "Always the schemer." He looked down, deciding whether to engage in the latest gossip with him or to avoid encouraging his vices. "There's a pretty couple that's been staying with Aristo the fuller," he said, giving in to his weaker side. "I've heard the wife is something to look at, even though she's pregnant. Or so Kaliphon says."

"Tell me more. Why are they staying with Aristo? And why hasn't that living carcass kicked off yet?"

"Maybe the pungency of urine keeps him alive. I don't know. But Kaliphon says that one of them, at least, is a distant relative of Aristo."

"A relative? I didn't know he knew a single living person in the entire world. He's such a bore."

"He doesn't need to be exciting. He's rich."

"I suppose. Still, *I* wouldn't want to spend time with him. Anyone else I should know about?"

"Kaliphon says another young fellow showed up at Aristo's a few weeks ago."

"Another one, eh? Maybe Aristo is not so boring. Or maybe the vultures are just circling before he keels over. I think I'll pay him a visit, especially if his young female guest is worth looking at. Anything I should know about the second fellow?"

"Kaliphon hasn't told me much. All three guests arrived from Sicily. That much I know."

"You don't say—the dullest place on earth." Demaratos responded as flatly as he could, though that was the very piece of evidence he sought to gain from the conversation.

"But I thought you just came from there yourself," said the magistrate.

"Yes. And more's the pity. It's a small world; and that island makes it even smaller," he responded, trying to sound disinterested again.

The magistrate then looked Demaratos right in the eye. "But you listen here, my annoying friend," he said, exasperated. "I don't want any trouble from you while you're here. Don't be meddling with Aristo or any of his guests, or there'll be consequences. You can be sure."

"Then why did you tell me about his guests to begin with?" Demaratos asked.

"Mostly because you bring out the worst in people. I should have known better," responded the magistrate. "But I'm also bored, and I need something to do."

"So there are no jobs you need assistance with while I'm here?" Demaratos asked. "No policing, spying, quelling of public unrest?"

"None," responded the magistrate. "If anything, *you're* going to be our job for the next few days. I'll be watching. So I'd be careful if I were you."

"Not too careful. I want to give you plenty of excitement," Demaratos responded.

After leaving the magistrate's office, Demaratos ambled about town, catching something to eat at one of Herculaneum's many taverns. While he was eating, the first explosion from the mountain occurred, initiating the column of smoke and sending a shockwave reverberating through the air. The diners, utterly startled, all stared out the window, and for half an hour talked in circles over what it could mean and what they should do. Some people left to get back to their families. Others stayed and panicked. Some thought it was nothing and that it would soon blow over. Others viewed it as an omen of death. For Demaratos, it meant only one thing: that it afforded him a smokescreen to pursue his prey and that he needed to move quickly in case the situation either grew worse or ended too soon.

He invited three of his cronies to his lord's vacation home to confer with them about a course of action.

"This is the perfect moment," said one of his cronies—one with whom Demaratos shared his love of the hunt. "Everyone's attention is on the mountain, which is probably nothing. And I know exactly which couple you are talking about: the ones staying with the grumpy old fuller."

Another chimed in. "It's the husband you want," he said. "Though the woman would garner a pretty penny too. And you say she is an escapee as well."

A third interjected. "It shouldn't be difficult to pick them up. She's pregnant and he looks docile. He actually works at the fuller shop. And get this: he sometimes helps with the urine collection."

"Of course he does. What a bafoon!" laughed Demaratos. "It's just like I always say: a freedman doesn't know how not to be a slave anymore. That's why we have to help him get back into the profession he really wants."

The four men laughed.

Demaratos then said, "I want you to go to Aristo's house. Offer the couple assistance in the current crisis. If they don't want your help, tell them that for their own good, the town magistrate has asked everyone to make their way down to the wharfs and boat houses to await instructions. Mention that you've been personally sent to escort the aged fuller and his guests to the rendezvous point at Kaliphon's request. The old windbag will buy that line. Then, once you get them out of the house, bring them here and we'll figure out what to do with them, though I already have a few plans for the girl."

"But what if the other young man is there?" one of them asked. "Do we bring him too?"

"You have to. There's no other option."

"But what are we going to do with him? Kill him?" one of the men asked. "And what about Aristo? Won't he be missed?"

"Listen: if every one of the four of them ends up going missing by the end of today, no one will even bat an eye. A quarter of the town has left because of that smoke already. We'll find out where Aristo stashes his money, then we'll bash him in the head. It will be a pleasure. As for the other young man, no one knows he's here. He's completely anonymous, so we can sell him or kill him. It doesn't matter. Either way, if it all works, there will be plenty of profit for each of you. Just don't arouse suspicion. Think you can do that? Put on more charm than you ever have in your entire miserable lives. If you do, we might actually end up with the proceeds from three slaves as well as the old windbag's money."

As they turned to exit the door, the mountain let out another explosion, and one of the men looked back at Demaratos. "Are you sure this is a good time to be doing this?"

"If I thought we were in danger," Demaratos answered, "I'd be the first one out of here. But just in case you're right—which I doubt—and we need to speed things up a bit, maybe one of you should walk to Aristo's by way of the fuller shop first, in the event the freedman is running a urine collection. Since the new emperor banned the urine tax, I'm sure our man is doing an extra run right now. If the freedman is alone, you might be able to take him by force and get him back here without having to bother with the other three. Then we can decide whether we want to leave here or not. As long as I have the freedman, I don't really care about the other two."

The men then left.

Back at Aristo's, Nathan tried to describe Kaliphon's suggestions to his impatient host, but he ignored him. "Yeah, yeah," Aristo said. "Just do whatever Kaliphon tells you. Spare me the details." Aristo then turned to Ducetius, wanting to put his affairs in order in the event of an evacuation. "Ducetius," he said, "I need you to make the rounds before we go."

Nathan said, "Cousin, it looks bad out there. It would not be wise to do that now."

"How would *you* know?" snapped Aristo. "Now would be a *perfect* time. Looking at that pillar of smoke, I'm sure every bloke in town is peeing about now."

"Yes, but…"

"And when they return with dirty clothes in a few days," continued Aristo, "I'll have plenty of fluid to clean them."

Ducetius did not wish to counter Aristo but agreed with Nathan that harvesting urine at the moment was ill-advised. Nathan continued to argue with Aristo, but the elder would not back down.

"All right," surrendered Nathan. "You win. But *I* am going to make the rounds. I am not letting Ducetius out there."

"Please, Patrón," Ducetius complained, "that is not necessary."

"You have a wife and baby to tend to," answered Nathan. "*I* am doing it."

"But you don't know *how* to do it," scowled Aristo.

"I certainly do," retorted Nathan. "You think that after a month here I haven't helped Ducetius? It's a disgusting job, and I don't really understand why it needs to be done. But I certainly know how to collect urine from vats and piss pots."

"Are you deprecating my profession?" reprimanded Aristo. "Because if you are, you can find yourself another place to loaf."

"I meant no disrespect," responded Nathan, smiling. "I know how important your profession is. Everyone in town knows Aristo the fuller. I'm just not used to it. I never had to deal with urine. I always had…" He could not finish his sentence.

"Had what?" argued Aristo. "Ducetius? You always had Ducetius to do it for you? You primped up, over-indulged brat!"

"Cousin, please," interjected Ducetius. "The mountain is exploding, and we're arguing about urine."

"You're right," said Nathan. "I'm sorry. I'm going to go do the rounds now. But before I go, what *is* the urine for?"

"You want a science lesson right now?" yelled Aristo. "It's got an element in it that gets stains out. Good enough? Now go!"

"I'm going," said Nathan, laughing. "I'm going."

Nathan and Aristo had a love-hate relationship. It was entirely Aristo's fault, of course, in Nathan's eyes. Aristo was such a bellyacher it was no surprise he never married. In a few years, thought Nathan, people will start saying that about me if I continue working for a fuller.

As he walked down the hill from Aristo's, he collected a number of piss pots and pulled them in a little wagon to one of the corner urine vats distributed at various stations in the neighborhood. He then poured the urine from the smaller vessels into the larger one and wheeled the larger one to the shop.

"Yeeecchhh," winced Nathan as he turned his face away with squinted eyes from the pungent odor. Delivering the unsavory cargo to the shop, he picked up an empty vat lined up along the shop wall to replace the one he had taken. He then left the shop to return the vat to its proper corner and the piss pots to their locations. He then started the process all over again in another neighborhood.

No one was on the street, and Nathan felt a little spooked. He wanted to walk back to Aristo's and get their evacuation underway. The sky looked ominous and grew darker every minute.

"Where is everybody?" he said to himself. Some had already fled the city, but most were still waiting, like Kaliphon, to ascertain the best time to depart.

II

One might assume that the eruption of Mount Vesuvius on that fateful autumn day of AD 79 precipitated a mass exodus of people from the cities around it. And such was generally the case. But not everyone thought it was necessary to flee. Every town found itself in a different situation, some more dire than others. For Pompeii, Oplontis, Boscoreale, and Stabiae, the smoke from the eruption headed directly toward them, though they were far removed from the source. Falling ash and pumice from the collapsing cloud of debris early alerted the inhabitants of those towns to the seriousness of their situation. People had to strap pillows to their heads to avoid getting struck. And if they thought staying indoors kept them safe, the accumulated pumice on their rooftops caused their houses to collapse on them. But in towns like Herculaneum, the signs of danger were not imminent. Herculaneum was closer to the volcano than other towns, but for most of the day, the smoke from the vent blew away from the town, and the people believed they could wait out the event. Others, too old or infirm to move, chose to accept whatever fate would bring them. Some ran back and forth into the town on rescue missions, convinced that everyone needed to leave. Others wished to take advantage of the situation and loot abandoned homes, break into cash boxes, and steal foodstuffs from kitchens. Still others, who might have preferred to flee, met an untimely fate because they waited too long.

Nathan did not wish to be caught in the latter category and decided to make this second neighborhood his last before returning to Aristo's. As he was about to pour the final pisspot into the final vat, he was approached by a man who seemed determined to block his path.

"Can I help you?" he asked the man.

"Are you the fellow staying with Aristo the fuller?" the man asked.

"Who wants to know?" Nathan answered, sensing something instantly suspicious about him.

"Umm…" the man stuttered, "the magistrate wants everyone in town to umm…come down to the docks…to evacuate."

"I have not heard anything regarding that," Nathan responded.

"That is because we were just asked to spread the word throughout the town."

Nathan did not like the man and wished to end the conversation then and there. "I will walk down to the docks when I am ready," he said, returning to his task.

The man would not leave, however. In fact, he stepped closer and said, "Would you like some help completing your rounds?"

"No. I would not."

The man had the audacity to step even closer.

"Take one more step," Nathan warned, "and this urine is going down your throat."

"I am only trying to help."

"I don't need your help." Nathan grabbed the wagon handle and began to walk toward the *fullones*.

The man was already breaking Demaratos's cardinal rule not to arouse suspicion. He stepped back and tried to think of what to say next. "The reason I ask if you are the man staying with Aristo," he began, "is that your neighbor Kaliphon specifically requested me to escort you to the docks for your own personal safety since you are new in town."

With that information, Nathan's defenses lowered a bit. Seeing that happen, the man then thought that perhaps he was winning Nathan over. But Nathan was not convinced.

"If that is the case," Nathan responded, "Kaliphon can tell me that himself. I just spoke to him a little while ago, and I know how to make my way to the waterfront. Now if you truly wish to help me, leave me alone so I can complete my rounds and get home."

It was clear to the man that Nathan was not so 'docile' as supposed. But even though he feared it might annoy Nathan, he persisted in asking him, "But why do you need to return home? You should simply come with me. I am sure the other messengers will escort the rest of your family momentarily, so you can all meet safely down at the boathouses."

Nathan glared at the man and stated in no ambiguous terms, "Get away."

The man began to say something else, and Nathan, in a rage, kicked the entire vat of urine onto him. "Maybe now you understand what 'get away' means." The man fell backward onto the ground, his entire body soaked in the putrid fluid. As he thrashed and flailed on the ground, yelling obscenities, Nathan turned around and walked home.

Meanwhile, Ducetius was engaged in a similar debate with the other pair of Demaratos's henchmen. More compliant than Nathan, Ducetius set about readying himself to go with them. Aristo remarked to his young relative regarding the personal escort, "I guess you can see how important I am in this town." Ducetius, though annoyed by the remark, was also duly impressed. In the final analysis, however, the two 'messengers' were ill-equipped to transport a non-ambulatory old man down to the docks at that moment and had to tell him so.

"We do not have a stretcher to carry you on just yet, sir," they said. "But we will bring your young relatives down to the boathouses where everyone else is. Then we'll return with a stretcher to get you."

"That will not work," said Ducetius. "I cannot leave my old cousin here by himself while that mountain is exploding."

Aristo argued back. "I'll be fine, Ducetius," he said, sounding nicer than he ever did to Nathan. "Nathan will hopefully be home shortly, and Kaliphon is right next door if I need anyone. Just go. Better to take care of that pretty wife and child of yours than an old sack of barley like me. I will be fine."

After further argument, Ducetius and Lois relented. They finished packing a few emergency belongings and joined the two men.

As they walked down the hill in one direction, Nathan made his way up on a parallel street, and they passed each other completely unaware.

Nathan entered Aristo's house and yelled out for Ducetius and Lois. Aristo answered, "What are you yelling for? They're not here!"

"What do you mean 'they're not here'?" Nathan responded.

"What do you think it means? It means THEY ARE NOT HERE. Should I repeat it in Aramaic? I don't know Aramaic, but it might get better results."

"*Why* are they not here?" Nathan clarified.

"Some men from the town, if you can understand me, came to escort us down to the docks. Apparently the magistrate is orchestrating an evacuation for the entire city. I don't know if it's really necessary, but maybe. And Kaliphon sent the two men specifically to take care of us."

"Then why didn't you go with them?"

"The men didn't have a stretcher to carry me on, so I'm waiting for them to return with one."

"You're telling me," said Nathan, "that Kaliphon specifically sent men to escort you down to the docks but didn't instruct them to bring a stretcher?"

"Maybe he thought they knew."

The entire scenario did not sit right with Nathan, especially after his run-in with the annoying messenger by the fuller shop.

"I'll be right back," Nathan told Aristo. "And don't go anywhere until I return."

"Where are you going?" he yelled back. "And where would I go?"

Running out the door and down the hill without answering, Nathan passed a number of people walking in the same direction. The town was suddenly alive now, as if something had awakened everyone to the potential danger afoot.

Before going far, he heard Kaliphon call him from behind. "Nathan!"

Nathan ran back and asked him what was going on.

"I'm organizing an evacuation for the entire town," Kaliphon said. "I've sent out word to the magistrate that every able-bodied man is to help in a rescue effort. We'll be sailing people north up to Naples, then coming back for more."

"There were already two men up at Aristo's house who said you sent them to escort Aristo down to the docks."

"How could that be? I only discussed the plan moments ago with the magistrate and didn't mention anything about Aristo."

"Huh," responded Nathan. "And I was nearly accosted by a man who claimed he was sent by you and who wanted to help *me* down to the docks."

"That is strange," replied Kaliphon. "I am not sure what to make of it. But the plan is going into effect now, and I trust you and your companion can volunteer to help transport people."

"We certainly can." He paused. "But I don't know where my friend Ducetius is since those messengers took him."

"I would go down to the boathouses to find him. He's probably there," Kaliphon responded.

So the entire 'messenger' episode was a lie, Nathan thought. But why would someone want to abduct Aristo? And *himself*, for that matter. He had to find Ducetius and Lois before something bad happened to them.

Running several blocks, he saw Ducetius in the distance. He also saw the annoying man, still drenched with urine, talking to a middle-aged fellow just outside an impressive home. The home was only a block or two from the boathouses. Nathan remembered seeing that very house when he first arrived.

Nathan caught up to them as they approached the impressive home, and the middle-aged man was walking toward them.

Nathan called out, "Ducetius! Lois!"

The two turned around. "Patrón!" they smiled.

The middle-aged man appeared unnerved by Nathan's presence. The older gentleman added to his agitation by coming right up behind him and putting his hand on his shoulder.

"Our good magistrate!" the middle-aged man said to the older gentleman, trying to feign a smile. "How good to see you!"

"I'm sure," the magistrate responded sarcastically. He looked at the young couple in the care of Demaratos's friends, and said, "I see you have found our young out-of-towners."

"Yes," replied Demaratos.

"And where were you about to escort them, if I might ask?"

One of the henchmen answered, "We were just taking them down to the boathouses to await further instructions, sir."

"Oh, I see. So you heard somehow that I am arranging an evacuation?"

"Yes," he responded haltingly, hoping his answer was convincing.

"Very good, very good," responded the magistrate.

"Well, of course, my dear magistrate," said Demaratos, "where else would we be escorting them?"

"Who knows?" the magistrate answered. "But I expect every one of you to volunteer for the evacuation team I am putting together."

"Of course," said Demaratos. "We are at your service."

The magistrate turned around and began walking away, not quite satisfied that everything was in order. He swung around again, looked directly at Nathan and said, "Come on. I'll finish escorting the three of you down to the boathouses myself."

Demaratos spoke up and complained, "But magistrate, I was just going to invite them into the house for refreshments before the evacuation."

"That will not be necessary," he answered. "All hell is breaking loose, and you are thinking about refreshments? I have plenty of bread down at the waterfront for everyone." He paused. "If you survive this debacle, maybe they'll take you up on your offer. But for now, I'll see you down at the docks."

Nathan, Ducetius, and Lois followed the magistrate, all too eager to put some distance between themselves and Demaratos, who stayed behind with his cronies.

As they walked, Nathan asked the magistrate, "Who is that man?" referring to Demaratos.

"He's just a Roman who visits every summer," the magistrate responded. "No one you need worry about. Though"—he whispered privately into Nathan's ear— "I would keep your friend's wife out of his reach. He'll sleep with any unattended damsel he can find. And your friend's wife is attractive."

Nathan wanted to ask what the man's name was, but the magistrate began to speak again. "One thing I *will* tell you about him is that he is a distant descendant of the Tarquinii, and he will remind you of that fact if you ever talk to him for long enough."

With that, the magistrate's attentions refocused on the smoking mountain and his evacuation procedure. "We are almost at the boathouses," he said. "And when we arrive, I will be inundated." Nathan's only thought was to ask more about Demaratos's identity, but there was no graceful moment to return to that topic. He would have to content himself with the fact that he was a Roman and that his name was probably Tarquinius. Within another minute they reached the wharf, and the magistrate was thronged by people eager to hear his plan.

Demaratos, meanwhile, was occupied with his friends, trying to revise their scheme for Ducetius's capture, since Nathan and the magistrate had foiled them.

As they talked, the man drenched with urine spoke up first. "So you're telling me," he said, "that the guy I tried to abduct wasn't even the guy you were looking for?"

"That's right, you idiot," said one of the other cronies. "It was the docile one, not the bigger fellow. You couldn't tell that guy didn't match our description? What are you, blind?"

"I think he might be," said the third minion. "And clearly he can't smell either. You stink! Go take a dip in the bay, and spare us all!"

"All right, I will!" replied the man, angry and frustrated. "But I'll tell you this: before the night is out, I'm getting my revenge on the bastard who did this to me. We're either selling him into slavery, or we're dumping his body parts into the bay one by one—and I can tell you which part I'm slicing off first." He then marched down the hill toward the water, cursing and gesticulating.

Demaratos stood silent, watching his comrade strut away, and puzzling over what to do. "It's really not that complicated, boys," he concluded. "We simply need to get the freedman alone and into a boat. And if it's easier to kill his 'Patrón' instead of capturing him alive, that is perfectly fine with me. Let Urine Boy deal with him as he sees fit. As for the girl, I'd say she is a lost cause already. They'll probably sail her to Naples their first trip out of here. If one of us is able to capture her there once she is alone, all the better. But if not, it's fine. Any questions?"

"Yes," said one of the men. "Do we actually have to help with the evacuation?"

"Absolutely," answered Demaratos. "It gives us the best excuse to stay near the freedman—whose name is Ducetius, by the way. And, frankly, I think we have no other choice but to help. It keeps me in good with the magistrate. He's already watching me like a hawk. So we have to put on a good show for him till he lets up on me. Then we can do what we want."

Down at the boathouses, nearly a thousand people crowded around the magistrate to hear the evacuation plan.

"My fellow townsmen," the magistrate began, speaking from a makeshift platform with Kaliphon at his side, "my chief concern is the safety of everyone in this town. According to our records, we are currently home to five thousand, and have several hundred boats. That is enough boats for us to save every single one of you, if we cooperate with each other, take our time, and evacuate in a logical fashion. We are not in any immediate danger from the mountain, like some of our neighbors to the south, who no doubt can barely see 3 steps in front of them from the smoke. So I am asking all you able-bodied men who own a boat to volunteer to transport your neighbors to safety in Naples. You can transport your wives and children first, along with anyone else you can accommodate. If each boat-owner can make two or three trips to Naples and back, we can vouchsafe the lives of every inhabitant in this city. I have already sent word to the magistrate in Naples to prepare for refugees. And I myself will remain here until the last shipload departs.

"I know some of you may deem it unnecessary to evacuate, but I would rather err on the side of caution. So I am asking some of you to go back into town and urge everyone to make his way down to the waterfront. And if the rest of you would kindly step up to the tables here and register your names and the number of passengers you can carry, we will begin the evacuation immediately.

With that, the tables were swarmed with men enlisting to help. Others went back into town to warn the others. The magistrate looked on with pride that so many responded to his call.

"My goodness!" Nathan suddenly exclaimed to Ducetius and Lois, as they looked on. "We have to get Aristo! He's still back at the house!"

"My poor cousin!" responded Ducetius.

Without another word, Nathan ran up the hill. Ducetius tried to follow but did not want to leave Lois behind. "Patrón," he yelled. "I will catch up with you in a few minutes!" Nathan nodded in agreement and stayed his course.

"I can make it," said Lois, as she began to walk as quickly as she could.

Halfway up the hill, Nathan saw Demaratos and two of his friends walking across the street toward the waterfront. He began to look for something, anything, that he could use to defend himself in the event they made a move toward him. He found a piece of wood about three feet long with a nail sticking out of one end. "Perfect," he said.

Ducetius and Lois trailed behind, but Nathan could see Demaratos eyeing them as they made their way up the street. Nathan ran back down the block to intimidate them, and yelled, "You go near them and you're dead!"

Demaratos, surprised by Nathan's sudden appearance, tried to act innocent and answered back, "What are you talking about, friend? I mean no harm."

"Then stay away. If you go near them, you'll have to kill me first. And if you leave me alive, the magistrate will hear about you."

"Hear about what?"

"Just stay away," Nathan warned. "And you'd best hurry. The magistrate is already looking for you."

"Of course," Demaratos responded. "That is precisely where we are heading—as you can see."

Nathan waited for Ducetius and Lois to catch up. On their way, they had to pass directly across the street from Demaratos, who assiduously avoided even looking at them.

When Ducetius and Lois were finally close enough, Nathan whispered. "I do not trust those men. I am not sure what they are up to, but they want something from us. We have to be on our guard. Do you understand, the two of you?"

"Yes, Patrón," they both answered.

Sensing it was no longer necessary to run, Nathan walked apace with Ducetius and Lois, who was now feeling the strain of being in her seventh month. "I need to sit for a while," she said. She and Ducetius rested on a wall while Nathan continued up the hill.

On reaching the house, Nathan called for Aristo.

"It's about time you got back," the old man squawked. "You forgot all about me, didn't you?"

"How could I forget?" Nathan replied. "The sweet tones of your voice beckoned me back."

"What did you say?" the curmudgeon demanded. "I can't hear

you. It was something snide, I'm sure. How did my young cousin ever befriend the likes of you?"

Nathan came closer so Aristo could see him.

"Oh, that's right," continued Aristo in his own line of conversation. "You *owned* Ducetius. He didn't befriend you. You were his *master.*"

"That's right," responded Nathan. "And as his beloved former master, I need to get you out of here."

"But you don't even have a stretcher!" shrieked Aristo. "How are you supposed to transport me without a stretcher?"

Ignoring him, Nathan grabbed Aristo's bed, threw the matting off it, and carried the bedframe outside the door. "We're using your bedframe for the stretcher," Nathan announced.

"You'd better be careful with that," said Aristo. "I'm going to need it when we get back. It might get ruined!"

Nathan grabbed Aristo around his middle and flung him over his shoulder.

"Can't you *tell* me you're going to fling me over your shoulder?"

"Aristo, I'm flinging you over my shoulder," Nathan replied. "Just let me do what I need to do. I'm going to carry you outside and put you on the bedframe. Ducetius and I will carry you down to the waterfront. If this doesn't work, we'll use a wagon from your shop. All right?"

"What?" came the reply. He hadn't heard a word.

Without responding, Nathan carried Aristo across the room, out the door, and onto the bedframe. He dropped the piece of wood with the nail in it nearby on the ground.

Just then, Nathan saw someone creep up behind him in his periphery. "Who are you?" he asked angrily.

There was no reply.

Paranoid that it was one of Demaratos's men, Nathan picked up the piece of wood and swung it at the stranger, ripping his arm open. The young man, who was simply passing by, screamed out in pain.

"Aaaaahhh! Why did you do that?" he cried. "My arm!"

Nathan turned around and saw the young man bleeding profusely from the wound.

From a few yards away, another young man who had accompanied the first one yelled out to Nathan, "What are you doing?" The young man ran at Nathan with a clear intent to attack him. Nathan swung the piece of wood directly at his head, with the nail turned away from the recipient. The impact sent the young man flying to the ground, completely unconscious, with his head wading in blood.

"You're a madman!" yelled the first victim, futilely trying to stanch his arm. "What did you do to my friend?" He looked down at his companion in utter despair. Then he screamed, "Help! Help!" and backed away from Nathan in case he decided to swing at him again.

Just then, the mountain let out another explosion, deadening the sound of the young man's pleas.

"Get out of here before I kill you!" grunted Nathan. The young man, not sure what to do, ran away to find help.

"I didn't mean to kill anyone," thought Nathan aloud, as he looked down at the bloody skull he had just bludgeoned. "Is he dead? I hope not. I am sorry. If you are not one of that man's men, I am sorry."

Aristo, who had lain silent on the bedframe up to that moment, suddenly spoke. "What exactly are you doing?" he asked.

"Trying to get us out of here alive and in one piece."

"Well, that's more than I can say about *that* poor fellow."

"I know. I did not mean to hurt him."

"It sure looks like you did."

Nathan explained, "A group of thugs has been after us this entire afternoon, and I thought he was one of them."

"What are you talking about? You must be paranoid," responded Aristo.

"No, I'm not paranoid. There are people after us, and I think after you too."

"Why would someone want to attack us now when the entire city, and all of us in it, are on the brink of annihilation?"

"It makes no sense to me either. But ask Ducetius when he gets here."

About ten minutes later, Ducetius and Lois arrived. Lois sat down on another wall to rest, suddenly letting out a gasp upon seeing the motionless carcass on the ground.

"What happened, Patrón?" Ducetius asked.

"Your masterful friend here," said Aristo, "swung a beam at that innocent young fellow and sailed him into the next world."

"Did you think he was after you?" Ducetius asked.

"I thought he was," answered Nathan. "I haven't seen him

before, and I can't be sure of anyone. I attacked him when I saw him come up behind me. I didn't mean to kill him."

"I'm sure you didn't," comforted Ducetius.

"So you also think that men are after you?" Aristo asked Ducetius.

"I believe there are," Ducetius answered. "Their behavior around us has been strange all afternoon, cousin, as if they want to capture us or rob us, or something, when no one is looking. I don't know who they are, or why they would want to attack us in the midst of all that's happening, but they want us for something. And Patrón is trying to keep us all safe."

"Is *that* what he's doing?" responded Aristo sarcastically.

Nathan smiled.

"Well, then," Aristo continued, "if you and your Patrón could perhaps carry me to the waterfront without bloodying up the rest of the neighborhood, maybe we can make our way to Naples."

III

While logic dictated flight from Vesuvius, some stalwarts sailed right for it. One such was Pliny the Elder, the Roman author who not only once decried Sicily's latifundium system but was now in the Bay of Naples about to risk his life to save his friends. His death during his rescue mission, occurring simultaneously with Nathan's escape from Herculaneum, occasioned the only written account of the Vesuvius eruption—penned by his own nephew, Pliny the Younger.

While Nathan and Ducetius struggled to reach the waterfront and put Aristo and Lois in a boat to head north, Pliny ordered a ship south to inspect the dark cloud hovering over the bay. He did not understand, as Nathan did, that Vesuvius was involved; and no one understood until that day that Mount Vesuvius was a volcano, since it had not erupted for 800 years.

The growing turbulence of the waters on the bay made navigation to Naples a long, arduous and life-threatening endeavor for

Nathan and Ducetius, who were making their maiden voyage. For Pliny, in charge of the local Roman fleet, and with the current in his favor, the journey into the darkness was all too swift, and the cloud was collapsing back to earth laden with ash and pumice. The tide along the entire coastline was pulling the water out to sea, making it difficult to maneuver between the coast and current. The presence of falling debris, crashing waves, and sudden shallows strewn with beached marine life made Nathan's 8.5-mile nautical trek to Naples nearly impossible at times. One moment his boat was hit by a wall of water threatening to capsize it; the next moment, it was nearly run aground. The constant balancing act between the two proved exhausting to him and to all who sailed that day.

At the rate Nathan and Ducetius had to row, it would have been faster to walk to Naples, if walking were possible with aged Aristo, pregnant Lois, and the other elderly with them. For Pliny, sailing south and approaching the town of Stabiae to pick up his stranded friend Pomponianus, his ship was incessantly bombarded with burning rocks and cinders from the volcano. When asked if he wished to turn back, he was recorded as saying, "Fortune favors the brave. Steer to where Pomponianus is."

On Nathan's boat, a couple of young men and women assisted as best they could to forge ahead. When the waters were shallow enough, they jumped ship and pushed on foot, which proved faster than rowing. Kaliphon remained close to Nathan and kept an eye on him in case he needed help. At the same time, however, Demaratos and his men were also in a boat within view of Nathan, adding to the unrelenting stress of the ordeal. Demaratos remained at a distance and was often detained, but Nathan was continuously conscious of his presence. In the end, after a grueling six-hour voyage, they all reached Naples. Kaliphon had lost one passenger enroute when his boat overturned, but Nathan, who, as usual, had a sort of beginner's luck, disembarked his entire crew safely.

After depositing their precious human cargo, Nathan, Ducetius, and Kaliphon took a respite, discussing the wisdom of a return trip for a second rescue. A second trip was expected, since there were still many trapped back in the town. But the exhaustion of all three men cast doubt on their abilities to proceed. It was already nine o'clock at night, and they had not rested one minute since noon. It was one of the longest days Nathan could recall—and he could recall a number of them—but it promised to continue for ten more hours of overtaxing activity. Kaliphon mentioned that the return ride south would be easier since the current was on their side. His only fear was trying to steer out of the current when they reached Herculaneum so they would not overshoot the town completely. For Nathan, his greatest fear was leaving Lois and Aristo unattended at Naples, especially with Demaratos's men landing there as well. He told Kaliphon he would not leave unless he knew Lois and Aristo were safe. To that end, Kaliphon inquired among locals and used his political connections to find an official to take them in, as well as his own family.

By the time arrangements were made, another half hour had passed, and Nathan felt pressed to leave. Unbeknownst to him, or any of them at that moment, time had already run out for most of the inhabitants of the bay south of Herculaneum and north of Stabiae. Ten feet of pumice and ash already covered most of the towns. People's roofs had already fallen in on them, people's heads had already been bashed in by falling objects, people's oxygen had already diminished from the black smoke and fumes so that it was difficult to breath or light a torch in the darkness. Only in Stabiae, where Pliny had landed, and in Herculaneum, where Nathan, Ducetius, and Kaliphon were now heading, could the sound of human activity still be heard: in Stabiae because its distance spared it from the volcano's worst effects, and in Herculaneum because the smoke column and volcanic heat had not headed in its direction—yet. But everywhere else, there was a deathly silence, except for the muffled screams of those entombed alive under the debris—and even those would cease by morning.

Meanwhile, Demaratos and his men still cast their eye on Nathan and Ducetius, who kept their distance from them as best they could. They stayed close to Kaliphon, whose presence seemed to act as a deterrent, as the magistrate's had back in the town. Questions as to who the men were and why they were following them filled Nathan's brain, but he did not ask Kaliphon. In his fatigued mind, he somehow concluded that asking would show weakness, delusion, or paranoia. So he kept silent.

As dozens of ships began putting out into the bay again, Nathan, Ducetius, and Kaliphon prepared to do so as well. Nathan saw no sign of Demaratos, and he hoped that he could be back on the water long before *he* was. Then out of the corner of his eye, Nathan spotted him and his three cronies scuddling their provisions together so as not to lag too far behind. Nathan was relieved that all four men were leaving Naples, since it meant they couldn't bother Aristo and

Lois. But it also meant they would all remain in pursuit of him and Ducetius, and that lent a simultaneous sense of fear and resolve in him. He was going to best that stranger, whoever he was.

Of the three groups readying to depart, Nathan and Ducetius pushed off first into the bay. Kaliphon went next, to Nathan's relief. Demaratos, who was still not ready, pushed off last. Other ships followed.

Within five minutes on the water, Nathan could feel the current riding them effortlessly to their destination, just as Kaliphon said it would. Kaliphon had estimated it would take a mere quarter of the time it had taken to trudge upstream. But at such a velocity, Nathan knew he had to be ready at a moment's notice to turn into the shore when Herculaneum came into view. With that in mind, he and Ducetius practiced to see if they could do it. They could. However, it slowed them down so that Demaratos caught up with them. Demaratos could not do anything to Nathan while they were still out on the water, since one slip up could send him crashing onto a shoal or overshooting the turn-off. But once all three groups spotted Herculaneum and turned toward the shore together, Nathan and Ducetius prepared themselves for a possible conflict.

Back at the boathouses, the magistrate was still orchestrating the evacuation. About 1500 people still awaited rescue, and from a rough estimate of ships coming in at the same time as Nathan, there would still be 300 left who would have to wait for yet a third round. The magistrate spoke to everyone, reminding them that those who were about to set sail for the first time needed to come back to pick up the remaining people and that he himself would stay with the refugees until the last of them had boarded.

Nathan and Ducetius's plan was to grab passengers as quickly as they could and hurry off before their pursuers could cause them any trouble. But just as they were loading people aboard, Demaratos and his men suddenly grabbed them from behind, two men on one.

"What are you doing?" said Nathan. "Who are you? And what do you want?"

Just then, someone getting into the next boat a few feet away on the beach pointed his finger at Nathan in the torchlight and yelled out, "He's the man I was talking about!"

"What?" Nathan exclaimed.

"He's the man who killed my friend," the person repeated. It was the young man whom Nathan had regrettably attacked that morning. "He ripped my arm clean open," he continued, "and he attacked my friend, just leaving him there to die! Then he threatened me if I stayed!"

Everyone in the boats began to grumble. Some of the people, relatives and friends of the dead young man, began hurling insults and threats at Nathan. One man had to be restrained from attacking him. Nathan was dumbfounded and did not know how to defend himself. He was so physically and mentally spent from the day that he had completely forgotten about the incident.

Demaratos was dumbfounded as well. He had no idea what anyone was talking about, but he could not believe how fortune had smiled on him in such a way that the situation played Nathan right into his hands.

Nathan looked at Demaratos and said, "Is that what this is all about? Is that why you have been following us all day?" Nathan was so delirious with fatigue, he could not remember that his attack on the boy with the beam had occurred *after* the middle-aged man had started stalking him and Ducetius.

Demaratos spoke to the crowd, "We will take it from here." Looking at the young man with the gashed arm, he said, "Thank you for confirming the identity of the murderer."

The father of the young man with the ripped arm spoke up. "We are going with you to the magistrate right now."

"That will not be necessary," responded Demaratos. "Our city is in peril, and we will take care of this incident ourselves with the magistrate. The most important duty you have at the moment is to get yourself and your family on that boat and out of here. When this is all over, we will call on you."

The man and the rest of the crowd backed down, agreeing that survival was perhaps paramount if justice were ever to occur. And with that, Demaratos and his men tied Nathan's and Ducetius's hands behind their backs and led them into their boat at the far end of the beach. They then pushed off into the water as the others did. But as the others rowed away, the water in their sector of the beach was too shallow, and they remained grounded. It did not matter to Demaratos, however. He simply stared at his prey with lustful delight, not thinking about anything else.

"Who *are* you?" Nathan asked him, being held by the arms by Demaratos's men.

Ducetius asked the same, being held by the third man, and adding, "You couldn't possibly have been following us because of that incident with the boy. You were following us before that. In fact, you are the reason my Patrón even attacked that young man. So what is it that you want?"

Demaratos continued to stare at Ducetius. "You really don't know who I am?" he asked.

"Your name is Tarquinius," said Nathan, remembering what the magistrate had told him.

"Tarquinius!?" laughed Demaratos. "Tarquinius?! You buffoon. Who told you that?" All the men laughed in mockery.

Nathan said, "The magistrate said you were a descendant of the Tarquinii who ruled Rome. So why is that funny? And what do you want with us, and by what right are you holding us?"

"By every right," Demaratos responded. Then jabbing his index finger into Ducetius's chest, he said, "By every right I own *you*."

"What?" answered Ducetius, completely befuddled.

"You still don't know who I am?" he asked Ducetius again. "I have the same name as the ancestor of the Tarquinii, Demaratos of Corinth."

Nathan and Ducetius mindlessly repeated the name to themselves as though it meant nothing to them, "Demaratos of Corinth?" Then all of a sudden, reality struck, and both their mouths dropped open.

"You are Demaratos?" said Nathan, "From the latifundium in Enna?" In all their time in Sicily, they had never once laid eyes on him.

Demaratos smiled so devilishly, Nathan felt transported back to his nightmare in Pergusa. And Ducetius's bowels felt like they had dropped out of his torso as his mind relived the horrific life-altering night that man had caused.

"You see, my boy," Demaratos said to Ducetius, "you are mine. I am the one who sold you when you were a cowering child, and now I am going to sell you again. You will be a slave for the rest of your life, as you should have remained all along. Your family was justly condemned, and it is not right that you should ever have been freed."

"What are you talking about?" said Nathan. "*I* was his …"

Demaratos slapped Nathan so hard in the face it forced his head to reel to one side. "Shut up!" he yelled at Nathan. "And as for you," Demaratos said pointing at Nathan, whose eyes were involuntarily watering from the blow, "my friend here has a special treat for you. You will be cut into pieces one by one until you are dead: first your genitals, then your lips, then your hands, then your feet, then your eyes, and so on. We will cut you into pieces and throw you into the water. We originally thought of sparing you, or selling you, or just killing you. But my friend here wants revenge for the piss you covered him with. And so the source of your piss will be the first to go." Then turning again to Ducetius, he said, "And you, my boy, can watch as your Patrón, your ticket to freedom, ceases to exist, increment by increment, till your only link to freedom disappears and there will just be me and you."

The two men on either side of Nathan used one hand each to begin to disrobe him, while the man who had been drenched in urine took out a blade to commence the cutting. Nathan tried to break free, but it was no use. He was strong, but so were they; and there were two of them, and his hands were tied. How was it, he thought, that this was going to be his end? He was only thirty. But then again, thirty, he thought, was the age of reckoning for most men: the period in which they started movements or began wars or got into enough trouble to get killed or change the world.

But he wasn't just going to let them kill him, and neither was Ducetius.

Ducetius tried to break free from his bonds to help his Patrón. Then Nathan, springing to action, leaned on his two captors for leverage and lifted his legs to kick the urine-drenched man so hard in the knees that his knees became hyperextended. The urine-drenched man then yelped in pain, dropped his blade, and lost his balance, falling backward out of the boat. Nathan and one of his accosters then fell out the other side and into the shallow water. The three who still remained in the boat, which was now wobbling from all the movement, also lost their balance and stumbled to regain their footing.

Ducetius jumped loose from the grasp of the man who was holding him, but before he could get away, the man grabbed his legs and flung him to the deck. "Don't damage him too much," Demaratos cautioned. "We need to sell him mostly intact." Meanwhile, Nathan managed to hoist himself up in the shallow water, his hands still tied. He jumped first to his knees, then to his feet. After he managed to stand upright, he jumped into the air and landed with both his knees directly on the face of the man still lying in the water. A rock must have lain underneath the man's head, because the impact instantly sent blood to the surface of the water, and the man lay motionless. Nathan then stood up again and tried to shimmy back into the boat to help Ducetius.

Just then, Kaliphon appeared on the beach, desperately calling out to all of them. He could see that something was amiss between them—though he could not tell what. For the moment, however, the most pressing matter was that an enormous wave was about to engulf them all and demolish their craft. "Demaratos! Nathan!" he yelled to them, pointing toward the water. "Watch out!"

The men in the boat, as well as Nathan, who was straddling the rim with one leg in and one leg out, all turned their heads just in time to see a ten-foot curl come crashing down upon them. As it made impact, it bent the necks of each of them backward or forward or to the side and enveloped them in a wild fury of swirling liquid darkness. It shattered the boat into pieces, which shot out in every direction, knocking the men in their heads, lacerating their limbs, scraping across their flesh, or all three. Then it sent all six of them—the dead man included—tumbling in submarine somersaults toward the beach or the sandy bottom or a rock or wherever it decided to send them. Some of them collided into each other as they flipped around, and some were flung far away from the others. The dead man slapped directly into Nathan, but he did not realize who or what it was. None of them could tell which end was up, down, forward, or back. The primary thought in each of them was whether they could hold their breath long enough to survive. Even Kaliphon, who was on the beach, was knocked down by the wave as it drove inland, and he became alarmed.

After the water began to abate, rushing madly back into the bay, each of the men who was still alive slowly reemerged from the foam.

Nathan popped his head out first, gasping and landing close to where Kaliphon was. As soon as he caught his breath, Nathan said to him, in no uncertain terms, "Kaliphon, those men are trying to kill us." He gasped again for air. "Get us out of here." His hands were untied from the force of the wave toss, and he began desperately searching for Ducetius, who was still bound and helpless. Another shadowy figure emerged, but it was hard to tell who it was. Whoever it was, he could barely walk and was pulling himself along the sand, whimpering and cursing. Then from a distance, in a couple of feet of water, Nathan could hear a choking and gurgling voice call "Pa…trón!"

"Ducetius!" Nathan called back. "Where are you?"

"He…here!" came the response, interrupted by a glottal gulp, barely audible amid the water and volcano.

Ducetius had managed to survive but was fumbling back and forth, his hands still tied, between standing, kneeling, and falling back down.

"I am coming!" called out Nathan. Running through the water, then diving to skim the surface, Nathan propelled himself to Ducetius and untied him.

"Patrón!" smiled Ducetius.

Nathan smiled back and plastered a kiss on Ducetius's face. "I don't know how you are still alive," Nathan observed, reckoning Ducetius should have perished four catastrophes ago, "but you are."

As the last man resurfaced and came into view, Nathan turned again to Kaliphon, and said, "You must get us out of here. That man Demaratos has been trying to kill us all day. Do you still have a boat we can take?"

"My boat is here," he replied, "but it is the last one available."

"I tell you Kaliphon, you must take us and leave them. Demaratos is a murderer and a slave catcher."

"I know," Kaliphon concurred, as they hurried toward the boat.

As they climbed in, Demaratos yelled back across the beach. "Kaliphon! What are you doing? Wait for me! Wait for me!" Colliding with the man who was still pulling himself along the sand, Demaratos kicked him with disgust and tripped.

Kaliphon pushed off into the bay, ignoring Demaratos's pleas. "What are you doing?" Demaratos screamed to him at the top of his lungs as the ship sailed away. "You can't just leave me here! I work for the magistrate! I should have sold you back years ago! Years ago! You don't deserve to be free! If it weren't for the magistrate… Come back here! You don't deserve…Come…back…" As Demaratos's voice faded into the distance, Nathan could hear it breaking into sobs.

Nathan turned to Kaliphon and observed, "So he was after you too."

Kaliphon looked directly at Nathan, but barely responded. "It's complicated."

"Thank you for rescuing us," responded Nathan, needing no more to be said.

They all then looked back to watch Demaratos and his crippled associate—the one who had been drenched in urine—make their slow and separate treks back to the boathouses from the beach.

If the men in the boat had been within earshot, they would have heard Demaratos saying to his crony, "We'll get them tomorrow. There's nowhere they can escape. And if it takes years, or even if we never succeed, they'll be looking over their shoulders the rest of their lives. And that is power. They will remember me."

Meanwhile, the three in the boat found themselves too exhausted to row north to Naples. Kaliphon surprised them both by saying, "Let's just drift south with the current. If we go north, we'll never make it. And if the mountain explodes on our way there, we'll be too close to escape." Nathan and Ducetius agreed. The three of them then simply drifted into the current and for an hour headed straight south till they ran aground on the beach near Stabiae.

Back in Herculaneum, Demaratos and his man joined the remaining refugees for the night in the boathouses. More ships were expected, though no one could be sure. But the magistrate was there, and he seemed confident that everyone would be rescued before the night was out.

About 11:45 pm, however, as about half of the three hundred remaining refugees slept in the boathouses and the other half lay awake talking, Demaratos went for a brief jaunt, leaving his crippled associate behind. While he was walking, a sudden pyroclastic surge, or cloud of molten rock and superheated gases, came cascading down the slopes of Vesuvius at a mile a minute and a thousand-degrees in temperature. Its heat was so intense that if anyone had taken the time to look, they would have witnessed a terrifying wave of death devouring everything in its path between the mountain and the town as leaves disappeared from trees, burning right off their branches, and small animals suddenly vaporized.

When the surge reached Herculaneum, it instantly cooked every living organism in the region within a radius of several miles. It occurred so rapidly that none of its victims knew anything was happening to them. Demaratos's head split open as his brains boiled, and the man drenched in urine twitched in a single convulsion as all his bones fractured and his skin burned off him completely. It did not matter whether one was out in the open, sought shelter in the boathouses, or was indoors. From such heat, there was no escape. The surge hit Herculaneum before it reached the other towns. But throughout the night, six later surges ripped through Pompeii, Boscoreale, and Oplontis, finishing off whatever or whoever remained.

The next morning, everyone in the bay area was dead, except for those who had managed their way north to Naples and Misenum and those in the south around the western portion of Stabiae. Ironically, Pliny lay dead on the Stabiae beach himself—not from a pyroclastic surge, pumice, ash, or fumes, but from a heart attack brought on by his heroic attempt, despite asthma and excessive weight, to save his beloved friends.

A thousand feet away on the same beach, Nathan, Ducetius, and Kaliphon lay asleep in the sand under their upturned craft, which they had arranged as a lean-to.

IV

Little could Nathan realize when he sailed to Italy that summer of AD 79 that Rome was in transition and set to undergo a series of catastrophes never to be repeated in such rapid succession again. Titus had just become emperor when Nathan arrived, and the Vesuvian eruption set a foreboding tone for both men as they embarked on a new era in their lives. Although they did not know each other and would never meet, their lives would be intertwined by several common circumstances, and they would unwittingly tread the same exact ground on more than one occasion. They had, in fact, already done so when both men fought atop the Temple Mount in the days just before the fall of Jerusalem. At that time, Nathan was in his early twenties and following in the footsteps of his brother. Titus was a young general in his late twenties and was following in the footsteps of his father. Fate had now brought them twenty-five hundred miles from the Temple, but close to each other yet again. Nathan was about to enter the birth city of Titus, just as Titus had once entered the birth city of Nathan. Their outward situations would always lay at opposite ends of the social spectrum: one an unemployed alien and refugee; the other, arguably the most important political figure in the world. But just like Jerusalem had touched both of them, so would the eruption of Mount Vesuvius and a pair of other disasters soon to strike.

A plague and a great fire followed on the heels of Vesuvius all in the course of two brief years. Those years corresponded to the twenty-six months Titus sat on the throne, at the end of which he would unexpectedly die. They also corresponded to Nathan's first two years in the imperial capital.

The Jews would always believe that Titus's misfortunes were signs of divine retribution for destroying the Temple. Titus often believed that himself. Since he was kinder than almost any other emperor in all Roman history, people thought he behaved so as to make amends for his earlier sins. He not only passed helpful laws, such as banning the urine tax instituted by his overly pecuniary father, but he put a stop to chronic senatorial witch hunts and even ended his controversial liaison with the Jewish princess Berenice.

The Rome that Nathan entered under Titus would only then come to possess many of the features for which it became known. The Colosseum, which did not exist during Nathan's childhood, would be completed within a year of his arrival. The imperial palace and the Circus Maximus would begin to take on their better-known forms. And the arch of Titus would soon be erected as well, becoming not only one of the most prominent monuments in the Forum, but a showcase for the iconic and oldest surviving depiction of the destruction of Jerusalem, including the Temple's seven-pronged menorah—all executed in fine Roman high relief.

As Nathan, Ducetius, and Kaliphon regained consciousness on the beach at Stabiae the day after the eruption, they realized they had awakened to a new world. They foraged along the shore for shellfish and cooked them over a fire to assuage their ravenous hunger. It barely made a dent. They then set off north for Naples, anxious to reunite with Lois, Aristo, and Kaliphon's family. All along the route, they witnessed the devastation wrought by Vesuvius. They did not even recognize the coastline where Herculaneum had once stood until they espied certain rock formations well past it. Only then did they realize that the beach and the boathouses had disappeared. Even Vesuvius itself had eerily morphed. It no longer came to one majestic point but stood cloven and gouged out in the middle. It put a pit in their stomachs to see how the entire bay had altered and to understand that probably no one who had remained in Herculaneum during the night had survived. It crossed Nathan's mind that perhaps that meant Demaratos was dead and that perhaps even a tragedy could have a positive ending if one landed on the proper side of it. But he dared not voice his thoughts to his rowing comrades.

The three did not reach Naples for two days. They camped overnight on another beach a few hours south of it, then they set off again in the morning after roasting more clams, urchins, and sand crabs. The three men somehow looked both worn out and ruggedly improved by all the crude living.

By mid-afternoon, they had found Lois and Kaliphon's family in Naples, all safe and sound. Lois told them that Aristo had died a few days prior, and they told Lois and Kaliphon's family the unsettling news that Herculaneum was no more. All around, the news was tough.

No one believed at first that the towns of the bay had disappeared. "What do you mean Herculaneum is gone?" everyone asked. "How can a city simply vanish?" But it had. People were grateful to be alive, but many had lost their homes, businesses, and families. Among the wealthy who simply had one less vacation destination, the news was alarming enough. But for others, they had lost everything and would have to start their lives over from nothing.

For Nathan, he cared about just one thing: had Demaratos survived the eruption.

"No one has seen him," said Lois. "And according to everyone we've spoken to, no one has seen the magistrate either. I think it is safe to say that madman is dead—though it is sad to think that about the magistrate."

With that, Nathan, Ducetius, and Lois made preparations to leave for Rome a few weeks later. They needed to find a caravan heading north. Just before their departure, however, Lois went into labor. It was a little premature, but Lois was thankful that the event occurred in the safety of the city worker's home and not on the road. As for Nathan and Ducetius, they both wondered who the child would look like, since it could have been sired by any of at least fifty men. Would it be Vitus, Sos, one of the latifundium managers, one of the many field hands who had taken his turn with the defenseless girl in her early days in Sicily, or possibly even Ducetius himself? "I do not think I am the father," Ducetius told Nathan. "I came around too late."

"You have loved her, though, I assume," said Nathan.

"She is my wife."

But the baby looked exactly like Sos when it was born—to a degree that even Lois herself barely seemed to have contributed a gene to it. "I am not surprised," said Nathan and Ducetius in conversation with each other. In the world of in-utero competition, they remarked, as well as in most masculine venues, a specimen like Sos was not to be outdone. To everyone around them in Naples, however, including Kaliphon's family and the other refugees, the baby belonged to Ducetius, and Ducetius was his proud father.

If Ducetius ever doubted his right to claim the baby as his own, Nathan reminded him that it owed its life to him even more than to Sos. He retraced the difficult circumstances Ducetius had navigated through to bring that baby's birth to fruition. As Ducetius recounted the story to Nathan, he had taken on the custody of pregnant Lois at the port of Thermae in northern Sicily when Sos suddenly announced that he was not going to continue on to Herculaneum with them but was heading back to the latifundium. Sos reminded them that George would be put to death if he did not return, and that he could not have George's death on his conscience. But he also had the protection of Lois on his conscience. So he made Ducetius swear to be Lois's protector. And if Sos might not survive, he told them, he made Lois swear that she would let Ducetius become her husband if she would have him. And that is what happened, despite all the tears and difficulty of Sos's and Lois's parting.

When Nathan arrived at Herculaneum with the news of Sos's diabolical end, Lois swore she would fulfill her vow to Sos by marrying the man he had chosen for her. She and Ducetius never had an official wedding, but they promised each other, in Nathan's and Aristo's presence, that they would live together and be man and wife. Until that time, they had put on the charade of marriage. It was safer and simpler as they traveled together. In Herculaneum, only Aristo knew the truth about the young couple, and he kept it discreet for family honor and love. But now Ducetius and Lois took on a common-law marriage, which would be officially recognized under Roman custom after a year's time. Long before that anniversary arrived, however, Ducetius had proven again and again his husbandly and protective role with Lois and her baby as he dodged the machinations of Demaratos, the tempests of the bay, and the fury of Mount Vesuvius.

V

"This city is magical," exclaimed Nathan.

Like tourists for millennia, Nathan was awed by his first sight of Rome. "If Jerusalem is the joy of the whole earth, Rome is the marvel. Look at these buildings!"

Nathan, Ducetius, and Lois traveled nearly a month to reach the Eternal City from the devastated bay. Joining another caravan of refugees from Herculaneum, they intersected the Appian Way just north of Naples and followed it 140 miles between the Tyrrhenian coast and the Appenine mountains till they reached a gate at the southern end of the city.

"*Was* the joy of the whole earth," Ducetius reminded Nathan, continuing their conversation. "Jerusalem is in ruins. But I agree that *this* place is a marvel."

"I have never seen anything like it," concurred Lois.

"Where do we go now? What do we do?" asked Ducetius.

"According to Kaliphon," answered Nathan, "we have to look for an enormous amphitheatre that's under construction, then continue north from there into an area called Subura."

"I haven't seen Kaliphon for days. Where is he?"

"He went on to Ostia," Nathan answered. "He said he has some connections there. I was hoping he would end up in Rome near us."

"At least Ostia is not too far away. But I will miss him. And he suggested that we look for an apartment in the Subura?"

"Yes. He said it would probably be the only neighborhood we could afford. I don't know how nice it is, but it's affordable. And he said there is a synagogue there."

"Really?" questioned Ducetius.

"I would imagine there is a temple to every god in the world in this place," responded Lois, adjusting baby Kalo in her arms.

"But probably not the Christian God," said Ducetius. "Romans do not like him."

"Give them time," mused Lois, never guessing how prophetic her statement would be.

"Look over there. Could that be the amphitheatre?"

The three of them glanced to their right, the view of which was largely obscured by the enormous Acqua Claudia aqueduct, which provided several sectors of the city with water and was the largest such structure in Rome. The three reached a vantage point in its arches where they could see what appeared to be the amphitheatre from the other side. It was so gargantuan, however, that it defied reality; and their piecemeal view of it only fed their imaginations as to what it looked like as a whole. It was, in fact, not even as large as the Temple in Jerusalem had been, but its height and circular shape lent it a surreal aura as it began, from their changing point of view, to tower above the rest of the skyline. It was known as the Flavian Amphitheatre at the time but was later dubbed the Colosseum.

"The theatre in Enna is a pauper's shack compared to that thing!" said Nathan. "I did not realize the Romans liked theatre so much."

"I didn't either. Maybe the new emperor is trying to promote it."

"Do you know that the new emperor," said Nathan, "is the same man as the young general who destroyed Jerusalem during the war?"

"I thought he might be," answered Ducetius. "But I must say that does not bode auspiciously for our arrival. He doesn't still hold a grudge against us, does he?"

"Kaliphon did not seem to think so. We discussed it back in Naples. And until recently, the emperor was carrying on an affair with Agrippa's sister Berenice, so he doesn't dislike *all* Jews."

"But he is no longer having an affair with her, I heard Kaliphon say," recalled Lois. "So his attitude could slant either way."

"We will see," said Nathan.

"It is strange," continued Ducetius, "that all those years ago we fought against him so far away. And now we're going to live right in his vicinity again."

"It is strange, isn't it?" responded Nathan. "But I suggest we keep that old connection between us to ourselves. The less people know about us here, the better. I have no idea what life in this city will be like. But I think we should play up our connections with Herculaneum and Sicily, if need be, and downplay our connections to anywhere else."

"I agree," responded Lois.

"The Julii and Claudii disliked the Christians," said Nathan, "but the Flavii dislike the Jews. Maybe we should pick another faith while we're here. Kaliphon says that Isis, Orpheus, and Mithra are popular. Maybe we can try one of those … whoever they are."

"We all know about Isis," said Ducetius. "And we learned about Orpheus in Sicily. He is the god who entered Hades to rescue Eurydice."

"You remember that?"

"I thought it was a touching story. But the other name, Mithra, I've never heard of."

They continued walking parallel to the aqueduct with the amphitheatre beyond it to their right. The Appian Way, which for the previous half mile or so had been within the city confines, then ended at a perpendicular at which the trio made a right directly toward the amphitheatre. Before turning, they caught a glimpse of the Circus Maximus almost straight ahead of them: a building of such immensity that there was no way to view it in its entirety amid the bustle and close-set structures surrounding it. What little they could see of it looked like a monster of titanic proportions. If they had thought the amphitheatre was large, the Circus Maximus was three times its size, though not as tall.

As they followed the road to the right, with the amphitheatre now straight ahead of them, they entered the very heart of the city. To their left they now passed the Palatine, the most central of Rome's seven hills. The other hills—the Quirinal, Viminal, Capitoline, Esquiline, Caelian, and Aventine—roughly formed a circle around it. Atop the Palatine stood the royal complex of governmental, religious, and other buildings at the political epicenter of the empire: the palaces of Augustus and Livia, the Domus Tiberiana, the House of the Vestals, a temple of Apollo, Nero's Golden House, and a series of cloistered gardens between them all.

"Look at these buildings!" pointed Nathan again. "They are like I always imagined Mount Olympus. How could the Romans, who are so violent, build such beautiful buildings?"

"I assume that is where the emperor lives," said Lois.

"It seems likely," responded Nathan.

"If it is," said Ducetius, "then all the rulers we have heard about our entire lives from thousands of stadia away, lived within mere feet of where we are standing right now: Augustus, Tiberias, Gaius, Claudius, Nero, and the rest."

"I'm impressed," said Nathan. "I didn't know you knew or cared who the emperors were."

"I have always known the emperors. They affect our lives,"

responded Ducetius. "I was born during the reign of Claudius, and so were you," he said, pointing to Nathan.

"And I know I was born during the reign of Nero," said Lois. "It is hard to believe," she added, "that all the decisions of our world are made in these buildings and in the Senate, which I assume must be close by. Somehow, I always thought of Rome as more of an idea than an actual city."

"I know exactly what you mean," agreed Nathan. "It has become an idea, I think, greater than its physical dimensions."

Continuing on, they passed directly under the Acqua Claudia and came into full view of the amphitheatre. Although surrounded by scaffolding and workers, it was an awesome sight.

"I want to see that place inside sometime," said Nathan. "But not today. We still have to find the Subura." Walking over to a passerby, he asked the man where the *Argiletum* was: the road to the neighborhood they sought.

"The Argiletum?" answered the man. "What do you want with *that* place?"

"We were told to find it. Could you please direct us?"

The man smirked. "I take it you are foreigners. Where is that accent from?" he asked with a twinge of disdain in his voice.

Nathan became impatient. "No matter. We'll ask someone else."

"No, no," responded the man. "Go left here and enter the Forum. Then before you reach the Senate, the road is directly to your right."

"Thank you," said the three, parting with the man.

"What an unpleasant fellow, thinking he is better than we are," said Nathan, as soon as the man was out of earshot. "Do I really have an accent?"

"Of course," answered Ducetius. "We've lived in so many places, I shudder to think what our accent sounds like. Do you remember me having an accent when we were young?"

"No. You were just always Ducetius, so if you had an accent, it was simply part of you, not another place. I didn't even know you came from another place until you were old enough not to have an accent anymore." They walked a little further. "Lois, you have a lovely accent," he added.

"Yes. It makes me want to go to Pontus," said Ducetius.

"Maybe one day we will," responded Lois. "I would love to see my home again, like you were able to."

They then entered the Forum. The congestion, commerce, politicking, haggling, and entertainment transpiring all around them in the foreground formed a stark contrast to the majesty of the graceful, pillared edifices towering above them in every direction. It was pedestrian and spectacular all at once.

With all they had seen so far—the Servian Walls, Appian Gate, aqueduct, circus, Palatine, amphitheatre, Forum—it was difficult to grasp that so much splendor could be compressed within a two-square-mile area. No wonder Rome was master of the world.

The three could have gawked and dawdled in the Forum all day, but took a right turn onto the cobblestone Argiletum where the unpleasant stranger had directed them. And suddenly they found themselves in a vastly different setting. The Subura looked more rough-hewn and dangerous than any sector they had walked through thus far.

Situated in the lowlands between the Viminal and Esquiline hills, the Subura's main thoroughfare was lined with *tabernae*: workshops, bookmakers, fullones, barbershops, blacksmiths, textile merchants, cobblers, and food markets of every kind. As a whole, the neighborhood evinced a strange admixture of wealth and poverty, quaintness and squalor, merchant-class and criminal. Although most of the Subura's residents were lowly plebeians, there were occasional patricians who lived in or frequented the area. Julius Caesar had hailed from the Subura and was its most famous son. He bore the marks, all his life, of the street-smart, gang-memberish existence he was exposed to in his youth there. Whether as a political novice who bribed and clawed his way into office, an ambassador who slept with his enemy to gain his friendship, a young captive who brutally avenged himself on his nappers by charming and later crucifying them, or a seasoned general who relentlessly plotted his opponents' demise, Caesar embodied all the complexities of the Subura, with a conniving mind and a thin veneer of patrician civility. He was a creation of the very neighborhood the little trio was about to take on as their new home.

The Subura utterly intrigued them. It also made them nervous. Could they rebuild their lives there? Who would they ask for an apartment? Was it safe for Lois and the baby?

They passed by a fuller and found themselves reminiscing about Aristo. "He was such an irascible old fellow," said Nathan, "I don't know why I miss him, but I do."

"He could be very difficult," said Lois, "but he welcomed us into his home, understood our situation, and acted as a witness to our vows. I will always be grateful to him."

"I wish he were still with us," said Ducetius. "He would know exactly how to negotiate an apartment in this neighborhood."

"Yes, he would trade *me*," chuckled Nathan. "Anything to get his darling little Ducetius whatever he needed."

"He certainly did love you," Lois said to Ducetius. "You could do no wrong."

"And I could do no right," said Nathan.

Continuing on, they passed the storefront of a taberna bookmaker. As they took a glance, the door to the shop suddenly flew open, and a woman, full of blast and fury, pushed a young man out onto the cobblestone, reprimanding him with every step. Nathan muttered, "It sounds like me and Aristo."

"You were a mistake from the first day we hired you!" the woman yelled at the young man. "But my husband, of course…Get out!" She shoved him again. "And don't think you're getting paid for this week!" She kicked him from behind while he was still within reach. "Who knows what else you've taken!" The young fellow stumbled away, angry and discountenanced, as people in the crowd began to stare or jeer at him. He returned a few expletives of his own on his way up the street.

"And don't ever come back!" she belted out in a final volley.

Watching the entire scenario, Nathan gazed admiringly at the woman, who was attractive and feisty; and he made a move to approach her to inquire about the neighborhood and a job.

Ducetius stopped him. "Are you really going to talk to that woman right now?"

"Why not?" responded Nathan.

"Because she looks rather perturbed at the moment."

"I think she looks good," responded Nathan.

Allowing her a moment to shake off the whole ordeal and calm herself, Nathan approached her as she stared blankly down the street, her face alit by the sun. "Pardon me," he said, "but I was just on my way to your shop to inquire about employment. If this is an inopportune time, I can return later." He looked directly into her eyes as he spoke.

She glared at him, giving him a once over from head to foot. Nathan was unsure how she meant that but took it as a compliment. She then asked, "What qualifications do you have?"

He answered, "I have excellent penmanship and can write Latin, Greek, Aramaic, and Hebrew."

"Hebrew, eh? I'd keep that one quiet." She then paused, looked him over again, and said, "Come back later."

Surprised, but hoping to speak to her again, Nathan answered, "I will, thank you." He then tipped his head and turned to leave, then swung back around again just as the woman was reentering the shop. "One more thing," he asked, before the door shut. "Could you recommend a good building where we might find an apartment?"

The woman stuck her head back outside. "Who is 'we'?" she asked, mimicking Nathan's phraseology.

"'We' is myself, and the three of them," he said, pointing to Ducetius and his little adopted family.

She responded, "Two entrances down," nodding her head. She then went back inside and let the door slam behind her.

The landlord they found two entrances down proved considerably kinder than the bookseller. His name was Manus, and he had a little son named Justin with him. Nathan expected all the inhabitants of the Subura to have the temperament of the lovely, short-tempered harpy they had just witnessed in action, but Manus was not like her at all. He was gentle and kind. "Can I help you?" he asked.

"We have just moved into town," answered Nathan, "and are looking for an apartment. The bookseller two doors down recommended that we look here. Is it possible you might have a vacancy?"

"We might. Come inside." he said.

The four of them, with baby Kalo, entered the building and climbed a stairway to a small landing on the second floor. The landlord's apartment was there, and he invited them inside. "Please take a look," he said. It was a pleasant, though not overly spacious or fancy dwelling, featuring basic furnishings and a shelf of scrolls. But since it was on the second story directly above the tabernae, it was considered ideal: able to have running water, and easy to escape in case of fire.

After a cursory tour, introductions, and small talk, they all sat down.

"Tell me about yourselves and your situation," continued the landlord, "and we will see what we can do. Why did you come to this neighborhood, and what are you looking for?

Nathan did all the talking. "We are from out of town. We came here on the recommendation of a friend."

"And he recommended the Subura?"

"He said it might be affordable."

"And where are you coming from?"

"Herculaneum. Maybe you heard of the catastrophe there."

"I certainly did. Refugees have been pouring into the city for over a month talking about it. The only hint we had that something was afoot prior to that was that the sky was dark for several days when it happened. We didn't know what it was until the refugees arrived. And the refugees have continued to stream in to the point where, if there were any vacant apartments in this area, they have mostly been taken by now. We're overflowing." He paused. "So you were in Herculaneum when the eruption occurred?"

"Yes. It was terrible. But are you telling us that you do not have any rooms left?"

"We may have an apartment. But I need to know about your finances before we can discuss that. How will you earn a living in order to pay the rent if I grant you a vacancy?"

"Ducetius and I both have construction experience. We worked in a number of buildings just like this one back in Sicily, repairing walls and roofs, fixing leaks, framing windows, building sheds, etc. We also oversaw the renovation of a local amphitheatre."

"Very good. So you lived in Sicily for a while as well as Herculaneum. I detected the Sicilian accent on your friend—Ducetius is it? However, with you and the young lady, I hear other ethnic strains. May I ask where from?"

Nathan hesitated to answer. They had only been in Rome a matter of hours, and already he was divulging more than he wished. "Let's just say, for the moment, that Sicily, like Rome, draws residents from everywhere."

"In that case," the landlord explained, "you will fit right in. The Subura is known for its eclectic mixture. And your experience in construction and supervision will go far here."

"I am actually interested," Nathan responded, "in finding work as a scrivener. I'm sure Ducetius would be interested in that as well. I spoke to the bookseller two doors down about it. She told me to come back and speak to her later. But, if I may ask, what is your opinion of that profession, if you know anything about it. Is it a worthwhile one? I see you have a number of scrolls on your shelf, so I figured you've had some dealings with the local booksellers."

"Bookmaking and copying? I would say that the work can be most tedious. But it has its upsides. You can gain an entire education from reading the manuscripts you copy and learn things you would otherwise never be exposed to. I have always enjoyed it, despite the minutiae it involves. And the pay is not bad."

"So you have worked as a copyist yourself?" asked Nathan.

"I am the owner, or I should say, co-owner of that copy shop you stopped at. The woman you spoke to is my wife, Valeria. She is the other co-owner."

Nathan smiled. "No wonder she pointed us in your direction when we asked her about an apartment."

"If she spoke to you at all she must have liked you. She doesn't like most people. However, to my knowledge, we do not have any openings at the moment, so I am not sure why she suggested you come back."

"I believe a position may have opened up while we were waiting to speak to her."

"What do you mean? Was she firing someone—again?"

"That seemed to be the case," Nathan said smiling.

Manus looked downward in awkward resignation. "That is my wife. And that is her specialty. My wife is a shrewd judge of character. That quality has its upsides, though sometimes it can be difficult to live with. It's hard to find good help these days. Most of the workers in the shop are slaves. We rent them from a number of places in the area. But I insist on employing at least a couple of free men as well. Not enough free men in the city have work these days. Romans have grown too dependent on government handouts for everything, and it has been to our detriment as I see it. On the other hand, our free hires usually prove more difficult than the slaves, though they often have more drive. That would be the second worker she has fired this month."

Nathan was surprised at the landlord's candor. Nathan needed, however, to square away the question of lodgings before continuing. "If you find us acceptable," he said to Manus, "and if you and your wife might be willing to try us out for at least one day of work tomorrow, either as copyists, if you need, or as carpenters—or both—is it possible that you might have an apartment we can stay in at least for tonight, if not longer? We have nowhere else to stay, so at the very least, we would like to pay for a room tonight with the cost of services rendered tomorrow, if you could use us; then we can continue our search elsewhere for work and a room if you decide you cannot accommodate us."

Manus looked directly into Nathan's eyes. "I believe Valeria might be amenable to one of those two arrangements. If you would step outside with me, back to the copy shop, I will go speak with her."

The three of them returned to the street and waited in the late afternoon sunlight in front of the bookseller while Manus went to speak to Valeria alone. Five minutes later, Valeria came outside to speak to them. With no further ado, she stated, "My husband and I will make the following arrangement with you: You and your friend," alluding to Ducetius, "will work part time in the copy shop, as needed, and part time as repairmen in our building, as needed. There is always something awry in the apartments, and you will be responsible for fixing things. And you," she said, pointing to Lois, "will watch over our little son Justin while you are caring for your own son, so that my husband can spend more time in the shop. In return, you can rent our last remaining vacancy, on the third floor. But this arrangement is probationary. If you do not prove satisfactory, starting with tomorrow, there are others who can take your place within an hour. Is that agreeable to you all?" She almost sounded kindly with that last question.

"We are agreeable to it," they each said in their own way.

"Good," she said, with the faintest glimmer of a smile.

VI

But life in Rome was tough. It required daily strategy. The apartment they took had no toilet, so they had to use chamber pots or a public latrine. It had no kitchen, so they had to cook in the insula courtyard or eat in a taberna. It had no bathtub, so they had to use a bathhouse. It had no laundry facilities, so they had to use a fuller.

For at least his first month in the capital of the world, Nathan was daunted by the logistics of simply readying himself in the morning for the day's tasks. It was a far cry from his childhood in Jerusalem, where Ducetius prepared his clothes, his bowl of hot water, and his shaving blade, even if he wasn't shaving that day. In Nathan's experience, it was easier to camp outside, as he had done during his several migrations, than it was to live in the big city. At least while camping, everyone lived under the same conditions, was dirty, slept and cooked outside, and had low expectations for personal cleanliness. In the Subura, however, everyone lived in close quarters, and work often took place indoors between physical laborers, who sweated on the job, and sedentary workers, who did not. For Nathan and Ducetius, who jockeyed back and forth between both, the mix was uncomfortable. Nathan could not remember another place he had lived in all his life where the ability to be clean and the expectation to be clean were at such odds. Back in Sicily, the amphitheatre was near the palaestra, which had bathing facilities, and Auntie Ayathe had a toilet room and bathtub as well. In Herculaneum, Aristo possessed all the civil amenities, and Nathan could clean up after work. But here in Rome, he had to walk for blocks to undertake basic hygiene, only to spend part of the day doing repairs and then later enter the copy shop sweaty. The only consolation was that Valeria seemed not to mind at all whatever condition he was in when she encountered him.

Compounding the logistics of Roman life was the discomfiture for Nathan of having to bathe circumcised among Gentile men. If Efstathios, back in Sicily, had found Nathan 'strange down there,' as he put it, the Romans found his exposed glans at the baths a downright affront to public decency. Circumcision was no badge of honor in the empire, nor was it a mere indicator of one's faith. It was an immoral defacing of the human form, and something that ought not be done. In the Middle East and Africa the practice was common, and if Nathan had migrated there after the war, his appearance would have found ready acceptance. In Sicily, the Grecofied Ennans viewed circumcision askance, but the lone venue where Nathan's Jewishness might be on display there—the palaestra—boasted so few visitors that it barely mattered. On the Italian mainland, however, it was a different story.

For weeks after they started utilizing the local *thermae*, both Nathan and Ducetius, who had bravely endured circumcision after his sale to Opal at the age of ten, were shunned in the pools and steam rooms as if they had an open festering wound. Manus later explained that despite Rome's ethnic eclecticism, Jews were still a rarity in the public baths. He told Nathan that it was becoming vogue among coreligionists to undergo an epispasm surgery to cosmetically reverse the condition. He mentioned that even Gentiles unfortunate enough to suffer from a naturally shortened foreskin underwent the procedure. Manus described to Nathan a non-surgical option called a *fibula*, developed by the Greeks centuries before for such a circumstance, but it was painful and complicated, involving the pulling of one's loose penile flesh over the end of one's glans and tying it closed with a clasp through a piercing. But Nathan would not hear of it. He took pride in his body as it was, despite approaching middle age, and weathered whatever reaction he received until his neighbors grew accustomed to it. He also became adept, as did Ducetius, at learning to conceal it under a towel or sponge. And if any neighbor challenged his dignity over the matter, he was more than ready to defend himself and Ducetius as well.

The inconveniences of urban life aside, Nathan, Ducetius, and Lois all enjoyed the actual tasks involved in their workaday existence. Lois adored both the little boys in her charge, brought them to the market almost daily, and either bought street food or prepared food for everyone, Manus and Valeria included. And Nathan and Ducetius found both aspects of their day—copy and repair work—personally gratifying. Although copying entailed the very tedium that Manus had described, conversation at the shop, whether by slave or free man, achieved a level of erudition that everyone took pleasure in and that few venues outside academic circles could match. On any given day, one scrivener might be working on a scientific theory of botany, another Aristotle, and a third a play by Terence. It was wonderful. Nathan thought numerous times how much Efstathios would have relished the intellectual atmosphere and could have used the services of a copy shop in Enna while trying to acquire his play for the opening day.

Copy work provided more variety from day to day than Nathan expected. On some occasions, a large number of copies would be on order for a wealthy client, and the entire shop worked in concert, practicing similar penmanship for uniform products, while one of them dictated aloud from the original. At other times, individual scriveners were given latitude to be creative with calligraphy and illustrations, and Nathan would try his hand at design. Sometimes he and another copyist would work off two discrepant originals and debate over which wording seemed more plausible. At other times, if there was a lacuna or missing word in a manuscript due to age or damage, there ensued either a mad and often futile scramble through other copy shops along the Argiletum or nearby Vicus Sandalarium to find an undamaged version, or a discussion would begin to decide how best to fill in the missing word. Although many booksellers sold scrolls at a discount if they contained inaccuracies,

Manus and Valeria prided themselves on high-quality copies and allowed more discussion among their workers than their competitors, in order to minimize errors.

The amount and level of discussion on a given day depended on which of the two co-owners was on duty. Manus enjoyed intellectualizing and took an interest in the content of the pieces. Valeria took more of an interest in efficiency and completion of the task. Not that she lacked intellect. But she had only so much patience until the point of diminishing returns propelled her to a decision. Under the one, the workers felt more philosophical; under the other, more productive. There was an upside to each, and the undulation between the two kept the work interesting.

Despite their differences in philosophy, management style, and personality—or maybe because of them—Manus and Valeria ran a top-notch outfit. They sold their wares at a higher price than others along the strip, but their reputation warranted it. They kept abreast of what books were being advertised on other storefronts and usually found, to their content, that although they sold less popular works, and therefore fewer scrolls in general, their clientele was more prestigious and willing to pay. They were also the only shop along the strip willing to produce works in codex form, with pages and a binding, rather than as scrolls. Few clients other than the young poet Martial ever requested that experimental format, but Valeria saw potential in its compactness and transportability, and other scriveners, like the freedman Secundus down the block, later followed her cue.

Beginning a few months into their stay, Nathan and Manus would go for a walk together after work. Manus was often in no particular rush to get home, and Nathan had no particular someone to come home to. Although Manus was ten years Nathan's senior—unlike Valeria, who was younger than Nathan—they had a great deal in common. One evening while walking together, Manus pointed out the synagogue in the Subura. Nathan had not seen a synagogue in years—Enna did not have one, and he never knew of one in Herculaneum—and the one in the Subura looked so inconspicuous, he could not tell it was a synagogue at all.

"This is the synagogue?" asked Nathan. "How do you know?"

Manus lowered his voice. "My mother was a Jewess who grew up here," he said, "and my father was a Roman."

"Is Valeria Jewish also?" Nathan asked, lowering his voice.

"No. She is Roman. So little Justin is similar to myself, only with his parents in reverse. But we do not discuss such things. It is dangerous, at times, to be a Jew in Rome."

"I imagined it would be."

"For the most part, we are left alone. But once in a while, an emperor casts an evil glance our way. My mother told me that Tiberius expelled the Jews from Rome before I was born. And when I was old enough to remember, Claudius did the same."

"Why were you expelled?"

"I don't know, exactly, especially in the case of Tiberius. I know they were lumped in with an expulsion of the Isis cult. But with Claudius, I always suspected that it was because of some trouble the Christians were causing. Romans have a hard time distinguishing between Christians and Jews. But I also think it may have had to do with the emperor's friend, King Agrippa, being proclaimed a god or messiah by some of his Jewish followers."

"I vaguely remember that story. And when the Jews were expelled, did you have to leave?"

"Since my father was Roman, we were spared. But we knew other people in the city who were forced out, especially from the Transtiberim region, across the Tiber, where most of the Jews live. Eventually they came back. There are plenty of us here now, but who knows when the next expulsion will come? The Flavii are not great fans of the Jews. The current emperor destroyed Jerusalem and the Jewish Temple years ago."

"I am familiar with that fact." Nathan did not wish to reveal just how familiar.

"I assumed so," Manus said. "Because with a name like Nathan, you must be one of us."

Nathan almost started at Manus's remark. "I forget that my name can give me away," he said. "I figure in an eclectic city like Rome, people hear non-Latin names all the time and can't distinguish one type from another."

"That is generally true. But there are always those who know. So you, we, must be careful. There is a cloud over our people in the city these days."

"Do you mean because of the Flavii?"

"Yes. We are being singled out by them, not only with the special Jewish tax and other laws but because of the amphitheatre as well."

"There's a tax for being Jewish?"

"Yes. You've never paid it?"

"No one ever mentioned it in Sicily."

"We have to pay a special Jewish tax for the upkeep of the Jupiter Capitolinus every year."

"What is that?"

"It's the enormous temple to Jupiter on the Capitoline Hill, not far from here. It's the largest Roman temple in the world. When Titus destroyed Jerusalem, his father Vespasian ended our tithe for the Jerusalem Temple and turned it into an equivalent tax to upkeep Capitolinus. Whether we supported the war or not, we have to pay it. And the collectors are notorious."

"They always are."

"But one of the men who oversees the collection is my own brother-in-law. He works for the special fiscal procurator's office in Ostia. And he checks up on me every year to make sure I've paid it."

"Your own brother-in-law?"

"He doesn't want Valeria to get in trouble."

"He can't just overlook it since you're married to his sister?"

"He would never do a favor like that for me. We barely get along."

"Is it bad?"

"We manage. But the amphitheatre situation is what really bothers me. Taxes come and go. If Vespasian could have taxed the air, he would have. But every time I see the amphitheatre, it makes me shudder."

"What do you mean? What's the connection between being Jewish and the amphitheatre?"

"Really? You don't know?"

"Know what?"

"You don't know who is building the amphitheatre, and how it is being paid for?"

"No. I do not. I assume it is being built by slaves along with some free laborers and artists. When I oversaw the renovation back in Sicily, that is the mix of workers we had."

Manus bent close to Nathan to whisper into his ear. "But all of the slaves in the Flavian Amphitheatre are Jews."

"What?" Nathan started. "How is that possible?"

"It is. There are 12, 20, 50, 70,000 of them, some say. And they were all captured at the fall of Jerusalem."

Nathan's mouth dropped open. He could not speak for almost half a minute, simply staring at Manus.

"I had no idea. And they have been kept alive in there all this time," Nathan asked, "just to work on that structure? Jerusalem fell years ago."

"Yes. It's been ten years. The actual building began about eight years ago or so. Who knows where they were between the fall and then. Partially in transit, no doubt. But for eight years I have watched that building go up from a distance, knowing and feeling queasy about it. And it was the captives' property and the confiscated treasures from the Temple that are financing the project."

"Are you sure?"

"Of course I'm sure. Ask anyone on the street. They will tell you."

"Have you ever been there? Have you ever seen any of them?"

"I wouldn't dare. Who knows if they wouldn't take one look at me and say, 'He's one of them too,' and lash me under the whip as well. Sometimes I think that one of these days the emperor is going to issue an edict to have us all rounded up throughout the city to join them. It's entirely possible. Every time the door of the shop opens, I think that moment has come. But there are other times when I almost want to volunteer to join their ranks. I feel guilty that I am free and they are not. And they only lost their freedom because they fought so hard trying to gain it; something I never did. Why are they being punished and I am not?"

"I do not understand the workings of fate. But I certainly know the guilt you describe. I have experienced it too," recalled Nathan. "I have seen so much injustice. But what can one do? We could suffer for other people, but what would it accomplish? If we died, it would only be one life, and it wouldn't amount to anything. But what will happen to all those slaves when the building is completed?"

"I don't know. Some will probably be sold. I'm sure many of them will be slaughtered in the games on the opening day."

"How horrible: worked and then killed in the very building they built. How is it that the rulers of the world who dispense justice to the people of half the world do such things? I take it, then, that the amphitheatre is not for plays, but for games."

"It is not for plays, Nathan. This is Rome. There are theatres here, but they are dwarfed by Rome's true love. The Flavii would not spend eight years on a monument to perform Sophocles or Terence. The people crave blood and suffering. They want to see the worst a person might experience in life so they can subconsciously prepare for it and sit safely in their seats while preparing."

VII

But Nathan dared. He had to know. Despite all the logistics he had put into readying himself that morning, he was already sweating. Every step closer to the amphitheatre made him nervous and stronger or weaker in his resolve. One moment he was thinking he would talk to someone in charge to find out if there was some way he could help some of them, buy some of them, speak to some of them; the next moment he thought, as did Manus, that they would look at him and say, 'he is one of them' and chain him to a work gang as well. But he had to go. Someone among them might have fought by his side all those many lifetimes ago. He might even recognize one of them.

As he walked closer to the walls that currently trapped the slaves inside and he outside, he wondered at the twist of fate that had separated him from them. He had wanted Manus to join him but had been afraid to ask. When he came to the outskirts of the site, several guards and an overseer eyed him with suspicion. Walking up to a lone guard, he asked if he could have permission to take a look around. He had come prepared with money to offer a bribe if he needed to. He had also come prepared with a fabrication to tell the manager that he was in search of a new slave for the Funisulanus estate in Sicily. One of the few items that had survived Nathan's migration from Enna to Herculaneum to Naples to Rome was the receipt of sale for Lois. It had Funisulanus's name on it and the signature of Vitus. In the event Nathan needed a political connection to gain access to the amphitheatre, he brought those papers with him. And if he did not need them, he felt at least that they lent him confidence and a feeling of status as though he were not merely another potential Jew who could be forced into servitude.

The guard took the bribe and waved his hand as though swatting a fly to allow Nathan to pass. Showing him the papers had not been necessary. Entering the complex, he was hit by the smell of sweat and smoke, the sound of chisels and hammers, and the sight of bodies moving with apathy. The eyes of the laborers stared vacuously as the windows of souls with no future: victims of an imperial fury with muscles strained and growing tanner, with minds ever dimming in the futility of perpetual servitude.

As Nathan watched, one nameless wretch crossed his line of vision walking along an upper story of the structure, pushing a heavy-laden wheelbarrow. All sinew, with a gaze that no doubt once burned with a tenacity since snuffed out, he struck Nathan with the nobility with which he must once have been possessed. But whoever he was in the past, no one would know. His face had been scarred so badly that his features were almost indiscernible, at least on the side generally closest to Nathan, with one eye either missing or seared shut. Nathan could not tell. As he disappeared from Nathan's view into an archway, the thought of him lingered, though other slaves and sights caught his attention.

Then a moment later he heard a call echo across the arena that sent a shockwave through him. "Younger brother!" he heard.

Nathan froze. What had that voice just said? Younger brother? Did he really hear that, or was he imagining it? And had he heard it properly? Or was he so psychologically primed to hear a voice from the past that his brain had culled random sounds into a recognizable phrase? Nathan could not believe his ears, if, in fact, they had actually heard the phrase at all. He stood silent like a predator waiting to hear it again. Mere seconds later the words cut through the air once more. "Younger brother!" There was no mistaking it. It was the words 'younger brother.'

Was someone playing a joke on him? Was the callout even directed at him? Or was there perhaps a set of slave or managerial brothers on the jobsite paging one another in the same manner he and his brother had last agreed to? But if that was the case, was the term 'younger brother' so common among siblings that it was mere coincidence that it was being used in his presence when he half-expected to hear a familiar phrase? Or could it be, perhaps, that Amram actually was somewhere in that stadium, still alive, and just recognized him?

Nathan did not know what to do first. The second call was followed by an audible reprimand, most likely from an overseer, followed by the crack of a whip cutting through the air as clearly as the call. Both sounds emitted from the area where he had last seen the scarred slave, indicating to Nathan that the scarred slave had called to him and was reprimanded for it. But did that mean that Amram was the slave with the scarred face? The slave's general visage, build, and height ran through Nathan's brain. With sunburn, scarring, weight loss, wear and tear, and a decade of time all conspiring to obfuscate, Nathan concluded it really could have been Amram.

But could Amram still be alive? Yes, he concluded again, he could be. Amram had last disappeared from Nathan's sight during the battle on the Temple Mount in the midst of soldiers and flames. If he somehow survived, that could have been when his face was seared. If Amram really was that scar-faced slave, Nathan had to find him. Although Amram barely made it onto Nathan's subconscious list of people he ever expected to see alive again, and he had sometimes found his emotions conflicted over the years on the subject of how he would feel if Amram ever stepped into his life again, he suddenly found himself overwhelmed by the hope that someone—anyone—from his past still lived.

He made his way across the construction site to find the stairs that led to the upper level where he thought he had seen the possible Amram. Although it looked like a couple of guards and overseers along the way were ready to ask his business or halt his progress, they did not. He walked with the surety of his supervisory days in Enna, and it did the trick. Everyone left him alone. His manner of strut did not help him find the man he sought, however. He asked a few slaves if they knew an Amram, but they all said no. Either they had never met him, Amram went by a different name, or they were trying to protect him.

After almost an hour, Nathan gave up his search. He had circumnavigated the entire third tier, peered into openings, leered around pillars, squinted through smoke, picked through labor crews, and watched for signs of him on other levels, but all to no avail. It was as though he had vanished. Perhaps he had been scurried off the jobsite temporarily, thrown into a detention pit for yelling, and was either having his tongue ripped out or was being put out of his misery. Discouraged after so much hope had arisen in him and having convinced himself of a happy ending to the day, Nathan made his way out of the amphitheatre. He continued to look around till he found himself completely off the premises and reentering the Subura.

He couldn't wait to tell everyone what had happened. He thought Valeria would not be interested. But he told Ducetius and Lois, who shared his excitement and frustration, even though Lois had never met his brother. Later that evening, he went for a walk with Manus and filled him in on the incident.

Manus reprimanded Nathan for attempting so foolhardy an

endeavor and cautioned him against ever going back to the amphitheatre.

"But how could I not go back?" countered Nathan. "I have to rescue my brother." He explained to Manus his plan to use the paperwork he still had from Sicily to at least attempt to purchase Amram's freedom. Manus was of the opinion that the plan could possibly work, but that Nathan was, under no circumstances, to return alone. He also reminded him that he had no money to purchase a slave.

"Might it be possible," Nathan asked, "to borrow a loan from you?"

"I would have to confer with Valeria about that. And I cannot imagine she would agree to it."

When the three of them—Nathan, Manus, and Valeria—discussed the idea, however, Valeria was not entirely averse to the proposition. But she posed some pointed and unexpected questions for Nathan that he did not readily know how to answer.

"What is your brother like?" she asked.

"What does that matter?" Manus remonstrated.

"I would like to know if purchasing him is wise and worth the risk."

Nathan was at a loss as to how to paint his brother in a positive light. The first words that came to his mind were impossible, obstinate, difficult, unrelenting, driven, and opinionated. He couldn't help but think that he could apply some of those very terms to Valeria, and on that score thought better of the idea. "He is leaderly," he finally answered, "and knows what he wants."

"Then why is he still a slave?" she asked. "With such qualities, I would expect him to be either dead or free. Why isn't he one or the other?"

It was uncanny how quickly Valeria could put someone on the defensive. Nathan again had to think about an answer. "I do not really know how long he has been enslaved. It might have occurred recently. And if not, he is no doubt biding his time for the right moment to escape."

"If I buy him," Valeria continued, "will he work for us?"

Nathan was again at a loss. "He is not really suited to desk work. And he would not be content repairing roofs and walls either. In fact, I cannot imagine him following the directives of any employer." He mused over how very different he and Amram were, and how he, Nathan, suffered by comparison.

"Then what does he do well?" she asked.

Nathan again had to ponder but gave up trying to mince words. "To be honest," he answered, "he excels at leading insurrections. That is why he is in the situation he is. He is a leader of men. I would say he would be good at running your copy shop, but only if it had a thousand employees and if he had the option of galvanizing them into a legion."

"Interesting. And one more question," she said. "Do you *want* him to be free?"

"What kind of question is that?" objected Manus. "He is his brother!"

But Nathan understood the question. He had been pondering it himself all day. "I don't know," he answered. "He can be meddlesome and overbearing, as older brothers are apt to be. But he is my brother. And he should be at liberty to take his station in the world as I am to take mine."

Valeria seemed content with all his answers. Now it was her time to ponder. Manus interrupted her by stating that none of her questions really pertained to the issue at hand. She countered by saying she had obtained the very information she sought. She then concluded: "I am of the opinion, Nathan, that we had best purchase your brother's freedom. Given his disposition and background, he may be fomenting another Servile War from inside the amphitheatre as we speak. And we must preempt that from happening. Since you lived in Sicily and Jerusalem, you understand insurrection. If insurrection happens here, it will ruin business, and we cannot have that. In addition to all of those considerations, he is, after all, your brother. So if my goodly husband agrees, we will put up the funds for his release. You can pay us back over the next year."

Nathan smiled. "Thank you for your consideration. Your offer sounds reasonable. And your motivation for releasing him is not unfounded."

"If we do this, however," she added, "I would like to meet him before he flitters off to who knows where."

It took Manus and Valeria several days to collect the funds Nathan needed. Nathan asked Valeria if she wished to join them when they returned to the worksite. He thought that perhaps between her thoroughgoing Roman-ness and business acumen, it might bring them advantage.

"No," she answered, in her usual definitive, but almost charming, tone. "I do not wish to be gawked at by all those men. Not that they haven't seen fairer. But I would rather not. Such things are better handled by your gender." Nathan disagreed. But there was no arguing with Valeria.

When Nathan and Manus returned to the amphitheatre, they offered the same guard a slightly higher bribe, and he shooed them in with another swat of his hand.

They ambled about a bit, and asked a lone slave if he knew the man with the scarred face. The slave shook his head cautiously as if any answer he gave might cause him trouble.

Nathan then asked him again in colloquial Aramaic, and a decidedly Jerusalemite accent. "Do you know the man I mean? The whole side of his face, or maybe his whole face…"

The slave stared directly into Nathan's eyes upon hearing such familiar tones and responded in kind with the question, "Were you there too? Are you from there?"

"I just need to know where the man with the scarred face might be. I may know him, and I promise I do not mean him any harm."

"He isn't here anymore."

"Where did he go?"

"Someone came and took him away. Yesterday. He's gone. I know who you mean, but he isn't here. He was bought, and they took him. They looked very official, and they took him."

"Thank you." Nathan and Manus then walked over to the guard house and asked the soldier on duty if anyone had bought a slave who had a scarred face.

"What's it to you?" said the guard. "You're a Jew yourself, right? Half of Transtiberim has been here trying to buy these slaves. We can't sell them all, or there'll be no one left to do the work."

"I am not from Transtiberim. It's just that the man helped me once, a long time ago, and I wanted to buy his freedom if he could be purchased."

"Well you're out of luck," said the guard. "But he must have been quite a fellow, that scar-face. The man who bought him yesterday said the same thing."

Nathan was flabbergasted. What? The purchaser had said the same thing? Someone else in the city knew the scarface, who was possibly, maybe even probably, his brother? Who could it possibly be? And how could his timing be so bad? How could that other person just happen to have discovered his brother in the midst of all these captives within a week of his own discovery? If he had just come a day earlier, he might have had a chance. Now it was too late. But who had bought him? He had to know.

"Any clues as to the name of the buyer? I will certainly pay you for the information."

"Aaaaghh," the guard complained, not wanting to work. "I suppose."

The guard put out his palm for the money before beginning his search. Nathan handed him a paltry amount. "You'll have to do better than that," said the guard.

"They'll be more upon receipt of the information."

"Fair enough," responded the guard. "Let me look here. There was a royal inspection here yesterday. The buyer was part of the emperor's retinue." He fumbled through some papers on a table. "There's documentation somewhere around here for it. I wrote it myself." With his back turned, he continued to rummage while explaining the purchase to Nathan. "The overseer yesterday told the guy he could just take the grunt. But he insisted on paying for him. Who knows why? Rich people…" He then found the paper. "Here it is. I actually found it. Can you read?"

He handed it to Nathan, who eyed the scribble: '1500 denarii. Jewish slave. Flavius Josephus.'

Nathan handed him back the parchment with 20 denarii, or about half a day's wages, underneath it. "Thank you for your help," said Nathan.

"Glad to be of service."

Someone in the emperor's retinue named Flavius Josephus knows Amram, he thought. How could that possibly be?

VIII

"You see what I have to contend with?" started Manus during their next walk. "She's impossible. My problem is that I'm too nice, and she needs someone who can rein her in. The contest of wills between us is discouraging. We share views on raising our son, maintaining an excellent shop, what to eat, keeping the apartment orderly; but in the day-to-day working out of our relationship, we fight like gladiators. Observing us could season one for a debut at the arena. I am never quite enough for Valeria. She doesn't trust me or see me as an initiator. If I plan to do something in the next three minutes, she starts doing it in two, so she always thinks that what we do is her idea. I explain to her that if she waited mere seconds longer before she spoke or made a move, she would find me doing her very ideas first. We do not have much in common in terms of what interests us, but on the other hand, we are not that different, except in terms of timing and aggression."

"How do you know each other?"

"Our fathers arranged our marriage even though my father was a Jew and hers a Roman. They both lived in Ostia. My parents moved to Ostia shortly after Tiberius lifted the ban on Jews. They still all live there. My father passed away, but her parents and brother are still there. My father owned a shop. Her father was a retired soldier who gained his citizenship after 25 years of service, married late, and settled there. They befriended each other, and that is how it happened. Ostia is a beautiful city. Sometimes Valeria still visits there with little Justin. As for me, I have tried to grow in love with Valeria. And I have. But she has not reciprocated. I care for her. She is quite a woman. Not shallow, incapable, or uneducated, as you have seen. Just the opposite. Sometimes too much so. But I just do not seem able to reach her. Have you ever been married, and do you understand what I am experiencing?"

"No. I have never been married. The Jewish War interrupted my life. If it hadn't come along, there was a girl—a fine girl—I was going to marry. She had a good family; our fathers were friends, we were neighbors, and they planned on our marriage from the time we were small. But we became separated due to the war for years, and she ended up marrying someone else."

"How unfortunate. Do you still love her?"

"Yes. I still love her. She passed away this last year. And, if it is permissible for me to say, she still loved me till her dying day."

"How do you know?"

"I was there."

"You were there when she passed?"

"Yes."

"That sounds like a complicated scenario: you were not married, but you still loved each other, and you were present on her dying day."

"Yes. Our life in Sicily was complicated. And so was my life before that."

Nathan was ready to let his guard down and tell Manus everything about his past. He doubted the wisdom of doing so, but the mention of Elisheva weakened his resolve. Manus was candid with him; why should he not be candid with Manus.

"So you were not always in Sicily?" he asked

"No."

"I assume you were in Jerusalem then."

"Yes."

"And did you fight under your brother's leadership?"

"Yes. And Ducetius did too."

"But Ducetius is from Sicily. Did he go to Jerusalem to fight for the cause?"

"No. He was my slave."

"Yes, of course he was! He calls you Patrón. I knew that. But a Sicilian in Jerusalem? Usually it's the other way around. And his wife, Lois?"

"She is neither Sicilian nor Jewish. She is a Christian from Pontus. She was another slave's wife. He was a Christian too. But he was executed in Sicily."

"My, my. Your little circle converged from all over the world. And it seems like there is nothing straightforward about it or your life, is there?"

"I'd say there is at least one straightforward thing: I am trying to find my life. But I'm not sure how to get there. I keep waiting for life to happen, but instead it is simply passing me by, and the direction toward my goal keeps changing. But my life must be out there somewhere, and I am going to find it. Some day."

"Is it out there?" responded Manus. "Have I found my life? All the trappings of a life are there for me. I have a wife, a son, a shop, a decent income, rent from our insula, and I live in the heart of the greatest city in the world. But have I found my life? It all found me, and I am not sure that what found me matches what I would have sought, had I thought about it."

"I have always defined life around the woman I loved. Only God and that matter to me. I don't know what else there is. But politics, war, duty, loyalty, and trouble came into play to confuse things and set up obstacles. Then the deaths of people around me changed the course of my life, my attitude, and my options."

"What do you mean?"

"When the war for freedom began," Nathan answered, "my hopes ran high for the future. I was young, we had a plan, and I was part of something bigger than myself. But then my father was executed by the Romans, I was separated from my mother, thousands perished, Jerusalem was destroyed, and our cause was lost. I regained some hope when I found my mother and sister in the aftermath, and we resettled in Sicily in Ducetius's hometown. Elisheva also found her way there a few years later, to the same town we were in, believe it or not, along with her brother and her husband. We were able to find lucrative work there on the amphitheatre. But that fell apart as well. Ducetius's family came under threat from an old local situation, and then Elisheva died after a difficult pregnancy. All of a sudden, in the midst of an existence that again held some promise, I was left with nothing. So I followed Ducetius when he fled Sicily to Herculaneum. I was hoping we could start our lives over yet again, in Rome. But you know what befell us in Herculaneum. And now we are here."

"And anything can happen here," said Manus, smiling.

"That is for sure. I can even find my long-lost brother enslaved on a major building project after a decade of believing he was dead." He paused. "So that is what has happened to me these past ten years and how death has accompanied and altered every step and stop along the way." Changing subjects, Nathan added, "By the way, I have been thinking about the whole 'Flavius Josephus' conundrum."

"Yes. I have given it some thought as well. What are you thinking?"

"The only sense I can make out of it is the possibility that he might be an old friend and associate of ours named Joseph whom we knew back in Jerusalem. He was a general in the Judaean army, and both my brother and I had close contact with him. I worked for him as an adjutant during the Galilean campaign. But he was captured by General Vespasian, and the last time I saw him he was working with Emperor Titus—General Titus at the time. Is it possible that Flavius Josephus could be him?"

"You had connections with a Judaean general?"

"Yes. I told you that my brother was one of the ringleaders of the rebellion. And my father was a member of the Jewish Council."

"So you were of some importance. You were not simply an average fellow back then."

"I wasn't important," responded Nathan, further regretting

that he had divulged so much of his past. "I was young, and I just happened to be connected to important men. In any case, I am now definitively a well-below-average fellow. My life as a triple refugee from Jerusalem, then Sicily, and then from Herculaneum indicates a rather luckless life, and places me on the level of a mere scavenger and survivor. So whatever importance I may have had—which was next to none, and happenstantial—was lost in the shuffle a long time ago. You, on the other hand, are an established businessman, property owner, husband, and father. I am none of those things and may live and die without accomplishing one of them."

"I doubt it. Your story remains to be written. You are young. At least young-ish. But as for your theory about Flavius Josephus being your old associate, it seems unlikely to me. I assumed by his name that he was a distant member of the royal family."

"I thought about that very thing myself but concluded that it is improbable. For one thing, the fact that he has a Hebrew name like Joseph makes it unlikely that he is a blood member of the Flavii. Second, the fact that he knew my brother puts him in Judaea at least at some point in his life, because my brother never left Judaea until his capture—at least that I know of. Third, he has the same name, Joseph, as our close associate during the war. And fourthly, if our associate was captured and then freed by Vespasian and Titus, so that the last time I saw him he was working for them, doesn't it make sense that he would take the *nomen* of his Patrón, and Latinize Joseph to Josephus?"

Manus mulled the theory over in his mind. "You have some compelling arguments there."

"I think I am right. But even if so, how can I ever make contact with him? If he is a member of the emperor's retinue, as the guard the other day indicated, there is no way I could send a message to him on Palatine Hill."

"Not necessarily," said Manus. "There may be a way. In our line of business, we have connections to important people, just like you used to. Not that I have met many important people like you have—though an occasional senator ambles in for a book. But servants of important people come to the shop on a regular basis to have the works of their lords copied or to purchase important works for them. I would guess that I know a servant or two who might know someone who might be familiar with this Flavius Josephus—even if he is not the man you suppose he is. Next to being in the army, the best way for a plebeian to access the Palatine is through a copy shop. And our copy shop in particular, thanks to Valeria, has the most upscale clientele on the Argiletum."

"My, my," smiled Nathan. "I did not realize…"

"So I am not quite as unimportant as you think you are…and you are certainly not as luckless."

IX

"Look at these lines, Patrón," said Ducetius, showing Nathan a document he was working on. Nathan read the following:

> 'So I tell you, do not worry about your life,
> what you will eat or drink, or about your body,
> what you will wear. Is not life more important
> than food, and the body more important than
> clothing? Look at the birds of the air. They do not
> sow or reap or store away in barns, and yet your
> heavenly Father feeds them. Are you not much
> more valuable than they?"

"What is this?" Nathan asked.

"Just keep reading a little more, Patrón."

Nathan continued. "'… If that is how God clothes the grass of the field, which is here today, and tomorrow is thrown into the fire, will he not much more clothe you, O you of little faith? Which of you by worrying can add a single hour to his life?' How much of this do you want me to read?" asked Nathan.

"Just read one more line," said Ducetius, pointing to another passage.

Nathan then read, almost losing his patience: "Whoever wants to find his life will only lose it, but whoever loses his life for my sake will find it. For what does it profit a man if he gains the whole world but loses his soul?"

Nathan looked up again when he was done. "It's a good read. But you're about to lose your soul if you ask me to read anymore.

Who is the author? Just the other day I was talking to Manus about finding my life. This writer seems to concur that I will not be able to find it."

"I don't know," Ducetius answered, "His name is simply Matthaios."

"Matthaios? You mean like Greek for Mattathias?" Nathan started. "Could the writer be Joseph? He is certainly Jewish. We were just talking about Joseph the other day too, like I told you. Is that why you are showing me this?"

"The author is not Joseph. It is simply Matthaios. That is not why I am showing this to you. But I agree that the writer seems Jewish. He's writing about Joram's messiah, and those are quotes by him."

"Oh," responded Nathan, disappointed at the subject matter and rethinking his original positive reaction to it.

"I wish you were working on this book with me," said Ducetius. "It helps me understand why Joram believes the way he did."

"Why would that matter to me? I am glad we are not working on it together," retorted Nathan, wishing to end the conversation. "You were always more enthralled with Joram's ideas than I was."

Valeria, who was in the shop that day and apparently overheard their discussion, came over to them. She took a look at the manuscript Ducetius was working on and tossed it back onto the table in disgust. "Did Manus give you this document to work on?" she asked.

"Yes, he did. Am I not doing a satisfactory job?"

"You are doing a fine job. But my husband seems to think we are running a charity here. Who is paying for this?"

"I assume the author."

Valeria then walked over to Manus, who was at the other end of the shop, and asked him to step into the back storage room. The door shut, and all the workers could hear the curt tones of an argument, though none of the specific words were audible.

Later that evening, Nathan and Manus discussed the episode during their walk.

"What was the problem with Ducetius's manuscript this morning?" Nathan asked.

"It's been an ongoing battle with Valeria," Manus explained. "Occasionally, I get my hands on a document from one of the eastern mystery religions around the empire, and I want to have a copy of it. I am fascinated by that type of thing. I have a small library of those documents in the apartment."

"So that's what's on your shelf."

"Yes. I've been able to find writings by Stoics, Epicureans, Jews, Magi, some tidbits about the Eleusian Mysteries, Orphic Mysteries, Mithra, a bit of the Book of the Dead from Egypt, some of the Sybilline writings. Last week I came across that Christian manuscript, and I thought I should add it to my collection."

"Does Valeria not approve of that creed, or is it the collection itself she objects to?"

"She couldn't care less about the creed, and she tolerates the collection. But she disapproves of me asking our scriveners to make the copies for me. No one is paying for it. It is for my own private edification. So really, she and I are paying for it. She says it is 'an inefficient use of manpower.' I know she's right. She usually is—which I find so annoying. Sometimes I do the copying for the collection myself. But since things were slow this week, I gave it to Ducetius. I'm actually making a second copy of it myself for the man I borrowed it from."

"So the man *is* paying for it in this case."

"Not really. Only sort of. Don't tell Valeria—though I'm sure she's going to find out anyway—but I offered to copy the document at half price if the owner was willing to give me the original right then, on the spot. And the copy Ducetius is making is, in fact, for free."

"Well, don't worry, Manus. Valeria won't find out from me."

"I appreciate that. I have enough trouble."

"But tell me a little about some of these mysteries you mentioned before. Are any of them credible?"

"Sometimes I think I believe them all," said Manus. "I'm trying to cover my bases, and I read as many different beliefs as I can. I figure that someone out there has the answers to the universe. If I haven't been able to find my life either, as you say, maybe somebody else has. I know that the messiah in that manuscript Ducetius and I have been copying says that anybody who wants to find his life will only lose it."

"Yes," responded Nathan. "Ducetius just showed me that very line this morning."

"And I just copied that line the other day and have been thinking about it ever since. But, he adds, 'whoever loses his life for my sake will find it.'"

"But Manus, how can you lose your life for the sake of someone you don't even know? That is a preposterous proposition."

"Maybe. But I've been getting to know the man in that manuscript a little better as I keep copying. He is quite a fellow, though I don't know what became of him."

"I believe you'll find out at the end of the story. He was executed by the Romans. He's dead, just like everyone else. And that's all there is to it."

"What a shame. He had good things to say. The Romans have killed and enslaved too many good people. But whatever happened to that fellow, I want to add that manuscript to my collection. It's because of how they are—the Romans, I mean—that people keep searching for something beyond them, like that man did. If the Romans could have created a world like he described, with people praying for their enemies and the last being first, we wouldn't feel the need to search so hard in life for meaning."

"Then we should thank the Romans for being the way they are, because I would miss all the philosophizing," he added sarcastically.

"Speaking of philosophizing, those mysteries and rituals you were asking about are all quite interesting. The Eleusinian rites deal with a reenactment of the story of Ceres and Proserpina."

"Oh, I know that story!" exclaimed Nathan with delight. "I heard it on a regular basis in Sicily. But they call the characters Demeter and Persephone."

"It is an incredible story: one of gift and loss, searching and finding, death and resurrection."

"Like all the great stories."

"Perhaps. But they say that those who partake in the Eleusinian mysteries are assured eternal life." He paused. "On the other hand, the Orphic mysteries say the same thing. I have never been to an Eleusinian rite. They used to be much more popular a long time ago than they are now, though the Sicilians still live on that story since it took place right on their doorstep. But an Orphic rite: that I have been to. And it was magical—full of redemption, love, hope of escape from death, and discussion about the beautiful, lyrical, heroic Orpheus. If we could only be like Orpheus, we could live forever."

"And what about Mithra? He is the most mysterious one of all. I'd never heard of him before recently. Or is Mithra a her?"

"He is a him. And most of his devotees are men. He is a most masculine god, slayer of the primordial evil beast from the beginning of the world. Many Roman soldiers follow him. I have been to one of the mithraea that is right here in the city. Maybe I will be allowed to go to one again sometime, and you can come with me. They have beautiful statues and imagery. They have banquets and lots of discussions and fun. They have a very serious side to them too, and they slaughter a bull and fill up the floor of the mithraea with its blood. It can be an intense and messy affair. But really, despite my having gone to one of their rites, I know very little about them, and no one is allowed to divulge their secrets.

That's actually how it is with all of the mystery cults. Even important men have been condemned for letting out ritual secrets. One of the Greek playwrights was partially stoned for revealing a mystery in one of his plays. And with the followers of Mithra, there are levels and levels of secrecy that one is initiated into while being swallowed up into its depths. I find them all fascinating. Maybe they are all true. I don't know. Or maybe that man who was executed had it right after all, since he was killed."

"Why? Do you think his being killed adds credibility to him?"

"I think he must have been onto something, and it was too true to accept. Otherwise he would have lived to write his tale like all the others. But he didn't. After all, as they say, who can see the face of God and live? Right? It can't be done."

"You attribute too much to him, I think," Nathan countered. "Don't forget that Moses saw God's backside."

"Yes. He did. And lived," Manus chuckled. "So I take it from that remark that Judaism still holds all the answers for you then."

"I have not found another creed more believable. And it doesn't pride itself in being secretive. It's just the opposite; though ironically, most people don't want it."

"People like to be in on secrets. It's human nature. So even after all your travels and experiences and discussions with people, you still come right back to square one with Judaism? That is not the Roman way. Here eclecticism is the ultimate truth. It's one of the reasons we Jews, and even the Christians, sometimes get into trouble. But nothing else has drawn you?"

"Not as much."

"Then I would say that despite all your whining, you already have found your life. And that means you really should start paying the *fiscus* tax."

X

When Rome caught fire during Titus's reign, plague broke out as well. Even for Romans who normally did not attribute disasters to the gods, the continuing onslaught of troubles from volcano to fire to plague during Titus's reign gave them cause to start.

When the fire ignited, Titus was visiting the ruins of Pompeii, still reeling from the first calamity of his regime. But even in the midst of the devastation, and while facing new threats that emerged like blows from an unseen hand, Titus handled it with grace, lending his personal presence where people were in need and displaying a generosity rare in a Caesar. His disposition made him popular during his brief reign and left his reputation singularly untarnished among Roman emperors. He was a servant of the people like his hard-working father who, when asked to rest for health reasons, said that 'an emperor should die on his feet.'

But if Vespasian found that working for the good of the empire meant running it along Draconian lines to return it to fiscal solvency after Nero and the Year of the Four Emperors—even to the point of enacting the very tax on urine that Titus later rescinded—Titus took the approach of serving the empire through public appearances and personal largesse: a largesse afforded him by the surplus and stability his father had bequeathed him. Different as they were, though, Vespasian and Titus formed two sides of the same coin and proved the most successful father-son team in the entire panoply of Roman history. The one provided, and the other knew how to utilize.

When Titus returned to the capital from the bay to find it smoldering and infirm, he again reached into his own pocket to help restore order and a sense of security. He performed sacrifices to propitiate the gods on the people's behalf and sought out medical advice to stanch the epidemic. The damage from the fire was extensive, decimating the entire western portion of the city, spreading to the Capitoline Hill, and hitting major structures like the Pantheon, Jupiter Capitolinus, and Pompey's Theatre. If it had traveled further east, it would have consumed the forum, Argiletum and Subura, as did the fire during Nero's reign, when the Subura proved the epicenter. It was during its reconstruction that Manus and Valeria had been able to take advantage of newly available lots to purchase their building.

When news of the fire began to spread, Valeria's older brother traveled from Ostia to check on his little sister. Several years' Valeria's senior, the older brother fit right into the category of 'meddlesome and overbearing,' which Nathan had used to describe his own brother. But the brother was devoted to his kin and came to bring Valeria and Justin back 'home' with him for a while. It did not matter how Manus felt on the subject. Manus was too middle-aged, Jewish, and uninteresting for the brother's taste. But by the time the brother arrived, the plague had set in, and Manus agreed that Valeria should leave. He himself was already showing symptoms— or so he believed—in the form of a mild fever, so he insisted on remaining in Rome. In any case, Valeria's brother did not extend an invitation to him.

When Nathan heard Manus's decision, he insisted on remaining also, to tend to his boss-friend as well as the shop. Ducetius followed suit. Valeria then insisted that if the rest of them refused to leave, at least Lois and baby Kalo should travel with her and her brother to safety. Ducetius secretly wished to leave with his little family but sensed that Valeria's brother would not welcome him. And he was right. Despite everyone's desire for Ducetius to join Lois and Valeria, with Lois even weeping at the idea of leaving her lovable husband behind, the brother insinuated in his every gesture that the women and toddlers were welcome, but the men were on their own.

Within a few hours, the brother, Valeria, Lois, and the two little boys booked a river transport down the twelve miles of the Tiber to the port of Ostia. They were not alone in choosing that destination. The long line to purchase the fare, as well as the overcrowding on the ship, made the brief journey long and uncomfortable. But they ultimately reached their goal and remained there free from danger for the duration of the outbreak.

Not so the men. The disease proved especially rife in the Subura, and Nathan and Ducetius watched corpses mount up in the streets, occasionally lit up on a pyre to dispose of them. They also observed Manus's appearance daily grow worse, which alarmed them. The incubation period typically took a week, followed by fever, a rash, chills, swelling of the lymph nodes, and vomiting. At first they moved in with Manus to watch over him, but they soon moved back upstairs. After several more days, they merely cracked the door open to see Manus lying on the floor under a pile of blankets, with a chamber pot nearby and a spittoon next to his head, as they left food for him. Sometimes Nathan would sit outside in the hallway and talk to him through the door, but there was little direct contact. Manus could only speak briefly before tiring or growing delirious.

After a couple of weeks, Nathan and Ducetius found themselves simply waiting for their friend, neighbor, and boss to die. They could only speculate what would become of them, their job, and their rental situation if that happened. They spoke daily on the subject and concocted scenarios that rarely ended well. Sometimes they believed their situation would simply restabilize, and that Valeria would maintain the status quo even if Manus were to pass. At other times, they convinced themselves that she would remain in Ostia, sell the property and shop, and not give a care what befell them. Nathan thought there might be a possibility she would let him and Ducetius run the shop and insula while she continued as an absentee landlady; but they really had no idea what their fate would be.

In addition, Nathan was fond of Manus. He was also secretly, and not-so-secretly, fond of Valeria. If Manus died and Valeria remained in Ostia, he would lose both of them. And if Lois fared better in Ostia than in the Subura, which was almost certain to be the case, then he might lose Ducetius to Ostia as well. He even dared mention once to Ducetius that if Manus died, he might try for Valeria's hand, and he wanted to know what Ducetius thought of that possibility. The idea, of course, led down a whole new avenue of horror stories and hypotheticals, from Nathan being accused of pursuing Valeria only for her money, to criminal neglect while he cared for Manus in the hopes that he would die. Thus Nathan lived on pins and needles day after day, not knowing how to feel, what to say, and how to proceed, hoping for the best and the worst, and not always sure which was which.

After three weeks, it became apparent that Manus was not going to die, however, and that he was on the mend. Most victims of the plague developed such swollen and painful lymph nodes that it looked like fists were emerging from their groins and armpits. Blackening of the skin also set in due to necrosis, especially in the tenderer portions of the body like lips, noses, fingers, and toes. Within a week, and sometimes much less than that, the victim was dead. Manus, however, lingered. That was a sign that he would survive, but Nathan had nothing with which to compare Manus's symptoms so that he could be sure. Everyone assumed that if a poor wretch caught the dreaded disease, only one conclusion lay in store, but there was always a small number that recovered from a plague. As Manus improved, Nathan's horror stories and marital hopes awkwardly tucked themselves back into the silence of his thoughts again.

XI

"Do I have a problem, Ducetius?" asked Nathan. "I only seem to fall in love with married women."

"That is not true, Patrón," answered Ducetius. "You loved Elisheva for years before she got married. It's not your fault she ended up with Efstathios. And you've eyed single female passersby on the street since you were nine. Probably younger. And as for Valeria, you do not love her because she is married. I understand exactly why you feel the way you do about her: she's smart, she's impossible, she's challenging, she's beautiful, and she's somehow fun."

"That's it, isn't it? I couldn't have said it better. Still, I feel like it's more than a coincidence that both the women I have been drawn to are, or were, taken by other men."

"Your problem isn't that you only love married women. Your problem is that you don't meet any other women except ones that are married. You've always been that way. Between saving yourself for Elisheva your whole childhood, then working in Galilee during the war, then migrating across the entire Mediterranean and living in an obscure outpost in central Sicily—though it is the most beautiful, interesting, endearing, obscure little outpost in the world— you have never had much chance to meet many single women. I fell in love with a married woman too."

"Yes, but who could help that? Lois is … you know…" he faltered for words.

"Yes, I know. But I hope you're not going to include her in your list of married loves," laughed Ducetius. "She's taken! I know you like her. I can tell. And there's no one I'd rather give her to than you in the event something was to happen to me, just like Sos passed her on to me when something happened to him. But while I'm still around, I hope you realize you can't have her, and I'm not going to share. That's not part of the manumissions contract. You're stuck with me in the picture, whether we face war, flight, volcanic eruptions, tidal waves, or the plague. I am apparently never going to die no matter what life-threatening situations you continue to throw me into. So, in short, you've got to find your own woman. Forget about finding your life. Find your own wife. They are often, though not always, one and the same. I will help you, Patrón."

"I suppose you're right. But part of me still thinks I should hold out for Valeria. I know Manus has recovered, but he looks terrible. I may still have a chance."

"You can't think like that. It sounds evil. And he's your friend."

"I know, I know. You're the only person in the world I would be this frank with. And I'm half kidding. Forgive me."

"It's fine. If it happens, it happens. But don't be wishing it, or you'll feel guilty the rest of your life even if you win the prize."

"You're right. I hadn't thought of that. The fact is, I love Manus, and we *are* friends, and I should never have said what I said."

"No, you shouldn't have. But I'm not going to hold it against you or tell anybody. Meanwhile, you and I will be on the lookout."

"What's happening to me? I used to be a good person. I think I am not a good person anymore."

"You still have a lot of good in you, Patrón. Who would know better than I would? But you've grown up, and growing up is hard and sometimes brings out the worst in a person at the same time it brings out our best. We've all changed. And you've been through a lot. I know that too, because I was with you. Life can be disappointing. But your life isn't over yet."

"You sound like Manus. And it might as well be over. I'm middle-aged, and I am nowhere."

He had changed, Nathan thought to himself, and not for the better. If once he had been idealistic, he no longer was. If he had been prayerful and conscious of the holy, that attitude had faded long ago. If he had idolized men like Joseph and his father, there were no more heroes to look up to in his life. If people had once relied on his innate goodness, he had grown sarcastic and biting in the course of the last decade, starting with his relationship with

Efstathios, and now even more so in his death wish for Manus. He had become cynical, pessimistic, and self-centered. His entire world revolved around himself and the things he had not achieved. He felt purposeless, where before he had been full of hope and energy. He was thirty-plus, and it did not feel good.

Compared to other people, he had always considered himself bland and boring and thought that everyone else around him had a more distinct character than he had. He looked at himself and only saw that he lacked the heroism of Joseph, the zeal of Amram, the good looks of Efstathios, the wisdom of his father, the humble charm of Ducetius, the imposing persuasiveness of Sos, and the open-mindedness of Manus. He was neither high nor low, brilliant nor dullard, happy nor morbid, deep nor shallow, skilled nor hampered, young nor old, flippant nor philosophical. He was non-descript. People liked him, but it did not get him anywhere. And they only liked him because he was wishy-washy and could blend into any setting. He had abilities but never in quantities that gained him notoriety or respect in any given field. His brother had led an insurrection. His father led the council. Joseph led the army. What, if any, accomplishments or qualities marked him? He did not make things happen but let things happen to him instead. He was middling in all he did. He had no strong opinions. He would never change the world. He was non-committal. Amram had been a Zealot, his father a conservative, Elisheva a Christian. They knew who and what they were. He did not. He never made definitive decisions on anything. No wonder he fell in love with married women. That way he could feel but never need to commit.

Is that what he was all about: an inability to commit to anything? Is that why he fled in the opposite direction from Pella after the war—because heading toward Pella would mean marrying Elisheva? Could that, indeed, have been his subconscious agenda? Maybe he had to cut himself a little slack in that regard, since he was caught after the war between finding his mother and finding his love, and he knew the former might need him, while the latter could wait. But the very idea that the latter could wait showed his lackadaisical attitude toward marriage, at least at the time. And it had cost him. Or had it instead placed him right in the very vacillating position for the rest of his life where he wanted to be, and in fact felt most comfortable: right in the middle, always wanting and not wanting, trying and not trying, believing and not believing? Maybe that was his truth. He had fought in the war but had given neither his life nor his freedom. He worked for Joseph, but never arose to save the day as Joseph did. He 'rescued' his mother in Joppa but had no qualms about leaving her behind in Sicily. He was a dabbler in letters but never penned a book. He could be a do-er and a man of action, but merely to solve the predicament of the moment and never to achieve the next step in any overall plan. He had no overall plan.

And what was the mark of a man if not to know himself and where he was headed? He was a failure. He had never even given himself over to debauchery, to sin boldly, even when he had the chance. Would not Elisheva have given in to his advances had he pressed his suit? Could they not have carried out a clandestine affair and run away together if they so chose? Could he not have sought out illicit trysts with other women or have visited the prostitutes among the workers' quarters in Enna? Why could he not even decide to cast his lot with pleasure or immorality? Would that have been so difficult? Even Efstathios had dived headlong into what he considered flagrancy for years, only then to commit to change. Efstathios was a hero compared to him, yet he belittled Efstathios at every opportunity. It was not Efstathios who was the half-man. It was him.

What was he, Nathan, afraid of? He didn't know. But it was becoming apparent to him as he thought about his life that at the very heart of his behavior lay fear. He wouldn't have guessed it. And no one looking at him from the outside could ever detect it. But it was true. And he realized that his lack of commitment was how his fear played itself out. On the other hand, commitment meant acknowledging the possibility of mistakes, taking responsibility for poor choices, and possessing the strength to live with the consequences, all while assigning blame solely to oneself. But he did not want to blame himself for anything. He still believed that somehow, despite all the evidence to the contrary, he was good. Other people were responsible for the ills of the world. Not him. He needed to be good in his own mind. That was all he had going for him, he thought. If he didn't have at least that to commend him, he had nothing, he believed.

The more he thought about the manner in which he had passed the prior twenty years, the more he realized he had merely skimmed the surface of life, only to touch down when someone else's life was in peril, like his father's or Joseph's or Elisheva's or Ducetius's. Those were the times, in fact, when Nathan had felt the most alive. And of all of the people in his life, it was Ducetius who had given him the greatest impetus and most opportunities to spring into action to save him. As a result, Nathan had always thought that Ducetius was dependent on him. But it was apparent now that it was actually Nathan who needed Ducetius in order to keep him going and give him a reason to take the next step. To look at the two of them living side by side as friends, no one would ever have supposed that such was the case. Nathan was larger, louder, and more leaderly. But when given the choice, it was to Ducetius's home in Sicily that Nathan sought refuge after the war. And when Ducetius fled to Herculaneum, Nathan followed after him, not vice-versa. Could it be, then, that Nathan never really was as good or as strong as he supposed? Could it be that his life only made sense when someone else was the focus of it? Could it be that that was why one could only find his life if it was lost for someone else?

XII

"We're going to be late," urged Manus.

"Do we have to attend opening day?" complained Nathan.

The Flavian Amphitheatre was now complete, and the inaugural ceremonies were about to commence. No one in the city could talk of anything else.

"It was your idea to go!" retorted Manus. "You said you'd never been to the games, and you thought that since the emperor was going to be there, your mystery man, Flavius Josephus, might be there as well—and perhaps your brother."

"But do we need to be there on time?"

"We might not get in at all if we're too late."

Valeria, who had returned from Ostia escorted by her brother, voiced her opinion. "Manus, my dear," she said. "You don't look well. Heaven has spared you. You should not attend a whole-day affair and tire yourself out."

It had been months since the plague had subsided. People were returning home, reconstruction had begun on the Capitoline, businesses were recovering, and the anticipation of a hundred days of games at the new amphitheatre made the populace forget its recent woes. Titus stood at the crest of his career in terms of public opinion.

"But they're giving out prizes at the opening ceremony," said Manus.

"But they may also be slaughtering those Jewish slaves," added Lois. "Do you really want to see that?"

"They have it coming to them," Valeria's brother said.

"You have a point there," responded Manus—not to his brother-in-law's comment but to Lois's.

"Well, I for one am going now," stated the brother. "Is Justin coming along?"

"Not yet. I'd like him to wait a few more years before seeing the games," said Valeria.

"You're going to make him soft," responded the brother. "He should come. Anyway, I'm off. No need to look for me there. I'll be on my own. Good-bye."

After the brother left, they all sat down and sighed in relief. "He is difficult," said Valeria. "But I appreciated him coming to get me and bringing us back safely."

"Yes," they all agreed, unable to think of anything else positive to say.

"*You* were certainly in no position to help get us," Valeria reminded Manus.

"No, certainly not. I am grateful to have survived."

"Thank you again," said Valeria, facing Nathan and Ducetius, "for taking care of my husband and the shop while I was gone." Valeria sounded kindlier than she ever had before, though it was hard to tell if it was from gratitude for her husband's life or simply the desire to speak gently to Nathan.

/////

Inhabitants from every quarter of the city converged on the amphitheatre that morning. Although the stadium seating may have accommodated up to eighty-seven thousand, according to some ancient reports, the arena was insufficient to house everyone wishing to attend that opening day. Titus accounted for such a contingency by arranging a second venue at the Groves of Lucius and Gaius, built and named for Emperor Augustus's prematurely deceased grandsons, where a spectacle of almost equal magnificence awaited the audience there.

As the populace funneled through the seventy-two entrances of the Colosseum-Amphitheatre to begin the day, ushers assigned each attender a ticket with a designated seat number according to their social status and class—status partly gauged by one's dress and comportment. Tickets were free, since the emperors traditionally paid the fare for everyone, but no one could proceed through the labyrinth of painted halls and stairways to the *vomitoria* without a ticket. The seat numbers were etched into the marble of each seat, and marble diagrams located in the vestibules guided everyone to their sector. Everyone was expected to sit in his assigned location. The passageways were color-coded according to class in order to further help ticket-holders to their proper tiers. Upper-class passageways were decorated with paintings and mosaics; lower-class with basic red and white.

The first tier of seats, closest to the action in the arena, was called the *podium* and was reserved for the upper echelons: the emperor and his guests, Roman priests, members of the administration, the Vestal Virgins, and senators. The emperor occupied a special box called the *cubiculum*, and he and the Vestal Virgins entered and exited the arena through two special entrances among the seventy-two. The entrances stood at the north and south sides of the stadium, one on each long side of the oval-shaped structure. The emperor could also access his seat through a special tunnel connected directly to the imperial palace.

The second tier was reserved for the equites, also known as the knightly class, as well as other nobles. The equites formed the least known of the three Roman classes, sandwiched between the patricians and the plebeians. Above them and behind them arose a third tier for the average citizenry, divided into two groups. Wealthier plebeians sat in the lower group of seats, and above them, furthest from the action, sat the poorest plebeians. Women and slaves were technically forbidden to attend the games by royal decree of Augustus, but it was seldom enforced.

Nathan, Manus, and Ducetius followed the red and white passages to their seats in the tier called the *maenianum secundum imum*, designated for wealthier plebeians. They were placed in Section XXIX. Their view was good, even from that high up. The emperor's box stood across the arena from them, roughly straight ahead but down and to the left. Nathan figured that if Flavius

Josephus sat near the emperor, and if he was indeed Joseph, and if Joseph hadn't changed too much in terms of weight, facial hair or balding, that he would recognize him even from that distance—though that was a lot of ifs. The Vestal Virgins were located on the same side as Nathan, Manus, and Ducetius, though down and more sharply to their left, directly across from the emperor's box.

As the crowd settled in, a preliminary show began in the arena. There were trees temporarily staged throughout the entire stadium floor to mimic a natural setting. Then onto the stage among the trees a long wooden train carrying a cargo of caged cranes was pulled into view by slaves. Afterward, a hundred dwarves trotted out from the various entrances on goats, releasing the cranes from the cages. The freed cranes then coursed through the air across the entire breadth of the stadium as though they had practiced a dance formation. But the dwarves opened little satchels of food to fling tidbits onto the ground and attract them. The cranes swooped downward to reach the food, and the dwarves waged battle against them as they flew near. Some had bows and arrows; others had spears, clubs, or sling shots. It was a reenactment of the battle of the cranes and pygmies from the Iliad, in which Homer described a stunted race of men only a forearm high, perennially beset by the winged creatures. The Romans loved reenactments, especially with exotic animals and unusual combatants—and most especially if the reenactments ended in death. A reenactment without the death of something would seem a cheap and useless waste of time.

The battle of the cranes continued until one after another of the birds plummeted to its demise and the dwarves exited the stage till only one of each remained. While the audience watched, the master of ceremonies appeared in order to explain the literary allusion of the battle, make other announcements, and direct the audience after a trumpet salute to the emperor's box, where the emperor and his retinue then entered. The cheers from the throng then crescendoed to such a pitch and furor it matched no other sound Nathan or Ducetius had ever heard in their lives. After the applause quelled, the last dwarf pelted his prey, and a roar arose from the bleachers again. The dwarf exited with a bow and a smile. The next act then awaited the signal to commence.

"I never knew there were this many people in the whole world," said Ducetius to Nathan, astounded at the size and sound of the audience in the wake of the applause.

"This place is spectacular," replied Nathan. "Almost as impressive as our theatre in Enna."

Ducetius laughed. "Maybe. Though I believe the mountains in Enna formed a finer backdrop, if I do say so myself."

"I agree, I agree. Sicily was beautiful. But I doubt if anyone in this audience would take it over Rome. We are in the center of the world, my friend, right here where we are sitting."

"If that is really the case," Manus interjected, "then maybe someone in the audience has the answer to the universe."

"I daresay someone might," Nathan responded, making light of the comment. "In the meantime, I'm scouring every face, and especially the ones in the emperor's box, for our mystery man."

"You can see that far?" asked Manus.

"You can't?" answered Nathan.

"He must be here somewhere," said Ducetius, "or all we came here to see was a sedge of cranes die."

"You will see a lot more die than cranes by the end of the day," said Manus. "Rome may not hold the secret to life, but it will teach you a great deal about death."

As they finished speaking, the next show was announced: a mini reenactment of the Carthaginian Wars. Cheers arose from the crowd again as four elephants made their way onto center stage, manned by Africans dressed in Carthaginian garb. A circle of gladiators dressed as Roman soldiers followed them into view and surrounded them, beginning to prod the elephants so that they not only attacked the soldiers but each other as well. The Africans then shot a number of the gladiators through with arrows and spears, but as the fight continued, the riders proved no match for the Romans or even for the elephants. As the mammoth creatures reared on their hind legs, the Africans held onto their reins for dear life, and two of them quickly fell to the ground, one crushed underfoot so that his brain, blood, and other organs splatted onto the sand. The other had his legs crushed so that he cast a terrified screaming glance at his flattened lower extremities but could not move them. He was mercilessly left alive by the others so that the audience could watch him be pounced upon again and again as the stomping continued in every direction around him, and all he could do was cringe and hope to die.

After more fighting, the third and fourth Africans were downed as a Roman spear impaled one on his descent to the sand, and the other was lassoed and yanked forward over the fourth elephant's tusks. The elephant bowed its head as the African slid down its face and was ripped open by its ivory skewers before tumbling onto the sand. But the agony of the fallen African did not end there. The rope around his neck was now entwined around the elephant's legs by the Roman soldiers, so that the African was incessantly kicked, crushed and broken as the animal tried to extricate itself. The Romans continued to prod the creatures so that they slipped and slid on the increasingly unrecognizable remains of the four original riders while trying to annihilate each other. Then in a grand finale, the Romans surrounded the four ailing beasts and rained a torrent of arrows and spears into them till they collapsed onto the arena floor, bellowing and heaving or lying in massive lifeless heaps.

Nathan watched spellbound, impressed by the human fortitude and pageantry of the event yet wincing with horror and empathy at what befell the pathetic participants. He had never seen such meaningless violence before or witnessed civilized men doing such things to other men. "That was a gruesome show," he observed, not quite knowing how to feel. He was not squeamish. He knew what death entailed. He had seen it and imposed it on others. But the heartless infliction of it on the Colosseum victims raised questions in his mind that he could not decide whether to utter or merely ponder. For instance, what was this place, this cauldron of death, where he now found himself, and what was he doing there in the middle of it? Was Rome, he asked himself, really the standard of civilization in the world? Was it really the culture that had brought peace, prosperity, a common language, and stable economic system to millions of otherwise lowly, disparate and warring nations, as his father Opal believed? Or did it, as did all empires, starting with Babel, merely sanction tyranny and murder under the guise of civility?

He looked over at Ducetius, whose face betrayed similar thoughts. "Patrón," he said, "I've never seen men killed like that before."

"It is a lot to take in," Manus feebly comforted. "But fortunately, or unfortunately, you will get used to it."

"You once said to me," commented Nathan, "that watching you and Valeria fight with each other would season me for my debut in the arena. But let me tell you, Manus, nothing in the shop has prepared me for today." He grew angry as he continued to speak. "You Romans are animals, and we were right to have fought for our freedom against you."

"Keep your voice down," warned Manus; though, in fact, Nathan was doing just that. "And remember, I am only half Roman."

"I fought in a war for three years," continued Nathan, "but it was nothing like this. In war, there is a reason to kill, but what I've seen here today had no reason to it. Those poor men died for nothing but to entertain a mob. That is no way to die, and no reason to have lived."

"They didn't live for that moment," countered Manus, "and their lives are not defined by that moment, even if that's all we see of them. Something happened to each of them that led them to their end here. And, most likely, it was something criminal. I don't want to justify the bloodshed you've seen here today, but remember that most of the people who will die here broke the law. There is a reason they will be put to death. Some are volunteers also, hard as that is to believe. But in either case, criminal or not, the crazy hope in it all is that if they distinguish themselves here today, even if they were guilty of a crime, they have a chance to gain their freedom. And that is what keeps them going: that every one of them has that chance."

"I am familiar with that fact," stated Nathan. "Ducetius and I were captured at the fall of Jerusalem. The general, Joseph, who I think is Flavius Josephus, recognized us among the captives, and he was allowed to set us free. That is the only reason we are still alive today. But while we were still captives, I figured out that Ducetius and I were placed in a particular grouping destined to slay each other in the arena. And I thought to myself, 'At least in the arena, we have a chance to survive.' So I know what you are talking about. But let me remind you, in terms of those whom Rome considers criminals, that Ducetius and I were numbered among them. So the argument that today's victims deserve to die holds little weight with me. Were Ducetius and I criminals? Did we deserve to die an ignominious death because we fought for our nation and faith? I do not think so. Instead it is Rome that is the criminal. Rome is the thief of the world."

"I cannot defend Rome's faults," said Manus. "They are many."

"I was ready to love this city," continued Nathan, "and I did when we first arrived. I was awed by Rome's grandeur and its power. I never saw or even imagined a place like this before, even coming from Jerusalem. But if the arena is the heart that fuels the body of this empire, then this empire is sick and needs a remedy. I wish we had won our war. I know that Elisheva, the woman I loved, used to say that it was futile fighting merely for a little plot of land like Judaea. But I think now that even if there were only one little patch of sod where the idea of loving God and one's neighbor as oneself reigned, it would be better than a world where *this* ruled everywhere."

Just then, the master of ceremonies interrupted both the entertainment and Nathan's philosophizing with an announcement that raffle balls were about to be cast into the audience.

"We will resume our discussion later, Nathan," said Manus. "This is the primary reason I came here today."

"It wasn't for the killing and brain splatting?"

"And are raffle balls what I think they are?" asked Ducetius.

Suddenly, from above and behind them, little wooden spheres dropped onto the audience like giant brown hail, from the topmost rim of the amphitheatre. Looking up and back, Ducetius and Manus could see workers stationed along the rim of the entire arena with basketfuls of raffles. The workers were primarily there to man the mechanisms for a huge awning to block the sun from the audience, if need be; but they seemed to enjoy their current task, beaning attenders they didn't like in the head while trying to award other attenders whom they did like.

"I got one!" yelled Manus. "I actually got one! Look, it dropped right into my lap!"

"What does it say?" asked Nathan and Ducetius, almost at once.

"Silver cup," answered Manus.

"So you won a silver cup?"

"Yes. I won a silver cup. How nice!"

"But where do you get it?"

"The announcer said before that you have to go to the dispensary on the ground floor of your section."

"So let's go get it."

"But I don't want to miss anyone else getting dismembered while we're gone."

"Don't worry. They'll wait till we get back."

"Look, everyone is leaving their seats to get their prizes. Let's go."

Like three boys at a sporting event, they waited on the dispensary line, happy to be at the stadium, and momentarily forgetting the philosophical implications of the morning. The people around them discussed the fact that they had either won a goat, a donkey, a tunic, or an article of food. "A goat would have been nice for milk and wool," said Manus, "but I'd have to feed it and take care of it. So I'm glad I won a silver cup. It's much less demanding." If they had been privy to the discussions in the upper-class lines, they would have heard about winning gold vessels, horses, cattle, or slaves.

"Do they always give out prizes at these events?" asked Nathan.

"Always. Sometimes they just throw loaves of bread into the audience."

"That's what keeps people coming to the arena. 'I don't mind if a few poor slobs are annihilated,'" said Nathan, imitating a Roman citizen, "'so long as I get a loaf of bread.'"

"Joram's messiah did a similar thing with bread in the story I am copying."

"No he didn't. Don't be ridiculous."

"He doesn't throw the bread. But he feeds five thousand people with just a few loaves."

"That's hardly the same thing. And I'm sure that didn't really happen. It sounds symbolic of something."

"I'm sure it is symbolic. But it doesn't say what. In the story, though, it keeps the people coming back to him, just like here."

"There's nothing like a good loaf of bread."

After picking up the silver cup, which Manus found small but delightful, mostly because it was free and he had won it, the three men resumed their seats just in time for an animal hunt. The hunt would consume the rest of the morning and entail the slaughter of thousands of beasts. The kickoff to the event, as recorded by Martial the poet, was a battle between a bull and an elephant in which the elephant won and seemingly bowed on its knees before the emperor in the cubiculum. Whether the creature had been trained to perform this trick or it was truly a spontaneous response to the greatness of Titus, as some believed, the crowd went wild with cheers. Afterward, other animals from every corner of the empire were released onto the stage in groups of about fifty at a time. Some were tame, some were wild. Hunters also appeared. Some of the hunters were men, others were women.

"I don't even know what half those species are!" said Nathan, marveling at the array below.

"Where do they even get them?"

"And I didn't know there would be females in the show."

"They don't allow females in the audience, but they allow them on stage?"

"Females being on stage is discouraged by good society,"

explained Manus. "But sometimes even upper crust women become huntresses and gladiators."

"Why would a rich woman want to do that if it ruins her reputation?"

"Mostly because they can. They like the challenge. And some of them worship the men and want to be near them. None of the women performing today are wealthy or important, however, or they would have announced who they were."

As they continued to watch, a number of the hunters, both male and female, were mauled and devoured by the animals. The audience moaned or showed momentary dismay, especially if it was a momentary favorite, but that was all part of the show.

"Could you imagine being eaten alive by an animal? How horrific."

"It was done to Christians in Nero's day on a regular basis."

"So is it the Jews' turn now?"

"I would not say that any of these hunters are Jewish prisoners. Usually the prisoners are killed during the lunch break. We will probably see it happen after the hunt. And prisoners are rarely given weapons to defend themselves like these hunters are."

"Speaking of the Jewish prisoners, have you spotted Joseph or your brother yet?"

"I've been looking for them but haven't seen anyone like them."

"Have you spotted your brother-in-law?"

"I haven't been looking for him. But if I know him, he's probably itching about now to watch the Jewish prisoners dispatched at half-time."

As it turned out, only a small number of the original tens of thousands of Jewish prisoners were brought out during lunch. Part of the ignominy of dying a criminal in the arena was that it often occurred during the lull in the day when people couldn't care less that someone was experiencing his final moments. The saltiness of the garum or the quality of the bread was of greater importance. The first two hundred slaves brought out were trapped in a fight to the death with a fellow slave, usually one they knew. It was a despicable requirement of the Romans to make someone kill and then die in that manner, but the criminals were not considered human. And because of the lack of attention from the audience, when a slave vanquished his foe or plunged a spear into the heart of his best friend, there were no cheers, tears, or notice at all. No one was rooting for any of the slaves. They simply died before they could forge any human connection with the audience—the only way to survive—and they needed to die quickly so that the regularly scheduled program could recommence for the afternoon.

Thirteen hundred other Jewish prisoners marked for death appeared in batches of two hundred or so after the first group, and were either tied to posts to be consumed for lunch by an animal or left to run around undefended until they were ripped apart in flight by a gorilla, bear, wild dog, hyena, crocodile, or lion.

Although by lunchtime Nathan and Ducetius had become acclimated to the ubiquitous spector of heinous slaughter, they found the death of the Jewish slaves difficult to watch. They knew that some of the victims could have been neighbors they had never met. They also knew that none of the victims had committed a crime other than defying servitude to Rome. They also knew that they themselves could have been among them, and couldn't help but study how each man died, to try to imagine how they would face such a death themselves if they ever had to.

When they asked some nearby spectators why so few Judaeans perished when there had been enough to fill the entire stadium, one man complained that the Jews in Transtiberim had managed to raise sufficient funds to purchase the majority of the captives. The Roman administration would not allow all of them to go free, however. They needed an ample showing for the opening day at the amphitheatre. All except fifteen hundred were spared. It was a pity, the man said.

Nathan couldn't help but think that if the scar-face, his possible brother, had not been purchased before the opening day, he would have been hand-picked to die in the arena based merely on his unusual visage.

The afternoon show featured a reenactment of the naval Battle of Sybota between the Corcyraeans and Corinthians, a battle that precipitated the Peloponnesian War. The entire stadium was flooded with water, and not only were ships and men employed, but horses, bulls, and other animals that were trained ahead of time to swim. By the end of the bloody engagement, most of the combatants, and a goodly portion of the menagerie, had either drowned or died at spear or arrow point. All in all, from a Roman perspective, and certainly from Titus's, the opening day at the Colosseum was a monumental success and could not have gone any better.

XIII

The entire shop went abuzz when Manus ran over to Nathan.

"Nathan! Look at the author of this manuscript!"

Nathan read the name 'Flavius Josephus.'

"You think it is the same man we have been discussing?" Nathan asked.

"I do. Look at the subject matter."

"The Jewish War," Nathan read. "It must be."

"Do you know what this means, my friend?" asked Manus. "It means you were right that your mystery man Josephus was the general you used to know. Read some of the content he wrote, if there is any doubt."

Nathan skimmed through the scroll. It was true. He homed in on a section entirely about the campaign in Galilee and Joseph's part in it. Tarichaea, Cana, Sepphoris, Tiberias, Jotapata—they were all mentioned. He remembered years ago discussing with Joseph whether they would ever live to write about all they had accomplished. Now Joseph was actually doing it.

Ducetius came over to read with Nathan. He could see that his Patrón was moved by the narrative, changing facial expressions regularly as he re-lived the events with every word. "But he never mentions you," said Ducetius after several minutes. "Weren't you there at Tarichaea and the fall of Jotapata?"

"Yes…I was," replied Nathan.

"He mentions himself plenty of times, though," observed Ducetius.

"Perhaps in his memory he fought the entire campaign alone. I know that's how I feel when I look back."

"No wonder you have difficulty with relationships," quipped Ducetius. "But really," he said, referring back to the scroll, "Lord Joseph weaves a riveting tale. It almost makes you wish you were there."

"Especially since, according to him, I wasn't," replied Nathan. "Let's see if he mentions Amram or abba or other people we know."

They read further, pouring over unfurled yards of the scroll across two desks to skim for any mention of Nathan. They found two references to Amram and at least one to 'the father of Amram' but none to Nathan himself. "How could this be?" Nathan expressed in frustration. "Maybe I was only dreaming."

Manus returned to Nathan, after having given him time to peruse. "Well?" Manus asked. "What do you think?"

"I'm a bit perturbed."

"About what?" asked Manus.

"Josephus completely omits me from the narrative."

"What?"

"I'm not mentioned at all in this scroll."

"How could that be? And you would expect to be?"

"Yes, I would."

"Maybe you just haven't gotten to the right section yet," said Manus.

"I was there throughout the entire northern campaign, which is the very part I've been reading, and there's not a word about me. He mentions my brother, who never came up north"—except for one notable visit, which Nathan wasn't going to mention—"and he had the audacity to refer to my father merely as 'the father of Amram,' and not as mine at all. But I am nowhere in the story."

"There must be a reason," counseled Manus.

"What reason could there possibly be?"

"In my experience, authors omit people they either really hate or really want to protect. Did he really hate you?"

"No."

Ducetius chuckled.

"Then he must want to keep you out of the public eye."

"But he mentions my brother. Why wouldn't he mention me?"

"Maybe he thought your brother was dead."

"Why would that make a difference?"

"Because if someone is dead, they probably don't need anonymity or protection from public scrutiny anymore. But since he knew, or thought, that you might still be alive—you told me he rescued you after the fall of Jerusalem, correct?—he might have thought you needed protection."

"Hmmph. But for the last six months, Joseph has known that my brother is alive. So unless he wrote this section before he discovered that and simply forgot to edit it—which is entirely possible—it doesn't make sense. Also, I don't know why I, in particular, would need protection or anonymity."

"You should ask him, if you ever meet."

"And speaking of that, my dear Manus, I wish you had at least introduced me to the person who delivered this manuscript to you."

"In hindsight," replied Manus, "I probably should have."

"Was it a slave of Joseph's?" Nathan asked. "I assume Joseph didn't come here himself."

"Correct. It was a servant," answered Manus. "He said that his master, Flavius Josephus, needed this portion of his manuscript copied and that it is a small part of a larger whole."

"Did you at least bother to mention me or my situation to the servant or send a greeting from me back to Joseph?"

"I did not," replied Manus.

"But why? Between you and my omission in this scroll, I'm beginning to feel a bit jilted."

"Not at all. I simply felt uncomfortable discussing your situation on the first encounter with a new client. It was a business decision," explained Manus.

"Well, I am relieved," Nathan replied, "to hear it's only because I am bad for business and not because you actually forgot about me."

"When the young man returns in two weeks," said Manus, "I will make sure you speak to him and arrange a meeting. Don't you think I was anxious to say something about you? But I did not think it wise."

"I have waited a year and a half, since I first saw his name, to establish contact with him," said Nathan, a bit flustered. "But I suppose it can wait two more weeks."

/////

The slave, however, did not return in two weeks. He was delayed for more than a month by the sudden death of Titus, the news of which rocked the entire city.

Titus's death was the fourth and final tragedy of the emperor's brief reign. As word of it spread, rumor accompanied it that his younger brother Domitian had poisoned him. Titus was resting at a farmhouse at the end of the hundred days of entertainment when he suddenly took ill. And then, according to one report, Domitian sent a physician to the farmhouse who thought it would be wise to encase Titus in ice to lower his fever. To top it off, Titus's attendants began, perhaps at Domitian's suggestion, to play on the emperor's superstitious nature by reminding him that his father had died in that very farmhouse. After that, no remedy could cure him.

Whatever the case, Emperor Titus, vanquisher of Judaea, destroyer of the Temple, and one of the most popular men ever to don the Roman purple—despite a volcano, a fire, and a plague—died heirless at the age of forty-two. It was autumn, AD 81. And Rome now had to brace itself for a whole new imperial timbre under his little brother Domitian.

XIV

One warm day after the turn of the year, while Rome was still adjusting to the imperial turnover, Amram appeared sitting in the Argiletum across the street from the copy shop just as Nathan came out for an afternoon jaunt.

"Hello, younger brother," he said, as if not a day had passed since Jerusalem.

"Amram!" Nathan exclaimed. "You're here! You're alive! And you're free! So it *was* you that I saw in the amphitheatre."

"It was me," he responded. "And it was you."

Nathan walked over and threw his arms around his brother, who arose but only partially returned the embrace. "I tried to find you after you called out to me that day," Nathan said, "but you had disappeared. I looked for you for an hour, but you were nowhere to be seen."

"I know. They silenced me, chained and gagged. It was part of the daily routine."

"But you're alive," continued Nathan. "I went back to find you a week later, after I had borrowed some money to buy your freedom..."

"But I had disappeared for good by then."

"Yes. One of the guards told me you had been purchased, and by Joseph, no less."

"Don't even mention that name. Besides, it's Josephus now:

that worthless, feckless bag of scum. If I ever see him again, I'll kill him."

"Really? He purchased your freedom, and now you want to kill him? I have been trying to track him down for months in the hopes of finding you. I was only able to confirm what his new name was a few days ago, and I may possibly have found a way to meet him. But it ends up you would not have been with him even if I had succeeded. You have to explain to me why you are still so angry with him at this point."

"What's to explain? You forgot that he is a traitor? And that I beaned him with a rock last time I saw him? And that he is now a Roman and an enemy?"

"You know I have a different view of him."

"A delusional view."

They were already arguing, and it was their first conversation in eleven years.

"But he did everything he could to save us and the city at the end of the war."

"He saved no one but himself," retorted Amram.

"But he tried to save you by your purchase. Doesn't that mean something? I saw the receipt for your sale in the amphitheatre. He spent 1500 denarii to save your skin."

"He was a fool to spend that much. I refused to go with him."

"What do you mean you refused?"

"When I found out who had purchased me, I refused to meet him or go with him. He had apparently shown the guards a list of men he wanted to set free, and I was the only one of them who was still alive. He had them show me to him from a distance so that he could confirm my identity. But when I learned who it was—he looked so pudgy and beardless I didn't recognize him—I spat on the ground and wouldn't budge. I still had plenty of work to do against Rome in that amphitheatre. I wasn't going to leave it in order to go with that worthless waste of a life."

"So how did you get out?"

"After he left, the guards kicked me out. They said I was free, that I had been legitimately purchased, that they didn't care what happened to me, and good riddance. So I left."

"But where did you go? Where have you been living all this time?"

"Transtiberim. I found a place within a day. With our own kind."

"I've heard of Transtiberim but have not been there."

"I've been raising the battle cry there. If the traitor ever shows up, he'll be mobbed and cut to shreds. And I'll make the first incision."

"Amram," said Nathan, trying to reason with his brother, "the war is over."

"Not for me."

"The Temple is gone. Judaea Capta. Vespasian and Titus are dead."

"When our last enemy is dead, I will lay down my arms."

"You mean Joseph?"

"He can't be that hard to find. He left the Palatine to inspect the amphitheatre. He may even have an apartment somewhere in the city that he commutes to on occasion. And now that I am free, I will find him, just like I found you."

"And then you will lay down your arms?"

"I will."

"But I think you wouldn't know what to do with yourself if the war were truly over. It's your life."

"And you have never had a life, dear brother, because you have never woken up to the reality that life is a war."

"It's only a war if you fight."

"What a weakling you are."

"I am not weak. And I am still alive, just like you. I have fought when I have needed to; and in the years since we spoke last, I have needed to. But my life has gone differently than yours. I will tell you about it sometime, if you ever care to hear, which I doubt you ever will. But I am curious about one point that you raised. You said that you had plenty of work to do against Rome in the amphitheatre. What did you mean by that?"

"I killed dozens of Romans while I was there—and they never punished me for it. It was an opportunity I did not expect to have in captivity. But I killed more there than in any single battle back in Judaea."

"How did that happen?"

"A few days after I arrived in the amphitheatre, I wrestled and killed a huge guard who attacked me, and instead of the Romans executing me, they said they liked the way I fought. Those Romans are savages. Anyway, they started taking bets on me that I could kill anybody, but I refused to fight any of my fellow Jews. They threatened to kill me if I didn't, but I told them I didn't care. They threatened to slaughter my entire work gang, but I ordered my gang to kneel on the ground and prepare to die, and they did."

Nathan recalled a similar story about their grandfather, which Amram had probably never heard of.

"Then the Romans relented. I told the guards that even though we would not fight any fellow Jews, we would fight any Romans they brought our way. So for the last eight years a few of my fellow captives and I have been killing Romans for sport in the amphitheatre. Between the five of us, we are up to eighty-eight victims: twenty-six by myself."

"They allowed that?"

"The Romans are imbeciles. Bloodthirsty imbeciles. Once the overseer found out what was going on, he actually started recruiting new guards just for the fights. It was beautiful: Romans setting up Romans to die. And it was my idea, not theirs. We should have won that war against them. I don't know how we didn't. But that self-centered traitor is partly to blame, and that is why I will despise him till the day I die."

"So is that where your scars and burn marks come from?"

"No. They mostly came from the last battle on the Temple Mount. But the amphitheatre guards and the fighting added to it."

Amram was so disfigured on half of his face, he almost looked magnificent.

"I searched for you on the Mount that night at that battle," said Nathan, "but you disappeared then too."

"I don't remember what happened. Somebody must have dragged me to safety."

"But somehow," Nathan marveled, "you always reappear, whether it's fire, battle, or captivity. I think reappearing is your specialty."

Amram almost smiled at that remark. "But look," he said, "discussing my life story is not why I came here."

"So you're here just to lend a little holiday cheer to my new neighborhood?"

Amram caught the reference but ignored it. "No," he said. "I wanted to reestablish contact with you to find out if you knew the whereabouts of the traitor and to invite you back into the cause with me."

"Invite me back into the cause?" exclaimed Nathan with horror. "Amram, I am glad to see you alive again. I have been anxious about you for years and thought you had perished. But I am not interested in the cause anymore. Every time I see you, you require my life from me. And frankly, I have my own life now. And you know your cause is lost."

"Really?" attacked Amram. "You have a life now? What life do you have? Are you married? Do you have children? Do you own the copy shop that you just walked out of?"

It was amazing how quickly the eleven years since their last conversation did not seem long enough for Nathan. Amram could never simply carry on neutral banter. There was always a consequence for the listener, especially if it was Nathan. Amram had been after him to join forces his entire life. In a way, Nathan knew it was a compliment and that that's how Amram expressed brotherly affection and loyalty. But Nathan did not wish to have any part of it. Fires, plagues, and volcanoes might eventually reach the limits of their fury, and Nathan might be able to navigate his way around them all, but Amram never ceased in his scheming, and as long as he was alive, he felt compelled to lasso Nathan into whatever he was doing.

"I am none of those things," Nathan confessed openly. "But I have plans,"—he lowered his voice—"and they do not include an assassination on the Palatine."

Amram stared straight into his brother's eyes with his only remaining one and almost smiled again. "Then at least come back to Transtiberim with me," he said, softening his approach, "and hear what some of my associates have to say on that subject. They may inspire you." Amram waited for a response from Nathan, then continued: "During these past six months, I've become acquainted with a fellow named Zadok from Tiberias, whom you may remember from the campaign in Galilee. He also goes by the name Justus."

"What?" exclaimed Nathan. "You know Justus from Tiberias?"

"I do. And he remembers you."

"And none too kindly, I'm sure. He caused us nothing but trouble in our dealings with him. I can't believe he's still alive and living in Rome."

"Does that really surprise you? You survived, and so did the traitor. And I've been with thousands of survivors in the amphitheatre the last ten years."

"True. But what is your connection with Justus?"

"He has been writing a history of our campaign against Rome, and you should read it. It would set you straight on the real dealings of that quisling, who you still think is a hero."

"I was there, Amram. No one's account of Joseph will set me straighter than my own."

"When you're too close to a subject, it's hard to be objective. Zadok is objective."

"No, he's not. He's just as slanted as everyone else, including you and me," responded Nathan. He then added, "Joseph is writing an account of the war himself, which I've read a portion of in our copy shop."

"Yes. Zadok has informed me of his counterwork."

"It's not a counterwork, Amram," Nathan replied. "It's an accurate portrayal of the events."

"Is it, now? So not everyone is equally slanted in your view."

"The portion of Joseph's book that I've read matches my memory exactly, excep ..."

Nathan stopped himself mid-sentence, and Amram clearly caught it.

"Yes?" Amram said. "You were about to say ...?"

"Nothing," replied Nathan. "Just that Joseph's narrative is completely accurate. So if Justus's account differs from it, it is wrong."

"Wrong," Amram imitated Nathan. "Without reading it, you assume it is wrong. But you didn't finish your original sentence. What were you going to say, Nathan? Except ...what?"

Nathan thought it best simply to come out with it, so as not to make it as big an issue as it, in fact, was in Nathan's mind. "I was going to say that Joseph's account matches my memory of the events exactly, except he did not include any mention of me in his writing."

Amram was taken aback by that revelation. Nathan could not recall ever having seen a look of surprise on his brother's face like he saw at that moment. "Really now," Amram responded.

As Nathan squirmed to think of what to say next, Amram relished the discomposure.

"He mentions *you*," Nathan added simply to say something, and to at least weakly attempt a defense of Joseph. "He just doesn't mention me."

"And you still find him objective and think he is your friend," said Amram. "I think this should demonstrate just how wrong your mentor was on so many counts."

Nathan simply looked down, with no response.

"Did he at least speak well of me in his book?" asked Amram.

"Yes. He did."

"Now that is astounding. Here I desire no association with him whatsoever, but he mentions me in his book favorably. And you, who probably warrant mention as the confidant who knew him better than almost anyone in the world—and I say almost—he completely ignores." Amram paused as the thought sank into Nathan's mind. "All the more reason," Amram added, "for you to come back to Transtiberim with me tonight and hear about him from another vantage. The bottom line is, Joseph should have died honorably ten years ago instead of conniving to save his own skin. He'd be a hero to us all. But instead, he's still alive and is writing a book that doesn't even mention one of the war's true unspoken heroes. It's despicable what he did, and you should not admire him for it. He needs to pay. And if you're concerned that his book won't ever be completed because he's dead, remember that Zadok is writing a book as well, and one book is all the world needs. Besides, I believe Zadok mentions you in his account. You should ask him about it if we see him."

Nathan juggled the pros and cons of venturing to Transtiberim with his brother. He wanted to see the Jewish quarter and was curious to hear the wider Roman-Jewish perspective on Joseph. He even thought he might have a chance to share some of his own views with Amram's co-conspirators, though the strengths of his convictions about Joseph were waning at the moment.

"All right," he finally said. "I will come back with you for one night and listen to some of your friends. But even if I am inspired, I will tell you right here and now that I am excusing myself from any commitment to your plans. I am going with you merely as a courtesy to my elder brother."

"Do you think," Amram retorted, "that I expected any other response from you? Do you think I expected commitment from you? You will live and die never knowing what that word means, just like your heroes Joseph and abba. Your only commitment is to live. But let me ask you: what is life without a cause?"

"True as that may be," Nathan replied, "those are my terms."

"Fair enough."

"But one more thing," added Nathan. "I told my employer, who lent me money to buy you, that if you were ever freed, I would introduce you to her."

"Her?"

"Yes. It's a her. But she is quite a her. You will see. Her husband, my other employer, wants to meet you also, but he is seriously ill.

He is always ill, ever since the plague hit eight months ago. He never fully recovered. So before I can go with you, we will stick our head in the copy shop door, I will introduce you, and I will tell her I will not be returning to work till the day after tomorrow. Then I will go with you to Transtiberim."

Amram shook his head in uncharacteristic agreement.

Nathan did as he had said, only experiencing a delay when Amram and Ducetius expressed surprise at seeing each other. Valeria then told the brothers to leave, as they no doubt had important business to attend to.

Once they were outside, Nathan said to Amram, "You would like Valeria. She's a lot like you."

"She is Roman. I would not like her, and she is not like me."

All the way to Transtiberim, through the Forum, into the lowlands between the Capitoline and the Palatine to the waterfront on the Tiber and beyond, Nathan and Amram spoke to each other like never before. Amram let Nathan do most of the speaking, which is what made the biggest difference; and most of the speaking was simply about Nathan's life—of which Amram knew very little. He spoke about ima in Joppa and Ducetius's family in Sicily, the work on the amphitheatre in Enna and Joram marrying Adah, and Elisheva marrying Efstathios, and Sos and Lois, and the flight to Herculaneum, and the escape from Mount Vesuvius, the migration to Rome, and the job at the copy shop with Manus and Valeria. Amram actually took interest in Nathan's tale as if they had made a genuine human connection. He even expressed a respectful remorse upon learning of Opal's fate. Of course, it worried Nathan that his brother's attentiveness was simply a ploy to lure him into his trap, but he decided to enjoy the fraternal moment for all it was worth; and for Nathan, after all the years of difficulty between them, it was worth a great deal.

When they reached Transtiberim, it did not match Nathan's vision of a Jewish quarter. He figured it would emit an aura of holiness like the Temple precinct in Jerusalem. Instead, it resembled the *tohu vabohu* of the central market district he had been chased through by his brother's henchmen as a teenager, only on a more labyrinthine and industrial scale. After having crossed the Pons Judaeaorum or "Jews' Bridge" over the Tiber, Nathan was struck by the low-class seediness and fishmongering stench of the dock area where longshoremen loaded and unloaded goods from all over the world, including—ironically, and unbeknownst to Nathan—

wheat from the Funisulanus latifundium. As he and Amram continued further on, the scents, smoke, and soot of iron-smelting furnaces, blacksmith shops, glassmakers, tanners, and perfumers began to dominate, mixing for a time with the dock aromas in a strange ambient estuary. And equal to the smells was a confluence of race. Nathan espied faces from every province in the empire: Syrian, Numidian, Arab, and possibly even German.

The narrow circuitous streets reminded Nathan of Enna. There the resemblance ended, however. The unkempt dinge before Nathan, so antithetical to his sense of *kashrut*, took him by surprise. 'This is the Jewish quarter?' he asked himself. But despite its dense population and utilitarian gray, it had been gaining a reputation as a trendy part of the city—Jewish, immigranty, artsy and fashionable—and it began to attract a certain upscale set similar to the Subura. Caesar himself had once owned a villa in Transtiberim, and Cicero had contemplated buying one there. And right at the quarter's center, Flavius Josephus himself owned the very insula next door to the wretched one Amram lived in—a fact Amram did not yet know.

Throughout the evening, Nathan met his brother's friends, some of whom had served in captivity with him, and some of whom, like Nathan, had arrived in Rome from Palestine long after the war, and some of whom had ancestors who had lived in the Jewish quarter since the time of the Maccabees. He was impressed by their mixture of rough-hewn practicality, occasional piety, knowledge of foreign trade, and definitive political views. Nathan learned that the Transtiberim Jews had always had a voice in government, and that even Caesar had shown them great respect. He also learned that they not only targeted Joseph as a political enemy, but also King Agrippa, who was still alive and occasionally in residence in the city.

Nathan had hoped in the past that if there were ever a reunion between himself, Amram, and Joseph, that it would be a happy one. But the night in Transtiberim showed him that dream could never be. Although the three had come so far in life, and years had elapsed, and the political situation had changed significantly, and they were thousands of miles away from home, time and circumstances had managed only to reopen old wounds rather than heal them, and their common past and survival drove them apart instead of drawing them together.

By the morning, after many hours of late-night conversation, including one with Zadok Justus, Nathan almost felt a twinge of affinity with the Jewish resistance, as he knew he would. In keeping with their bargain, however, Nathan left Amram's overly-testosteronic and overcrowded tenement in the early afternoon with no promise of commitment to any cause, and Amram simply allowed his brother to leave the insula without a hitch—almost.

Just as the two brothers were parting and Nathan could taste the air of freedom two yards from Amram, Amram suddenly asked Nathan to stay in touch and to inform him if he ever found Joseph's whereabouts.

"I cannot promise you that," Nathan responded. "I want peace."

Amram merely nodded in silence, restraining himself in order to honor their deal. But as Nathan continued to walk homeward, he could sense the serpent coiling tighter around him again.

XV

"Is he?"

"He is."

It had been two years in coming, but Manus was finally dead.

"He never complained. He just let it happen."

"It was inevitable."

"He hadn't been well in years."

He left everything in order. Or rather, Valeria made sure everything was in order before it happened. Manus helped.

Valeria was not without emotion. "He was a good man," she said.

Her brother was there and saw to all the funerary arrangements: the priest, the pyre, the sacrifice of a sow, and the final feast at the end of the *novendialis* or nine days of mourning. He oversaw everything diligently and thoroughly, not because he cared for Manus, but because it was the proper thing to do. Valeria appreciated that.

At the end of the nine days, the brother said to Valeria, "I will help you make arrangements to come back home again."

"I *am* home," she answered. "My life and business are here. But thank you for the offer."

The brother was surprised and disapproved. He knew, however, that there was no point in arguing with Valeria. She was just like him. "So will you maintain the copy shop and insula on your own, or with what's-his-name?" he asked incredulously.

"Yes. What's-His-Name is rather competent. He knows the business in and out. And What's-Her-Name is wonderful with little Justin, as you've seen. So there is no need to worry, big brother. I will be fine."

In a few days the brother was gone, and the rest of them had to figure out how to proceed without Manus. It was not easy. He had been a husband, father, business owner, and landlord; he had provided a job and an apartment for Nathan; Nathan had enjoyed his many walks with him and had learned about the Jewish captives in the amphitheatre, Mithra, the fiscus Judaica, the Subura synagogue, death in the arena, and the art of publishing from him. But as had been the case with so many other losses in his life, he was able to fill in the practical daily voids from the loss but found it difficult to fill the emotional ones. Nathan began to fear, unattached as he was, that his own end would leave no void at all for those he would eventually bereave. Who would miss him? Everyone who loved or admired him most—his father, mother, Elisheva, Joram, Joseph, George, Auntie Ayathe, and Efstathios—were either dead or far away. He started to believe he would become just another Jotapata or amphitheatre victim whose absence healed over only too quickly till he was completely forgotten. The only person he thought might miss him was Ducetius. And the one he hoped might miss him most was Valeria—though so soon after Manus's passing, he dared not entertain that thought too seriously.

To clear his mind, Nathan started going for walks after work with Ducetius. But they weren't the same. Ducetius was not Manus, and he did not learn as many new ideas from Ducetius. Nathan knew Ducetius so well, and vice versa, that there was little of anything new Ducetius could add to the mix like Manus could. Of course, there was the occasional new insight about Joram's messiah, but Nathan found that uninteresting, so Ducetius barely mentioned it.

On their fourth walk, however, Ducetius brought up the topic, having just finished copying the Matthaios manuscript. "Joram's messiah said once that you will know people by their fruit."

"What does that even mean?" retorted Nathan, trying to dismiss it.

"That people are like trees," answered Ducetius, "and you will know what kind of life they led by what their lives produced or what fruit they left behind. At least that is my understanding. I've been thinking about it for weeks."

"With all that's going on, you're thinking about that?"

"Yes. The emperor's death, your reunion with your brother, Manus's passing, and your upcoming meeting with lord Joseph have made me think about what our lives mean. I want my life to count for something, and I don't know if it does. I think you think about that too."

Ducetius was right. Nathan thought about that often. "But what my mind has been thinking about much more these days" Nathan said, "is…"

"…Valeria. I know."

"Yes. Valeria. How did you know?"

"Patrón, I know you better than you know yourself."

Nathan laughed. "I think you're right. So what do I do about her at this juncture? How do I talk to her about what I'm feeling?"

"Do you mean to say that you are still in love her, even though she's not married anymore?"

"Don't be clever."

"Well, do you?"

"Not as much."

"Really?"

"No, not really. My feelings have not lessened. I think they have increased."

"Then I think you should tell her."

"But it's only been a month…"

"It's been more like two years, ever since she gave you that once-over in the street that day."

"You saw that?"

"Lois did too. I do not think Valeria would be averse to discussing things with you. In fact, if she doesn't bring up the topic before you do within the next week or so—and she'll only wait that long for propriety's sake—I'd be surprised. Or so Lois says."

And that is exactly how it happened. A week after, when work was done and the shop stood vacant of all but two, Valeria approached Nathan at his table and said, "Nathan, we need to discuss the future."

Nathan arose from his seat and stood directly over Valeria just like he had hoped and imagined he would some day. He always thought she was taller than she was, since he primarily saw her from a seated position, and she could be so bossy. But her height was just right compared to his at close range, and he knew exactly what to do.

"Does the future involve this?" he asked, as he tilted his face downward so their lips touched.

Valeria did not move. Neither did Nathan. He couldn't believe it. He expected she would move, but she did not. They stood *neged*, opposed and against and before and compressed. He stared into her eyes, and she into his.

He kissed her with a gentleness so tantalizing it could only have come from his years of inexperience and expectant expectation. Then he pressed against her again, and their lips interlocked in a perfect fit. For one second Nathan thought to himself, who is this woman I barely know, who is not Elisheva, and not even a Jewess, whose world and dreams are so different from mine? But he answered the question by picking her up and carrying her manfully to the wall.

She surrendered to his embrace, and they lost themselves in each other a long time. Then suddenly, as if his earnestness and utter abandon triggered a shut-off valve in her, he felt her deflate away from him. No! not yet! he thought. What's wrong? Have I gone too far and forgotten myself? How are you not liking this? Am I doing something incorrectly? I thought this is what was supposed to happen. But he could sense her leaving the world of his dream and resuming her terrestrial form as employer again. And he devolved back from being king of the universe to the boss's errand boy. Why did it have to end so soon? Were there any other people in the world to whom they were accountable at that moment? Could they not have remained in that dream another few minutes?

"My original intention," Valeria said coyly, smiling and looking up into Nathan's eyes, "was to discuss fiscal matters."

"Really?" responded Nathan with a boyish smile. "I'm sorry. I thought you wanted to discuss *physical* matters."

Valeria let out a small burst of laughter, which Nathan had never seen her do. She looked beautiful when she did that. "You idiot," she said.

"But don't tell me we're done with this conversation," Nathan said. "Because I have a lot more to say." He brought his lips close to hers and kissed her again but eased up so she would have the option to continue or not.

She opted not, which he found incomprehensible. But such was the case.

"Be patient, my sweet Nathan," she spoke gently to him. "It will happen. But you must let me lead on the timing."

"Of course, of course." He barely knew what she even meant by that remark, but he was willing to agree to anything just to keep her close.

"There is my family and the shop to consider."

"I know, I know," he mindlessly responded.

"I cannot risk any problems with either of them."

"Certainly, certainly."

They continued in embrace, person to person, man to woman, heartbeat to heartbeat, lip to lip, enjoying the intensity and comfort and excitement of it all. He sandwiched her between himself and the copy shop wall for a long time. It grew dark outside. How had this not happened years ago, thought Nathan. I've always had the ability, and women are everywhere. And this one has been right here for two years.

In the end, maternity won the final say, however. "I must get back to Justin," whispered Valeria, sweetly, trying to let Nathan down easily. "I do not want to leave from here, but I must."

"All right, all right," relinquished Nathan. And, still shaking a little from the sheer pleasure of what had transpired, the two of them released each other and clumsily and laughingly closed the shop together.

Nathan thought to himself later as he lay in bed that perhaps Valeria had played things right after all. There was more exhilaration in expectation than in culmination, frustrating as it was; and what more could he reasonably ask for at this point than what had already happened? Expectation was good. It kept him interested. It was also probably what kept him young and immature even into adulthood. But for good or bad, expectation and lack of fulfillment had been two major themes in his life. He spent hours in sleeplessness that night reliving what had just happened.

He felt sixteen all over again.

XVI

"It's just around the corner," the slave remarked.

Despite the months he had waited, through the period of mourning for Titus's death, followed by that of Manus, and followed again by his newfound relationship with Valeria, Nathan eventually met up with Joseph's slave at the copy shop and arranged for a meeting with his old mentor. Nathan and the slave were now ambling through neighborhoods Nathan had never seen before. He thought he knew Rome, but he could only guess where they currently were.

"Is this the Quirinal?" he asked.

"Yes, lord," the servant responded.

Like other writers and poets on the Flavian dole, Joseph had been granted an apartment in the city for private use, just as Amram had guessed. The Quirinal lay just north of the Subura and had originally been inhabited by the Sabines, whose women the early Romans had abducted and raped to solve their bachelorhood and tiny population problem. Since then it had become an upscale residential district where Cicero's famous friend Atticus had lived and where Vespasian resided before assuming the throne. During Vespasian's reign, Joseph lived in an apartment within Vespasian's house. Now under Titus, he was granted his own residence, which lay a few blocks from that of Martial the poet on Pear Street.

Nathan felt a pit in his stomach. He had no idea what to expect from his meeting with Joseph. Joseph was a Roman now, and a writer, and connected to the royal family's social circle. He had a new set of societal pressures and standard of etiquette to comply with, and he apparently had a whole new attitude toward Nathan, whom he had omitted in his narrative.

As he neared Joseph's apartment, Nathan worried he was being followed by one of Amram's henchmen. Amram had sent him two messages over the previous weeks insisting that he contact him about when the meeting with Joseph was taking place, asking him to divulge the location. Nathan returned only a vague and minimal reply, which likely meant his brother had hired someone to surveil him. Nathan could not detect any surveillance, but that did not mean it wasn't happening. He had never suspected that Benjamin—who was now one of Amram's apartment mates in the Transtiberim—had been a spy. For all Nathan knew, Amram already had a plant in the copy shop or knew Joseph's address and was set to ambush him. But what could Nathan do? He had to take life as it came.

Nathan was also fretting over his upcoming wedding in Ostia, meeting Valeria's parents and meeting again her unfriendly brother. If Nathan wasn't so nervous about his current circumstances, he would have been impressed that he, who had ostensibly accomplished so little in life, stood at the vortex of so much attention from the ilks of historians like Flavius Josephus, notorious rebels like Amram bar Opal, new heads of fiscus magistracies, and formidable women publishers on the Argiletum.

"That is my master's home," the servant said, pointing ahead to a gated insula. The slave had said little else during their lengthy walk together.

As they entered the gate, Nathan thought, 'What will I find in there? Is Joseph really pudgy and beardless? Does he have any idea that Amram is after him?'

Once in the house, the servant asked Nathan to remain in the entryway while he found his master. After what felt a long time, Joseph suddenly appeared.

"Joseph! You are still alive!" exclaimed Nathan, not able to believe the vision he was seeing.

"Yes! But you know I always find a way," said Joseph, smiling and embracing his old friend.

"You could have smooth-talked your way onto the ark."

"But come in, come in," said Joseph. "Take a look around. This is my new world." Nathan soaked in Joseph's surroundings, impressed by its finery. It even had a second floor, an almost unheard feature in an insula. The atrium lacked a *compluvium*, or opening in the ceiling, since there were other apartments above it. But it possessed all the other features of a high-class domus, including a full dining area and study.

Joseph asked a servant to bring in some food and bade Nathan recline on one of the sofas. "It is hard to believe," Joseph began, taking some morsels from the table, "that we are both still alive and in Rome."

"It could not have happened," responded Nathan, "if you hadn't freed Ducetius and I on the Temple Mount that day."

"That was one of the hardest days of my life, Nathan. I wish I could have freed you all."

"The Romans would never have allowed that."

"No. But they allowed *some*." Joseph paused. "Is Ducetius still with you? Did he make it through the decade as well?"

"Yes. He is here with me, and he is a freedman now."

"Very good."

"And he is married as well."

"You are a kind Patrón. And what about you? Did you ever marry the woman Elisheva who made such an impact on you?"

"I could not," answered Nathan, touched that Joseph remembered her name.

"What happened? Did things change between you? Or was it the war? Or would you rather not say?"

"She married another man during our separation after the war. We saw each other since she lived nearby, but she passed away just before I came to Rome."

"That is too sad. It is not every day that one meets a woman of the caliber with which you described her. I regret to hear of her passing."

"She was one of the finest women I have ever known. It would not be possible to replace her."

"So you have never tried?"

"No. I have not. But I did meet a woman after my arrival here, and we are set to be married soon, after she completes the ten months for her first husband."

"So she is a widow?"

"Yes."

"But ten months? Does that mean she is a Roman and not Jewish?"

"Yes. She is a Roman. About 27. Her name is Valeria, and she has a little son from her previous marriage. Her old husband was a Jew, and she and her family are willing to take on a Jew again."

"We must make a good impression on women then. But I would never have imagined you'd marry a Roman."

"It seems strange, now that you say it. But things happen in life step by step so that I hardly noticed." He thought of his conversation with Joram his first night in Sicily.

"True."

"The truth is, I grew tired of being alone for so long."

"So this is your first marriage? You never married before this?"

"I did not. The war and circumstances kept it from happening. It has been a tumultuous decade with a great deal of moving around. But I take it, then, that you are married?"

"I've had four wives," responded Joseph almost sheepishly.

"Four!?" exclaimed Nathan. "No one I know has had four wives, except Emperor Claudius and King Herod. That is quite an accomplishment! And all in ten years!"

"It was tough, but the fourth one made the work all worth it."

They continued to speak of the past for a long time, with Nathan describing his years in Sicily and Herculaneum. They then turned to the topic of Amram, and Nathan recounted the day he saw his brother in the amphitheatre and how it led to his quest to find Joseph in the city.

"But I do not understand," said Joseph. "You have spoken to your brother? And your brother is living freely somewhere in the city?"

"Yes."

"But why has he not come to see me?" asked Joseph.

"He doesn't know where you are."

"But he should know. I left word with the head of the guard at the amphitheatre how he could contact me on the Palatine. I was staying there at the time. I expected him to show up within a few days."

"He never mentioned any of that to me," Nathan responded, surprised by this new information. "You have to explain to me," he asked, "what exactly happened that day you purchased Amram."

"The emperor allowed me to submit a list of names to the guard," Joseph responded, "so that I could free a few captives. I did it discreetly, since I knew many of the captives might consider me an enemy. In fact, had they recognized me, they probably would have pelted me, like someone did back in Jerusalem, with a rock. But my shaven chin and extra poundage"—Joseph patted his belly—"kept me incognito. In any case, your brother was the only name on the list that they could find. When they showed him to me from about a hundred feet away, I verified his identity, even with that major disfigurement on his face. He refused to come with me, but I figured that might be the case. I told the guard to release him later, after I was gone, since your brother couldn't be seen walking away with a traitor. But I left word how he could contact me, and he never did."

"So Amram knew your whereabouts? And you know how the Jews feel about you?"

"Of course. A few years ago, one of the eunuchs in my own household ended up being an informant for the Jewish resistance. So I am well aware that I am surrounded by enemies."

"Do you think the eunuch could have been a plant from my brother?"

"I don't think that's possible. I handpicked him from the market myself, and your brother was still in captivity."

Nathan thought again about Benjamin but said nothing.

"But not everyone sees me as an enemy," Joseph continued. "You are a Jew, and you do not. And there are others who consider me a hero and understand that I am writing my books to defend us in a way I could not during the war itself."

"I wish you could explain that to my brother."

"You think he doesn't know that?"

"He doesn't appear to, but I couldn't say. Amram and I speak, but I never know what he is thinking. I shudder to imagine how he will react when he learns I'm marrying a Roman."

"You know exactly how he will react. And in regard to me, he may have to maintain the pretense of enmity toward me in the amphitheatre and in the public eye till he figures out how to utilize what he knows about me, but he and I have always had an understanding. He knows we are fighting on the same side. And he knows I couldn't continue to fight if I had died back in Jotapata."

That is what I always thought too, Nathan said to himself. But how can you say he understands you after he had you sniped with a rock, hired me to spy on you, wanted you summoned before the council, and asked me to report back to him after this meeting?

"I suppose you are right," Nathan verbalized. "After all, what do I know? I do not have the mind of a leader like you and my brother have."

"I disagree. You were a leader at sixteen. And if you managed to forge a new life for your family in Sicily and rescue them from Herculaneum, you are a veritable hero. But you and I are in different stages of leadership, and our circumstances have imposed different requirements on us. I have to make decisions in Roman society and as a literary defender of our people that I would never have made before."

At that, Nathan wondered if that was why Joseph had omitted him in his narrative. And Joseph, who was uncannily perceptive, could sense that very thought and began to address the topic.

"For instance," Joseph continued, "you may have noticed in the portion of my book that you copied that you are not mentioned in my narrative."

Nathan shook his head in assent, waiting to hear the explanation.

"That was a deliberate decision to protect you in the event you were still alive, as I hoped you were. I did not want you incriminated with some of the more unreasonable elements of the Jewish leadership, like Gischala or bar Giora. I also needed to play up my own heroics in the story, to defend myself before a critical and unkind world that has more than once attempted my demise."

"I can understand that. And to be honest, I was wondering about that very thing."

"I am sure you were. But the truth is, you played such a crucial role in the war, whether you realize it or not, that you would have stolen too much of my thunder to have included you. Can you understand that? I hope so."

"Yes." It didn't explain his inclusion of Amram, but Nathan stayed silent on that topic.

"But to be candid, my young friend, I tire of the fight and posturing in life. Maybe I have outlived my usefulness, as perhaps your brother thinks. I write but am still despised, and I wonder if my books will ever garner the favor of the world I toil so hard to gain for our people."

"They will. They must. And what a story they tell."

"You have always been an encouragement to me. I wish I had your hopefulness and devotion. But the power of Rome makes me think I and our cause are lost. Rome is the world, and I think we had best awaken to that."

"Joseph, Rome is not the world any more than Egypt or Babylon was. And I am not devoted. I wish I could be. Everyone I have admired in life has had a singular focus, including Amram, Elisheva, and yourself. But I'm not like that."

"If I once was," Joseph responded, "I no longer am. I have straddled too many worlds to stay singular. Besides, you only think you vacillate. But you are as unswerving as anyone I have ever known, including your brother. Amram thinks he is committed to the faith, but it isn't the faith he loves; it's the love of conflict, which he believes his faith justifies."

"That is interesting, Joseph," Nathan responded. "I am the exact opposite. For me, the faith provides a safety net to avoid conflict in my confusions. The worlds I have straddled—Romaphile,

Zealot, Christian, Greek, Sicel, Roman—have left me feeling like an intellectual prostitute, open to any idea that comes along—not to espouse it, but to play with it for a while and allow it to complicate my thoughts. But when I get tired of trying to reconcile my worlds, I simply return to the original, since I know it best. It's sheer inertia that keeps me tied to my faith, not commitment."

"I wouldn't be so hard on yourself. We've all had to retreat from the bombardments of a cosmopolitan world. But I find it comforting that at least we can talk like we always did, though the world flung us apart for years."

The two men fell silent, reclining on the sofas, mulling over their conversation. They had talked all day.

When Nathan left Joseph's apartment, he felt closer and further from his old mentor than he ever had. Joseph was not the hero he had once been in Nathan's eyes, but he was more human. Nathan didn't know what he would report to Amram, if such a report ever occurred. But he knew that he had neither achieved the reconciliation between Joseph and Amram he had hoped might result, nor sensed the enmity with Joseph that Amram thought he would. Instead, he sensed himself again on his usual tightrope, flailing between the two extremes of his world—Joseph and Amram— knowing that wherever he landed, it would not be happy ground.

XVII

Months after their wedding, Nathan and Valeria sat spooned on the sofa in their apartment. Valeria read to her new husband from one of Manus's scrolls.

"When Iesous entered Cafarnaum," she read aloud, "a centurion came to him asking for help. 'Lord,' he said, 'my servant lies at home paralyzed, suffering terribly.' Iesous said to him, 'Shall I come and heal him?' The centurion replied, 'Lord, I do not deserve to have you come under my roof. But just say the word, and my servant will be healed. For I myself am a man under authority, with soldiers under me. I tell this one, 'Go,' and he goes; and that one, 'Come,' and he comes. I say to my servant, 'Do this,' and he does it.'

"When Iesous heard this," Valeria continued, "he was amazed and said to those following him, 'Truly I tell you, I have not found anyone in Israel with such great faith. I say to you that many will come from the east and the west, and will take their places at the feast with Abraam, Isaak and Iakobos in the kingdom of heaven. But the subjects of the kingdom will be thrown outside, into the darkness, where there will be weeping and gnashing of teeth.' Then Iesous said to the centurion, 'Go! Let it be done just as you believed it would.' And his servant was healed at that very moment."

Valeria set the scroll down in her lap, opened to where she had stopped. "This is my favorite scroll in the apartment," she announced.

"I don't care for it," responded Nathan.

"Have you ever read it?"

"I know the basics."

"And that's enough to dismiss it?"

"It is."

"I thought it would be a waste of time myself," responded Valeria, "especially since it's a scroll our dear Manus copied at our expense. But once I started it, it kept my interest."

"So you've been reading it through? Why?"

"Why not? Do I question your literary choices? I read it because I had never heard of it before, it was lying right there on the shelf, and it says some practical things."

"You think that scroll is practical?"

"It has its moments. Marriage, divorce, neighbors, politics: it has tidbits on everything. It discusses law vs. morality, which is a novel idea. It quotes Jewish prophecies, which I know nothing about, even though I've been married to two Jews. And I like that Iesous talks to foreigners and women. Most philosophers don't speak to either."

Little Justin, who was playing with a toy on the floor a few feet away, looked up and asked, "Does he talk to people like me?"

"Yes, he does," responded Valeria, in a motherly tone different from how she spoke to everyone else in the world. "In one of the stories it describes a conversation he had with little people. I'll read it to you some time."

"He sounds nice."

"But right now, my darling," Valeria said, "you need to take your nap. And daddy Nathan and I need to talk."

With that, Justin, who was a sweet, compliant boy, put down his playthings, stood up, waved to Valeria and Nathan, and went into his bedroom to sleep.

"He's such a good little fellow," said Nathan.

"He is," agreed Valeria. "But I don't know how. He didn't get it from me. Maybe Manus. But getting back to this scroll, I think that if I had met him—the man in the story—he would have spoken to me, and I would have had a similar conversation to the one he had with that centurion."

"You think so?"

"I do. For I myself am a woman under authority," she said, imitating the man in the story. "I say to this scrivener, 'Go!' and he goes, and that scrivener, 'Come,' and he comes. And to this scrivener"—she said, pointing to Nathan—"'Kiss me,' and he does it."

Nathan laughed and obliged.

"Another thing I like," Valeria continued, "is that it's not just philosophical. He steps into people's lives even though he has high standards and most of the people he speaks to are not so great. He is strong and forgiving all at the same time. I tend only to be strong and not very forgiving."

"And you think that's going to change now that you've read this scroll?"

"It might. I always thought forgiveness showed weakness. But now I think differently."

"Hmmph. Since when did you become so impressionable?"

"I didn't. I just know a good book when I read one," corrected Valeria.

"Is that why you married me?"

"You mean because you were a good book? I can see now that I'm not always as keen a judge of character as I thought. But yes. You were the finest piece of merchandise on the Argiletum. But don't let that go to your head. There might be a better one tomorrow.

"And as for this scroll, I know nothing about it except the words I've read from it. That's really why I wanted to read it to you, to find out more. It's simply called 'Matthaios,' but I can't figure out why."

"Matthaios is the author."

"But who was he? The name barely shows up in the entire book."

"I really don't know, other than the fact that he is an author of the Way. And I only know that from Ducetius. He copied it. He was working on it the day you and Manus had that argument about his collection in the back room."

"What do you mean 'the day'? There were a hundred days like that."

"Ha."

"But you are at least a little familiar with Iesous, aren't you? He is Jewish, so I figured you must know something."

"That's like saying because you are Roman, you must know about…Tarquinius Superbus."

"And so I do. But he wasn't Roman, Nathan. He was Etruscan. Don't you know anything? What *was* I thinking when I married you?"

"I know what *I* was thinking."

"We'll get to that later. Right now, let's stick to this scroll. Anything else on that?"

"Only a thing or two more."

"Enlighten me."

"I know that numerous people, even ones I am close to, have been duped into thinking Iesous is a god."

"But he was an actual person who lived fairly recently, right? How could he be a god?"

"Precisely what I think! But nobody listens to me. He is simply a man."

"On the other hand," replied Valeria, "one never knows when a god might be among us. Look at Emperor Gaius."

"Oh, please. You don't really think Gaius was Zeus, do you?

"I was joking. Still, if I believed in that sort of thing, I could see how one might concede the man in the scroll is divinity."

"How!?"

"He is so clever. No matter what people ask him, he responds in a way I would never have thought of. So either the author Matthaios thought of all those quips himself, in which case he must have been brilliant, or he was enchanted, as I am becoming, by Iesous's dialogues and felt compelled to transmit them to posterity."

"So you think wit can qualify someone as a god? Then surely my own divine birth has not gone unnoticed. Never mind Emperor Gaius. But I find your reasoning about Iesous childish."

"Well, what do the people who think Iesous is a god have to say? Are they all childish too?"

"No. They're only childish in their mystifying faith in him. Otherwise they're rather intelligent people: my sister—well, she isn't really that intelligent. But there's my brother-in-law with a commanding intellect, who was raised right alongside me in Jerusalem. And Ducetius and Lois, who were raised in Sicily and Pontus, and who are no slouches either."

"Jerusalem, Sicily, and Pontus? Well, there you have it," smiled Valeria. "They were all bound to follow him, weren't they; especially Ducetius and Lois, coming from Sicily and Pontus."

"Why do you say that?"

"Because he mentions in the story that people will come from the east and the west to join his kingdom. Isn't Pontus sort of east, and Sicily west? But you, who lived right where Iesous did as a fellow Jew—you want to be thrown out into the darkness and do not wish to join his ranks."

"And rightly so."

"'O you of little faith!'—he used that phrase somewhere in the story. I don't really believe in him myself either. But I could be persuaded. When I read his words, he is speaking right to me. And his kingdom, wherever it is, is the only one I've heard of where a Jew like you and a Roman like me could build a home together and there would be no distinction between us."

"There is no distinction between us anyway."

"How can you say that? The whole world makes a distinction."

"I don't," asserted Nathan.

"My brother does," replied Valeria. "And your brother does. And the Flavii do. And the whole empire does."

"Then the whole empire is wrong. And as for our brothers, they are pigheaded and deserve to meet each other one of these days. And what a sparring match that would be: Mr. Impossible vs. Mr. Impossibler. Which of them do you think is worse? At least my brother talks to me once in a while, unlike your brother, who barely spoke to me at all during our entire stay in Ostia."

"He talked to you about the fiscus, didn't he?"

"That was not a conversation."

"No. He's not a conversationalist. But when he does speak, you know exactly what is important to him."

"Yes. *You* are important to him."

"Not just me; our entire family."

"But I am not considered family, even though I married you."

"No. You are not Roman. Neither was Manus. So don't think you are alone in being treated like an outsider by my brother. But he will come around. I will work on him harder with you than I did with Manus."

"I won't hold my breath."

"No. I won't either. But regarding the fiscus, it is an important issue. Not to me; but it's the law. And following the law is the second rung on my brother's priority ladder, just under family. My brother doesn't want me to get in trouble. Making sure you pay the fiscus is, in his eyes, a way that he can protect the family as well as follow the rules. It's in his nature. Don't hold it against him. People like him keep the empire functioning. It is a big deal under the Flavii not to pay the fiscus ... if you are a Jew, that is."

"I suppose ..." Nathan conceded.

"But, of course," Valeria added, "if you and I were both to give up our cultural identities and families and throw caution to the wind and become childish and follow this scroll ..."

"Follow that scroll!? And what? I wouldn't be a Jew anymore, so I wouldn't have to pay the fiscus? Is that what you are saying? As if I would, for any reason, believe in that man, let alone for a hypocritical, pecuniary one. Are you mad? We just got married, and already you are trying to alter the footing on which our relationship is based. You just said before you don't believe in him either. Please don't tell me you have shifted in these last three minutes. He's just a man, Valeria. I don't know if I could take another person falling prey to him. I'm certainly not going to. Your brother would sooner go to synagogue with me up the street than I would turn to this nonsense," said Nathan, flicking at the scroll like an annoying gnat.

"I've heard of crazier things," said Valeria, picking up the scroll again to read.

XVIII

"Is it true?"

"Is what true?"

After three years of silence between the two brothers, Amram appeared at the copy shop door just as Nathan was leaving again.

"Can't you say hello when you see me?" asked Nathan, already annoyed.

"I could," answered Amram. "But I'm not sure I'm welcome, so I don't want to waste your time."

"Since when have you ever cared about that? You're always welcome. It's been a long time."

"Yes, it has. I only hear about you through the grapevine."

"I'm sure you do," responded Nathan snidely. "That must be how you always know when I'm leaving work, no matter what time I leave, or what year it is."

"But," said Amram, ignoring Nathan's snidery, "I doubt if you ever inquire about me."

"It's not that I don't care, Amram," responded Nathan. "It's just that we have little in common these days, and it's safer to keep my distance."

"That's why I came to talk to you."

"You asked me before if something was true. What do you want to know the truth of?"

"Let's go for a walk," said Amram. "Better yet, let's go eat in one of these tabernae around here."

"All right. Let's do that. But let me tell Valeria first. Want to come up and meet my wife?"

"I'd rather not," responded Amram. "And we met before."

Nathan disappeared through the insula door, ran to the second floor, informed Valeria, and returned to street level in less than two minutes. "Want to try that taberna a couple of buildings down on the right?" suggested Nathan upon reappearing. "It's a good one."

"No. Let's try this one right here."

Why can't we try the one I recommended, asked Nathan to himself. Is it because you always have to be in control? Or you think you know this taberna is better than the other one? Or perhaps one of your henchmen works here, and that's how you already know whatever it is you are about to ask me?

Whatever the case, the two brothers went to the taberna Amram chose and sat down in the innermost corner. A candle on the rough-hewn table between them lent an air of coziness completely incommensurate with the diners.

"So what is it you want to know?" asked Nathan.

Amram paused before answering while a young worker placed bread, garum, wine, munchables, and a handcloth on the table.

Amram then asked Nathan, "So what game are you playing with me, with us, and with your life?"

"What are you talking about?" retorted Nathan, already on the defensive.

"You have distanced yourself from the cause, married a Roman woman, and been heard speaking in favor of the Way. Have you gone completely mad?"

"You've known about my marriage for two years."

"Yes, and I've had to make excuses for you ever since."

"Why do you have to make excuses?" responded Nathan impatiently.

"Do you think my associates don't clamor to cross the Tiber to end your life just to save me face?" asked Amram.

"Save you face for what?" responded Nathan.

"Because you cavort and cohabit with the enemy," Amram explained. "They want you dead, and I am the only thing standing between you and oblivion."

"I don't believe you," said Nathan. It was too monstruous to be true. "You're talking nonsense. I don't ever see you, but your friends want me dead? The very ones I met when I visited Transtiberim with you?"

"Most of them. Not all of them. Benjamin speaks up for you. But he is losing ground, I can tell you that."

"How can they care that much?"

"They care that much."

Nathan questioned the possibility of his situation really being as precarious as Amram described. "And is it the same with Joseph?" he asked.

"I'm not discussing him," answered Amram.

"But I want to know."

"Still panting after him like a little whore?"

"That is over the top!" exclaimed Nathan, getting angry. "And completely unnecessary."

"Perhaps. But if *I* know anything about him at all," continued Amram, "it's not through any help of yours, dear brother. So you must forgive me my attitude. I trusted you to tell me his whereabouts years ago. I trusted you, but you couldn't trust me with that information." He paused. "But did you really think I wouldn't find him anyway? I found you, even though you are of no consequence whatsoever. Joseph, on the other hand, is famous. Though for how much longer, I couldn't say."

"You wouldn't dare…"

"Dare what?"

"You know what. Who are you to play judge over other people and decide who lives or dies?"

"I only decide if someone is still of use to me."

"So if Joseph is still alive, it's only because he is still of some use?" responded Nathan. "And myself as well, I suppose. You evil…"

"I'm evil because I said that? I shudder to imagine what you would think of me, dear brother, if I had informed you that he is already dead. I know you speak to him every now and then. Go and see for yourself."

"I will. It has been a while."

"But not as long as the silence between you and me. But enough about the traitor. The more important issue is your recent leanings toward theological suicide. Have you lost all sense of truth and proportion subscribing to that sect? If I have been able to quell some of my associates' fanaticism over your marriage, I have barely been able to contain them over that."

Infuriated over his friends' presumption to interfere with his political, marital and inner life, Nathan stated, "The loss of proportion and truth is entirely on your end. What business is it of yours, or anyone else's, what I believe or do?"

"Younger brother," said Amram, lowering his voice, "you have always been my business."

"I'm almost thirty-seven," Nathan responded, pushing himself away from the table. "I do not need protection, and you do not need to be your brother's keeper any longer."

"Prove it," demanded Amram.

"I proved it for ten years," responded Nathan, "when you weren't anywhere to be seen in my life, from the time the war ended till I saw you in the amphitheatre. I was completely on my own, and I survived very well. You, on the other hand, were in chains.

"You tell me my life is in peril, but it's only because of you, if it's even true. You are not saving me from anything. So don't flatter yourself. My life is safer and more settled than it has been since I was fifteen."

"But we are not talking about surviving volcanoes. The odds are fifty-fifty against nature. We are speaking about treachery and changing sides, from which the odds are considerably lower. To follow your wife's lead—your Roman wife's lead—regarding your faith, I am astounded you could have let something like that occur. The first man learned the price of that, and the calamity of the universe rests on his uxorious error. But instead of avoiding his example, you follow it. When there is the final showdown between us and Rome—and there will be—where will you stand? Who will protect you when you are neither Roman nor Jew? People caught in the middle have been put to death for decades under the Caesars, and rightly so."

"You're talking nonsense Amram. The showdown has already occurred. Your cause is finished. And I don't need protection. We live in a different world than the one we fought for twenty years ago. When will you see that? And I'm tired of being watched. I'm tired of being tethered to the past. If my silence over these past three years hasn't made it obvious, I want out. I love you, and you are my brother. But I can't live in or on the outskirts of your circle anymore. I want to follow my own life and live the way I want to live and believe what I want to believe. Why can't I be my own man?"

"The fact that you ask that question is why it will never happen."

"Only so long as you are around," responded Nathan. "When I am on my own, I am fine. I wish I could both have you in my life, since you are my brother, and not have you, all at the same time." He recalled Elisheva speaking similarly about *him*.

"But life doesn't work that way," Amram answered. "And you are not the only one tethered. None of us lives on his own. We may be deluded that we are free, but in reality, there is only the ability to have more or less control over everyone around us. There is no freedom. Even the powerful are controlled. Am I free? Do I live independently? So long as Rome and Joseph and my circle and you exist, I am not free.

"And as for the past, younger brother, you set out to find both Joseph and myself on your own. No one forced you to do it. Neither of us knew you were searching for us, nor that you knew anything about our whereabouts, nor that you were even alive or anywhere near enough to attempt a search. You looked for us of your own volition. And you found us. You wanted to be tethered to the past, whether you thought you wanted it or not. You brought us back into your world, and here we are. I can walk away, and you can believe what you want and live as you want, and things can resume the way they have been for these past three years. But there will be consequences to that. And it will not be freedom. No one and nothing is ever free."

Nathan did not know how to respond or whether he even cared to. In the scroll Valeria had eventually persuaded him to read, the main character, who was somehow supposed to rescue the world like Orpheus his Eurydice, did not answer his accusers when charged with indictment. Pilate the procurator, the very one in front of whom Nathan's father and grandfather had lain prostrate so many years before, was the very one who questioned him in the scroll, and he did not utter a word. And so Nathan wished to remain silent as well. Yes, he had denied the cause. Yes, he had married a Roman wife. Yes, he had turned to the Way. He was guilty on all three counts, and guiltiest, in Amram's eyes, of the last. But what of it? Was he not free in having made that decision? According to Amram, there is no freedom. But wasn't the decision to follow his conscience the one free thing he had done his entire life? Had it merely been Valeria who had brought him to it? It had certainly not been. It had been a long time in coming; the culmination of Joram's talks about prophecy, Efstathios's take on Abram, Elisheva's geo-theology and pleadings, the concept of the threeness on the trail from Pergusa, the unsalvific nature of Jovian visitations, Ducetius's insight on Hell and his lone and terrible confrontation at the Gate to the Underworld. How could he not have decided as he did in the face of all those things? Valeria was the final tug from the precipice. But none of the others had forced him into it. They had never given him an ultimatum or turned against him as he felt Amram often had. Instead, they loved him all the more in his intransigence. That enabled him to decide of his own free will. He had finally chosen to choose something because of that. And it was a choice that did not tether him to the past or to his brother or to Joseph or to Rome or to Jerusalem. It was not to a particular plot of land or ideology. It was, as he saw it, to the only one who could possibly extricate him from all those things, as well as the slavery to his own good-ness and the internal rules and petty squabbles that keep people lashed down in the muck of self-absorption and empty causes and a chasing after the wind.

So no, he did not wish to speak. He thought his silence would be to the amazement or consternation of his brother. But it was not. His brother, rather strangely and coolly, simply waited in the silence as Nathan continued to think to himself; as if he suddenly understood for the first time that he, Nathan, was man enough to need no further explanations from him, and that all had been said, and that if he had truly decided to strike out on his own, so be it.

They were equals now, and Nathan was allowed to part ways with him.

Nathan got up from the table to leave. "It is as you say, brother," he said. "But I must do what I must do."

"And I as well," Amram responded.

Nathan left the taberna, knowing it was probably at the price of enmity with his past and his brother and could unleash an aspect of the war he barely knew existed so long as he had remained subservient.

XIX

Nathan could not hide the fact forever, though he rarely gave it a thought. Then one day at the baths, two men eyed him from across the pool, one younger and one older.

"What do they want?" Nathan asked Ducetius, who was sitting next to him in the water.

"I don't know," answered Ducetius. "But last time I was here, they kept glancing at me as well."

"Did they ever say what they wanted, or did they threaten you?"

"No."

"We'll have to watch out for them, then. Who knows what they're up to. It reminds me a little too much of Herculaneum."

"Why do we get into trouble everywhere we go? I thought we were safe here."

"Safe in Rome?"

"So far it's been safe."

"If you like fires, plagues, and fiscus laws, I suppose it's safe."

"I forgot about those. I guess it hasn't been that safe. But sometimes I think it's you, Patrón. You always get us into trouble."

"Me?! I didn't cause any of those issues. And if I remember correctly, it was *you* who got us into trouble the last two places we lived. And even here, those guys were staring at *you* before I even showed up."

"You're right," Ducetius smiled sarcastically. "You're always right."

Nathan had not been to a public thermae for two years. Since his marriage to Valeria, he had access to running water in their apartment. However, the water feed to the insula was currently in disrepair, and he and Ducetius had spent the entire day prior unsuccessfully trying to fix it.

They waited for the two voyeurs to leave, but the men took their time. When they could wait no longer, Nathan and Ducetius climbed out of the water, concealing their middles. The looks on the strangers' faces, however, indicated that their discretion hadn't succeeded.

Nathan and Ducetius walked out onto the Argiletum sensing eyes upon their backs from every crevice. They stopped for a snack at one of the tabernae to throw off any would-be followers, and left when they felt it was safe. Ducetius returned to his apartment, and Nathan went into the shop to warn Valeria that something might be amiss.

As Nathan exited back onto the street to return home and Valeria stood at the door watching him, four soldiers strode down the Argiletum and surrounded him.

The soldiers grabbed Nathan's arms to lead him away, and Valeria flew into action. Storming up to the soldiers in a huff, she demanded, "What is your business with my husband? I am the daughter of a Roman citizen and the sister of a Roman magistrate in Ostia, and this man is my husband. What charge are you pressing against him?"

"Ma'am," answered one of the soldiers, "we have our orders to take this man into custody. We do not know the nature of the charge. But I suggest you cooperate with our efforts and return inside. Otherwise, we may be obliged to escort you with us as well, civic connections notwithstanding."

"Where are you taking him?" she asked.

"The castra up the street," answered the soldier.

"The Praetorium?" she started, thinking they meant the intimidating Praetorian headquarters a mile away.

"No. The smaller office right here in the Subura, on the right."

"Don't worry, Valeria," said Nathan. "Whatever the charge is, I'm sure it will be cleared up once I speak to the commanding officer." They then took him away.

About 20 paces up the street, they backtracked. Valeria, watching again from the door, could hear Nathan protest. "Whatever accusation you have against me," he said, "I assure you my friend had nothing to do with it." She then looked on while two of the soldiers entered the insula, reappeared momentarily with Ducetius in custody, and disappeared up the street in a sixsome.

Lois, who ran out of the insula almost frantic, rushed over to Valeria. "Do you know what is going on? What's going to happen?" she asked.

"I don't know," Valeria responded sternly. "But I'm sending word to my brother."

As Nathan and Ducetius walked with their hands tied behind their backs to the local castra, Nathan couldn't help but think his brother Amram lay behind his predicament. The timing of his arrest came right on the heels of their last discussion, and he couldn't imagine how else an accusation could have arisen against him in a city where so few people knew him. He racked his brain trying to think of what his infraction could be. His best guess involved the fiscus, based on the way the men at the baths were eyeing him. Nathan had originally paid the fiscus—a fee of two drachma, or two days' wages—to his brother-in-law during the first year he and Valeria were married. However, under Domitian's most recent law update, the fee had increased, requiring a Jew to pay for each member of his family, young or old, whether they were Jewish or not. Thus Nathan had to pay for Valeria and Justin, and Ducetius had to pay for Lois and Kalo. And if he and Ducetius claimed they were Christians and not Jews, they were still obliged to pay the fiscus; for another revision of the law stated that people who lived a hidden Jewish lifestyle—which basically amounted to being circumcised and abstaining from pork—while adhering to another faith, were subject not only to the fiscus but also to possible confiscation of their property, deportation, or an agonizing execution in the arena.

If Nathan's arrest was, in fact, Amram's doing, his brother had managed to land him in the heart of a perfect storm from which there was no escape. He would most likely face execution. Nathan imagined that within the next few days, his brother would also machinate an equally fiendish trap for Joseph and be rid of both his enemies at once. He realized that bringing Joseph down might be harder, since he had the emperor's support. But Domitian was taciturn and could not be trusted. And if Amram had succeeded in planting one of his men in Joseph's household, it was not impossible. As Nathan reckoned it then, especially now with the castra looming in full view, Amram's lifelong war was about to be won, and Amram was about to win it.

Despite the desperate thoughts coursing through Nathan's head, the soldiers escorting him and Ducetius were a friendly lot. They told Nathan he would probably be fine, since he and Ducetius seemed like decent, ordinary fellows, unlike the usual riffraff they dealt with. They even stopped in a taberna for a drink and offered both prisoners a sip. All four of the soldiers belonged to Rome's local police force, the Cohortes Urbanae, founded by Augustus to maintain civil order decades before. It consisted of more than one thousand highly trained soldiers, answerable to a chain of centurions, tribunes, and ultimately the urban prefect.

The prefect in charge when Nathan was arrested was Titus Aurelius Fulvus, a new appointee who had just replaced a prefect recently executed by Domitian. Youthful, ambitious, fated to sire a future Roman emperor and die young, Fulvus wished to gain favor with Domitian with a reputation for toughness. Had Nathan been arrested under the previous prefect, he stood a chance to receive clemency. Under Fulvus, his fate was sealed.

When Nathan and Ducetius reached the castra, the soldiers deposited them into the care of the lone legionnaire on duty. After speaking to the legionnaire about the case, they left, and the legionnaire locked Nathan and Ducetius in the holding cell. "What is happening to us?" Nathan asked the legionnaire through the slammed door.

"You'll be questioned and sentenced in the morning." he responded flatly, his voice muffled by the door.

"Do you know what charge is being brought against us?"

"Not in the least," the legionnaire responded in as uncaring a tone as he could muster.

"And, perchance, do you have something to eat?" Nathan asked. "We've only had a snack since morning."

With that, the soldier laughed. "Something to eat? Where do you think you are, an inn?" But despite the jailor's cavalier attitude, he unbolted the cell door and tossed something onto the floor.

"It's bread," said Ducetius, who split the dirtied morsel in the dark with Nathan.

"Thank you, officer!" yelled Nathan through the door. "That was very kind."

"If you girls need anything else…" came the muffled reply.

Starting that evening and throughout the night, other prisoners joined Nathan and Ducetius at regular intervals as the Cohortes Vigilum rounded up hoodlums and burglars. From the smell, look, and vocabulary of the newcomers, Nathan understood why their original escort viewed him and Ducetius as different from the rest. As the inmate mix became uncomfortable, Nathan and Ducetius spoke little, and only in Aramaic or Hebrew when they did. By morning, there were a dozen in the cell, and they all looked mean, avoided interaction, and waited for their interrogation and sentencing.

⁜

By mid-morning, Nathan could hear the muffled voices of women in the outer office. "Is that Valeria?" he said. "And Lois?" asked Ducetius. It was. The two wives had found their way to the castra, toddlers in tow, to check on their wayward husbands. The jailor, who had replaced the earlier legionnaire at sunrise, unbolted the cell, held his hand to his nose, and called for Nathan and Ducetius. He shackled them and let them talk to their visitors in the main office.

"Do not touch them," warned the jailor as the women reached out to hug their forlorn, unwashed, sleep-deprived, and hungry men.

"Is there any news about the charge?" Valeria asked Nathan with desperation.

"None. We still do not know why we are here."

"I sent word to my brother last night. I'm sure he will send help."

"He won't send it on my account," responded Nathan.

"But he will on mine."

Valeria and Lois then produced food from their satchels, asking the jailor to partake before giving some to their husbands. The jailor obliged.

Within a minute, a flurry of soldiers entered the office, led by a centurion who asked the room cleared of all but the detainees.

The jailor said, "These two women are the wives of these two detainees." But the centurion responded, "All but the detainees. Out! Out!" and he shooed Valeria and Lois to the exit.

Nathan and Ducetius thought their interrogation was about to commence, but instead they were returned to the holding cell, still

403

chained. After waiting two more hours in the putrid-smelling dark, the soldiers began calling prisoners one by one into the office for questioning and sentencing—except for Nathan and Ducetius.

As the two listened to the proceedings as best they could, they found it terrifying how quickly some of the prisoners were apprised of their fate. Nathan had always assumed that sentencing involved a defense for each victim. But that was only the case for elites. The condemnation of most of the prisoners in the castra was a foregone conclusion not only because they had been brought to the castra, but also because they were all plebes or non-citizens. Although Nathan and Ducetius could not hear every word spoken by the centurion through the cell door, the sentencing they caught wind of struck them as utterly capricious and arbitrary and not equal for the same crime. Half the men were condemned to death in the arena, whatever their misdemeanor, and two received the sentence *damnatio ad bestia*, or death by being fed alive to wild animals. Others were to be burned to death, banished, or to have all their property confiscated. Only one was released with six months of civic duty, like road maintenance.

Of all the punishments, being fed to animals or being burned alive seemed the most heinous to Nathan at first. But even worse, he concluded, would be having to watch Ducetius undergo any of those punishments first.

It wasn't until near the end of the centurion's shift in the late afternoon that Nathan and Ducetius were finally brought into the main office for questioning. By then, all the other prisoners had been taken away; and their hope was that this perhaps signified their case was of a special nature, leading to a lighter sentence.

"Have the witnesses obtained the proper credentials yet?" asked the centurion of his assistant.

"They have, sir," answered the soldier.

"Then bring them in, and let's be done with it."

The two men whom Nathan and Ducetius recognized as the voyeurs from the thermae walked into the castra, followed by another middle-aged man. As Nathan and Ducetius looked at the three men in tandem, Nathan suddenly recognized them, after compensating for maturation in the young man's face. He felt a pit in his stomach. Trying to whisper their identity to Ducetius, he was cut off when the centurion barked at him to remain silent.

The centurion asked the three witnesses to produce their identification bronzes confirming that they were Roman citizens. They produced four altogether, to the utter dismay of Nathan, who realized how hopeless their citizenship made his case.

The centurion then spoke directly to Nathan and Ducetius. "You two stand accused of murdering a Roman citizen, the son of a Roman citizen."

It was only with this disclosure that Ducetius, too, recognized that the three men hailed from their final traumatic moments near the boats at Herculaneum. One was the father of the boy Nathan had accidentally killed, one was the friend of the boy, and the other was the father of the friend. Who could have imagined that after seven years, those three would end up in the same neighborhood and therma as Nathan and Ducetius? It seemed almost impossible. But Rome was, after all, the capital of the world, and refugees from the bay were still trickling in to start a new life there, and the Subura was the most affordable neighborhood in it. So it was not implausible. But it was catastrophic for Nathan.

The centurion spoke again. "There is an extenuating circumstance in this case, in that one of you is noted by my officers as being the in-law of a Roman citizen and magistrate. The other of you is noted by the witnesses as having been absent during the actual act of murder but is identified as a likely accomplice."

In Roman society, there was no official punishment for murder. An investigation was not even called for, unless a citizen was murdered by a non-citizen, as was the case in this situation. Had Nathan merely killed a fellow nobody, there would have been no charge, no trial, and no penalty. The victim's family, if they had the means, would simply have hired a hitman from one of the Subura's many local gangs and taken vengeance that way.

"If I may speak, my lord..." said the father of the victim.

"You may," answered the centurion.

"If my lord is considering a lenient sentence for this murderer due to the status of his in-laws, my lord should know that both the accused are also Jews."

"Is that so?" asked the centurion, almost smiling.

"If I may speak, my lord..." Nathan asked.

"You may not!" barked the centurion again. "You will speak when addressed."

Nathan bowed his head in submission.

"Yes," continued the father. "We noticed Jewish bodily defacement on both men at the baths."

The centurion stared at Nathan and Ducetius. "Do you deny this?" he asked. "It would be easy enough to confirm."

"We are circumcised," answered Nathan, "however…" he hesitated.

"However what?" snapped the centurion. "Are you not Jews?"

An assistant suggested they were perhaps originally Jews, but currently practiced another religion, like Mithraism or the Way.

"Have you converted," asked the centurion, "to Mithras or the Way or to some other cult?"

"Yes," they each answered. "We are members of the Way."

"And have you paid the Fiscus Judaica for this year?"

"No," they both answered. "We have not."

"Then you are fools as well as murderers," rebuked the centurion. "If you had merely committed murder, I might have spared *your* life on account of your wife's connections and *your* life because you were not present at the time of the killing—though all of your property would still be confiscated and surrendered to these men. But given the fact that under the Fiscus laws, as well as those of Maiestas, you are concurrently guilty not only of murder but of 1) non-payment of the Fiscus, 2) maintaining a private Jewish lifestyle, and 3) converting to an illegal religion that affronts the person and divinity of the emperor, I am compelled by my station to condemn both of you to death in the arena by whatever means the master of ceremonies deems best for the entertainment of the day; and all of your property is to be handed over to these men the morning after your deaths."

Nathan, who wanted to scream, rallied himself to ask, "Please may I speak, my lord?" There was nothing more he could possibly lose by asking.

"You may," answered the centurion, slightly moved by the condemnation of two well-mannered young men, distinct from the typical rabble.

"My wife," said Nathan, "did not know me when I accidentally killed the young man in question—whose death I heartily regretted even then—nor was I living in Rome at the time. I was in Herculaneum. And my wife was living in Rome and married to another man. My wife has never been informed of my past wrongdoing and is completely innocent. I thus ask for clemency regarding the property on her behalf, so that she will have means by which to live." No separate plea was needed for Ducetius, since he owned no property.

The centurion remained silent for a moment, mulling over his response. "Your request is denied," he finally said. "It would mean a lack of compensation for the victim's family to which they are entitled." He stopped, then resumed: "This case is now closed. The witnesses may leave, making sure to return in one week's time to sign the paperwork for the property transfer. And due to the late hour, the prisoners will remain in custody here, being moved to the holding chamber at the amphitheatre tomorrow."

With that, the assistant took Nathan and Ducetius back into the cell. As the two accused stood alone in the dark too stunned to move, their emotions were interrupted by the sound of the outer door opening again and someone entering. The name "Kaliphon" could clearly be heard upon the stranger's entrance, uttered by more than one person in the office, and with some surprise. A muffled brief discussion then ensued. A minute later, the office went silent again as all the men but the lone legionnaire on evening shift exited the building for the night.

XX

As Amram appeared at the gate, Joseph's new house slave walked out to the courtyard to open it. From the look of their conversation from the window, Joseph suspected that the two already knew each other. It seemed Nathan was right. Amram really was an enemy.

Joseph ordered his household manager to quickly rally the domestics to entertain their guest. He then went to his upper chamber to prepare. To all appearances, Amram was alone and unarmed. But who knew how many in his household might come to Amram's aid if he issued the command to turn his visit into an assassination? Was this the moment when it would all happen? He had waited for Amram to visit him for five years, and now he showed up unannounced. The very fact that he knew Joseph would be home was a clear indication that something nefarious was afoot. As he finished dressing, Joseph hid a dagger in his robes, recalling former days when he wielded it with lethal swiftness. Now he was close to fifty, overweight, and slow of hand. Maybe it would be best, he thought, if Amram succeeded in his task.

Joseph waited for a servant to announce the visitor and send a message up to his quarters. He had to appear surprised by the visit.

He descended the staircase to the entranceway just as a guard was patting Amram down. "That won't be necessary," Joseph said for appearance's sake. "Amram bar Opal!" he then declared. "I have waited years to see you again. Welcome to my home." Though an embrace may have been in order, both men refrained.

Joseph led Amram to a seat in the *triclinium* and asked a slave to serve refreshments.

"To what do I owe this pleasure? And why haven't you visited sooner?"

"I am not here on a social call," said Amram, cutting to the chase. "I am here on business that concerns us both."

"Tell me," responded Joseph, dispensing with all protocol, as if back in the days of the rebellion.

"My brother has been arrested on charges of murder, and based on my contacts in the cohort, things are not going well for him."

"Murder? How? When?" asked Joseph.

"It happened years ago during his escape from Herculaneum. He briefly mentioned it to me. It was an accident. But the victim ended up being a Roman citizen, and the man's family ran into Nathan by chance here in the city. They've pressed charges. He will most likely be condemned by the end of the day."

"And your connections cannot get him released?" asked Joseph.

"No," answered Amram. "I need your connections."

"But yours are far more direct. I am willing, but do not understand why or how you need my help."

"Let's just say Nathan's recent defections have rendered him persona non grata in my circles. No one will lift a finger on his behalf."

"So you need *my* help?"

"Not for me, but for Nathan."

"So you want me to go directly to the emperor?"

"Yes. That is what I am asking," stated Amram.

Joseph thought through his words carefully before responding. "Amram," he explained, "my relationship with Domitian is rather tenuous these days. You know he is a difficult man, and my welcome with him is wearing thin. He's not like Titus, who was like a friend.

If I overstep my bounds with Domitian, I may not survive to make the request you are asking."

"If that is the case," Amram responded, "then, frankly, that is the case. You may not survive. But what is that to either you or me in the midst of war?"

"Amram, the war is over."

"The war is not over. I hear you say you still fight, but with quill and ink now. You think you have lived up to your name and have saved lives by what you have written. But I ask you now to stop being Joseph and to step into the fray like Esther. And if you die, you die."

"Esther?" Joseph exclaimed confounded, till he figured it out.

"And if you live," Amram continued, "it will exonerate you among the resistance."

"But how could that be? You said yourself that Nathan is considered an enemy."

"But in a few months," said Amram, "I can change that. Especially if Nathan is deported out of the city far from my circle. That is what I am asking of you: I want him to live, but I want him out of the city and my vicinity and out on his own. And once that is accomplished," Amram said slowly and thoughtfully, "I swear to you that this war will come to an end."

XXI

For what promised to be the last time, Ducetius awakened Nathan with his old call: "Samson, Samson, the Philistines are upon you."

This time it was true.

"Are you scared, Ducetius?" asked Nathan.

"Yes. But I am not alone. Are you, Patrón?"

"Yes. But I feel the same way."

Nathan had not slept much during the night, but he clearly had slept some. He hoped that like Samson, he would be strengthened one more time to face what he needed to face, and Ducetius too. The only way through death to the other side, if there was another side, was through it. And all he had to do in order to get there was to live through one more day. In the silence of the night, he had calculated that he had lived about thirteen thousand days. Now he only had to live through one more. Then it would be over.

When he imagined what it would be like to look into the drooling and devouring mouth of a wild animal, it was hard for him to believe that his life would all funnel down to that. When he was a child and all the hope of the world lay before him and there was fun to be had and a family that protected him, he couldn't imagine the incremental changes that would bring him to this point. Was there something he would have done differently? Most likely. The pivotal change might have been to have married Elisheva. But given who he was, he realized he would have done the same things all over again. And given all he had experienced, he considered that, ultimately, he had had a good run just the way things were.

Still, he wanted to choreograph his final moments, to go out well and not shamefully. But when the whole purpose of the method was to shame the victim, he thought, was there any way to avoid it? Was the crucifying of mashiach noble while it was happening? No. It was bloody, painful, unjust, humiliating. Nobility was attributed to it in hindsight because of its meaning. But his own death would mean nothing to anyone. It would not change a single life or aspect of the universe. It would not bring the temple of Dagan crashing down on Israel's enemies or open the floodgates of forgiveness. It would not even reconcile Amram to him or to Joseph. He would die never having achieved peace, or a family, or ever having known Elisheva—though he loved Valeria too. He would not even achieve what Manus had achieved. He would leave no voids that could not easily be filled.

To him, the most important thought he had to avoid in the upcoming days was that his last minutes in the arena would be the summation of his life. Manus had said something about that— that his end would not define him, his legacy, or his experience in the world. He had not lived merely for the purpose of providing a meal for an animal. When the thought that such had been his purpose came into his mind, it made him vomit, and that happened twice during the night. It happened to Ducetius too. And it certainly did not help the already unbearable stench in the holding cell. He had faith, and so did Ducetius. But somehow, even though he knew there was more to life and he had a hope of eternity, it made him squeamish to think that all of his strivings, ideas, dreams and achievements would be confronted by a beast whose salivary glands did not register that his life meant something to him. Meaninglessness can overcome faith, he thought, and his stomach could not sustain it. Nathan assumed that some people might get used to the idea of meaninglessness and live under the assumption of it their whole lives. But now that he was contemplating his last day on earth, he found it hard to believe that anyone, in thinking about the imminent ending of their life in the arena, would not have at least a fleeting bout of nausea when confronted with just how meaningless meaninglessness was, as if their nihilistic lifelong ideology had been a mere mental game compared to the reality.

He found some comfort in the idea that millions had passed through death's portal long before him and that others would join him that day, as well as in the future. He also had Ducetius with him. Ducetius kept him going, and he kept Ducetius going. Most of the prisoners in the holding cell were alone, which would make their deaths unbearable. So he felt fortunate. He would have to discuss with Ducetius, in fact, how they should fight each other to the death in the amphitheatre, in the event they were forced to do so. Nathan had strategized over this many times, ever since their capture at the end of the war. In Nathan's mind, there was no question that Ducetius needed to die first and at Nathan's hand. He would not permit Ducetius to survive him to be maimed or choked or dismembered slowly by some brute who didn't know who he was. Ducetius could come at him with everything he had—he wanted him to impress the audience and die with dignity—but Nathan would deliver him a final blow, the force of which would let him know how much he loved him and wished things could have ended differently.

But there would be much left undone for Nathan when his end would come that day. He had always hoped to have a son or daughter to provide a posterity for abba and ima. Maybe after he was gone Valeria would discover that she was carrying his child. He dreamed that would be the case, though there had been no sign of it despite two years of nuptial fervor. To date he did not know if either of his siblings had ever become parents. Perhaps if there was a delay in his execution, he would write them. But he doubted it. Some things would always remain undone; and such was life.

It bothered him in these final moments that human existence seemed as hampered and unfree as Amram had claimed. Between Qohelet's time and chance, the mandate of heaven, and his brother's puppeteering behind the scenes, it was hard to make sense of free will and fate. Had Nathan ever been free to control his own destiny? From his family, to Judaea, to the War, to the Empire, to Nature, to Death, to God, there were systems within systems, and layers upon layers that hemmed in every movement within confined parameters. It was as if each soul was born into a terrestrial cage, the size of which differed from individual to individual, but always within a cage. A peasant enjoyed certain freedoms that a noble did not, and a noble enjoyed freedoms unknown to a peasant. But all were trapped by one limitation or another.

As Amram had said, even the powerful were not free. So in the end, one could either find his life by losing it, or simply lose it without finding it. But in either case, one had to lose his life. There was no way out, only the freedom to make that choice. Nathan decided that if that was all there really was, he would have to content himself with it. It saddened him that his life would end at thirty-seven, however. Others would make it to their nineties, and others would not outlive childhood. Still, all that mattered was that one choice, and everyone was equally subject to it.

If only Nathan could have foreseen the future, it might have added some cheer to his final thoughts. He had faith that Rome would one day fall and that the Jews would somehow survive. And he trusted that the fledgling Way, which he had first learned about through his beloved Elisheva, would continue to grow and change the world as it had him. But he could not know for sure, and he knew he would not live long enough to see it.

XXII

The cell door opened. Nathan and Ducetius looked at each other, then tried to steel themselves for the next step in their final journey.

The jailor asked them to come out into the office, where he shackled their ankles together for the transfer to the amphitheatre holding chamber.

During the shackling, Nathan and Ducetius watched a man at the centurion's desk who had his back toward them but had a familiar voice. Nathan whispered to Ducetius if he recognized him, but the centurion once again yelled out, "Silence!"

The man's head then turned to see who was being silenced, and almost in unison Nathan and Ducetius blurted out, "Kaliphon?"

The centurion was about to reprimand them again, but the man at the desk did a double take and returned the prisoners' greeting. "Nathan! Ducetius! What are you doing here? You're in prison?"

"You know these prisoners?" asked the centurion.

"Yes," he responded, almost sheepishly. "They were, I always thought, up until this moment, fine men. Perhaps not. But yes, I know them! May I speak to them?"

The centurion consented with a hand wave.

"So," said Kaliphon to Nathan and Ducetius, "it is *your* case that I have been asked to intervene with."

"You are intervening in our case?" asked Nathan, incredulously.

"Yes," Kaliphon responded. "But I am a bit confused. I work for the fiscus office in Ostia, for, apparently, the man who is your wife's brother, Nathan. He sent me here on his authority to plead your case with the tribune. But I had no idea that the Nathan I was pleading for was you. I can't believe it's you, and you're here in prison. A few facts about the case, though, are making sense to me now that I know it is you." Suddenly changing his tone, Kaliphon said, "If you two will excuse me, this new information requires me to continue my conversation with the centurion in private for a moment."

"Put them back in the cell," ordered the centurion.

The jailor obliged, and the two prisoners found themselves in the dark again, though with their ears against the door.

They waited for several minutes, and Nathan eventually whispered to Ducetius, "They must be using hand gestures out there because I can't hear a thing."

The cell door then opened and Kaliphon walked in.

"Listen, Nathan and Ducetius," he said, waiting for them to ready themselves for the news, "I was able to commute your sentence, but not to the full extent I would have liked. Because of the numerous strikes against you, the tribune would not discuss with me last night the idea of sparing your lives. Had I known your full identity, it would have brought more urgency and evidence to the discussion. But there is no guarantee it would have changed anything. The tribune is a tough man, and his boss is even tougher. But after several hours with him, I was able to at least expunge the confiscation of your property from the sentence. I want you to know that."

Nathan closed his eyes in relief upon hearing that news. At least Valeria and Lois would be safe when they were gone. "Thank you for your efforts on our behalf," he and Ducetius said. The truth of the matter was, however, that Kaliphon's efforts were not for Nathan and Ducetius at all, but for Valeria. Valeria's brother could not have cared less what happened to Nathan, so long as the property remained intact within the family. The thought had entered Nathan's mind that such might be the case, but he did not dare mention it to Kaliphon, nor did Kaliphon deem it wise to mention it to Nathan.

"I also just spoke to the centurion," Kaliphon continued, "about mitigating your punishment in the arena. Although he does not have the authority to spare your lives, he has the power to soften the method of execution and has agreed to do so. The two of you are to fight each other to the death, and you are forbidden to be subject to anything worse that the master of ceremonies may have in mind. The centurion is rewriting the paperwork right now to that effect, and you should thank him heartily for doing so. In fact, I will suggest that your wives present him with a gift over the next few days for his magnanimity. He was under no compulsion to show mercy other than as a favor to me."

Upon hearing that additional information, the two became noticeably choked up. "Thank you, Kaliphon. Thank you!" That was all they could manage to say.

"I regret I could not do more," continued Kaliphon. "The paperwork for your case had already been filled out by the centurion last night when I arrived, and the tribune had approved it by the time I got to speak to him. If it had gone up the chain to the next level and been signed by the prefect, I would not have been able to do a thing. Even the emperor is constrained by protocol from commuting a sentence given by the prefect. But at least I gained you some dignity and a future for both of your wives."

"We appreciate it," said both Nathan and Ducetius. "It is more than we could have hoped for."

"It's time to leave now," said the jailor.

Nathan and Ducetius walked out of the cell and passed the centurion, who at first did not give them a second glance. But just before they reached the front door, he called them back to his desk and asked them, "Why didn't you simply tell me you had paid the fiscus?"

"Sir?" responded Nathan, not quite understanding the question.

"I could have spared your lives," said the centurion.

Both Nathan and Ducetius were surprised that it would have been that easy to get away with it. But Nathan responded, "How could we lie? Wouldn't it go badly at the final reckoning?"

"This is your final reckoning," he responded. He then motioned them to leave.

Once out the door, Kaliphon followed them to the street, where a wagon with an iron cage awaited them. The wagon driver unlocked the cage, held the door for the prisoners to enter, then bolted them inside. Kaliphon said to them from outside the cage, "I want you to know that I will be there at the arena to applaud you at your final battle. If no one else is watching, I will be. Rome should regret the loss of men like you. It doesn't know what it's doing. And just so you know, I will always look back on the work the three of us did together saving all those people during the eruption as the proudest moment of my life. I will tell that to your wives.

"By the way, your wives know that you were sentenced and that I was able to commute the property issue. I spoke to Valeria the moment I arrived from Ostia, and I also spoke to her after my negotiations with the tribune, even though it was close to midnight. They do not know about the commutation of your punishment to battle to the death, but I will inform them of that now. I am also going to negotiate with the centurion to allow your wives to see you one more time in the next couple of hours. If it works, I will escort them to the holding chamber myself, and I will see you there. And one more point: I will be returning to the castra and your homes over the next two days to see that the property transfer is canceled and that your wives and children are safe."

"Thank you, thank you for all you've done for us, Kaliphon," replied Nathan. "And if I may ask, what were some of the facts that started to make sense to you when you found out it was us?"

Kaliphon answered, "All of the witnesses mentioned that they had never seen you in town before that day, and the young one said you had a funny accent."

"That's what they remembered?"

"Yes. But that is not what I will remember. I will remember your tirelessness, faithfulness, and ability to survive not only three days in a boat, but also the wiles of that monster, Demaratos. That is what I will remember. You are the only people in the world who have ever known about that. Your brother-in-law often speaks ill of you, Nathan, I must tell you, but I will be setting the record straight when I return to Ostia."

With that, Nathan and Ducetius were carted off to the amphitheatre.

XXIII

"So I have a funny accent? And my brother-in-law speaks ill of me?"

"I think you knew that, Patrón."

The ease of tension they felt over not having to die by burning or *damnatio ad bestia* made Nathan and Ducetius almost giddy, as if they were not going to die at all but merely had to prepare for an athletic event. Nathan took the transport time to describe to Ducetius his ideas on how best to conduct their fight, and Ducetius was both touched and surprised that Nathan had had it planned out for years. Ducetius admitted that he had thought about it a few times since the Temple Mount, but not to the level of detail Nathan had. But the 'now,' as Joseph would have said, was upon them, and they needed to prepare their strategy. They also needed to keep their minds off the raw reality that they were going to die, for that was hard to take. When the wagon driver stopped in front of the holding chamber, they both began to dry heave as if they might vomit again. But they did not.

If it weren't for Ducetius, Nathan thought, he did not know how he could have faced that moment with any decorum. It was easy to be strong for someone else, and he thought about how seldom in his life he had ever needed to be strong for himself. But that was all right. Time, chance, and heaven had happened to them both.

The driver let the prisoners out of the cage and loosened their ankle shackles so they could walk more easily to the entrance. Near the entrance, about half a dozen guards were posted. Then suddenly, Nathan saw Joseph walk out of their midst toward him.

"Joseph, what are you doing here?" asked Nathan, half angry that he would see him in this state but half-elated that he cared.

"Nathan," said Joseph, "I must talk to you. You are no longer prisoners. I was able to have your sentence commuted by the emperor."

"What?" responded Nathan, completely confused. "*You* had our sentence commuted? We already know about the commutation. But we did not know you were involved. If that is the case, thank you. But I know that we are still prisoners."

Joseph was now confused himself. He had expected Nathan to be stunned by the news and to embrace his old friend in thanks. But that was not the case. "I don't follow you, Nathan," he said befuddled. "I worked on the commutation alone, by myself. I went to speak to the emperor on your behalf. I went myself, alone. Do you understand what I'm saying? And the emperor commuted your sentence. You are not condemned any longer. You are free to go. How could you possibly have known about the commutation already?"

"Because we were told already that it was commuted," answered Nathan. "But you have it wrong, Joseph. We are not free. We are still going to die. The only commutation in our sentence had to do with the confiscation of our property. So I'm not sure why you are saying that we are free to go. I wish that were the case, but it is not."

"Nathan, you are wrong," responded Joseph. "I have a scroll in my hand signed by the emperor, which states that your sentence is limited to banishment and confiscation of property. You are free to go and are not to be incarcerated or executed by any means."

At this point, Nathan began to feel delirious. He had not eaten in twenty-four hours and was light-headed. The convoluted conversation only made it worse.

Ducetius then came closer. "Lord Joseph, Patrón and I do not understand. We were just told before coming here that our sentence was commuted. We are still to die, but our property is not to be confiscated. But you are saying the opposite. I do not understand."

"Who told you your sentence was commuted already?" asked Joseph, trying to solve this puzzle.

"A magistrate named Kaliphon," answered Ducetius. "We knew him from Herculaneum before the eruption. He came to Rome and was able to negotiate a commutation for us. But it sounds like you are saying it wasn't really him. It was you."

"Perhaps," responded Joseph, "your man Kaliphon arranged a separate commutation for you from the one I arranged."

"So you are saying, my lord," asked Ducetius, "that you arranged a commutation completely separate from the one Kaliphon negotiated for us?"

"Yes, that is what I am saying," answered Joseph, growing a bit flummoxed. "Somehow you received two commutations. I do not know who Kaliphon is, but the commutation I have here in my hand is signed by the emperor himself, and it releases you from execution altogether. The commutation that Kaliphon negotiated for you is not signed by the emperor. But mine is, and it supersedes his. Here. Read it for yourselves," said Joseph, handing them the document.

Nathan and Ducetius read it together but still somehow felt it could not be true. Even Ducetius, who was normally clear-headed, was in a weakened mental state from the lack of food and the emotional jarring of the previous twelve hours.

"Is this for real?" Nathan asked.

"Yes!" responded Joseph, growing impatient.

"So we do not have to die?" asked Nathan, who had actually gotten used to the idea and was almost looking forward to the end of his troubles.

"No, you do not have to die," responded Joseph. "But you are obliged to surrender your property and leave Rome."

Nathan simply stared at Joseph with a stupefied expression on his face. "So we do not have to fight each other to the death in the arena?"

"No! It states it in writing. You will not be subject to any execution and are free to go. Look!"

Nathan read one more time and threw his chained arms around Joseph as best he could. "How can I ever thank you? You actually spoke to the emperor on our behalf? I remember you told me you were already out of favors with him. But you went anyway. What did I ever do to deserve that?"

"Everything. You are Nathan, the one given: son of the politician, brother of the rebel, hero of Jotapata. I don't know what Kaliphon knew about you, but he and I both thought you were worth the effort; and Ducetius too."

Ducetius waited for Nathan to attempt some witticism, but he did not.

"But how did you know I was even arrested?" he asked instead.

"Your brother told me."

"My brother?!" exclaimed Nathan. "How could that be? I absolutely do not believe that! How is that even possible? Are you telling me the truth?"

"Yes," said Joseph.

"Amram came to see you?" Nathan asked incredulously. "After all this time? And you are still alive to tell the tale?"

"Yes."

"Patrón," said Ducetius, "even Samson's death in the arena could not have accomplished that."

The moment was too good to be true. But it was, in fact, apparently, really happening.

"Ducetius," Nathan asked, "is this really happening, or am I just imagining this?"

"No Patrón," answered Ducetius. "It is really happening."

Joseph then said, "Someone is clearly watching out for you, Nathan. I find it hard to believe that your brother came to see me as well." Then, redirecting his next comments to the driver, he said, "Please unchain these men, by order of the Emperor…and Deity."

A few minutes later, Valeria, Lois, and Kaliphon arrived. There was much to explain and many introductions to be made. It took several hours to sort out the details. And even after that, Kaliphon and Joseph, or Joseph's household manager, had to make arrangements to spend part of the next day correcting the paperwork at the castra and Praetoria, including the transfer of all Nathan and Valeria's properties. As late afternoon approached, the entire group limped back to Nathan and Valeria's apartment, exhausted after coming down from such a height of terror, and not sure what their next steps would be. They only knew that as they discussed possible options for the future, they ate their last meal in Rome.

XXIV

The view over the north wall was as spectacular as he remembered. Valeria, seeing it for the first time, exclaimed. "This island is beautiful, Nathan."

Nathan was relieved. The deportation had not been easy for

Valeria since she had lost the most. The rest of them—he, Ducetius, and Lois—had already experienced devastation and migration four times in their brief lives. But for Valeria, rebuilding her life was a new and unsettling thing. She almost wept when they parted the Argiletum.

Spending a week with her family in Ostia before the deportation, Valeria learned of her brother's true intentions in sending Kaliphon—with whom the other three were staying at the time—to intervene in Nathan's legal case. She understood her brother's plan from a strictly economic point of view but was horrified from a human, wifely, and sisterly perspective. Despite Kaliphon's positive words about Nathan, her brother remained intransigent in his negative opinion of him. His views clarified for Valeria just how power-hungry her brother had become and how much he secretly hoped to utilize her, his sister, for personal and dynastic advancement in the future. She never accused him of such to his face. It was wiser to keep such things to herself. But she grew wary of him during that week.

Valeria also figured out from his expressed goals why he had never approved of her marriage to Manus, despite the fact that it had been arranged by their parents, and why he would never accept a penniless adventurer like Nathan either. Her brother was poised to embark on the fast track to Roman political success, and Nathan did not fit into his plans. He was an obstacle that had to be dealt with. Ironically, however, the brother had discovered something connected with Nathan that could potentially aid him in his meteoric rise. "Do you know that there's a latifundium for purchase near the town your beloved vagabond is thinking of going to?" he asked Valeria one day.

"He has mentioned it. What of it?" responded Valeria.

"I'm thinking of purchasing it myself," the brother explained. "I sent some of my people there several months ago to investigate."

"But why? You had no idea we were even considering relocating there several months ago."

"No, I did not. But I am applying for the position of quaestor on the island and will need somewhere to live if I get it—though it is a longshot. So if you end up in Sicily, we might be neighbors. Or, better yet, you and Justin should come share the estate with me."

"Don't even consider inviting me to live with you without my husband," Valeria stated adamantly.

"I'd consider my proposition carefully if I were you," he warned.

Valeria simply stared him down.

"In any case," he added, "it would only be temporary. No self-respecting Roman would consider Sicily as a permanent residence."

"I'll hold off on that judgment till I see it for myself," Valeria retorted.

When Valeria shared with Nathan that the latifundium was for sale and that her brother might buy it, it settled the matter for Nathan that they could return to Sicily without worry. They had been considering the wisdom or folly of such a move since leaving Rome. But if Funisulanus, and presumably Vitus, had moved on to greener pastures and Demaratos was dead besides, it meant that the island was safe even for Ducetius and that they could be reunited with their families, despite whatever complications his brother-in-law might possibly, and only possibly, present.

After they were back on the island for three months, it was as if they had never left. The rhythm of workaday life resumed almost too quickly for Nathan, who felt as though he was facing a long and much too peaceful denouement to his life. Within a week, he and Ducetius were repairing and maintaining George's rental properties again. They had hoped to be enjoying the banter and competition of Joram and Efstathios, but those two had been gone for several years on a missionary journey, copying letters of Paulos and Petros in codex form for redistribution, and spreading their message to new hearers in various locations.

When George learned that Valeria had once been a successful bookseller on the Argiletum, he commissioned Nathan and Ducetius to construct a shop for her out of the ground level of his most strategically located insula. Valeria was utterly thrilled at the idea, as was he, and as Efstathios would be, if he ever returned. She ended up having to delay the opening by several months due to pregnancy, but followed through after delivering a healthy son. Nathan, who named the baby Opal, postulated that his son's tiny life already loosely reflected, in backward order, his own. "Conceived in Rome, born is Sicily, and raised by a Jew," he said proudly. "He's quite the little international fellow, wouldn't you say?" he asked Ducetius. "Not to mention how cute he is. Doesn't he look just like me?"

"Not really, Patrón," answered Ducetius.

Almost two years later, shortly after Joram and Efstathios returned home from a difficult and fruitful journey, Valeria gave birth to a daughter. "Now *she* looks like me, doesn't she, Ducetius?" asked Nathan.

"Not in the least, Patrón," responded Ducetius again. "But she looks more like you than Kalo looks like me." They looked over at Kalo who, at the age of nine, was already gargantuan.

Auntie Ayathe's youngest, who had a secret crush on Kalo, asked if the little newborn, who was the first baby girl born among them, could be named after Elisheva, whose loss was still felt by all. Although Nathan could not imagine Valeria agreeing to such an idea, she consented. The family celebrated her naming with a little party at Auntie Ayathe's on the eighth day.

That night, Nathan lay in bed awake, taking stock of his life and all he had been through over the years. Between him and Adah, they had provided three grandsons and a granddaughter for ima and abba. George was still recovering from his financial setback and would finally have the bookshop he had always desired. Valeria was succeeding in her business and had set up a liaison with a scrivener in Syracuse to borrow and copy a Livy scroll, Aristotle, an Epicharmus play, and other works. Joram and Efstathios were home safe and sound, with inspiring tales about their journeys and trials. Auntie Ayathe was at peace with her beloved Ducetius nearby again and contemplated marriages between her girls with Justin and Kalo. And who knew? Maybe Elisheva's son Nathan would someday marry the newborn Elisheva and live out in the next generation what their parents could not in theirs.

For the moment, all seemed good. Work progressed, the family was growing, and the island lay tranquil in the moonlight. But just as Nathan's eyes began to shut, with the baby gently cooing at the foot of the bed, his mind unexpectedly turned to Amram and whether he would hold to his vow of ending the war; to Joseph and whether his book would win out against Justus of Tiberias's diatribe against him; to Domitian still on the warpath against the Jews; to the resistance in Transtiberim biding its time for vengeance; to Joram, who invited him to set out with them on their next mission; to Efstathios, who would wrestle between faith and physical happiness his entire life; to the Ennans, who had grown superstitious again about the amphitheatre; to Ducetius's parents, who might still be at large somewhere in the world; and to Valeria's brother, who had just received word of his appointment as quaestor and was about to notify his sister in the upcoming weeks. He contemplated the words of Qohelet, that time and chance happen to us all, and drifted off to sleep.

Afterword

Brothers' War was written to answer a simple question I had growing up: what happened to Jews and Christians after the Bible story ended in Acts? As a teenager living in the closing years of the hippie movement, I wanted to know. I also read George C. Brauer's historical work, *Judaea Weeping,* about the fall of Jerusalem, which partly answered my question, and I thought to myself, "this story needs to be told," and, "I wish I had lived through that event." And so I began writing *Brothers' War,* transporting my teenage self back to the Roman-Jewish world of the first century, along with some of my family members and other acquaintances.

Hailing from a Sicilian background, I had heard stories about that place my whole life, too, and wanted to investigate it as well. And so the story of Sicily and the Jewish War began to intertwine. In the end, I hoped to weave together a plausible epic of how a young Jewish escapee from the fall of Jerusalem became one of my Sicilian ancestors.

Appendix

Abba: Hebrew term for father

Andron: an exclusive room in a Greek house for men (only) to eat and socialize

Ergastulum/ergastula: Roman slave barracks where slaves worked and slept

Ima: Hebrew term for mother

Insula/insulae: Roman apartment building(s)

Kashrut: Jewish dietary restrictions, related to 'kosher'

Lar: Roman household idol

Lararium: Roman household shrine where lares, or household idols, were kept

Latifundium/latifundia: large Roman plantation(s) or estate(s) worked by slaves to grow crops

Neged: Hebrew term for next to, in front of, opposed to, against, alongside

Nomen: the family name of a Roman. It is often the second name listed for a male, as in Gaius Julius Caesar or Marc Antony, and it is often the only name used for a female, as in the case of Julia or Antonia.

Palaestra: a Greek type of gymnasium, primarily used for boxing or wrestling

Rab: Hebrew term of respect (sometimes Reb)

Qohelet: Hebrew name for the Book of Ecclesiastes, derived from a word meaning "teacher" used for king Solomon

<u>**Ostracon/ostraca**</u>: sherd(s) of pottery used to write something, be it a note or a vote, for or against someone. The word ostracize derives from it.

<u>**Quaestor**</u>: lowest ranking Roman official, who oversaw finances, expenditures, and occasionally murder investigations (> inquest)

<u>**Seleucids**</u>: Greek/Hellenistic rulers based in Syria who attempted to conquer Israel. Their invasion led to the rise of the Maccabees and the first Hanukkah.

<u>**Taberna/tabernae**</u>: Roman shop(s) or tavern(s) usually on the ground level of an apartment building (insula)

<u>**Thermae**</u>: Roman bathhouse

<u>**Transtiberim**</u>: Rome's Jewish quarter, known today as a quaint, artsy part of the city

ACKNOWLEDGMENTS

Several significant individuals must be acknowledged for their help in bringing this book to its completed form. I thank them all here from the bottom of my heart.

1. First and foremost is my wife, Dr. Evelyn Emma, professor of English, whose love of literature and willingness to enter the world of Brothers' War with me shaped it more profoundly than anyone apart from myself. Her every comment, from "I love this character" to "this chapter's got to go," guided my steps for a year before submitting my manuscript for review. She was also the first person who let me know that someone other than myself might possibly enjoy my story.

2. My son Maximilian Emma, whose photographs of Sicily—several of which can be seen on my website—provided reminders to me of the island as I wrote. I could also rely on his keen sense of human frailty and drama when needing a sounding board to discuss plot issues.

3. My son James Emma, whose enviable talents not only created the book cover, map, and other illustrations by hand (how did he draw all those little details?), but whose positive critique of the book demonstrated for the first time that the story could appeal to a younger audience as well as adult.

4. Frank Korn, scholar, long-established author, dear family friend, and relative of a relative, whose mentoring talks with me, extensive knowledge of Rome, experiences in the publishing world, and overall kindness to me—along with his wonderful wife Camille—inspired me to believe that publishing this book was a possibility. I couldn't have done it without him.

5. My publisher Rebecca Franks, whose encouragement, profes-

sional insights, humor, and friendship I did not expect from a business relationship. The complexities of publishing often discouraged me, but Rebecca explained them, broke them down, and prioritized them for me, equipping me to press on when I had come to her bereft.

6. My test readers, who willingly saddled themselves with the reading of my manuscript though they had committed no crime. Without any recompense for the task—they did not even know their names would appear here—they did it anyway.

    a. Chief among them is Scott Ingalls, "my most literary friend," as I call him, whose scientific mind probed every jot and tittle of my writing, and offered corrections and questions no one else did.

    b. My friends Ron and Laura Reinhart, who approached my work with the complimentary litmus tests of Germanic meticulousness and Sicilian exuberance, assuring me on both counts that the story passed muster. "This book is a gem," Ron exclaimed. "It should be made into a movie!"

    c. Two volunteers who only knew me secondhand, but who took on the challenge of reading out of the sheer goodness of their hearts. Vicki Daudelin, wife of a church friend, and Jim Kerschaver, father-in-law of a gym friend, critiqued my book while convalescing after major incidents in their lives. Vicki's comments on the chronology and female characters, and Jim's on the action sequences, helped me rethink several items.

    d. Pico Banergee, my dear former student, who was the first to perceive the humor I had hoped would come through in the story. "Even though it's a serious plot," he commented, "there are a lot of funny lines." My son James, the only other young reader besides Pico, corroborated his view.

    e. Jason Ritchie, who kindly read the book unsolicited and provided feedback on the spiritual elements of the story. His commentary on the story's cross-cultural dialogues about the Scriptures fueled my hope that the story could beckon the reader beyond the historical adventure.

f. Paul DeMena, a fellow author with his own amazing story (he's lived in China for 30 years), who introduced me to publisher Rebecca Franks on his own initiative. Without his thoughtful, unsolicited intervention in jumpstarting the publishing process for me, I might have deceased before this book ever came to print.

So thank you, thank you, one and all.

David Paul Emma

Photo Credit: Brian Kievning

DAVID PAUL EMMA grew up in the dense ethnic mix of northern New Jersey in the 1970s, a crucible of cultures, faiths, and politics that led him to study history and begin writing *Brothers' War* at the age of sixteen. After traveling the world, studying Chinese, Hebrew, and Sicilian, and joining an archaeological dig in Galilee, the author now teaches history and lives with his family near his hometown. He is currently working on a second historical novel.

If you've enjoyed this book and found it a worthwhile
read, please share your thoughts by leaving a review
on Amazon or with your favorite book retailer.

Thank you for reading.

David Paul Emma

Connect with David
davidpaulemma.com